ONE HUNDRED YEARS OF SOLITUDE

GABRIEL GARCÍA MÁRQUEZ

TRANSLATED FROM THE SPANISH
BY GREGORY RABASSA

PENGUIN BOOKS

PENGUIN BOOKS

Published by the Penguin Group
Penguin Books Ltd, 80 Strand, London WC2R ORL, England
Penguin Group (USA) Inc., 375 Hudson Street, New York, New York 10014, USA
Penguin Group (Canada), 90 Eglinton Avenue East, Suite 700, Toronto, Ontario, Canada M4P 2Y3
(a division of Pearson Penguin Canada Inc.)
Penguin Ireland, 25 St Stephen's Green, Dublin 2, Ireland (a division of Penguin Books Ltd)
Penguin Group (Australia), 707 Collins Street, Melbourne, Victoria 3008, Australia
(a division of Pearson Australia Group Pty Ltd)
Penguin Books India Pvt Ltd, 11 Community Centre, Panchsheel Park, New Delhi – 110 017, India
Penguin Group (NZ), 67 Apollo Drive, Rosedale, Auckland 0632, New Zealand
(a division of Pearson New Zealand Ltd)
Penguin Books (South Africa) (Pty) Ltd, Block D, Rosebank Office Park,
181 Jan Smuts Avenue, Parktown North, Gauteng 2193, South Africa

Penguin Books Ltd, Registered Offices: 80 Strand, London WC2R ORL, England

www.penguin.com

First published as *Cien Años de Soledad* 1967
This translation first published in Great Britain by Jonathan Cape 1970
Published in Penguin Books 1972
This edition published 2014

001

Copyright © Gabriel García Márquez, 1967
Translation copyright © Harper and Row, Publishers, Inc., 1970
All rights reserved

The moral right of the author and translator has been asserted

Printed in England by Clays Ltd, St Ives plc

ISBN: 978-0-241-97235-9

www.greenpenguin.co.uk

Penguin Books is committed to a sustainable
future for our business, our readers and our planet.
This book is made from Forest Stewardship
Council™ certified paper.

for jomí garcía ascot
and maría luisa elío

ONE HUNDRED YEARS OF SOLITUDE

José Arcadio Buendía
m. Úrsula Iguarán

José Arcadio
m. Rebeca

Amaranta

Colonel Aureliano Buendía
m. Remedios Moscote

17 Aurelianos

Aureliano José
(by Pilar Ternera)

Arcadio
(by Pilar Ternera)
m. Santa Sofía de la Piedad

Remedios the Beauty

Aureliano Segundo
m. Fernanda del Carpio

José Arcadio Segundo

Renata Remedios (Meme)

José Arcadio

Amaranta Úrsula
m. Gaston

Aureliano
(by Mauricio Babilonia)

Aureliano
(by Aureliano)

MANY YEARS LATER, as he faced the firing squad, Colonel Aureliano Buendía was to remember that distant afternoon when his father took him to discover ice. At that time Macondo was a village of twenty adobe houses, built on the bank of a river of clear water that ran along a bed of polished stones, which were white and enormous, like prehistoric eggs. The world was so recent that many things lacked names, and in order to indicate them it was necessary to point. Every year during the month of March a family of ragged gypsies would set up their tents near the village, and with a great uproar of pipes and kettledrums they would display new inventions. First they brought the magnet. A heavy gypsy with an untamed beard and sparrow hands, who introduced himself as Melquíades, put on a bold public demonstration of what he himself called the eighth wonder of the learned alchemists of Macedonia. He went from house to house dragging two metal ingots and everybody was amazed to see pots, pans, tongs, and braziers tumble down from their places and beams creak from the desperation of nails and screws trying to emerge, and even objects that had been lost for a long time appeared from where they had been searched for most and went dragging along in turbulent confusion behind Melquíades' magical irons. "Things have a life of their own," the gypsy proclaimed with a harsh accent. "It's simply a matter of waking up their souls." José Arcadio Buendía, whose unbridled imagination always went beyond the genius of nature and even beyond miracles and magic, thought that it would be possible to make use of that useless invention to extract gold from the bowels of the earth. Melquíades, who was an honest man, warned him: "It won't work for that." But José Arcadio Buendía at that time did not believe in the honesty of gypsies, so he traded his mule and a pair of goats for the two magnetized ingots. Úrsula Iguarán, his wife, who relied on those animals to increase their poor domestic holdings, was unable to dissuade him. "Very soon we'll have gold enough and more to pave the floors of the house," her husband replied. For several months he worked hard to demonstrate the truth of his idea. He explored every inch of the region, even the riverbed, dragging the two iron ingots along and reciting Melquíades' incantation aloud. The only thing he succeeded in doing was to unearth a suit of fifteenth-century armor which had all of its pieces soldered together with rust and inside of which there was the hollow resonance of an enormous stone-filled gourd. When José Arcadio Buendía and the four men of his expedition managed to take the armor apart, they found inside a calcified skeleton with a copper locket containing a woman's hair around its neck.

In March the gypsies returned. This time they brought a

2

telescope and a magnifying glass the size of a drum, which they exhibited as the latest discovery of the Jews of Amsterdam. They placed a gypsy woman at one end of the village and set up the telescope at the entrance to the tent. For the price of five reales, people could look into the telescope and see the gypsy woman an arm's length away. "Science has eliminated distance," Melquíades proclaimed. "In a short time, man will be able to see what is happening in any place in the world without leaving his own house." A burning noonday sun brought out a startling demonstration with the gigantic magnifying glass: they put a pile of dry hay in the middle of the street and set it on fire by concentrating the sun's rays. José Arcadio Buendía, who had still not been consoled for the failure of his magnets, conceived the idea of using that invention as a weapon of war. Again Melquíades tried to dissuade him, but he finally accepted the two magnetized ingots and three colonial coins in exchange for the magnifying glass. Úrsula wept in consternation. That money was from a chest of gold coins that her father had put together over an entire life of privation and that she had buried underneath her bed in hopes of a proper occasion to make use of it. José Arcadio Buendía made no attempt to console her, completely absorbed in his tactical experiments with the abnegation of a scientist and even at the risk of his own life. In an attempt to show the effects of the glass on enemy troops, he exposed himself to the concentration of the sun's rays and suffered burns which turned into sores that took a long time to heal. Over the protests of his wife, who was alarmed at such a dangerous invention, at one point he was ready to set the house on fire. He would spend hours on end in his room, calculating the strategic possibilities of his novel weapon until he succeeded in putting together a manual of startling instructional clarity and an irresistible power of conviction. He sent it to the government, accompanied by numerous descriptions of his experiments and several pages of explanatory sketches, by a messenger who crossed the mountains, got lost in measureless swamps, forded stormy rivers, and was on the point of perishing under the lash of despair, plague, and wild beasts until he found a route that joined the one used by the mules that carried the mail. In spite of the fact that a trip to the capital was little less than impossible at that time, José Arcadio Buendía promised to undertake it as soon as the government ordered him to so that he could put on some practical demonstrations of his invention for the military authorities and could train them himself in the complicated art of solar war. For several years he waited for an answer. Finally, tired of waiting, he bemoaned to Melquíades the failure of his project and the gypsy then gave him a convincing proof of his honesty: he gave him back the doubloons in exchange for the magnifying glass, and he left him in addition some Portuguese maps and several instruments of navigation. In his own handwriting he set down a concise synthesis of the studies by Monk Hermann, which he left José Arcadio so that he would be able to make use of the astrolabe, the compass, and the sextant. José Arcadio Buendía spent the long months of the rainy season shut up in a small room that he had built in the rear of the house so that no one would disturb his experiments. Having completely abandoned his domestic obligations, he spent entire nights in the courtyard watching the course of the stars and he almost contracted sunstroke from trying to establish an exact method to ascertain noon. When he became an expert in the use and manipulation of his instruments, he conceived a notion of space that allowed him to navigate across unknown seas, to visit uninhabited territories, and to establish relations with splendid beings without having to leave his study. That was the period in which he acquired the habit of talking to himself, of walking through the house without paying attention to anyone, as Úrsula and the children broke their backs in the garden, growing banana and caladium, cassava and

4

yams, ahuyama roots and eggplants. Suddenly, without warning, his feverish activity was interrupted and was replaced by a kind of fascination. He spent several days as if he were bewitched, softly repeating to himself a string of fearful conjectures without giving credit to his own understanding. Finally, one Tuesday in December, at lunchtime, all at once he released the whole weight of his torment. The children would remember for the rest of their lives the august solemnity with which their father, devastated by his prolonged vigil and by the wrath of his imagination, revealed his discovery to them:

"The earth is round, like an orange."

Úrsula lost her patience. "If you have to go crazy, please go crazy all by yourself!" she shouted. "But don't try to put your gypsy ideas into the heads of the children." José Arcadio Buendía, impassive, did not let himself be frightened by the desperation of his wife, who, in a seizure of rage, smashed the astrolabe against the floor. He built another one, he gathered the men of the village in his little room, and he demonstrated to them, with theories that none of them could understand, the possibility of returning to where one had set out by consistently sailing east. The whole village was convinced that José Arcadio Buendía had lost his reason, when Melquíades returned to set things straight. He gave public praise to the intelligence of a man who from pure astronomical speculation had evolved a theory that had already been proved in practice, although unknown in Macondo until then, and as a proof of his admiration he made him a gift that was to have a profound influence on the future of the village: the laboratory of an alchemist.

By then Melquíades had aged with surprising rapidity. On his first trips he seemed to be the same age as José Arcadio Buendía. But while the latter had preserved his extraordinary strength, which permitted him to pull down a horse by grabbing its ears, the gypsy seemed to have been worn down by some tenacious illness. It was, in reality, the result of multiple and rare diseases contracted on his innumerable trips around the world. According to what he himself said as he spoke to José Arcadio Buendía while helping him set up the laboratory, death followed him everywhere, sniffing at the cuffs of his pants, but never deciding to give him the final clutch of its claws. He was a fugitive from all the plagues and catastrophes that had ever lashed mankind. He had survived pellagra in Persia, scurvy in the Malayan archipelago, leprosy in Alexandria, beriberi in Japan, bubonic plague in Madagascar, an earthquake in Sicily, and a disastrous shipwreck in the Strait of Magellan. That prodigious creature, said to possess the keys of Nostradamus, was a gloomy man, enveloped in a sad aura, with an Asiatic look that seemed to know what there was on the other side of things. He wore a large black hat that looked like a raven with widespread wings, and a velvet vest across which the patina of the centuries had skated. But in spite of his immense wisdom and his mysterious breadth, he had a human burden, an earthly condition that kept him involved in the small problems of daily life. He would complain of the ailments of old age, he suffered from the most insignificant economic difficulties, and he had stopped laughing a long time back because scurvy had made his teeth drop out. On that suffocating noontime when the gypsy revealed his secrets, José Arcadio Buendía had the certainty that it was the beginning of a great friendship. The children were startled by his fantastic stories. Aureliano, who could not have been more than five at the time, would remember him for the rest of his life as he saw him that afternoon, sitting against the metallic and quivering light from the window, lighting up with his deep organ voice the darkest reaches of the imagination, while down over his temples there flowed the grease that was being melted by the heat. José Arcadio, his older brother, would pass on that wonderful image as a hereditary memory to all of his de-

6

scendants. Úrsula, on the other hand, held a bad memory of that visit, for she had entered the room just as Melquíades had carelessly broken a flask of bichloride of mercury.

"It's the smell of the devil," she said.

"Not at all," Melquíades corrected her. "It has been proven that the devil has sulphuric properties and this is just a little corrosive sublimate."

Always didactic, he went into a learned exposition of the diabolical properties of cinnabar, but Úrsula paid no attention to him, although she took the children off to pray. That biting odor would stay forever in her mind linked to the memory of Melquíades.

The rudimentary laboratory—in addition to a profusion of pots, funnels, retorts, filters, and sieves—was made up of a primitive water pipe, a glass beaker with a long, thin neck, a reproduction of the philosopher's egg, and a still the gypsies themselves had built in accordance with modern descriptions of the three-armed alembic of Mary the Jew. Along with those items, Melquíades left samples of the seven metals that corresponded to the seven planets, the formulas of Moses and Zosimus for doubling the quantity of gold, and a set of notes and sketches concerning the processes of the Great Teaching that would permit those who could interpret them to undertake the manufacture of the philosopher's stone. Seduced by the simplicity of the formulas to double the quantity of gold, José Arcadio Buendía paid court to Úrsula for several weeks so that she would let him dig up her colonial coins and increase them by as many times as it was possible to subdivide mercury. Úrsula gave in, as always, to her husband's unyielding obstinacy. Then José Arcadio Buendía threw three doubloons into a pan and fused them with copper filings, orpiment, brimstone, and lead. He put it all to boil in a pot of castor oil until he got a thick and pestilential syrup which was more like common caramel than valuable gold. In risky and desperate processes of distillation, melted

7

with the seven planetary metals, mixed with hermetic mercury and vitriol of Cyprus, and put back to cook in hog fat for lack of any radish oil, Úrsula's precious inheritance was reduced to a large piece of burnt hog cracklings that was firmly stuck to the bottom of the pot.

When the gypsies came back, Úrsula had turned the whole population of the village against them. But curiosity was greater than fear, for that time the gypsies went about the town making a deafening noise with all manner of musical instruments while a hawker announced the exhibition of the most fabulous discovery of the Naciancenes. So that everyone went to the tent and by paying one cent they saw a youthful Melquíades, recovered, unwrinkled, with a new and flashing set of teeth. Those who remembered his gums that had been destroyed by scurvy, his flaccid cheeks, and his withered lips trembled with fear at the final proof of the gypsy's supernatural power. The fear turned into panic when Melquíades took out his teeth, intact, encased in their gums, and showed them to the audience for an instant—a fleeting instant in which he went back to being the same decrepit man of years past—and put them back again and smiled once more with the full control of his restored youth. Even José Arcadio Buendía himself considered that Melquíades' knowledge had reached unbearable extremes, but he felt a healthy excitement when the gypsy explained to him alone the workings of his false teeth. It seemed so simple and so prodigious at the same time that overnight he lost all interest in his experiments in alchemy. He underwent a new crisis of bad humor. He did not go back to eating regularly, and he would spend the day walking through the house. "Incredible things are happening in the world," he said to Úrsula. "Right there across the river there are all kinds of magical instruments while we keep on living like donkeys." Those who had known him since the foundation of Macondo were startled at how much he had changed under Melquíades' influence.

At first José Arcadio Buendía had been a kind of youthful patriarch who would give instructions for planting and advice for the raising of children and animals, and who collaborated with everyone, even in the physical work, for the welfare of the community. Since his house from the very first had been the best in the village, the others had been built in its image and likeness. It had a small, well-lighted living room, a dining room in the shape of a terrace with gaily colored flowers, two bedrooms, a courtyard with a gigantic chestnut tree, a well-kept garden, and a corral where goats, pigs, and hens lived in peaceful communion. The only animals that were prohibited, not just in his house but in the entire settlement, were fighting cocks.

Úrsula's capacity for work was the same as that of her husband. Active, small, severe, that woman of unbreakable nerves who at no moment in her life had been heard to sing seemed to be everywhere, from dawn until quite late at night, always pursued by the soft whispering of her stiff, starched petticoats. Thanks to her the floors of tamped earth, the unwhitewashed mud walls, the rustic, wooden furniture they had built themselves were always clean, and the old chests where they kept their clothes exhaled the warm smell of basil.

José Arcadio Buendía, who was the most enterprising man ever to be seen in the village, had set up the placement of the houses in such a way that from all of them one could reach the river and draw water with the same effort, and he had lined up the streets with such good sense that no house got more sun than another during the hot time of day. Within a few years Macondo was a village that was more orderly and hard-working than any known until then by its three hundred inhabitants. It was a truly happy village where no one was over thirty years of age and where no one had died.

Since the time of its founding, José Arcadio Buendía had built traps and cages. In a short time he filled not only his own house but all of those in the village with troupials, canaries, bee eaters, and redbreasts. The concert of so many different birds became so disturbing that Úrsula would plug her ears with beeswax so as not to lose her sense of reality. The first time that Melquíades' tribe arrived, selling glass balls for headaches, everyone was surprised that they had been able to find that village lost in the drowsiness of the swamp, and the gypsies confessed that they had found their way by the song of the birds.

That spirit of social initiative disappeared in a short time, pulled away by the fever of the magnets, the astronomical calculations, the dreams of transmutation, and the urge to discover the wonders of the world. From a clean and active man, José Arcadio Buendía changed into a man lazy in appearance, careless in his dress, with a wild beard that Úrsula managed to trim with great effort and a kitchen knife. There were many who considered him the victim of some strange spell. But even those most convinced of his madness left work and family to follow him when he brought out his tools to clear the land and asked the assembled group to open a way that would put Macondo in contact with the great inventions.

José Arcadio Buendía was completely ignorant of the geography of the region. He knew that to the east there lay an impenetrable mountain chain and that on the other side of the mountains there was the ancient city of Riohacha, where in times past—according to what he had been told by the first Aureliano Buendía, his grandfather—Sir Francis Drake had gone crocodile hunting with cannons and that he repaired them and stuffed them with straw to bring to Queen Elizabeth. In his youth, José Arcadio Buendía and his men, with wives and children, animals and all kinds of domestic implements, had crossed the mountains in search of an outlet to the sea, and after twenty-six months they gave up the expedition and founded Macondo, so they would not have to go back. It was, therefore, a route that did not interest him, for it could lead only to the past. To the south lay the swamps, covered with an eternal vegetable scum, and the whole vast universe of the great swamp, which, according to what the gypsies said, had no limits. The great swamp in the west mingled with a boundless extension of water where there were soft-skinned cetaceans that had the head and torso of a woman, causing the ruination of sailors with the charm of their extraordinary breasts. The gypsies sailed along that route for six months before they reached the strip of land over which the mules that carried the mail passed. According to José Arcadio Buendía's calculations, the only possibility of contact with civilization lay along the northern route. So he handed out clearing tools and hunting weapons to the same men who had been with him during the founding of Macondo. He threw his directional instruments and his maps into a knapsack, and he undertook the reckless adventure.

During the first days they did not come across any appreciable obstacle. They went down along the stony bank of the river to the place where years before they had found the soldier's armor, and from there they went into the woods along a path between wild orange trees. At the end of the first week they killed and roasted a deer, but they agreed to eat only half of it and salt the rest for the days that lay ahead. With that precaution they tried to postpone the necessity of having to eat macaws, whose blue flesh had a harsh and musky taste. Then, for more than ten days, they did not see the sun again. The ground became soft and damp, like volcanic ash, and the vegetation was thicker and thicker, and the cries of the birds and the uproar of the monkeys became more and more remote, and the world became eternally sad. The men on the expedition felt overwhelmed by their most ancient memories in that paradise of dampness and silence, going back to before original sin, as their boots sank into pools of steaming oil and their machetes destroyed bloody lilies and golden salamanders. For a week, almost without speaking, they went ahead like sleepwalkers through a universe of grief, lighted only by the tenuous reflection of luminous insects, and their lungs were overwhelmed by a suffocating smell of blood. They could not return because the strip that they were opening as they went along would soon close up with a new vegetation that almost seemed to grow before their eyes. "It's all right," José Arcadio Buendía would say. "The main thing is not to lose our bearings." Always following his compass, he kept on guiding his men toward the invisible north so that they would be able to get out of that enchanted region. It was a thick night, starless, but the darkness was becoming impregnated with a fresh and clear air. Exhausted by the long crossing, they hung up their hammocks and slept deeply for the first time in two weeks. When they woke up, with the sun already high in the sky, they were speechless with fascination. Before them, surrounded by ferns and palm trees, white and powdery in the silent morning light, was an enormous Spanish galleon. Tilted slightly to the starboard, it had hanging from its intact masts the dirty rags of its sails in the midst of its rigging, which was adorned with orchids. The hull, covered with an armor of petrified barnacles and soft moss, was firmly fastened into a surface of stones. The whole structure seemed to occupy its own space, one of solitude and oblivion, protected from the vices of time and the habits of the birds. Inside, where the expeditionaries explored with careful intent, there was nothing but a thick forest of flowers.

The discovery of the galleon, an indication of the proximity of the sea, broke José Arcadio Buendía's drive. He considered it a trick of his whimsical fate to have searched for the sea without finding it, at the cost of countless sacrifices and suffering, and to have found it all of a sudden without looking for it, as if it lay across his path like an insurmountable object. Many years later Colonel Aureliano Buendía crossed the region again, when it was already a regular mail route, and the only part of the ship he found was its burned-out frame in the midst of a field of poppies. Only then, convinced that the story had not been some product of his father's imagination, did he wonder how the galleon had been able to get inland to that spot. But José Arcadio Buendía did not concern himself with that when he found the sea after another four days' journey from the galleon. His dreams ended as he faced that ashen, foamy, dirty sea, which had not merited the risks and sacrifices of the adventure.

"God damn it!" he shouted. "Macondo is surrounded by water on all sides."

The idea of a peninsular Macondo prevailed for a long time, inspired by the arbitrary map that José Arcadio Buendía sketched on his return from the expedition. He drew it in rage, evilly, exaggerating the difficulties of communication, as if to punish himself for the absolute lack of sense with which he had chosen the place. "We'll never get anywhere," he lamented to Úrsula. "We're going to rot our lives away here without receiving the benefits of science." That certainty, mulled over for several months in the small room he used as his laboratory, brought him to the conception of the plan to move Macondo to a better place. But that time Úrsula had anticipated his feverish designs. With the secret and implacable labor of a small ant she predisposed the women of the village against the flightiness of their husbands, who were already preparing for the move. José Arcadio Buendía did not know at what moment or because of what adverse forces his plan had become enveloped in a web of pretexts, disappointments, and evasions until it turned into nothing but an illusion. Úrsula watched him with innocent attention and even felt some pity for him on the morning when she found him in the back room muttering about his plans for moving as he placed his laboratory pieces in their original boxes. She let him finish. She let him nail up the boxes and put his initials on them with an inked brush, without reproaching him, but knowing now that he knew (because she had heard him say so in his soft monologues) that the men of the village would not back him up in his undertaking. Only when he began to take down the door of the room did Úrsula dare ask him what he was doing, and he answered with a certain bitterness. "Since no one wants to leave, we'll leave all by ourselves." Úrsula did not become upset.

"We will not leave," she said. "We will stay here, because we have had a son here."

"We have still not had a death," he said. "A person does not belong to a place until there is someone dead under the ground."

Úrsula replied with a soft firmness:

"If I have to die for the rest of you to stay here, I will die."

José Arcadio Buendía had not thought that his wife's will was so firm. He tried to seduce her with the charm of his fantasy, with the promise of a prodigious world where all one had to do was sprinkle some magic liquid on the ground and the plants would bear fruit whenever a man wished, and where all manner of instruments against pain were sold at bargain prices. But Úrsula was insensible to his clairvoyance.

"Instead of going around thinking about your crazy inventions, you should be worrying about your sons," she replied. "Look at the state they're in, running wild just like donkeys."

José Arcadio Buendía took his wife's words literally. He looked out the window and saw the barefoot children in the sunny garden and he had the impression that only at that instant had they begun to exist, conceived by Úrsula's spell. Something occurred inside of him then, something mysterious and definitive that uprooted him from his own time and carried him adrift through an unexplored region of his memory. While Úrsula continued sweeping the house, which was safe now from being abandoned for the rest of her life, he

14

stood there with an absorbed look, contemplating the children until his eyes became moist and he dried them with the back of his hand, exhaling a deep sigh of resignation.

"All right," he said. "Tell them to come help me take the things out of the boxes."

José Arcadio, the older of the children, was fourteen. He had a square head, thick hair, and his father's character. Although he had the same impulse for growth and physical strength, it was early evident that he lacked imagination. He had been conceived and born during the difficult crossing of the mountains, before the founding of Macondo, and his parents gave thanks to heaven when they saw he had no animal features. Aureliano, the first human being to be born in Macondo, would be six years old in March. He was silent and withdrawn. He had wept in his mother's womb and had been born with his eyes open. As they were cutting the umbilical cord, he moved his head from side to side, taking in the things in the room and examining the faces of the people with a fearless curiosity. Then, indifferent to those who came close to look at him, he kept his attention concentrated on the palm roof, which looked as if it were about to collapse under the tremendous pressure of the rain. Úrsula did not remember the intensity of that look again until one day when little Aureliano, at the age of three, went into the kitchen at the moment she was taking a pot of boiling soup from the stove and putting it on the table. The child, perplexed, said from the doorway, "It's going to spill." The pot was firmly placed in the center of the table, but just as soon as the child made his announcement, it began an unmistakable movement toward the edge, as if impelled by some inner dynamism, and it fell and broke on the floor. Úrsula, alarmed, told her husband about the episode, but he interpreted it as a natural phenomenon. That was the way he always was, alien to the existence of his sons, partly because he considered childhood as a period of mental insufficiency, and partly because he was always too absorbed in his fantastic speculations.

But since the afternoon when he called the children in to help him unpack the things in the laboratory, he gave them his best hours. In the small separate room, where the walls were gradually being covered by strange maps and fabulous drawings, he taught them to read and write and do sums, and he spoke to them about the wonders of the world, not only where his learning had extended, but forcing the limits of his imagination to extremes. It was in that way that the boys ended up learning that in the southern extremes of Africa there were men so intelligent and peaceful that their only pastime was to sit and think, and that it was possible to cross the Aegean Sea on foot by jumping from island to island all the way to the port of Salonika. Those hallucinating sessions remained printed on the memories of the boys in such a way that many years later, a second before the regular army officer gave the firing squad the command to fire, Colonel Aureliano Buendía saw once more that warm March afternoon on which his father had interrupted the lesson in physics and stood fascinated, with his hand in the air and his eyes motionless, listening to the distant pipes, drums, and jingles of the gypsies, who were coming to the village once more, announcing the latest and most startling discovery of the sages of Memphis.

They were new gypsies, young men and women who knew only their own language, handsome specimens with oily skins and intelligent hands, whose dances and music sowed a panic of uproarious joy through the streets, with parrots painted all colors reciting Italian arias, and a hen who laid a hundred golden eggs to the sound of a tambourine, and a trained monkey who read minds, and the multiple-use machine that could be used at the same time to sew on buttons and reduce fevers, and the apparatus to make a person forget his bad memories, and a poultice to lose time, and a thousand more

16

inventions so ingenious and unusual that José Arcadio Buendía must have wanted to invent a memory machine so that he could remember them all. In an instant they transformed the village. The inhabitants of Macondo found themselves lost in their own streets, confused by the crowded fair.

Holding a child by each hand so as not to lose them in the tumult, bumping into acrobats with gold-capped teeth and jugglers with six arms, suffocated by the mingled breath of manure and sandals that the crowd exhaled, José Arcadio Buendía went about everywhere like a madman, looking for Melquíades so that he could reveal to him the infinite secrets of that fabulous nightmare. He asked several gypsies, who did not understand his language. Finally he reached the place where Melquíades used to set up his tent and he found a taciturn Armenian who in Spanish was hawking a syrup to make oneself invisible. He had drunk down a glass of the amber substance in one gulp as José Arcadio Buendía elbowed his way through the absorbed group that was witnessing the spectacle, and was able to ask his question. The gypsy wrapped him in the frightful climate of his look before he turned into a puddle of pestilential and smoking pitch over which the echo of his reply still floated: "Melquíades is dead." Upset by the news, José Arcadio Buendía stood motionless, trying to rise above his affliction, until the group dispersed, called away by other artifices, and the puddle of the taciturn Armenian evaporated completely. Other gypsies confirmed later on that Melquíades had in fact succumbed to the fever on the beach at Singapore and that his body had been thrown into the deepest part of the Java Sea. The children had no interest in the news. They insisted that their father take them to see the overwhelming novelty of the sages of Memphis that was being advertised at the entrance of a tent that, according to what was said, had belonged to King Solomon. They insisted so much that José Arcadio Buendía

B*

paid the thirty reales and led them into the center of the tent, where there was a giant with a hairy torso and a shaved head, with a copper ring in his nose and a heavy iron chain on his ankle, watching over a pirate chest. When it was opened by the giant, the chest gave off a glacial exhalation. Inside there was only an enormous, transparent block with infinite internal needles in which the light of the sunset was broken up into colored stars. Disconcerted, knowing that the children were waiting for an immediate explanation, José Arcadio Buendía ventured a murmur:

"It's the largest diamond in the world."

"No," the gypsy countered. "It's ice."

José Arcadio Buendía, without understanding, stretched out his hand toward the cake, but the giant moved it away. "Five reales more to touch it," he said. José Arcadio Buendía paid them and put his hand on the ice and held it there for several minutes as his heart filled with fear and jubilation at the contact with mystery. Without knowing what to say, he paid ten reales more so that his sons could have that prodigious experience. Little José Arcadio refused to touch it. Aureliano, on the other hand, took a step forward and put his hand on it, withdrawing it immediately. "It's boiling," he exclaimed, startled. But his father paid no attention to him. Intoxicated by the evidence of the miracle, he forgot at that moment about the frustration of his delirious undertakings and Melquíades' body, abandoned to the appetite of the squids. He paid another five reales and with his hand on the cake, as if giving testimony on the holy scriptures, he exclaimed:

"This is the great invention of our time."

WHEN THE PIRATE Sir Francis Drake attacked Riohacha in the sixteenth century, Úrsula Iguarán's great-great-grandmother became so frightened with the ringing of alarm bells and the firing of cannons that she lost control of her nerves and sat down on a lighted stove. The burns changed her into a useless wife for the rest of her days. She could only sit on one side, cushioned by pillows, and something strange must have happened to her way of walking, for she never walked again in public. She gave up all kinds of social activity, obsessed with the notion that her body gave off a singed odor. Dawn would find her in the courtyard, for she did not dare fall asleep lest she dream of the English and their ferocious attack dogs as they came through the windows of her bedroom to submit her to shameful tortures with their red-hot irons. Her husband, an Aragonese merchant by whom she had two children, spent half the value of his store on medicines and pastimes in an attempt to alleviate her terror. Finally he sold the business and took the family to live far from the sea in a settlement of peaceful Indians located in the foothills, where he built his wife a bedroom without windows so that the pirates of her dream would have no way to get in.

In that hidden village there was a native-born tobacco planter who had lived there for some time, Don José Arcadio Buendía, with whom Úrsula's great-great-grandfather established a partnership that was so lucrative that within a few years they made a fortune. Several centuries later the great-great-grandson of the native-born planter married the great-great-granddaughter of the Aragonese. Therefore, every time that Úrsula became exercised over her husband's mad ideas, she would leap back over three hundred years of fate and curse the day that Sir Francis Drake had attacked Riohacha. It was simply a way of giving herself some relief, because actually they were joined till death by a bond that was more solid than love: a common prick of conscience. They were cousins. They had grown up together in the old village that both of their ancestors, with their work and their good habits, had transformed into one of the finest towns in the province. Although their marriage was predicted from the time they had come into the world, when they expressed their desire to be married their own relatives tried to stop it. They were afraid that those two healthy products of two races that had interbred over the centuries would suffer the shame of breeding iguanas. There had already been a horrible precedent. An aunt of Úrsula's, married to an uncle of José Arcadio Buendía, had a son who went through life wearing loose, baggy trousers and who bled to death after having lived forty-two years in the purest state of virginity, for he had been born and had grown up with a cartilaginous tail in the shape of a corkscrew and with a small tuft of hair on the tip. A pig's tail that was never allowed to be seen by any woman and that cost him his life when a butcher friend did him the favor of chopping it off with his cleaver. José Arcadio Buendía, with the whimsy of his nineteen years, resolved the problem with a single phrase: "I don't care if I have piglets as long as they can talk." So they were married amidst a festival of fireworks and a brass band that went on for three days. They would have been happy from then on if Úrsula's mother had not terrified her with all manner of sinister predictions about their offspring, even to the extreme of advising her to refuse to consummate the marriage. Fearing that her stout and willful husband would rape her while she slept, Úrsula, before going to bed, would put on a rudimentary kind of drawers that her mother had made out of sailcloth and had reinforced with a system of crisscrossed leather straps and that was closed in the front by a thick iron buckle. That was how they lived for several months. During the day he would take care of his fighting cocks and she would do frame embroidery with her mother. At night they would wrestle for several hours in an anguished violence that seemed to be a substitute for the act of love, until popular intuition got a whiff of something irregular and the rumor spread that Úrsula was still a virgin a year after her marriage because her husband was impotent. José Arcadio Buendía was the last one to hear the rumor.

"Look at what people are going around saying, Úrsula," he told his wife very calmly.

"Let them talk," she said. "We know that it's not true."

So the situation went on the same way for another six months until that tragic Sunday when José Arcadio Buendía won a cockfight from Prudencio Aguilar. Furious, aroused by the blood of his bird, the loser backed away from José Arcadio Buendía so that everyone in the cockpit could hear what he was going to tell him.

"Congratulations!" he shouted. "Maybe that rooster of yours can do your wife a favor."

José Arcadio Buendía serenely picked up his rooster. "I'll

be right back," he told everyone. And then to Prudencio Aguilar:

"You go home and get a weapon, because I'm going to kill you."

Ten minutes later he returned with the notched spear that had belonged to his grandfather. At the door to the cockpit, where half the town had gathered, Prudencio Aguilar was waiting for him. There was no time to defend himself. José Arcadio Buendía's spear, thrown with the strength of a bull and with the same good aim with which the first Aureliano Buendía had exterminated the jaguars in the region, pierced his throat. That night, as they held a wake over the corpse in the cockpit, José Arcadio Buendía went into the bedroom as his wife was putting on her chastity pants. Pointing the spear at her he ordered: "Take them off." Úrsula had no doubt about her husband's decision. "You'll be responsible for what happens," she murmured. José Arcadio Buendía stuck the spear into the dirt floor.

"If you bear iguanas, we'll raise iguanas," he said. "But there'll be no more killings in this town because of you."

It was a fine June night, cool and with a moon, and they were awake and frolicking in bed until dawn, indifferent to the breeze that passed through the bedroom, loaded with the weeping of Prudencio Aguilar's kin.

The matter was put down as a duel of honor, but both of them were left with a twinge in their conscience. One night, when she could not sleep, Úrsula went out into the courtyard to get some water and she saw Prudencio Aguilar by the water jar. He was livid, a sad expression on his face, trying to cover the hole in his throat with a plug made of esparto grass. It did not bring on fear in her, but pity. She went back to the room and told her husband what she had seen, but he did not think much of it. "This just means that we can't stand the weight of our conscience." Two nights later Úrsula saw Prudencio Aguilar again, in the bathroom, using the esparto plug to wash the clotted blood from his throat. On another night she saw him strolling in the rain. José Arcadio Buendía, annoyed by his wife's hallucinations, went out into the courtyard armed with the spear. There was the dead man with his sad expression.

"You go to hell," José Arcadio Buendía shouted at him. "Just as many times as you come back, I'll kill you again."

Prudencio Aguilar did not go away, nor did José Arcadio Buendía dare throw the spear. He never slept well after that. He was tormented by the immense desolation with which the dead man had looked at him through the rain, his deep nostalgia as he yearned for living people, the anxiety with which he searched through the house looking for some water with which to soak his esparto plug. "He must be suffering a great deal," he said to Úrsula. "You can see that he's so very lonely." She was so moved that the next time she saw the dead man uncovering the pots on the stove she understood what he was looking for, and from then on she placed water jugs all about the house. One night when he found him washing his wound in his own room, José Arcadio Buendía could no longer resist.

"It's all right, Prudencio," he told him. "We're going to leave this town, just as far away as we can go, and we'll never come back. Go in peace now."

That was how they undertook the crossing of the mountains. Several friends of José Arcadio Buendía, young men like him, excited by the adventure, dismantled their houses and packed up, along with their wives and children, to head toward the land that no one had promised them. Before he left, José Arcadio Buendía buried the spear in the courtyard and, one after the other, he cut the throats of his magnificent fighting cocks, trusting that in that way he could give some measure of peace to Prudencio Aguilar. All that Úrsula took along were a trunk with her bridal clothes, a few household utensils, and the small chest with the gold pieces that she had inherited from her father. They did not lay out any definite itinerary. They simply tried to go in a direction opposite to the road to Riohacha so that they would not leave any trace or meet any people they knew. It was an absurd journey. After fourteen months, her stomach corrupted by monkey meat and snake stew, Úrsula gave birth to a son who had all of his features human. She had traveled half of the trip in a hammock that two men carried on their shoulders, because swelling had disfigured her legs and her varicose veins had puffed up like bubbles. Although it was pitiful to see them with their sunken stomachs and languid eyes, the children survived the journey better than their parents, and most of the time it was fun for them. One morning, after almost two years of crossing, they became the first mortals to see the western slopes of the mountain range. From the cloudy summit they saw the immense aquatic expanse of the great swamp as it spread out toward the other side of the world. But they never found the sea. One night, after several months of lost wandering through the swamps, far away now from the last Indians they had met on their way, they camped on the banks of a stony river whose waters were like a torrent of frozen glass. Years later, during the second civil war, Colonel Aureliano Buendía tried to follow that same route in order to take Riohacha by surprise and after six days of traveling he understood that it was madness. Nevertheless, the night on which they camped beside the river, his father's host had the look of shipwrecked people with no escape, but their number had grown during the crossing and they were all prepared (and they succeeded) to die of old age. José Arcadio Buendía dreamed that night that right there a noisy city with houses having mirror walls rose up. He asked what city it was and they answered him with a name that he had never heard, that had no meaning at all, but that had a supernatural echo in his dream: Macondo. On the following day he convinced his men that they would never find the sea. He ordered them to cut down the trees to make a clearing beside the river, at the coolest spot on the bank, and there they founded the village.

José Arcadio Buendía did not succeed in deciphering the dream of houses with mirror walls until the day he discovered ice. Then he thought he understood its deep meaning. He thought that in the near future they would be able to manufacture blocks of ice on a large scale from such a common material as water and with them build the new houses of the village. Macondo would no longer be a burning place, where the hinges and door knockers twisted with the heat, but would be changed into a wintry city. If he did not persevere in his attempts to build an ice factory, it was because at that time he was absolutely enthusiastic over the education of his sons, especially that of Aureliano, who from the first had revealed a strange intuition for alchemy. The laboratory had been dusted off. Reviewing Melquíades' notes, serene now, without the exaltation of novelty, in prolonged and patient sessions they tried to separate Úrsula's gold from the debris that was stuck to the bottom of the pot. Young José Arcadio scarcely took part in the process. While his father was involved body and soul with his water pipe, the willful firstborn, who had always been too big for his age, had become a monumental adolescent. His voice had changed. An incipient fuzz appeared on his upper lip. One night, as Úrsula went into the room where he was undressing to go to bed, she felt a mingled sense of shame and pity: he was the first man that she had seen naked after her husband, and he was so well-equipped for life that he seemed abnormal. Úrsula, pregnant for the third time, relived her newlywed terror.

Around that time a merry, foul-mouthed, provocative woman came to the house to help with the chores, and she knew how to read the future in cards. Úrsula spoke to her about her son. She thought that his disproportionate size was something as unnatural as her cousin's tail of a pig. The

25

woman let out an expansive laugh that resounded through the house like a spray of broken glass. "Just the opposite," she said. "He'll be very lucky." In order to confirm her prediction she brought her cards to the house a few days later and locked herself up with José Arcadio in a granary off the kitchen. She calmly placed her cards on an old carpenter's bench, saying anything that came into her head, while the boy waited beside her, more bored than intrigued. Suddenly she reached out her hand and touched him. "Lordy!" she said, sincerely startled, and that was all she could say. José Arcadio felt his bones filling up with foam, a languid fear, and a terrible desire to weep. The woman made no insinuations. But José Arcadio kept looking for her all night long, for the smell of smoke that she had under her armpits and that had got caught under his skin. He wanted to be with her all the time, he wanted her to be his mother, for them never to leave the granary, and for her to say "Lordy!" to him. One day he could not stand it any more and he went looking for her at her house. He made a formal visit, sitting uncomprehendingly in the living room without saying a word. At that moment he had no desire for her. He found her different, entirely foreign to the image that her smell brought on, as if she were someone else. He drank his coffee and left the house in depression. That night, during the frightful time of lying awake, he desired her again with a brutal anxiety, but he did not want her that time as she had been in the granary but as she had been that afternoon.

Days later the woman suddenly called him to her house, where she was alone with her mother, and she had him come into the bedroom with the pretext of showing him a deck of cards. Then she touched him with such freedom that he suffered a delusion after the initial shudder, and he felt more fear than pleasure. She asked him to come and see her that night. He agreed, in order to get away, knowing that he was incapable of going. But that night, in his burning bed, he

26

understood that he had to go see her, even if he were not capable. He got dressed by feel, listening in the dark to his brother's calm breathing, the dry cough of his father in the next room, the asthma of the hens in the courtyard, the buzz of the mosquitoes, the beating of his heart, and the inordinate bustle of a world that he had not noticed until then, and he went out into the sleeping street. With all his heart he wanted the door to be barred and not just closed as she had promised him. But it was open. He pushed it with the tips of his fingers and the hinges yielded with a mournful and articulate moan that left a frozen echo inside of him. From the moment he entered, sideways and trying not to make a noise, he caught the smell. He was still in the hallway, where the woman's three brothers had their hammocks in positions that he could not see and that he could not determine in the darkness as he felt his way along the hall to push open the bedroom door and get his bearings there so as not to mistake the bed. He found it. He bumped against the ropes of the hammocks, which were lower than he had suspected, and a man who had been snoring until then turned in his sleep and said in a kind of delusion, "It was Wednesday." When he pushed open the bedroom door, he could not prevent it from scraping against the uneven floor. Suddenly, in the absolute darkness, he understood with a hopeless nostalgia that he was completely disoriented. Sleeping in the narrow room were the mother, another daughter with her husband and two children, and the woman, who may not have been there. He could have guided himself by the smell if the smell had not been all over the house, so devious and at the same time so definite, as it had always been on his skin. He did not move for a long time, wondering in fright how he had ever got to that abyss of abandonment, when a hand with all its fingers extended and feeling about in the darkness touched his face. He was not surprised, for without knowing, he had been expecting it. Then he gave himself over to that hand, and in a terrible state of exhaustion he let himself be led to a shapeless place where his clothes were taken off and he was heaved about like a sack of potatoes and thrown from one side to the other in a bottomless darkness in which his arms were useless, where it no longer smelled of woman but of ammonia, and where he tried to remember her face and found before him the face of Úrsula, confusedly aware that he was doing something that for a very long time he had wanted to do but that he had imagined could really never be done, not knowing what he was doing because he did not know where his feet were or where his head was, or whose feet or whose head, and feeling that he could no longer resist the glacial rumbling of his kidneys and the air of his intestines, and fear, and the bewildered anxiety to flee and at the same time stay forever in that exasperated silence and that fearful solitude.

Her name was Pilar Ternera. She had been part of the exodus that ended with the founding of Macondo, dragged along by her family in order to separate her from the man who had raped her at fourteen and had continued to love her until she was twenty-two, but who never made up his mind to make the situation public because he was a man apart. He promised to follow her to the ends of the earth, but only later on, when he put his affairs in order, and she had become tired of waiting for him, always identifying him with the tall and short, blond and brunet men that her cards promised from land and sea within three days, three months, or three years. With her waiting she had lost the strength of her thighs, the firmness of her breasts, her habit of tenderness, but she kept the madness of her heart intact. Maddened by that prodigious plaything, José Arcadio followed her path every night through the labyrinth of the room. On a certain occasion he found the door barred, and he knocked several times, knowing that if he had the boldness to knock the first time he would have had to knock until the last, and after an interminable wait she opened the door for him. During the day, lying down to dream, he would secretly enjoy the memories of the night before. But when she came into the house, merry, indifferent, chatty, he did not have to make any effort to hide his tension, because that woman, whose explosive laugh frightened off the doves, had nothing to do with the invisible power that taught him how to breathe from within and control his heartbeats, and that had permitted him to understand why men are afraid of death. He was so wrapped up in himself that he did not even understand the joy of everyone when his father and his brother aroused the household with the news that they had succeeded in penetrating the metallic debris and had separated Úrsula's gold.

They had succeeded, as a matter of fact, after putting in complicated and persevering days at it. Úrsula was happy, and she even gave thanks to God for the invention of alchemy, while the people of the village crushed into the laboratory, and they served them guava jelly on crackers to celebrate the wonder, and José Arcadio Buendía let them see the crucible with the recovered gold, as if he had just invented it. Showing it all around, he ended up in front of his older son, who during the past few days had barely put in an appearance in the laboratory. He put the dry and yellowish mass in front of his eyes and asked him: "What does it look like to you?" José Arcadio answered sincerely:

"Dog shit."

His father gave him a blow with the back of his hand that brought out blood and tears. That night Pilar Ternera put arnica compresses on the swelling, feeling about for the bottle and cotton in the dark, and she did everything she wanted with him as long as it did not bother him, making an effort to love him without hurting him. They reached such a state of intimacy that later, without realizing it, they were whispering to each other.

"I want to be alone with you," he said. "One of these days

I'm going to tell everybody and we can stop all of this sneaking around."

She did not try to calm him down.

"That would be fine," she said. "If we're alone, we'll leave the lamp lighted so that we can see each other, and I can holler as much as I want without anybody's having to butt in, and you can whisper in my ear any crap you can think of."

That conversation, the biting rancor that he felt against his father, and the imminent possibility of wild love inspired a serene courage in him. In a spontaneous way, without any preparation, he told everything to his brother.

At first young Aureliano understood only the risk, the immense possibility of danger that his brother's adventures implied, and he could not understand the fascination of the object. Little by little he became contaminated with the anxiety. He wondered about the details of the dangers, he identified himself with the suffering and enjoyment of his brother, he felt frightened and happy. He would stay awake waiting for him until dawn in the solitary bed that seemed to have a bottom of live coals, and they would keep on talking until it was time to get up, so that both of them soon suffered from the same drowsiness, felt the same lack of interest in alchemy and the wisdom of their father, and they took refuge in solitude. "Those kids are out of their heads," Úrsula said. "They must have worms." She prepared a repugnant potion for them made out of mashed wormseed, which they both drank with unforeseen stoicism, and they sat down at the same time on their pots eleven times in a single day, expelling some rose-colored parasites that they showed to everybody with great jubilation, for it allowed them to deceive Úrsula as to the origin of their distractions and drowsiness. Aureliano not only understood by then, he also lived his brother's experiences as something of his own, for on one occasion when the latter was explaining in great detail the mechanisms of love, he interrupted him to ask: "What does it feel like?" José Arcadio gave an immediate reply:

"It's like an earthquake."

One January Thursday at two o'clock in the morning, Amaranta was born. Before anyone came into the room, Úrsula examined her carefully. She was light and watery, like a newt, but all of her parts were human. Aureliano did not notice the new thing except when the house became full of people. Protected by the confusion, he went off in search of his brother, who had not been in bed since eleven o'clock, and it was such an impulsive decision that he did not even have time to ask himself how he could get him out of Pilar Ternera's bedroom. He circled the house for several hours, whistling private calls, until the proximity of dawn forced him to go home. In his mother's room, playing with the newborn little sister and with a face that drooped with innocence, he found José Arcadio.

Úrsula was barely over her forty days' rest when the gypsies returned. They were the same acrobats and jugglers that had brought the ice. Unlike Melquíades' tribe, they had shown very quickly that they were not heralds of progress but purveyors of amusement. Even when they brought the ice they did not advertise it for its usefulness in the life of man but as a simple circus curiosity. This time, along with many other artifices, they brought a flying carpet. But they did not offer it as a fundamental contribution to the development of transport, rather as an object of recreation. The people at once dug up their last gold pieces to take advantage of a quick flight over the houses of the village. Protected by the delightful cover of collective disorder, José Arcadio and Pilar passed many relaxing hours. They were two happy lovers among the crowd, and they even came to suspect that love could be a feeling that was more relaxing and deep than the happiness, wild but momentary, of their secret nights. Pilar, however, broke the spell. Stimulated by the enthusiasm that José Arcadio showed in her companionship, she confused the form and the occasion, and all of a sudden she threw the whole world on top of him. "Now you really are a man," she told him. And since he did not understand what she meant, she spelled it out to him.

"You're going to be a father."

José Arcadio did not dare leave the house for several days. It was enough for him to hear the rocking laughter of Pilar in the kitchen to run and take refuge in the laboratory, where the artifacts of alchemy had come alive again with Úrsula's blessing. José Arcadio Buendía received his errant son with joy and initiated him in the search for the philosopher's stone, which he had finally undertaken. One afternoon the boys grew enthusiastic over the flying carpet that went swiftly by the laboratory at window level carrying the gypsy who was driving it and several children from the village who were merrily waving their hands, but José Arcadio Buendía did not even look at it. "Let them dream," he said. "We'll do better flying than they are doing, and with more scientific resources than a miserable bedspread." In spite of his feigned interest, José Arcadio never understood the powers of the philosopher's egg, which to him looked like a poorly blown bottle. He did not succeed in escaping from his worries. He lost his appetite and he could not sleep. He fell into an ill humor, the same as his father's over the failure of his undertakings, and such was his upset that José Arcadio Buendía himself relieved him of his duties in the laboratory, thinking that he had taken alchemy too much to heart. Aureliano, of course, understood that his brother's affliction did not have its source in the search for the philosopher's stone, but he could not get into his confidence. He had lost his former spontaneity. From an accomplice and a communicative person he had become withdrawn and hostile. Anxious for solitude, bitten by a virulent rancor against the world, one night he left his bed as usual, but he did not go to Pilar Ternera's house, but to mingle in the tumult of the fair. After wandering about among all kinds of contraptions without becoming interested in any of them, he spotted something that was not a part of it all: a very young gypsy girl, almost a child, who was weighted down by beads and was the most beautiful woman that José Arcadio had ever seen in his life. She was in the crowd that was witnessing the sad spectacle of the man who had been turned into a snake for having disobeyed his parents.

José Arcadio paid no attention. While the sad interrogation of the snake-man was taking place, he made his way through the crowd up to the first row, where the gypsy girl was, and he stopped behind her. He pressed against her back. The girl tried to separate herself, but José Arcadio pressed more strongly against her back. Then she felt him. She remained motionless against him, trembling with surprise and fear, unable to believe the evidence, and finally she turned her head and looked at him with a tremulous smile. At that instant two gypsies put the snake-man into his cage and carried him into the tent. The gypsy who was conducting the show announced:

"And now, ladies and gentlemen, we are going to show the terrible test of the woman who must have her head chopped off every night at this time for one hundred and fifty years as punishment for having seen what she should not have."

José Arcadio and the gypsy girl did not witness the decapitation. They went to her tent, where they kissed each other with a desperate anxiety while they took off their clothes. The gypsy girl removed the starched lace corsets she had on and there she was, changed into practically nothing. She was a languid little frog, with incipient breasts and legs so thin that they did not even match the size of José Arcadio's arms, but she had a decision and a warmth that compensated for her fragility. Nevertheless, José Arcadio could not respond to her because they were in a kind of public tent where the gypsies passed through with their circus things and did their business, and would even tarry by the bed for a game of dice. The lamp hanging from the center pole lighted the whole

33

place up. During a pause in the caresses, José Arcadio stretched out naked on the bed without knowing what to do, while the girl tried to inspire him. A gypsy woman with splendid flesh came in a short time after accompanied by a man who was not of the caravan but who was not from the village either, and they both began to undress in front of the bed. Without meaning to, the woman looked at José Arcadio and examined his magnificent animal in repose with a kind of pathetic fervor.

"My boy," she exclaimed, "may God preserve you just as you are."

José Arcadio's companion asked them to leave them alone, and the couple lay down on the ground, close to the bed. The passion of the others woke up José Arcadio's fervor. On the first contact the bones of the girl seemed to become disjointed with a disorderly crunch like the sound of a box of dominoes, and her skin broke out into a pale sweat and her eyes filled with tears as her whole body exhaled a lugubrious lament and a vague smell of mud. But she bore the impact with a firmness of character and a bravery that were admirable. José Arcadio felt himself lifted up into the air toward a state of seraphic inspiration, where his heart burst forth with an out-pouring of tender obscenities that entered the girl through her ears and came out of her mouth translated into her language. It was Thursday. On Saturday night, José Arcadio wrapped a red cloth around his head and left with the gypsies.

When Úrsula discovered his absence she searched for him all through the village. In the remains of the gypsy camp there was nothing but a garbage pit among the still smoking ashes of the extinguished campfires. Someone who was there looking for beads among the trash told Úrsula that the night before he had seen her son in the tumult of the caravan pushing the snake-man's cage on a cart. "He's become a gypsy!" she shouted to her husband, who had not shown the slightest sign of alarm over the disappearance.

"I hope it's true," José Arcadio Buendía said, grinding in his mortar the material that had been ground a thousand times and reheated and ground again. "That way he'll learn to be a man."

Úrsula asked where the gypsies had gone. She went along asking and following the road she had been shown, thinking that she still had time to catch up to them. She kept getting farther away from the village until she felt so far away that she did not think about returning. José Arcadio Buendía did not discover that his wife was missing until eight o'clock at night, when he left the material warming in a bed of manure and went to see what was wrong with little Amaranta, who was getting hoarse from crying. In a few hours he gathered a group of well-equipped men, put Amaranta in the hands of a woman who offered to nurse her, and was lost on invisible paths in pursuit of Úrsula. Aureliano went with them. Some Indian fishermen, whose language they could not understand, told them with signs that they had not seen anyone pass. After three days of useless searching they returned to the village.

For several weeks José Arcadio Buendía let himself be overcome by consternation. He took care of little Amaranta like a mother. He bathed and dressed her, took her to be nursed four times a day, and even sang to her at night the songs that Úrsula never knew how to sing. On a certain occasion Pilar Ternera volunteered to do the household chores until Úrsula came back. Aureliano, whose mysterious intuition had become sharpened with the misfortune, felt a glow of clairvoyance when he saw her come in. Then he knew that in some inexplicable way she was to blame for his brother's flight and the consequent disappearance of his mother, and he harassed her with a silent and implacable hostility in such a way that the woman did not return to the house.

Time put things in their place. José Arcadio Buendía and his son did not know exactly when they returned to the laboratory, dusting things, lighting the water pipe, involved once more in the patient manipulation of the material that had been sleeping for several months in its bed of manure. Even Amaranta, lying in a wicker basket, observed with curiosity the absorbing work of her father and her brother in the small room where the air was rarefied by mercury vapors. On a certain occasion, months after Úrsula's departure, strange things began to happen. An empty flask that had been forgotten in a cupboard for a long time became so heavy that it could not be moved. A pan of water on the worktable boiled without any fire under it for a half hour until it completely evaporated. José Arcadio Buendía and his son observed those phenomena with startled excitement, unable to explain them but interpreting them as predictions of the material. One day Amaranta's basket began to move by itself and made a complete turn about the room, to the consternation of Aureliano, who hurried to stop it. But his father did not get upset. He put the basket in its place and tied it to the leg of a table, convinced that the long-awaited event was imminent. It was on that occasion that Aureliano heard him say:

"If you don't fear God, fear him through the metals."

Suddenly, almost five months after her disappearance, Úrsula came back. She arrived exalted, rejuvenated, with new clothes in a style that was unknown in the village. José Arcadio Buendía could barely stand up under the impact. "That was it!" he shouted. "I knew it was going to happen." And he really believed it, for during his prolonged imprisonment as he manipulated the material, he begged in the depth of his heart that the longed-for miracle should not be the discovery of the philosopher's stone, or the freeing of the breath that makes metals live, or the faculty to convert the hinges and the locks of the house into gold, but what had just happened: Úrsula's return. But she did not share his excitement. She gave him a conventional kiss, as if she had been away only an hour, and she told him:

"Look out the door."

José Arcadio Buendía took a long time to get out of his perplexity when he went out into the street and saw the crowd. They were not gypsies. They were men and women like them, with straight hair and dark skin, who spoke the same language and complained of the same pains. They had mules loaded down with things to eat, oxcarts with furniture and domestic utensils, pure and simple earthly accessories put on sale without any fuss by peddlers of everyday reality. They came from the other side of the swamp, only two days away, where there were towns that received mail every month in the year and where they were familiar with the implements of good living. Úrsula had not caught up with the gypsies, but she had found the route that her husband had been unable to discover in his frustrated search for the great inventions.

Pilar Ternera's son was brought to his grandparents' house two weeks after he was born. Úrsula admitted him grudgingly, conquered once more by the obstinacy of her husband, who could not tolerate the idea that an offshoot of his blood should be adrift, but he imposed the condition that the child should never know his true identity. Although he was given the name José Arcadio, they ended up calling him simply Arcadio so as to avoid confusion. At that time there was so much activity in the town and so much bustle in the house that the care of the children was relegated to a secondary level. They were put in the care of Visitación, a Guajiro Indian woman who had arrived in town with a brother in flight from a plague of insomnia that had been scourging their tribe for several years. They were both so docile and willing to help that Úrsula took them on to help her with her household chores. That was how Arcadio and Amaranta came to speak the Guajiro language before Spanish, and they learned to drink lizard broth and eat spider eggs without Úrsula's knowing it, for she was too busy with a promising business in candy animals. Macondo had changed. The people who had come with Úrsula spread the news of the good quality of its soil and its privileged position with respect to the swamp, so that from the narrow village of past times it changed into an active town with stores and workshops and a permanent commercial route over which the first Arabs arrived with their baggy pants and rings in their ears, swapping glass beads for macaws. José Arcadio Buendía did not have a moment's rest. Fascinated by an immediate reality that came to be more fantastic than the vast universe of his imagination, he lost all interest in the alchemist's laboratory, put to rest the material that had become attenuated with months of manipulation, and went back to being the enterprising man of earlier days when he had decided upon the layout of the streets and the location of the new houses so that no one would enjoy privileges that everyone did not have. He acquired such authority among the new arrivals that foundations were not laid or walls built without his being consulted, and it was decided that he should be the one in charge of the distribution of the land. When the acrobat gypsies returned, with their vagabond carnival transformed now into a gigantic organization of games of luck and chance, they were received with great joy, for it was thought that José Arcadio would be coming back with them. But José Arcadio did not return, nor did they come with the snake-man, who, according to what Úrsula thought, was the only one who could tell them about their son, so the gypsies were not allowed to camp in town or set foot in it in the future, for they were considered the bearers of concupiscence and perversion. José Arcadio Buendía, however, was explicit in maintaining that the old tribe of Melquíades, who had contributed so much to the growth of the village with his age-old wisdom and his fabulous inventions, would always find the gates open. But Melquíades' tribe, according to what the wanderers said, had been wiped off the face of the earth because they had gone beyond the limits of human knowledge.

Emancipated for the moment at least from the torment of fantasy, José Arcadio Buendía in a short time set up a system of order and work which allowed for only one bit of license: the freeing of the birds, which, since the time of the founding, had made time merry with their flutes, and installing in their place musical clocks in every house. They were wondrous clocks made of carved wood, which the Arabs had traded for macaws and which José Arcadio Buendía had synchronized with such precision that every half hour the town grew merry with the progressive chords of the same song until it reached the climax of a noontime that was as exact and unanimous as a complete waltz. It was also José Arcadio Buendía who decided during those years that they should plant almond trees instead of acacias on the streets, and who discovered, without ever revealing it, a way to make them live forever. Many years later, when Macondo was a field of wooden houses with zinc roofs, the broken and dusty almond trees still stood on the oldest streets, although no one knew who had planted them. While his father was putting the town in order and his mother was increasing their wealth with her marvelous business of candied little roosters and fish, which left the house twice a day strung along sticks of balsa wood, Aureliano spent interminable hours in the abandoned laboratory, learning the art of silverwork by his own experimentation. He had shot up so fast that in a short time the clothing left behind by his brother no longer fit him and he began to wear his father's, but Visitación had to sew pleats in the shirt and darts in the pants, because Aureliano had not acquired the corpulence of the others. Adolescence had taken away the softness of his voice and had made him silent and definitely solitary, but, on the other hand, it had restored the intense expression that he had had in his eyes when he was born. He concentrated so much on his experiments in silver-work that he scarcely left the laboratory to eat. Worried over his inner withdrawal, José Arcadio Buendía gave him the keys to the house and a little money, thinking that perhaps he needed a woman. But Aureliano spent the money on muriatic acid to prepare some aqua regia and he beautified the keys by plating them with gold. His excesses were hardly comparable to those of Arcadio and Amaranta, who had already begun to get their second teeth and still went about all day clutching at the Indians' cloaks, stubborn in their decision not to speak Spanish but the Guajiro language. "You shouldn't complain," Úrsula told her husband. "Children inherit their parents' madness." And as she was lamenting her misfortune, convinced that the wild behavior of her children was something as fearful as a pig's tail, Aureliano gave her a look that wrapped her in an atmosphere of uncertainty.

"Somebody is coming," he told her.

Úrsula, as she did whenever he made a prediction, tried to break it down with her housewifely logic. It was normal for someone to be coming. Dozens of strangers came through Macondo every day without arousing suspicion or secret ideas. Nevertheless, beyond all logic, Aureliano was sure of his prediction.

"I don't know who it will be," he insisted, "but whoever it is is already on the way."

That Sunday, in fact, Rebeca arrived. She was only eleven years old. She had made the difficult trip from Manaure with some hide dealers who had taken on the task of delivering her along with a letter to José Arcadio Buendía, but they could not explain precisely who the person was who had asked the favor. Her entire baggage consisted of a small trunk, a little

c

rocking chair with small hand-painted flowers, and a canvas sack which kept making a *cloc-cloc-cloc* sound, where she carried her parents' bones. The letter addressed to José Arcadio Buendía was written in very warm terms by someone who still loved him very much in spite of time and distance, and who felt obliged by a basic humanitarian feeling to do the charitable thing and send him that poor unsheltered orphan, who was a second cousin of Úrsula's and consequently also a relative of José Arcadio Buendía, although farther removed, because she was the daughter of that unforgettable friend Nicanor Ulloa and his very worthy wife Rebeca Montiel, may God keep them in His holy kingdom, whose remains the girl was carrying so that they might be given Christian burial. The names mentioned, as well as the signature on the letter, were perfectly legible, but neither José Arcadio Buendía nor Úrsula remembered having any relatives with those names, nor did they know anyone by the name of the sender of the letter, much less the remote village of Manaure. It was impossible to obtain any further information from the girl. From the moment she arrived she had been sitting in the rocker, sucking her finger and observing everyone with her large, startled eyes without giving any sign of understanding what they were asking her. She wore a diagonally striped dress that had been dyed black, worn by use, and a pair of scaly patent leather boots. Her hair was held behind her ears with bows of black ribbon. She wore a scapular with the images worn away by sweat, and on her right wrist the fang of a carnivorous animal mounted on a backing of copper as an amulet against the evil eye. Her greenish skin, her stomach, round and tense as a drum, revealed poor health and hunger that were older than she was, but when they gave her something to eat she kept the plate on her knees without tasting anything. They even began to think that she was a deaf-mute until the Indians asked her in their language if she wanted some water and she moved her eyes as if she recognized them and said yes with her head.

42

They kept her, because there was nothing else they could do. They decided to call her Rebeca, which according to the letter was her mother's name, because Aureliano had the patience to read to her the names of all the saints and he did not get a reaction from any one of them. Since there was no cemetery in Macondo at that time, for no one had died up till then, they kept the bag of bones to wait for a worthy place of burial, and for a long time it got in the way everywhere and would be found where least expected, always with its clucking of a broody hen. A long time passed before Rebeca became incorporated into the life of the family. She would sit in her small rocker sucking her finger in the most remote corner of the house. Nothing attracted her attention except the music of the clocks, which she would look for every half hour with her frightened eyes as if she hoped to find it someplace in the air. They could not get her to eat for several days. No one understood why she had not died of hunger until the Indians, who were aware of everything, for they went ceaselessly about the house on their stealthy feet, discovered that Rebeca only liked to eat the damp earth of the courtyard and the cake of whitewash that she picked off the walls with her nails. It was obvious that her parents, or whoever had raised her, had scolded her for that habit because she did it secretively and with a feeling of guilt, trying to put away supplies so that she could eat when no one was looking. From then on they put her under an implacable watch. They threw cow gall onto the courtyard and rubbed hot chili on the walls, thinking they could defeat her pernicious vice with those methods, but she showed such signs of astuteness and ingenuity to find some earth that Úrsula found herself forced to use more drastic methods. She put some orange juice and rhubarb into a pan that she left in the dew all night and she gave her the dose the following day on an empty stomach. Although no one had told her that it was the specific remedy for the vice of eating earth, she thought that any bitter substance in an empty stomach would have to make the liver

43

react. Rebeca was so rebellious and strong in spite of her frailness that they had to tie her up like a calf to make her swallow the medicine, and they could barely keep back her kicks or bear up under the strange hieroglyphics that she alternated with her bites and spitting, and that, according to what the scandalized Indians said, were the vilest obscenities that one could ever imagine in their language. When Úrsula discovered that, she added whipping to the treatment. It was never established whether it was the rhubarb or the beatings that had effect, or both of them together, but the truth was that in a few weeks Rebeca began to show signs of recovery. She took part in the games of Arcadio and Amaranta, who treated her like an older sister, and she ate heartily, using the utensils properly. It was soon revealed that she spoke Spanish with as much fluency as the Indian language, that she had a remarkable ability for manual work, and that she could sing the waltz of the clocks with some very funny words that she herself had invented. It did not take long for them to consider her another member of the family. She was more affectionate to Úrsula than any of her own children had been, and she called Arcadio and Amaranta brother and sister, Aureliano uncle, and José Arcadio Buendía grandpa. So that she finally deserved, as much as the others, the name of Rebeca Buendía, the only one that she ever had and that she bore with dignity until her death.

One night about the time that Rebeca was cured of the vice of eating earth and was brought to sleep in the other children's room, the Indian woman, who slept with them, awoke by chance and heard a strange, intermittent sound in the corner. She got up in alarm, thinking that an animal had come into the room, and then she saw Rebeca in the rocker, sucking her finger and with her eyes lighted up in the darkness like those of a cat. Terrified, exhausted by her fate, Visitación recognized in those eyes the symptoms of the sickness whose threat had obliged her and her brother to exile themselves forever from an age-old kingdom where they had been prince and princess. It was the insomnia plague.

Cataure, the Indian, was gone from the house by morning. His sister stayed because her fatalistic heart told her that the lethal sickness would follow her, no matter what, to the farthest corner of the earth. No one understood Visitación's alarm. "If we don't ever sleep again, so much the better," José Arcadio Buendía said in good humor. "That way we can get more out of life." But the Indian woman explained that the most fearsome part of the sickness of insomnia was not the impossibility of sleeping, for the body did not feel any fatigue at all, but its inexorable evolution toward a more critical manifestation: a loss of memory. She meant that when the sick person became used to his state of vigil, the recollection of his childhood began to be erased from his memory, then the name and notion of things, and finally the identity of people and even the awareness of his own being, until he sank into a kind of idiocy that had no past. José Arcadio Buendía, dying with laughter, thought that it was just a question of one of the many illnesses invented by the Indians' superstitions. But Úrsula, just to be safe, took the precaution of isolating Rebeca from the other children.

After several weeks, when Visitación's terror seemed to have died down, José Arcadio Buendía found himself rolling over in bed, unable to fall asleep. Úrsula, who had also awakened, asked him what was wrong, and he answered: "I'm thinking about Prudencio Aguilar again." They did not sleep a minute, but the following day they felt so rested that they forgot about the bad night. Aureliano commented with surprise at lunchtime that he felt very well in spite of the fact that he had spent the whole night in the laboratory gilding a brooch that he planned to give to Úrsula for her birthday. They did not become alarmed until the third day, when no one felt sleepy at bedtime and they realized that they had gone more than fifty hours without sleeping.

"The children are awake too," the Indian said with her fatalistic conviction. "Once it gets into a house no one can escape the plague."

They had indeed contracted the illness of insomnia. Úrsula, who had learned from her mother the medicinal value of plants, prepared and made them all drink a brew of monkshood, but they could not get to sleep and spent the whole day dreaming on their feet. In that state of hallucinated lucidity, not only did they see the images of their own dreams, but some saw the images dreamed by others. It was as if the house were full of visitors. Sitting in her rocker in a corner of the kitchen, Rebeca dreamed that a man who looked very much like her, dressed in white linen and with his shirt collar closed by a gold button, was bringing her a bouquet of roses. He was accompanied by a woman with delicate hands who took out one rose and put it in the child's hair. Úrsula understood that the man and woman were Rebeca's parents, but even though she made a great effort to recognize them, she confirmed her certainty that she had never seen them. In the meantime, through an oversight that José Arcadio Buendía never forgave himself for, the candy animals made in the house were still being sold in the town. Children and adults sucked with delight on the delicious little green roosters of insomnia, the exquisite pink fish of insomnia, and the tender yellow ponies of insomnia, so that dawn on Monday found the whole town awake. No one was alarmed at first. On the contrary, they were happy at not sleeping because there was so much to do in Macondo in those days that there was barely enough time. They worked so hard that soon they had nothing else to do and they could be found at three o'clock in the morning with their arms crossed, counting the notes in the waltz of the clock. Those who wanted to sleep, not from fatigue but because of the nostalgia for dreams, tried all kinds of methods of exhausting themselves. They would gather together to converse endlessly, to tell over and over for hours on end the same jokes, to complicate to the limits of exasperation the story about the capon, which was an endless game in which the narrator asked if they wanted him to tell them the story about the capon, and when they answered yes, the narrator would say that he had not asked them to say yes, but whether they wanted him to tell them the story about the capon, and when they answered no, the narrator told them that he had not asked them to say no, but whether they wanted him to tell them the story about the capon, and when they remained silent the narrator told them that he had not asked them to remain silent but whether they wanted him to tell them the story about the capon, and no one could leave because the narrator would say that he had not asked them to leave but whether they wanted him to tell them the story about the capon, and so on and on in a vicious circle that lasted entire nights.

When José Arcadio Buendía realized that the plague had invaded the town, he gathered together the heads of families to explain to them what he knew about the sickness of insomnia, and they agreed on methods to prevent the scourge from spreading to other towns in the swamp. That was why they took the bells off the goats, bells that the Arabs had swapped them for macaws, and put them at the entrance to town at the disposal of those who would not listen to the advice and entreaties of the sentinels and insisted on visiting the town. All strangers who passed through the streets of Macondo at that time had to ring their bells so that the sick people would know that they were healthy. They were not allowed to eat or drink anything during their stay, for there was no doubt but that the illness was transmitted by mouth, and all food and drink had been contaminated by insomnia. In that way they kept the plague restricted to the perimeter of the town. So effective was the quarantine that the day came when the emergency situation was accepted as a natural thing and life was organized in such a way that work picked up its rhythm again and no one worried any more about the useless habit of sleeping.

It was Aureliano who conceived the formula that was to protect them against loss of memory for several months. He discovered it by chance. An expert insomniac, having been one of the first, he had learned the art of silverwork to perfection. One day he was looking for the small anvil that he used for laminating metals and he could not remember its name. His father told him: "Stake." Aureliano wrote the name on a piece of paper that he pasted to the base of the small anvil: *stake*. In that way he was sure of not forgetting it in the future. It did not occur to him that this was the first manifestation of a loss of memory, because the object had a difficult name to remember. But a few days later he discovered that he had trouble remembering almost every object in the laboratory. Then he marked them with their respective names so that all he had to do was read the inscription in order to identify them. When his father told him about his alarm at having forgotten even the most impressive happenings of his childhood, Aureliano explained his method to him, and José Arcadio Buendía put it into practice all through the house and later on imposed it on the whole village. With an inked brush he marked everything with its name: *table, chair, clock, door, wall, bed, pan*. He went to the corral and marked the animals and plants: *cow, goat, pig, hen, cassava, caladium, banana*. Little by little, studying the infinite possibilities of a loss of memory, he realized that the day might come when things would be recognized by their inscriptions but that no one would remember their use. Then he was more explicit. The sign that he hung on the neck of the cow was an exemplary proof of the way in which the inhabitants of Macondo were prepared to fight against loss of memory: *This is the cow. She must be milked every morning so that she will produce milk, and the milk must be boiled in order to be mixed with coffee to make coffee and milk.* Thus they went

48

on living in a reality that was slipping away, momentarily captured by words, but which would escape irremediably when they forgot the values of the written letters.

At the beginning of the road into the swamp they put up a sign that said MACONDO and another larger one on the main street that said GOD EXISTS. In all the houses keys to memorizing objects and feelings had been written. But the system demanded so much vigilance and moral strength that many succumbed to the spell of an imaginary reality, one invented by themselves, which was less practical for them but more comforting. Pilar Ternera was the one who contributed most to popularize that mystification when she conceived the trick of reading the past in cards as she had read the future before. By means of that recourse the insomniacs began to live in a world built on the uncertain alternatives of the cards, where a father was remembered faintly as the dark man who had arrived at the beginning of April and a mother was remembered only as the dark woman who wore a gold ring on her left hand, and where a birth date was reduced to the last Tuesday on which a lark sang in the laurel tree. Defeated by those practices of consolation, José Arcadio Buendía then decided to build the memory machine that he had desired once in order to remember the marvelous inventions of the gypsies. The artifact was based on the possibility of reviewing every morning, from beginning to end, the totality of knowledge acquired during one's life. He conceived of it as a spinning dictionary that a person placed on the axis could operate by means of a lever, so that in very few hours there would pass before his eyes the notions most necessary for life. He had succeeded in writing almost fourteen thousand entries when along the road from the swamp a strange-looking old man with the sad sleepers' bell appeared, carrying a bulging suitcase tied with a rope and pulling a cart covered with black cloth. He went straight to the house of José Arcadio Buendía.

Visitación did not recognize him when she opened the

C*

49

door and she thought he had come with the idea of selling something, unaware that nothing could be sold in a town that was sinking irrevocably into the quicksand of forgetfulness. He was a decrepit man. Although his voice was also broken by uncertainty and his hands seemed to doubt the existence of things, it was evident that he came from the world where men could still sleep and remember. José Arcadio Buendía found him sitting in the living room fanning himself with a patched black hat as he read with compassionate attention the signs pasted to the walls. He greeted him with a broad show of affection, afraid that he had known him at another time and that he did not remember him now. But the visitor was aware of his falseness. He felt himself forgotten, not with the irremediable forgetfulness of the heart, but with a different kind of forgetfulness, which was more cruel and irrevocable and which he knew very well because it was the forgetfulness of death. Then he understood. He opened the suitcase crammed with indecipherable objects and from among them he took out a little case with many flasks. He gave José Arcadio Buendía a drink of a gentle color and the light went on in his memory. His eyes became moist from weeping even before he noticed himself in an absurd living room where objects were labeled and before he was ashamed of the solemn nonsense written on the walls, and even before he recognized the newcomer with a dazzling glow of joy. It was Melquíades.

While Macondo was celebrating the recovery of its memory, José Arcadio Buendía and Melquíades dusted off their old friendship. The gypsy was inclined to stay in the town. He really had been through death, but he had returned because he could not bear the solitude. Repudiated by his tribe, having lost all of his supernatural faculties because of his faithfulness to life, he decided to take refuge in that corner of the world which had still not been discovered by death, dedicated to the operation of a daguerreotype laboratory. José

Arcadio Buendía had never heard of that invention. But when he saw himself and his whole family fastened onto a sheet of iridescent metal for an eternity, he was mute with stupefaction. That was the date of the oxidized daguerreotype in which José Arcadio Buendía appeared with his bristly and graying hair, his cardboard collar attached to his shirt by a copper button, and an expression of startled solemnity, whom Úrsula described, dying with laughter, as a "frightened general." José Arcadio Buendía was, in fact, frightened on that clear December morning when the daguerreotype was made, for he was thinking that people were slowly wearing away while his image would endure on a metallic plaque. Through a curious reversal of custom, it was Úrsula who got that idea out of his head, as it was also she who forgot her ancient bitterness and decided that Melquíades would stay on in the house, although she never permitted them to make a daguerreotype of her because (according to her very words) she did not want to survive as a laughingstock for her grandchildren. That morning she dressed the children in their best clothes, powdered their faces, and gave a spoonful of marrow syrup to each one so that they would all remain absolutely motionless during the nearly two minutes in front of Melquíades' fantastic camera. In the family daguerreotype, the only one that ever existed, Aureliano appeared dressed in black velvet between Amaranta and Rebeca. He had the same languor and the same clairvoyant look that he would have years later as he faced the firing squad. But he still had not sensed the premonition of his fate. He was an expert silversmith, praised all over the swampland for the delicacy of his work. In the workshop, which he shared with Melquíades' mad laboratory, he could barely be heard breathing. He seemed to be taking refuge in some other time, while his father and the gypsy with shouts interpreted the predictions of Nostradamus amidst a noise of flasks and trays and the disaster of spilled acids and silver bromide that was lost in the twists and turns it gave at every instant. That dedication to his work, the good judgment with which he directed his attention, had allowed Aureliano to earn in a short time more money than Úrsula had with her delicious candy fauna, but everybody thought it strange that he was now a full-grown man and had not known a woman. It was true that he had never had one.

Several months later saw the return of Francisco the Man, an ancient vagabond who was almost two hundred years old and who frequently passed through Macondo distributing songs that he composed himself. In them Francisco the Man told in great detail the things that had happened in the towns along his route, from Manaure to the edge of the swamp, so that if anyone had a message to send or an event to make public, he would pay him two cents to include it in his repertory. That was how Úrsula learned of the death of her mother, as a simple consequence of listening to the songs in the hope that they would say something about her son José Arcadio. Francisco the Man, called that because he had once defeated the devil in a duel of improvisation, and whose real name no one knew, disappeared from Macondo during the insomnia plague and one night he reappeared suddenly in Catarino's store. The whole town went to listen to him to find out what had happened in the world. On that occasion there arrived with him a woman who was so fat that four Indians had to carry her in a rocking chair, and an adolescent mulatto girl with a forlorn look who protected her from the sun with an umbrella. Aureliano went to Catarino's store that night. He found Francisco the Man, like a monolithic chameleon, sitting in the midst of a circle of bystanders. He was singing the news with his old, out-of-tune voice, accompanying himself with the same archaic accordion that Sir Walter Raleigh had given him in the Guianas and keeping time with his great walking feet that were cracked from saltpeter. In front of a door at the rear through which men were going and coming, the matron of the rocking chair was sitting and fanning herself in silence. Catarino, with a felt rose behind his ear, was selling the gathering mugs of fermented cane juice, and he took advantage of the occasion to go over to the men and put his hand on them where he should not have. Toward midnight the heat was unbearable. Aureliano listened to the news to the end without hearing anything that was of interest to his family. He was getting ready to go home when the matron signaled him with her hand.

"You go in too," she told him. "It only costs twenty cents."

Aureliano threw a coin into the hopper that the matron had in her lap and went into the room without knowing why. The adolescent mulatto girl, with her small bitch's teats, was naked on the bed. Before Aureliano sixty-three men had passed through the room that night. From being used so much, kneaded with sweat and sighs, the air in the room had begun to turn to mud. The girl took off the soaked sheet and asked Aureliano to hold it by one side. It was as heavy as a piece of canvas. They squeezed it, twisting it at the ends until it regained its natural weight. They turned over the mat and the sweat came out of the other side. Aureliano was anxious for that operation never to end. He knew the theoretical mechanics of love, but he could not stay on his feet because of the weakness of his knees, and although he had goose pimples on his burning skin he could not resist the urgent need to expel the weight of his bowels. When the girl finished fixing up the bed and told him to get undressed, he gave her a confused explanation: "They made me come in. They told me to throw twenty cents into the hopper and hurry up." The girl understood his confusion. "If you throw in twenty cents more when you go out, you can stay a little longer," she said softly. Aureliano got undressed, tormented by shame, unable to get rid of the idea that his nakedness could not stand comparison with that of his brother. In spite of the girl's efforts he felt more and more indifferent and terribly

53

alone. "I'll throw in another twenty cents," he said with a desolate voice. The girl thanked him in silence. Her back was raw. Her skin was stuck to her ribs and her breathing was forced because of an immeasurable exhaustion. Two years before, far away from there, she had fallen asleep without putting out the candle and had awakened surrounded by flames. The house where she lived with the grandmother who had raised her was reduced to ashes. Since then her grandmother carried her from town to town, putting her to bed for twenty cents in order to make up the value of the burned house. According to the girl's calculations, she still had ten years of seventy men per night, because she also had to pay the expenses of the trip and food for both of them as well as the pay of the Indians who carried the rocking chair. When the matron knocked on the door the second time, Aureliano left the room without having done anything, troubled by a desire to weep. That night he could not sleep, thinking about the girl, with a mixture of desire and pity. He felt an irresistible need to love her and protect her. At dawn, worn out by insomnia and fever, he made the calm decision to marry her in order to free her from the despotism of her grandmother and to enjoy all the nights of satisfaction that she would give the seventy men. But at ten o'clock in the morning, when he reached Catarino's store, the girl had left town.

Time mitigated his mad proposal, but it aggravated his feelings of frustration. He took refuge in work. He resigned himself to being a womanless man for all his life in order to hide the shame of his uselessness. In the meantime, Melquíades had printed on his plates everything that was printable in Macondo, and he left the daguerreotype laboratory to the fantasies of José Arcadio Buendía, who had resolved to use it to obtain scientific proof of the existence of God. Through a complicated process of superimposed exposures taken in different parts of the house, he was sure that sooner or later he would get a daguerreotype of God, if He existed, or put an end once and for all to the supposition of His existence. Melquíades got deeper into his interpretations of Nostradamus. He would stay up until very late, suffocating in his faded velvet vest, scribbling with his tiny sparrow hands, whose rings had lost the glow of former times. One night he thought he had found a prediction of the future of Macondo. It was to be a luminous city with great glass houses where there was no trace remaining of the race of the Buendías. "It's a mistake," José Arcadio Buendía thundered. "They won't be houses of glass but of ice, as I dreamed, and there will always be a Buendía, *per omnia secula seculorum.*" Úrsula fought to preserve common sense in that extravagant house, having broadened her business of little candy animals with an oven that went all night turning out baskets and more baskets of bread and a prodigious variety of puddings, meringues, and cookies, which disappeared in a few hours on the roads winding through the swamp. She had reached an age where she had a right to rest, but she was nonetheless more and more active. So busy was she in her prosperous enterprises that one afternoon she looked distractedly toward the courtyard while the Indian woman helped her sweeten the dough and she saw two unknown and beautiful adolescent girls doing frame embroidery in the light of the sunset. They were Rebeca and Amaranta. As soon as they had taken off the mourning clothes for their grandmother, which they wore with inflexible rigor for three years, their bright clothes seemed to have given them a new place in the world. Rebeca, contrary to what might have been expected, was the more beautiful. She had a light complexion, large and peaceful eyes, and magical hands that seemed to work out the design of the embroidery with invisible threads. Amaranta, the younger, was somewhat graceless, but she had the natural distinction, the inner tightness of her dead grandmother. Next to them, although he was already revealing the physical drive of his father, Arcadio looked like a child. He set about learning the art of silverwork with Aureliano, who had also taught him how to read and write. Úrsula suddenly realized that the house had become full of people, that her children were on the point of marrying and having children, and that they would be obliged to scatter for lack of space. Then she took out the money she had accumulated over long years of hard labor, made some arrangements with her customers, and undertook the enlargement of the house. She had a formal parlor for visits built, another one that was more comfortable and cool for daily use, a dining room with a table with twelve places where the family could sit with all of their guests, nine bedrooms with windows on the courtyard, and a long porch protected from the heat of noon by a rose garden with a railing on which to place pots of ferns and begonias. She had the kitchen enlarged to hold two ovens. The granary where Pilar Ternera had read José Arcadio's future was torn down and another twice as large built so that there would never be a lack of food in the house. She had baths built in the courtyard in the shade of the chestnut tree, one for the women and another for the men, and in the rear a large stable, a fenced-in chicken yard, a shed for the milk cows, and an aviary open to the four winds so that wandering birds could roost there at their pleasure. Followed by dozens of masons and carpenters, as if she had contracted her husband's hallucinating fever, Úrsula fixed the position of light and heat and distributed space without the least sense of its limitations. The primitive building of the founders became filled with tools and materials, of workmen exhausted by sweat, who asked everybody please not to molest them, exasperated by the sack of bones that followed them everywhere with its dull rattle. In that discomfort, breathing quicklime and tar, no one could see very well how from the bowels of the earth there was rising not only the largest house in the town, but the most hospitable and cool house that had ever existed in the region of the swamp. José Arcadio Buendía, trying to surprise Divine Providence in the midst of the cataclysm, was the one who least understood it. The new house was almost finished when Úrsula drew him out of his chimerical world in order to inform him that she had an order to paint the front blue and not white as they had wanted. She showed him the official document. José Arcadio Buendía, without understanding what his wife was talking about, deciphered the signature.

"Who is this fellow?" he asked.

"The magistrate," Úrsula answered disconsolately. "They say he's an authority sent by the government."

Don Apolinar Moscote, the magistrate, had arrived in Macondo very quietly. He put up at the Hotel Jacob—built by one of the first Arabs who came to swap knickknacks for macaws—and on the following day he rented a small room with a door on the street two blocks away from the Buendía house. He set up a table and a chair that he had bought from Jacob, nailed up on the wall the shield of the republic that he had brought with him, and on the door he painted the sign: *Magistrate*. His first order was for all the houses to be painted blue in celebration of the anniversary of national independence. José Arcadio Buendía, with the copy of the order in his hand, found him taking his nap in a hammock he had set up in the narrow office. "Did you write this paper?" he asked him. Don Apolinar Moscote, a mature man, timid, with a ruddy complexion, said yes. "By what right?" José Arcadio Buendía asked again. Don Apolinar Moscote picked up a paper from the drawer of the table and showed it to him. "I have been named magistrate of this town." José Arcadio Buendía did not even look at the appointment.

"In this town we do not give orders with pieces of paper," he said without losing his calm. "And so that you know it once and for all, we don't need any judges here because there's nothing that needs judging."

Facing Don Apolinar Moscote, still without raising his

voice, he gave a detailed account of how they had founded the village, of how they had distributed the land, opened the roads, and introduced the improvements that necessity required without having bothered the government and without anyone having bothered them. "We are so peaceful that none of us has died even of a natural death," he said. "You can see that we still don't have any cemetery." No one was upset that the government had not helped them. On the contrary, they were happy that up until then it had let them grow in peace, and he hoped that it would continue leaving them that way, because they had not founded a town so that the first upstart who came along would tell them what to do. Don Apolinar had put on his denim jacket, white like his trousers, without losing at any moment the elegance of his gestures.

"So that if you want to stay here like any other ordinary citizen, you're quite welcome," José Arcadio Buendía concluded. "But if you've come to cause disorder by making the people paint their houses blue, you can pick up your junk and go back where you came from. Because my house is going to be white, like a dove."

Don Apolinar Moscote turned pale. He took a step backward and tightened his jaws as he said with a certain affliction:

"I must warn you that I'm armed."

José Arcadio Buendía did not know exactly when his hands regained the useful strength with which he used to pull down horses. He grabbed Don Apolinar Moscote by the lapels and lifted him up to the level of his eyes.

"I'm doing this," he said, "because I would rather carry you around alive and not have to keep carrying you around dead for the rest of my life."

In that way he carried him through the middle of the street, suspended by the lapels, until he put him down on his two feet on the swamp road. A week later he was back with six barefoot and ragged soldiers, armed with shotguns, and an oxcart in which his wife and seven daughters were traveling. Two other carts arrived later with the furniture, the baggage, and the household utensils. He settled his family in the Hotel Jacob, while he looked for a house, and he went back to open his office under the protection of the soldiers. The founders of Macondo, resolving to expel the invaders, went with their older sons to put themselves at the disposal of José Arcadio Buendía. But he was against it, as he explained, because it was not manly to make trouble for someone in front of his family, and Don Apolinar had returned with his wife and daughters. So he decided to resolve the situation in a pleasant way.

Aureliano went with him. About that time he had begun to cultivate the black mustache with waxed tips and the somewhat stentorian voice that would characterize him in the war. Unarmed, without paying any attention to the guards, they went into the magistrate's office. Don Apolinar Mascote did not lose his calm. He introduced them to two of his daughters who happened to be there: Amparo, sixteen, dark like her mother, and Remedios, only nine, a pretty little girl with lily-colored skin and green eyes. They were gracious and well-mannered. As soon as the men came in, before being introduced, they gave them chairs to sit on. But they both remained standing.

"Very well, my friend," José Arcadio Buendía said, "you may stay here, not because you have those bandits with shotguns at the door, but out of consideration for your wife and daughters."

Don Apolinar Moscote was upset, but José Arcadio Buendía did not give him time to reply. "We only make two conditions," he went on. "The first: that everyone can paint his house the color he feels like. The second: that the soldiers leave at once. We will guarantee order for you." The magistrate raised his right hand with all the fingers extended.

"Your word of honor?"

"The word of your enemy," José Arcadio Buendía said. And he added in a bitter tone: "Because I must tell you one thing: you and I are still enemies."

The soldiers left that same afternoon. A few days later José Arcadio Buendía found a house for the magistrate's family. Everybody was at peace except Aureliano. The image of Remedios, the magistrate's younger daughter, who, because of her age, could have been his daughter, kept paining him in some part of his body. It was a physical sensation that almost bothered him when he walked, like a pebble in his shoe.

THE NEW HOUSE, white, like a dove, was inaugurated with a dance. Úrsula had got that idea from the afternoon when she saw Rebeca and Amaranta changed into adolescents, and it could almost have been said that the main reason behind the construction was a desire to have a proper place for the girls to receive visitors. In order that nothing would be lacking in splendor she worked like a galley slave as the repairs were under way, so that before they were finished she had ordered costly necessities for the decorations, the table service, and the marvelous invention that was to arouse the astonishment of the town and the jubilation of the young people: the pianola. They delivered it broken down, packed in several boxes that were unloaded along with the Viennese furniture, the Bohemian crystal, the table service from the

Indies Company, the tablecloths from Holland, and a rich variety of lamps and candlesticks, hangings and drapes. The import house sent along at its own expense an Italian expert, Pietro Crespi, to assemble and tune the pianola, to instruct the purchasers in its functioning, and to teach them how to dance to the latest music printed on its six paper rolls.

Pietro Crespi was young and blond, the most handsome and well-mannered man who had ever been seen in Macondo, so scrupulous in his dress that in spite of the suffocating heat he would work in his brocade vest and heavy coat of dark cloth. Soaked in sweat, keeping a reverent distance from the owners of the house, he spent several weeks shut up in the parlor with a dedication much like that of Aureliano in his silverwork. One morning, without opening the door, without calling anyone to witness the miracle, he placed the first roll in the pianola and the tormenting hammering and the constant noise of wooden lathings ceased in a silence that was startled at the order and neatness of the music. They all ran to the parlor. José Arcadio Buendía was as if struck by lightning, not because of the beauty of the melody, but because of the automatic working of the keys of the pianola, and he set up Melquíades' camera with the hope of getting a daguerreotype of the invisible player. That day the Italian had lunch with them. Rebeca and Amaranta, serving the table, were intimidated by the way in which the angelic man with pale and ringless hands manipulated the utensils. In the living room, next to the parlor, Pietro Crespi taught them how to dance. He showed them the steps without touching them, keeping time with a metronome, under the friendly eye of Úrsula, who did not leave the room for a moment while her daughters had their lesson. Pietro Crespi wore special pants on those days, very elastic and tight, and dancing slippers. "You don't have to worry so much," José Arcadio Buendía told her. "The man's a fairy." But she did not leave off her vigilance until the apprenticeship was over and the Italian left

Macondo. Then they began to organize the party. Úrsula drew up a strict guest list, in which the only ones invited were the descendants of the founders, except for the family of Pilar Ternera, who by then had had two more children by unknown fathers. It was truly a high-class list, except that it was determined by feelings of friendship, for those favored were not only the oldest friends of José Arcadio Buendía's house since before they undertook the exodus and the founding of Macondo, but also their sons and grandsons, who were the constant companions of Aureliano and Arcadio since infancy, and their daughters, who were the only ones who visited the house to embroider with Rebeca and Amaranta. Don Apolinar Moscote, the benevolent ruler whose activity had been reduced to the maintenance from his scanty resources of two policemen armed with wooden clubs, was a figurehead. In order to support the household expenses his daughters had opened a sewing shop, where they made felt flowers as well as guava delicacies, and wrote love notes to order. But in spite of being modest and hard-working, the most beautiful girls in town, and the most skilled at the new dances,.they did not manage to be considered for the party.

While Úrsula and the girls unpacked furniture, polished silverware, and hung pictures of maidens in boats full of roses, which gave a breath of new life to the naked areas that the masons had built, José Arcadio Buendía stopped his pursuit of the image of God, convinced of His nonexistence, and he took the pianola apart in order to decipher its magical secret. Two days before the party, swamped in a shower of leftover keys and hammers, bungling in the midst of a mixup of strings that would unroll in one direction and roll up again in the other, he succeeded in a fashion in putting the instrument back together. There had never been as many surprises and as much dashing about as in those days, but the new pitch lamps were lighted on the designated day and hour. The house was opened, still smelling of resin and damp whitewash, and the children and grandchildren of the founders saw the porch with ferns and begonias, the quiet rooms, the garden saturated with the fragrance of the roses, and they gathered together in the parlor, facing the unknown invention that had been covered with a white sheet. Those who were familiar with the piano, popular in other towns in the swamp, felt a little disheartened, but more bitter was Úrsula's disappointment when she put in the first roll so that Amaranta and Rebeca could begin the dancing and the mechanism did not work. Melquíades, almost blind by then, crumbling with decrepitude, used the arts of his timeless wisdom in an attempt to fix it. Finally José Arcadio Buendía managed, by mistake, to move a device that was stuck and the music came out, first in a burst and then in a flow of mixed-up notes. Beating against the strings that had been put in without order or concert and had been tuned with temerity, the hammers let go. But the stubborn descendants of the twenty-one intrepid people who plowed through the mountains in search of the sea to the west avoided the reefs of the melodic mixup and the dancing went on until dawn.

Pietro Crespi came back to repair the pianola. Rebeca and Amaranta helped him put the strings in order and helped him with their laughter at the mixup of the melodies. It was extremely pleasant and so chaste in its way that Úrsula ceased her vigilance. On the eve of his departure a farewell dance for him was improvised with the pianola and with Rebeca he put on a skillful demonstration of modern dances. Arcadio and Amaranta matched them in grace and skill. But the exhibition was interrupted because Pilar Ternera, who was at the door with the onlookers, had a fight, biting and hair-pulling, with a woman who had dared to comment that Arcadio had a woman's behind. Toward midnight Pietro Crespi took his leave with a sentimental little speech, and he promised to return very soon. Rebeca accompanied him to the door, and having closed up the house and put out the

64

lamps, she went to her room to weep. It was an inconsolable weeping that lasted for several days, the cause of which was not known even by Amaranta. Her hermetism was not odd. Although she seemed expansive and cordial, she had a solitary character and an impenetrable heart. She was a splendid adolescent with long and firm bones, but she still insisted on using the small wooden rocking chair with which she had arrived at the house, reinforced many times and with the arms gone. No one had discovered that even at that age she still had the habit of sucking her finger. That was why she would not lose an opportunity to lock herself in the bathroom and had acquired the habit of sleeping with her face to the wall. On rainy afternoons, embroidering with a group of friends on the begonia porch, she would lose the thread of the conversation and a tear of nostalgia would salt her palate when she saw the strips of damp earth and the piles of mud that the earthworms had pushed up in the garden. Those secret tastes, defeated in the past by oranges and rhubarb, broke out into an irrepressible urge when she began to weep. She went back to eating earth. The first time she did it almost out of curiosity, sure that the bad taste would be the best cure for the temptation. And, in fact, she could not bear the earth in her mouth. But she persevered, overcome by the growing anxiety, and little by little she was getting back her ancestral appetite, the taste of primary minerals, the unbridled satisfaction of what was the original food. She would put handfuls of earth in her pockets, and ate them in small bits without being seen, with a confused feeling of pleasure and rage, as she instructed her girl friends in the most difficult needlepoint and spoke about other men, who did not deserve the sacrifice of having one eat the whitewash on the walls because of them. The handfuls of earth made the only man who deserved that show of degradation less remote and more certain, as if the ground that he walked on with his fine patent leather boots in another part of the world were transmitting to her the weight and the temperature of his blood in a mineral savor that left a harsh aftertaste in her mouth and a sediment of peace in her heart. One afternoon, for no reason, Amparo Moscote asked permission to see the house. Amaranta and Rebeca, disconcerted by the unexpected visit, attended her with a stiff formality. They showed her the remodeled mansion, they had her listen to the rolls on the pianola, and they offered her orange marmalade and crackers. Amparo gave a lesson in dignity, personal charm, and good manners that impressed Úrsula in the few moments that she was present during the visit. After two hours, when the conversation was beginning to wane, Amparo took advantage of Amaranta's distraction and gave Rebeca a letter. She was able to see the name of the Estimable Señorita Rebeca Buendía, written in the same methodical hand, with the same green ink, and the same delicacy of words with which the instructions for the operation of the pianola were written, and she folded the letter with the tips of her fingers and hid it in her bosom, looking at Amparo Moscote with an expression of endless and unconditional gratitude and a silent promise of complicity unto death.

The sudden friendship between Amparo Moscote and Rebeca Buendía awakened the hopes of Aureliano. The memory of little Remedios had not stopped tormenting him, but he had not found a chance to see her. When he would stroll through town with his closest friends, Magnífico Visbal and Gerineldo Márquez—the sons of the founders of the same names—he would look for her in the sewing shop with an anxious glance, but he saw only the older sisters. The presence of Amparo Moscote in the house was like a premonition. "She has to come with her," Aureliano would say to himself in a low voice. "She has to come." He repeated it so many times and with such conviction that one afternoon when he was putting together a little gold fish in the workshop, he had the certainty that she had answered his call. Indeed, a short time later he heard the childish voice, and when he looked up his heart froze with terror as he saw the girl at the door, dressed in pink organdy and wearing white boots.

"You can't go in there, Remedios," Amparo Moscote said from the hall. "They're working."

But Aureliano did not give her time to respond. He picked up the little fish by the chain that came through its mouth and said to her:

"Come in."

Remedios went over and asked some questions about the fish that Aureliano could not answer because he was seized with a sudden attack of asthma. He wanted to stay beside that lily skin forever, beside those emerald eyes, close to that voice that called him "sir" with every question, showing the same respect that she gave her father. Melquíades was in the corner seated at the desk scribbling indecipherable signs. Aureliano hated him. All he could do was tell Remedios that he was going to give her the little fish and the girl was so startled by the offer that she left the workshop as fast as she could. That afternoon Aureliano lost the hidden patience with which he had waited for a chance to see her. He neglected his work. In several desperate efforts of concentration he willed her to appear but Remedios did not respond. He looked for her in her sisters' shop, behind the window shades in her house, in her father's office, but he found her only in the image that saturated his private and terrible solitude. He would spend whole hours with Rebeca in the parlor listening to the music on the pianola. She was listening to it because it was the music with which Pietro Crespi had taught them how to dance. Aureliano listened to it simply because everything, even music, reminded him of Remedios.

The house became full of love. Aureliano expressed it in poetry that had no beginning or end. He would write it on the harsh pieces of parchment that Melquíades gave him, on the bathroom walls, on the skin of his arms, and in all of it

Remedios would appear transfigured: Remedios in the soporific air of two in the afternoon, Remedios in the soft breath of the roses, Remedios in the water-clock secrets of the moths, Remedios in the steaming morning bread, Remedios everywhere and Remedios forever. Rebeca waited for her love at four in the afternoon, embroidering by the window. She knew that the mailman's mule arrived only every two weeks, but she always waited for him, convinced that he was going to arrive on some other day by mistake. It happened quite the opposite: once the mule did not come on the usual day. Mad with desperation, Rebeca got up in the middle of the night and ate handfuls of earth in the garden with a suicidal drive, weeping with pain and fury, chewing tender earthworms and chipping her teeth on snail shells. She vomited until dawn. She fell into a state of feverish prostration, lost consciousness, and her heart went into a shameless delirium. Úrsula, scandalized, forced the lock on her trunk and found at the bottom, tied together with pink ribbons, the sixteen perfumed letters and the skeletons of leaves and petals preserved in old books and the dried butterflies that turned to powder at the touch.

Aureliano was the only one capable of understanding such desolation. That afternoon, while Úrsula was trying to rescue Rebeca from the slough of delirium, he went with Magnífico Visbal and Gerineldo Márquez to Catarino's store. The establishment had been expanded with a gallery of wooden rooms where single women who smelled of dead flowers lived. A group made up of an accordion and drums played the songs of Francisco the Man, who had not been seen in Macondo for several years. The three friends drank fermented cane juice. Magnífico and Gerineldo, contemporaries of Aureliano but more skilled in the ways of the world, drank methodically with the women seated on their laps. One of the women, withered and with goldwork on her teeth, gave Aureliano a caress that made him shudder. He rejected her. He had discovered that the more he drank the more he thought about Remedios, but he could bear the torture of his recollections better. He did not know exactly when he began to float. He saw his friends and the women sailing in a radiant glow, without weight or mass, saying words that did not come out of their mouths and making mysterious signals that did not correspond to their expressions. Catarino put a hand on his shoulder and said to him: "It's going on eleven." Aureliano turned his head, saw the enormous disfigured face with a felt flower behind the ear, and then he lost his memory, as during the times of forgetfulness, and he recovered it on a strange dawn and in a room that was completely foreign, where Pilar Ternera stood in her slip, barefoot, her hair down, holding a lamp over him, startled with disbelief.

"Aureliano!"

Aureliano checked his feet and raised his head. He did not know how he had come there, but he knew what his aim was, because he had carried it hidden since infancy in an inviolable backwater of his heart.

"I've come to sleep with you," he said.

His clothes were smeared with mud and vomit. Pilar Ternera, who lived alone at that time with her two younger children, did not ask him any questions. She took him to the bed. She cleaned his face with a damp cloth, took off his clothes, and then got completely undressed and lowered the mosquito netting so that her children would not see them if they woke up. She had become tired of waiting for the man who would stay, of the men who left, of the countless men who missed the road to her house, confused by the uncertainty of the cards. During the wait her skin had become wrinkled, her breasts had withered, the coals of her heart had gone out. She felt for Aureliano in the darkness, put her hand on his stomach and kissed him on the neck with a maternal tenderness. "My poor child," she murmured. Aureliano shuddered. With a calm skill, without the slightest misstep, he left his accumulated grief behind and found Remedios changed into a swamp without horizons, smelling of a raw animal and recently ironed clothes. When he came to the surface he was weeping. First they were involuntary and broken sobs. Then he emptied himself out in an unleashed flow, feeling that something swollen and painful had burst inside of him. She waited, scratching his head with the tips of her fingers, until his body got rid of the dark material that would not let him live. Then Pilar Ternera asked him: "Who is it?" And Aureliano told her. She let out a laugh that in other times frightened the doves and that now did not even wake up the children. "You'll have to raise her first," she mocked, but underneath the mockery Aureliano found a reservoir of understanding. When he went out of the room, leaving behind not only his doubts about his virility but also the bitter weight that his heart had borne for so many months, Pilar Ternera made him a spontaneous promise.

"I'm going to talk to the girl," she told him, "and you'll see what I'll serve her on the tray."

She kept her promise. But it was a bad moment, because the house had lost its peace of former days. When she discovered Rebeca's passion, which was impossible to keep secret because of her shouts, Amaranta suffered an attack of fever. She also suffered from the barb of a lonely love. Shut up in the bathroom, she would release herself from the torment of a hopeless passion by writing feverish letters, which she finally hid in the bottom of her trunk. Úrsula barely had the strength to take care of the two sick girls. She was unable, after prolonged and insidious interrogations, to ascertain the causes of Amaranta's prostration. Finally, in another moment of inspiration, she forced the lock on the trunk and found the letters tied with a pink ribbon, swollen with fresh lilies and still wet with tears, addressed and never sent to Pietro Crespi. Weeping with rage, she cursed the day that it had occurred to her to buy the pianola, and she forbade the embroidery les-

70

sons and decreed a kind of mourning with no one dead which was to be prolonged until the daughters got over their hopes. Useless was the intervention of José Arcadio Buendía, who had modified his first impression of Pietro Crespi and admired his ability in the manipulation of musical machines. So that when Pilar Ternera told Aureliano that Remedios had decided on marriage, he could see that the news would only give his parents more trouble. Invited to the parlor for a formal interview, José Arcadio Buendía and Úrsula listened stonily to their son's declaration. When he learned the name of the fiancée, however, José Arcadio Buendía grew red with indignation. "Love is a disease," he thundered. "With so many pretty and decent girls around, the only thing that occurs to you is to get married to the daughter of our enemy." But Úrsula agreed with the choice. She confessed her affection for the seven Moscote sisters, for their beauty, their ability for work, their modesty, and their good manners, and she celebrated her son's prudence. Conquered by his wife's enthusiasm, José Arcadio Buendía then laid down one condition: Rebeca, who was the one he wanted, would marry Pietro Crespi. Úrsula would take Amaranta on a trip to the capital of the province when she had time, so that contact with different people would alleviate her disappointment. Rebeca got her health back just as soon as she heard of the agreement, and she wrote her fiancé a jubilant letter that she submitted to her parents' approval and put into the mail without the use of any intermediaries. Amaranta pretended to accept the decision and little by little she recovered from her fevers, but she promised herself that Rebeca would marry only over her dead body.

The following Saturday José Arcadio Buendía put on his dark suit, his celluloid collar, and the deerskin boots that he had worn for the first time the night of the party, and went to ask for the hand of Remedios Moscote. The magistrate and his wife received him, pleased and worried at the same time, for they did not know the reason for the unexpected visit, and then they thought that he was confused about the name of the intended bride. In order to remove the mistake, the mother woke Remedios up and carried her into the living room, still drowsy from sleep. They asked her if it was true that she had decided to get married, and she answered, whimpering, that she only wanted them to let her sleep. José Arcadio Buendía, understanding the distress of the Moscotes, went to clear things up with Aureliano. When he returned, the Moscotes had put on formal clothing, had rearranged the furniture and put fresh flowers in the vases, and were waiting in the company of their older daughters. Overwhelmed by the unpleasantness of the occasion and the bothersome hard collar, José Arcadio Buendía confirmed the fact that Remedios, indeed, was the chosen one. "It doesn't make sense," Don Apolinar Moscote said with consternation. "We have six other daughters, all unmarried, and at an age where they deserve it, who would be delighted to be the honorable wife of a gentleman as serious and hard-working as your son, and Aurelito lays his eyes precisely on the one who still wets her bed." His wife, a well-preserved woman with afflicted eyelids and expression, scolded his mistake. When they finished the fruit punch, they willingly accepted Aureliano's decision. Except that Señora Moscote begged the favor of speaking to Úrsula alone. Intrigued, protesting that they were involving her in men's affairs, but really feeling deep emotion, Úrsula went to visit her the next day. A half hour later she returned with the news that Remedios had not reached puberty. Aureliano did not consider that a serious barrier. He had waited so long that he could wait as long as was necessary until his bride reached the age of conception.

The newfound harmony was interrupted by the death of Melquíades. Although it was a foreseeable event, the circumstances were not. A few months after his return, a process of aging had taken place in him that was so rapid and critical that soon he was treated as one of those useless great-grandfathers who wander about the bedrooms like shades, dragging their feet, remembering better times aloud, and whom no one bothers about or remembers really until the morning they find them dead in their bed. At first José Arcadio Buendía helped him in his work, enthusiastic over the novelty of the daguerreotypes and the predictions of Nostradamus. But little by little he began abandoning him to his solitude, for communication was becoming increasingly difficult. He was losing his sight and his hearing, he seemed to confuse the people he was speaking to with others he had known in remote epochs of mankind, and he would answer questions with a complex hodgepodge of languages. He would walk along groping in the air, although he passed between objects with an inexplicable fluidity, as if he were endowed with some instinct of direction based on an immediate prescience. One day he forgot to put in his false teeth, which at night he left in a glass of water beside his bed, and he never put them in again. When Úrsula undertook the enlargement of the house, she had them build him a special room next to Aureliano's workshop, far from the noise and bustle of the house, with a window flooded with light and a bookcase where she herself put in order the books that were almost destroyed by dust and moths, the flaky stacks of paper covered with indecipherable signs, and the glass with his false teeth, where some aquatic plants with tiny yellow flowers had taken root. The new place seemed to please Melquíades, because he was never seen any more, not even in the dining room. He only went to Aureliano's workshop, where he would spend hours on end scribbling his enigmatic literature on the parchments that he had brought with him and that seemed to have been made out of some dry material that crumpled like puff paste. There he ate the meals that Visitación brought him twice a day, although in the last days he lost his appetite and fed only on vegetables. He soon acquired the forlorn look that one

D

sees in vegetarians. His skin became covered with a thin moss, similar to that which flourished on the antique vest that he never took off, and his breath exhaled the odor of a sleeping animal. Aureliano ended up forgetting about him, absorbed in the composition of his poems, but on one occasion he thought he understood something of what Melquíades was saying in his groping monologues, and he paid attention. In reality, the only thing that could be isolated in the rocky paragraphs was the insistent hammering on the word *equinox, equinox, equinox,* and the name of Alexander von Humboldt. Arcadio got a little closer to him when he began to help Aureliano in his silverwork. Melquíades answered that effort at communication at times by giving forth with phrases in Spanish that had very little to do with reality. One afternoon, however, he seemed to be illuminated by a sudden emotion. Years later, facing the firing squad, Arcadio would remember the trembling with which Melquíades made him listen to several pages of his impenetrable writing, which of course he did not understand, but which when read aloud were like encyclicals being chanted. Then he smiled for the first time in a long while and said in Spanish: "When I die, burn mercury in my room for three days." Arcadio told that to José Arcadio Buendía and the latter tried to get more explicit information, but he received only one answer: "I have found immortality." When Melquíades' breathing began to smell, Arcadio took him to bathe in the river on Thursday mornings. He seemed to get better. He would undress and get into the water with the boys, and his mysterious sense of orientation would allow him to avoid the deep and dangerous spots. "We come from the water," he said on a certain occasion. Much time passed in that way without anyone's seeing him in the house except on the night when he made a pathetic effort to fix the pianola, and when he would go to the river with Arcadio, carrying under his arm a gourd and a bar of palm oil soap wrapped in a towel. One Thurs-

74

day, before they called him to go to the river, Aureliano heard him say: "I have died of fever on the dunes of Singapore." That day he went into the water at a bad spot and they did, not find him until the following day, a few miles downstream, washed up on a bright bend in the river and with a solitary vulture sitting on his stomach. Over the scandalized protests of Úrsula, who wept with more grief than she had had for her own father, José Arcadio Buendía was opposed to their burying him. "He is immortal," he said, "and he himself revealed the formula of his resurrection." He brought out the forgotten water pipe and put a kettle of mercury to boil next to the body, which little by little was filling with blue bubbles. Don Apolinar Moscote ventured to remind him that an unburied drowned man was a danger to public health. "None of that, because he's alive," was the answer of José Arcadio Buendía, who finished the seventy-two hours with the mercurial incense as the body was already beginning to burst with a livid fluorescence, the soft whistles of which impregnated the house with a pestilential vapor. Only then did he permit them to bury him, not in any ordinary way, but with the honors reserved for Macondo's greatest benefactor. It was the first burial and the best-attended one that was ever seen in the town, only surpassed, a century later, by Big Mama's funeral carnival. They buried him in a grave dug in the center of the plot destined for the cemetery, with a stone on which they wrote the only thing they knew about him: MELQUÍADES. They gave him his nine nights of wake. In the tumult that gathered in the courtyard to drink coffee, tell jokes, and play cards, Amaranta found a chance to confess her love to Pietro Crespi, who a few weeks before had formalized his promise to Rebeca and had set up a store for musical instruments and mechanical toys in the same section where the Arabs had lingered in other times swapping knick-knacks for macaws, and which the people called the Street of the Turks. The Italian, whose head covered with patent leather curls aroused in women an irrepressible need to sigh, dealt with Amaranta as with a capricious little girl who was not worth taking seriously.

"I have a younger brother," he told her. "He's coming to help me in the store."

Amaranta felt humiliated and told Pietro Crespi with a virulent anger that she was prepared to stop her sister's wedding even if her own dead body had to lie across the door. The Italian was so impressed by the dramatics of the threat that he could not resist the temptation to mention it to Rebeca. That was how Amaranta's trip, always put off by Úrsula's work, was arranged in less than a week. Amaranta put up no resistance, but when she kissed Rebeca good-bye she whispered in her ear:

"Don't get your hopes up. Even if they send me to the ends of the earth I'll find some way of stopping you from getting married, even if I have to kill you."

With the absence of Úrsula, with the invisible presence of Melquíades, who continued his stealthy shuffling through the rooms, the house seemed enormous and empty. Rebeca took charge of domestic order, while the Indian woman took care of the bakery. At dusk, when Pietro Crespi would arrive, preceded by a cool breath of lavender and always bringing a toy as a gift, his fiancée would receive the visitor in the main parlor with doors and windows open to be safe from any suspicion. It was an unnecessary precaution, for the Italian had shown himself to be so respectful that he did not even touch the hand of the woman who was going to be his wife within the year. Those visits were filling the house with remarkable toys. Mechanical ballerinas, music boxes, acrobatic monkeys, trotting horses, clowns who played the tambourine: the rich and startling mechanical fauna that Pietro Crespi brought dissipated José Arcadio Buendía's affliction over the death of Melquíades and carried him back to his old days as an alchemist. He lived at that time in a paradise of disemboweled animals, of mechanisms that had been taken apart in an attempt to perfect them with a system of perpetual motion based upon the principles of the pendulum. Aureliano, for his part, had neglected the workshop in order to teach little Remedios to read and write. At first the child preferred her dolls to the man who would come every afternoon and who was responsible for her being separated from her toys in order to be bathed and dressed and seated in the parlor to receive the visitor. But Aureliano's patience and devotion finally won her over, up to the point where she would spend many hours with him studying the meaning of the letters and sketching in a notebook with colored pencils little houses with cows in the corral and round suns with yellow rays that hid behind the hills.

Only Rebeca was unhappy, because of Amaranta's threat. She knew her sister's character, the haughtiness of her spirit, and she was frightened by the virulence of her anger. She would spend whole hours sucking her finger in the bathroom, holding herself back with an exhausting iron will so as not to eat earth. In search of some relief for her uncertainty, she called Pilar Ternera to read her future. After a string of conventional vagaries, Pilar Ternera predicted:

"You will not be happy as long as your parents remain unburied."

Rebeca shuddered. As in the memory of a dream she saw herself entering the house as a very small girl, with the trunk and the little rocker, and a bag whose contents she had never known. She remembered a bald gentleman dressed in linen and with his collar closed by a gold button, who had nothing to do with the king of hearts. She remembered a very young and beautiful woman with warm and perfumed hands, who had nothing in common with the jack of diamonds and his rheumatic hands, and who used to put flowers in her hair and take her out walking in the afternoon through a town with green streets.

"I don't understand," she said.

Pilar Ternera seemed disconcerted:

"I don't either, but that's what the cards say."

Rebeca was so preoccupied with the enigma that she told it to José Arcadio Buendía, and he scolded her for believing in the predictions of the cards, but he undertook the silent task of searching closets and trunks, moving furniture and turning over beds and floorboards looking for the bag of bones. He remembered that he had not seen it since the time of the rebuilding. He secretly summoned the masons and one of them revealed that he had walled up the bag in some bedroom because it bothered him in his work. After several days of listening, with their ears against the walls, they perceived the deep *cloc-cloc*. They penetrated the wall and there were the bones in the intact bag. They buried it the same day in a grave without a stone next to that of Melquíades, and José Arcadio Buendía returned home free of a burden that for a moment had weighed on his conscience as much as the memory of Prudencio Aguilar. When he went through the kitchen he kissed Rebeca on the forehead.

"Get those bad thoughts out of your head," he told her. "You're going to be happy."

The friendship with Rebeca opened up to Pilar Ternera the doors of the house, closed by Úrsula since the birth of Arcadio. She would arrive at any hour of the day, like a flock of goats, and would unleash her feverish energy in the hardest tasks. Sometimes she would go into the workshop and help Arcadio sensitize the daguerreotype plates with an efficiency and a tenderness that ended up by confusing him. That woman bothered him. The tan of her skin, her smell of smoke, the disorder of her laughter in the darkroom distracted his attention and made him bump into things.

On a certain occasion Aureliano was there working on his silver, and Pilar Ternera leaned over the table to admire his laborious patience. Suddenly it happened. Aureliano made

78

sure that Arcadio was in the darkroom before raising his eyes and meeting those of Pilar Ternera, whose thought was perfectly visible, as if exposed to the light of noon.

"Well," Aureliano said. "Tell me what it is."

Pilar Ternera bit her lips with a sad smile.

"That you'd be good in a war," she said. "Where you put your eye, you put your bullet."

Aureliano relaxed with the proof of the omen. He went back to concentrate on his work as if nothing had happened, and his voice took on a restful strength.

"I will recognize him," he said. "He'll bear my name."

José Arcadio Buendía finally got what he was looking for: he connected the mechanism of the clock to a mechanical ballerina, and the toy danced uninterruptedly to the rhythm of her own music for three days. That discovery excited him much more than any of his other harebrained undertakings. He stopped eating. He stopped sleeping. Only the vigilance and care of Rebeca kept him from being dragged off by his imagination into a state of perpetual delirium from which he would not recover. He would spend the nights walking around the room thinking aloud, searching for a way to apply the principles of the pendulum to oxcarts, to harrows, to everything that was useful when put into motion. The fever of insomnia fatigued him so much that one dawn he could not recognize the old man with white hair and uncertain gestures who came into his bedroom. It was Prudencio Aguilar. When he finally identified him, startled that the dead also aged, José Arcadio Buendía felt himself shaken by nostalgia. "Prudencio," he exclaimed. "You've come from a long way off!" After many years of death the yearning for the living was so intense, the need for company so pressing, so terrifying the nearness of that other death which exists within death, that Prudencio Aguilar had ended up loving his worst enemy. He had spent a great deal of time looking for him. He asked the dead from Riohacha about him, the dead who came from the Upar Valley, those who came from the swamp, and no one could tell him because Macondo was a town that was unknown to the dead until Melquíades arrived and marked it with a small black dot on the motley maps of death. José Arcadio Buendía conversed with Prudencio Aguilar until dawn. A few hours later, worn out by the vigil, he went into Aureliano's workshop and asked him: "What day is today?" Aureliano told him that it was Tuesday. "I was thinking the same thing," José Arcadio Buendía said, "but suddenly I realized that it's still Monday, like yesterday. Look at the sky, look at the walls, look at the begonias. Today is Monday too." Used to his manias, Aureliano paid no attention to him. On the next day, Wednesday, José Arcadio Buendía went back to the workshop. "This is a disaster," he said. "Look at the air, listen to the buzzing of the sun, the same as yesterday and the day before. Today is Monday too." That night Pietro Crespi found him on the porch, weeping for Prudencio Aguilar, for Melquíades, for Rebeca's parents, for his mother and father, for all of those he could remember and who were now alone in death. He gave him a mechanical bear that walked on its hind legs on a tightrope, but he could not distract him from his obsession. He asked him what had happened to the project he had explained to him a few days before about the possibility of building a pendulum machine that would help men to fly and he answered that it was impossible because a pendulum could lift anything into the air but it could not lift itself. On Thursday he appeared in the workshop again with the painful look of plowed ground. "The time machine has broken," he almost sobbed, "and Úrsula and Amaranta so far away!" Aureliano scolded him like a child and he adopted a contrite air. He spent six hours examining things, trying to find a difference from their appearance on the previous day in the hope of discovering in them some change that would reveal the passage of time. He spent the whole night in bed with his eyes open, calling to

Prudencio Aguilar, to Melquíades, to all the dead, so that they would share his distress. But no one came. On Friday, before anyone arose, he watched the appearance of nature again until he did not have the slightest doubt but that it was Monday. Then he grabbed the bar from a door and with the savage violence of his uncommon strength he smashed to dust the equipment in the alchemy laboratory, the daguerreotype room, the silver workshop, shouting like a man possessed in some high-sounding and fluent but completely incomprehensible language. He was about to finish off the rest of the house when Aureliano asked the neighbors for help. Ten men were needed to get him down, fourteen to tie him up, twenty to drag him to the chestnut tree in the courtyard, where they left him tied up, barking in the strange language and giving off a green froth at the mouth. When Úrsula and Amaranta returned he was still tied to the trunk of the chestnut tree by his hands and feet, soaked with rain and in a state of total innocence. They spoke to him and he looked at them without recognizing them, saying things they did not understand. Úrsula untied his wrists and ankles, lacerated by the pressure of the rope, and left him tied only by the waist. Later on they built him a shelter of palm branches to protect him from the sun and the rain.

AURELIANO BUENDÍA and Remedios Moscote were married one Sunday in March before the altar Father Nicanor Reyna had set up in the parlor. It was the culmination of four weeks of shocks in the Moscote household because little Remedios had reached puberty before getting over the habits of childhood. In spite of the fact that her mother had taught her about the changes of adolescence, one February afternoon she burst shouting into the living room, where her sisters were chatting with Aureliano, and showed them her panties, smeared with a chocolate-colored paste. A month for the wedding was agreed upon. There was barely enough time to teach her how to wash herself, get dressed by herself, and understand the fundamental business of a home. They made her urinate over hot bricks in order to cure her of the habit of wetting her bed. It took a good deal of work to convince her of the inviolability of the marital secret, for Remedios was so confused and at the same time so amazed at the revelation that she wanted to talk to everybody about the details of the wedding night. It was a fatiguing effort, but on the date set for the ceremony the child was as adept in the ways of the world as any of her sisters. Don Apolinar Moscote escorted her by the arm down the street that was decorated with flowers and wreaths amidst the explosion of rockets and the music of several bands, and she waved with her hand and gave her thanks with a smile to those who wished her good luck from the windows. Aureliano, dressed in black, wearing the same patent leather boots with metal fasteners that he would have on a few years later as he faced the firing squad, had an intense paleness and a hard lump in his throat when he met the bride at the door of the house and led her to the altar. She behaved so naturally, with such discretion, that she did not lose her composure, not even when Aureliano dropped the ring as he tried to put it on her finger. In the midst of the murmurs and confusion of the guests, she kept her arm with the fingerless lace glove held up and remained like that with her ring finger ready until the bridegroom managed to stop the ring with his foot before it rolled to the door, and came back blushing to the altar. Her mother and sisters suffered so much from the fear that the child would do something wrong during the ceremony that in the end they were the ones who committed the impertinence of picking her up to kiss her. From that day on the sense of responsibility, the natural grace, the calm control that Remedios would have in the face of adverse circumstances was revealed. It was she who, on her own initiative, put aside the largest piece that she had cut from the wedding cake and took it on a plate with a fork to José Arcadio Buendía. Tied to the trunk of the chestnut tree, huddled on a wooden stool underneath the palm shelter, the enormous old man, discolored by the sun and rain, made a vague smile of gratitude and ate the piece of cake with his fingers, mumbling an unintelligible psalm. The only unhappy person in that noisy celebration, which lasted until dawn on Monday, was Rebeca Buendía. It was her own frustrated party. By an arrangement of Úrsula's, her marriage was to be celebrated on the same day, but that Friday Pietro Crespi received a letter with the news of his mother's imminent death. The wedding was postponed. Pietro Crespi left for the capital of the province an hour after receiving the letter, and on the road he missed his mother, who arrived punctually Saturday night and at Aureliano's wedding sang the sad aria that she had prepared for the wedding of her son. Pietro Crespi returned on Sunday midnight to sweep up the ashes of the party, after having worn out five horses on the road in an attempt to be in time for his wedding. It was never discovered who wrote the letter. Tormented by Úrsula, Amaranta wept with indignation and swore her innocence in front of the altar, which the carpenters had not finished dismantling.

Father Nicanor Reyna—whom Don Apolinar Moscote had brought from the swamp to officiate at the wedding—was an old man hardened by the ingratitude of his ministry. His skin was sad, with the bones almost exposed, and he had a pronounced round stomach and the expression of an old angel, which came more from simplicity than from goodness. He had planned to return to his parish after the wedding, but he was appalled at the hardness of the inhabitants of Macondo, who were prospering in the midst of scandal, subject to the natural law, without baptizing their children or sanctifying their festivals. Thinking that no land needed the seed of God so much, he decided to stay on for another week to Christianize both circumcised and gentile, legalize concubinage, and give the sacraments to the dying. But no one paid any attention to him. They would answer him that they had been many years without a priest, arranging the business of their souls directly with God, and that they had lost the evil of original sin. Tired of preaching in the open, Father Nicanor decided to undertake the building of a church, the largest in the world, with life-size saints and stained-glass windows on the sides, so that people would come from Rome to honor God in the center of impiety. He went everywhere begging alms with a copper dish. They gave him a large amount, but he wanted more, because the church had to have a bell that would raise the drowned up to the surface of the water. He pleaded so much that he lost his voice. His bones began to fill with sounds. One Saturday, not even having collected the price of the doors, he fell into a desperate confusion. He improvised an altar in the square and on Sunday he went through the town with a small bell, as in the days of insomnia, calling people to an open-air mass. Many went out of curiosity. Others from nostalgia. Others so that God would not take the disdain for His intermediary as a personal insult. So that at eight in the morning half the town was in the square, where Father Nicanor chanted the gospels in a voice that had been lacerated by his pleading. At the end, when the congregation began to break up, he raised his arms signaling for attention.

"Just a moment," he said. "Now we shall witness an undeniable proof of the infinite power of God."

The boy who had helped him with the mass brought him a cup of thick and steaming chocolate, which he drank without pausing to breathe. Then he wiped his lips with a handkerchief that he drew from his sleeve, extended his arms, and closed his eyes. Thereupon Father Nicanor rose six inches above the level of the ground. It was a convincing measure. He went among the houses for several days repeating the demonstration of levitation by means of chocolate while the acolyte collected so much money in a bag that in less than a month he began the construction of the church. No one doubted the divine origin of the demonstration except José

Arcadio Buendía, who without changing expression watched the troop of people who gathered around the chestnut tree one morning to witness the revelation once more. He merely stretched on his stool a little and shrugged his shoulders when Father Nicanor began to rise up from the ground along with the chair he was sitting on.

"Hoc est simplicissimus," José Arcadio Buendía said. *"Homo iste statum quartum materiae invenit."*

Father Nicanor raised his hands and the four legs of the chair all landed on the ground at the same time.

"Nego," he said. *"Factum hoc existentiam Dei probat sine dubio."*

Thus it was discovered that José Arcadio Buendía's devilish jargon was Latin. Father Nicanor took advantage of the circumstance of his being the only person who had been able to communicate with him to try to inject the faith into his twisted mind. Every afternoon he would sit by the chestnut tree preaching in Latin, but José Arcadio Buendía insisted on rejecting rhetorical tricks and the transmutation of chocolate, and he demanded the daguerreotype of God as the only proof. Father Nicanor then brought him medals and pictures and even a reproduction of the Veronica, but José Arcadio Buendía rejected them as artistic objects without any scientific basis. He was so stubborn that Father Nicanor gave up his attempts at evangelization and continued visiting him out of humanitarian feelings. But then it was José Arcadio Buendía who took the lead and tried to break down the priest's faith with rationalist tricks. On a certain occasion when Father Nicanor brought a checker set to the chestnut tree and invited him to a game, José Arcadio Buendía would not accept, because according to him he could never understand the sense of a contest in which the two adversaries have agreed upon the rules. Father Nicanor, who had never seen checkers played that way, could not play it again. Ever more startled at José Arcadio Buendía's lucidity, he asked him how it was possible that they had him tied to a tree.

"Hoc est simplicissimus," he replied. "Because I'm crazy."

From then on, concerned about his own faith, the priest did not come back to visit him and dedicated himself to hurrying along the building of the church. Rebeca felt her hopes being reborn. Her future was predicated on the completion of the work, for one Sunday when Father Nicanor was lunching at the house and the whole family sitting at the table spoke of the solemnity and splendor that religious ceremonies would acquire when the church was built, Amaranta said: "The luckiest one will be Rebeca." And since Rebeca did not understand what she meant, she explained it to her with an innocent smile:

"You're going to be the one who will inaugurate the church with your wedding."

Rebeca tried to forestall any comments. The way the construction was going the church would not be built before another ten years. Father Nicanor did not agree: the growing generosity of the faithful permitted him to make more optimistic calculations. To the mute indignation of Rebeca, who could not finish her lunch, Úrsula celebrated Amaranta's idea and contributed a considerable sum for the work to move faster. Father Nicanor felt that with another contribution like that the church would be ready within three years. From then on Rebeca did not say another word to Amaranta, convinced that her initiative had not the innocence that she attempted to give it. "That was the least serious thing I could have done," Amaranta answered her during the violent argument they had that night. "In that way I won't have to kill you for three years." Rebeca accepted the challenge.

When Pietro Crespi found out about the new postponement, he went through a crisis of disappointment, but Rebeca gave him a final proof of her loyalty. "We'll elope whenever you say," she told him. Pietro Crespi, however, was not a man of adventure. He lacked the impulsive character of his fiancée, and he considered respect for one's given word as a wealth that should not be squandered. Then Rebeca turned to more audacious methods. A mysterious wind blew out the lamps in the parlor and Úrsula surprised the lovers kissing in the dark. Pietro Crespi gave her some confused explanations about the poor quality of modern pitch lamps and he even helped her install a more secure system of illumination for the room. But the fuel failed again or the wicks became clogged and Úrsula found Rebeca sitting on her fiancé's lap. This time she would accept no explanation. She turned the responsibility of the bakery over to the Indian woman and sat in a rocking chair to watch over the young people during the visits, ready to win out over maneuvers that had already been old when she was a girl. "Poor Mama," Rebeca would say with mock indignation, seeing Úrsula yawn during the boredom of the visits. "When she dies she'll go off to her reward in that rocking chair." After three months of supervised love, fatigued by the slow progress of the construction, which he went to inspect every day, Pietro Crespi decided to give Father Nicanor the money he needed to finish the church. Amaranta did not grow impatient. As she conversed with her girl friends every afternoon when they came to embroider on the porch, she tried to think of new subterfuges. A mistake in calculation spoiled the one she considered the most effective: removing the mothballs that Rebeca had put in her wedding dress before she put it away in the bedroom dresser. She did it when two months were left for the completion of the church. But Rebeca was so impatient with the approach of the wedding that she wanted to get the dress ready earlier than Amaranta had foreseen. When she opened the dresser and unfolded first the papers and then the protective cloth, she found the fabric of the dress and the stitches of the veil and even the crown of orange blossoms perforated by moths. Although she was sure that she had put a handful of mothballs in the wrappings, the disaster seemed so natural that she did not dare blame Amaranta. There was less than a month until the wedding, but Amparo Moscote promised to sew a new dress within a week. Amaranta felt faint that rainy noontime when Amparo came to the house wrapped in the froth of needlework for Rebeca to have the final fitting of the dress. She lost her voice and a thread of cold sweat ran down the path of her spine. For long months she had trembled with fright waiting for that hour, because if she had not been able to conceive the ultimate obstacle to Rebeca's wedding, she was sure that at the last moment, when all the resources of her imagination had failed, she would have the courage to poison her. That afternoon, while Rebeca was suffocating with heat inside the armor of thread that Amparo Moscote was putting about her body with thousands of pins and infinite patience, Amaranta made several mistakes in her crocheting and pricked her finger with the needle, but she decided with frightful coldness that the date would be the last Friday before the wedding and the method would be a dose of laudanum in her coffee.

A greater obstacle, as impassable as it was unforeseen, obliged a new and indefinite postponement. One week before the date set for the wedding, little Remedios woke up in the middle of the night soaked in a hot broth which had exploded in her insides with a kind of tearing belch, and she died three days later, poisoned by her own blood, with a pair of twins crossed in her stomach. Amaranta suffered a crisis of conscience. She had begged God with such fervor for something fearful to happen so that she would not have to poison Rebeca that she felt guilty of Remedios' death. That was not the obstacle that she had begged for so much. Remedios had brought a breath of merriment to the house. She had settled down with her husband in a room near the workshop, which she decorated with the dolls and toys of her recent childhood, and her merry vitality overflowed the four walls of the bedroom and went like a whirlwind of good health along the porch with the begonias. She would start singing at dawn. She was the only person who dared intervene in the arguments between Rebeca and Amaranta. She plunged into the fatiguing chore of taking care of José Arcadio Buendía. She would bring him his food, she would help him with his daily necessities, wash him with soap and a scrubbing brush, keep his hair and beard free of lice and nits, keep the palm shelter in good condition and reinforce it with waterproof canvas in stormy weather. In her last months she had succeeded in communicating with him in phrases of rudimentary Latin. When the son of Aureliano and Pilar Ternera was born and brought to the house and baptized in an intimate ceremony with the name Aureliano José, Remedios decided that he would be considered their oldest child. Her maternal instinct surprised Úrsula. Aureliano, for his part, found in her the justification that he needed to live. He worked all day in his workshop and Remedios would bring him a cup of black coffee in the middle of the morning. They would both visit the Moscotes every night. Aureliano would play endless games of dominoes with his father-in-law while Remedios chatted with her sisters or talked to her mother about more important things. The link with the Buendías consolidated Don Apolinar Moscote's authority in the town. On frequent trips to the capital of the province he succeeded in getting the government to build a school so that Arcadio, who had inherited the educational enthusiasm of his grandfather, could take charge of it. Through persuasion he managed to get the majority of houses painted blue in time for the date of national independence. At the urging of Father Nicanor, he arranged for the transfer of Catarino's store to a back street and he closed down several scandalous establishments that prospered in the center of town. Once he returned with six policemen armed with rifles to whom he entrusted the maintenance of order, and no one remembered the original agreement not to have armed men in the town. Aureliano enjoyed his father-in-law's efficiency. "You're going to get as fat as he is," his friends would say to him. But his sedentary life, which accentuated his cheekbones and concentrated the sparkle of his eyes, did not increase his weight or alter the parsimony of his character, but, on the contrary, it hardened on his lips the straight line of solitary meditation and implacable decision. So deep was the affection that he and his wife had succeeded in arousing in both their families that when Remedios announced that she was going to have a child, even Rebeca and Amaranta declared a truce in order to knit items in blue wool if it was to be a boy and in pink wool in case it was a girl. She was the last person Arcadio thought about a few years later when he faced the firing squad.

Úrsula ordered a mourning period of closed doors and windows, with no one entering or leaving except on matters of utmost necessity. She prohibited any talking aloud for a year and she put Remedios' daguerreotype in the place where her body had been laid out, with a black ribbon around it and an oil lamp that was always kept lighted. Future generations, who never let the lamp go out, would be puzzled at that girl in a pleated skirt, white boots, and with an organdy band around her head, and they were never able to connect her with the standard image of a great-grandmother. Amaranta took charge of Aureliano José. She adopted him as a son who would share her solitude and relieve her from the involuntary laudanum that her mad beseeching had thrown into Remedios' coffee. Pietro Crespi would tiptoe in at dusk, with a black ribbon on his hat, and he would pay a silent visit to Rebeca, who seemed to be bleeding to death inside the black dress with sleeves down to her wrists. Just the idea of thinking about a new date for the wedding would have been so irreverent that the engagement turned into an eternal relationship, a fatigued love that no one worried about again, as if the lovers, who in other days had sabotaged the lamps in order to kiss, had been abandoned to the free will of death. Having lost her bearings, completely demoralized, Rebeca began eating earth again.

Suddenly—when the mourning had gone on so long that the needlepoint sessions began again—someone pushed open the street door at two in the afternoon in the mortal silence of the heat and the braces in the foundation shook with such force that Amaranta and her friends sewing on the porch, Rebeca sucking her finger in her bedroom, Úrsula in the kitchen, Aureliano in the workshop, and even José Arcadio Buendía under the solitary chestnut tree had the impression that an earthquake was breaking up the house. A huge man had arrived. His square shoulders barely fitted through the doorways. He was wearing a medal of Our Lady of Help around his bison neck, his arms and chest were completely covered with cryptic tattooing, and on his right wrist was the tight copper bracelet of the *niños-en-cruz* amulet. His skin was tanned by the salt of the open air, his hair was short and straight like the mane of a mule, his jaws were of iron, and he wore a sad smile. He had a belt on that was twice as thick as the cinch of a horse, boots with leggings and spurs and iron on the heels, and his presence gave the quaking impression of a seismic tremor. He went through the parlor and the living room, carrying some half-worn saddlebags in his hand, and he appeared like a thunderclap on the porch with the begonias where Amaranta and her friends were paralyzed, their needles in the air. "Hello," he said to them in a tired voice, threw the saddlebags on a worktable, and went by on his way to the back of the house. "Hello," he said to the startled Rebeca, who saw him pass by the door of her bedroom. "Hello," he said to Aureliano, who was at his silversmith's bench with all five senses alert. He did not linger with anyone. He went directly to the kitchen and there he stopped for the first time at the end of a trip that had begun on the other side of the world. "Hello," he said. Úrsula stood for a fraction of a second with her mouth open, looked into his eyes, gave a cry, and flung her arms around his neck, shouting and weeping with joy. It was José Arcadio. He was returning as poor as when he had left, to such an extreme that Úrsula had to give him two pesos to pay for the rental of his horse. He spoke a Spanish that was larded with sailor slang. They asked where he had been and he answered: "Out there." He hung his hammock in the room they assigned him and slept for three days. When he woke up, after eating sixteen raw eggs, he went directly to Catarino's store, where his monumental size provoked a panic of curiosity among the women. He called for music and cane liquor for everyone, to be put on his bill. He would Indian-wrestle with five men at the same time. "It can't be done," they said, convinced that they would not be able to move his arm. "He has *niños-en-cruz*." Catarino, who did not believe in magical tricks of strength, bet him twelve pesos that he could not move the counter. José Arcadio pulled it out of its place, lifted it over his head, and put it in the street. It took eleven men to put it back. In the heat of the party he exhibited his unusual masculinity on the bar, completely covered with tattoos of words in several languages intertwined in blue and red. To the women who were besieging him and coveting him he put the question as to who would pay the most. The one who had the most money offered him twenty pesos. Then he proposed raffling himself off among them at ten pesos a chance. It was a fantastic price because the most sought-after woman earned eight pesos a night, but they all accepted. They wrote their names on fourteen pieces of paper which they put into a hat and each woman took one out. When there were only two pieces left to draw, it was established to whom they belonged.

"Five pesos more from each one," José Arcadio proposed, "and I'll share myself with both."

He made his living that way. He had been around the world sixty-five times, enlisted in a crew of sailors without a country. The women who went to bed with him that night in Catarino's store brought him naked into the dance salon so that people could see that there was not a square inch of his body that was not tattooed, front and back, and from his neck to his toes. He did not succeed in becoming incorporated into the family. He slept all day and spent the night in the red-light district, making bets on his strength. On the rare occasions when Úrsula got him to sit down at the table, he gave signs of radiant good humor, especially when he told about his adventures in remote countries. He had been shipwrecked and spent two weeks adrift in the Sea of Japan, feeding on the body of a comrade who had succumbed to sunstroke and whose extremely salty flesh as it cooked in the sun had a sweet and granular taste. Under a bright noonday sun in the Gulf of Bengal his ship had killed a sea dragon, in the stomach of which they found the helmet, the buckles, and the weapons of a Crusader. In the Caribbean he had seen the ghost of the pirate ship of Victor Hugues, with its sails torn by the winds of death, the masts chewed by sea worms, and still looking for the course to Guadeloupe. Úrsula would weep at the table as if she were reading the letters that had never arrived and in which José Arcadio told about his deeds and misadventures. "And there was so much of a home here for you, my son," she would sob, "and so much food thrown to the hogs!" But underneath it all she could not conceive that the boy the gypsies took away was the same lout who would eat half a suckling pig for lunch and whose flatulence withered the flowers. Something similar took place with the rest of the family. Amaranta could not conceal the repugnance that she felt at the table because of his bestial belching. Arcadio, who never knew the secret of their relationship, scarcely answered the questions that he asked with the obvious idea of gaining his affection. Aureliano tried to relive the times when they slept in the same room, tried to revive the complicity of childhood, but José Arcadio had forgotten about it, because life at sea had saturated his memory with too many things to remember. Only Rebeca succumbed to the first impact. The day that she saw him pass by her bedroom she thought that

Pietro Crespi was a sugary dandy next to that protomale whose volcanic breathing could be heard all over the house. She tried to get near him under any pretext. On a certain occasion José Arcadio looked at her body with shameless attention and said to her: "You're a woman, little sister." Rebeca lost control of herself. She went back to eating earth and the whitewash on the walls with the avidity of previous days, and she sucked her finger with so much anxiety that she developed a callus on her thumb. She vomited up a green liquid with dead leeches in it. She spent nights awake shaking with fever, fighting against delirium, waiting until the house shook with the return of José Arcadio at dawn. One afternoon, when everyone was having a siesta, she could no longer resist and went to his bedroom. She found him in his shorts, lying in the hammock that he had hung from the beams with a ship's hawser. She was so impressed by his enormous motley nakedness that she felt an impulse to retreat. "Excuse me," she said, "I didn't know you were here." But she lowered her voice so as not to wake anyone up. "Come here," he said. Rebeca obeyed. She stopped beside the hammock in an icy sweat, feeling knots forming in her intestines, while José Arcadio stroked her ankles with the tips of his fingers, then her calves, then her thighs, murmuring: "Oh, little sister, little sister." She had to make a supernatural effort not to die when a startlingly regulated cyclonic power lifted her up by the waist and despoiled her of her intimacy with three slashes of its claws and quartered her like a little bird. She managed to thank God for having been born before she lost herself in the inconceivable pleasure of that unbearable pain, splashing in the steaming marsh of the hammock which absorbed the explosion of blood like a blotter.

Three days later they were married during the five-o'clock mass. José Arcadio had gone to Pietro Crespi's store the day before. He found him giving a zither lesson and did not draw him aside to speak to him. "I'm going to marry Rebeca," he told him. Pietro Crespi turned pale, gave the zither to one of his pupils, and dismissed the class. When they were alone in the room that was crowded with musical instruments and mechanical toys, Pietro Crespi said:

"She's your sister."

"I don't care," José Arcadio replied.

Pietro Crespi mopped his brow with the handkerchief that was soaked in lavender.

"It's against nature," he explained, "and besides, it's against the law."

José Arcadio grew impatient, not so much at the argument as over Pietro Crespi's paleness.

"Fuck nature two times over," he said. "And I've come to tell you not to bother going to ask Rebeca anything."

But his brutal deportment broke down when he saw Pietro Crespi's eyes grow moist.

"Now," he said to him in a different tone, "if you really like the family, there's Amaranta for you."

Father Nicanor revealed in his Sunday sermon that José Arcadio and Rebeca were not brother and sister. Úrsula never forgave what she considered an inconceivable lack of respect and when they came back from church she forbade the newlyweds to set foot in the house again. For her it was as if they were dead. So they rented a house across from the cemetery and established themselves there with no other furniture but José Arcadio's hammock. On their wedding night a scorpion that had got into her slipper bit Rebeca on the foot. Her tongue went to sleep, but that did not stop them from spending a scandalous honeymoon. The neighbors were startled by the cries that woke up the whole district as many as eight times in a single night and three times during siesta, and they prayed that such wild passion would not disturb the peace of the dead.

Aureliano was the only one who was concerned about them. He bought them some furniture and gave them some

96

money until José Arcadio recovered his sense of reality and began to work the no-man's-land that bordered the courtyard of the house. Amaranta, on the other hand, never did overcome her rancor against Rebeca, even though life offered her a satisfaction of which she had not dreamed: at the initiative of Úrsula, who did not know how to repair the shame, Pietro Crespi continued having lunch at the house on Tuesdays, rising above his defeat with a serene dignity. He still wore the black ribbon on his hat as a sign of respect for the family, and he took pleasure in showing his affection for Úrsula by bringing her exotic gifts: Portuguese sardines, Turkish rose marmalade, and on one occasion a lovely Manila shawl. Amaranta looked after him with a loving diligence. She anticipated his wants, pulled out the threads on the cuffs of his shirt, and embroidered a dozen handkerchiefs with his initials for his birthday. On Tuesdays, after lunch, while she would embroider on the porch, he would keep her happy company. For Pietro Crespi, that woman whom he always had considered and treated as a child was a revelation. Although her temperament lacked grace, she had a rare sensibility for appreciating the things of the world and had a secret tenderness. One Tuesday, when no one doubted that sooner or later it had to happen, Pietro Crespi asked her to marry him. She did not stop her work. She waited for the hot blush to leave her ears and gave her voice a serene stress of maturity.

"Of course, Crespi," she said. "But when we know each other better. It's never good to be hasty in things."

Úrsula was confused. In spite of the esteem she had for Pietro Crespi, she could not tell whether his decision was good or bad from the moral point of view after his prolonged and famous engagement to Rebeca. But she finally accepted it as an unqualified fact because no one shared her doubts. Aureliano, who was the man of the house, confused her further with his enigmatic and final opinion:

"These are not times to go around thinking about weddings."

That opinion, which Úrsula understood only some months later, was the only sincere one that Aureliano could express at that moment, not only with respect to marriage, but to anything that was not war. He himself, facing a firing squad, would not understand too well the concatenation of the series of subtle but irrevocable accidents that brought him to that point. The death of Remedios had not produced the despair that he had feared. It was, rather, a dull feeling of rage that gradually dissolved in a solitary and passive frustration similar to the one he had felt during the time he was resigned to living without a woman. He plunged into his work again, but he kept up the custom of playing dominoes with his father-in-law. In a house bound up in mourning, the nightly conversations consolidated the friendship between the two men. "Get married again, Aurelito," his father-in-law would tell him. "I have six daughters for you to choose from." On one occasion on the eve of the elections, Don Apolinar Moscote returned from one of his frequent trips worried about the political situation in the country. The Liberals were determined to go to war. Since Aureliano at that time had very confused notions about the difference between Conservatives and Liberals, his father-in-law gave him some schematic lessons. The Liberals, he said, were Freemasons, bad people, wanting to hang priests, to institute civil marriage and divorce, to recognize the rights of illegitimate children as equal to those of legitimate ones, and to cut the country up into a federal system that would take power away from the supreme authority. The Conservatives, on the other hand, who had received their power directly from God, proposed the establishment of public order and family morality. They were the defenders of the faith of Christ, of the principle of authority, and were not prepared to permit the country to be broken down into autonomous entities. Because of his humanitarian feelings

Aureliano sympathized with the Liberal attitude with respect to the rights of natural children, but in any case, he could not understand how people arrived at the extreme of waging war over things that could not be touched with the hand. It seemed an exaggeration to him that for the elections his father-in-law had them send six soldiers armed with rifles under the command of a sergeant to a town with no political passions. They not only arrived, but they went from house to house confiscating hunting weapons, machetes, and even kitchen knives before they distributed among males over twenty-one the blue ballots with the names of the Conservative candidates and the red ballots with the names of the Liberal candidates. On the eve of the elections Don Apolinar Moscote himself read a decree that prohibited the sale of alcoholic beverages and the gathering together of more than three people who were not of the same family. The elections took place without incident. At eight o'clock on Sunday morning a wooden ballot box was set up in the square, which was watched over by the six soldiers. The voting was absolutely free, as Aureliano himself was able to attest since he spent almost the entire day with his father-in-law seeing that no one voted more than once. At four in the afternoon a roll of drums in the square announced the closing of the polls and Don Apolinar Moscote sealed the ballot box with a label crossed by his signature. That night, while he played dominoes with Aureliano, he ordered the sergeant to break the seal in order to count the votes. There were almost as many red ballots as blue, but the sergeant left only ten red ones and made up the difference with blue ones. Then they sealed the box again with a new label and the first thing on the following day it was taken to the capital of the province. "The Liberals will go to war," Aureliano said. Don Apolinar concentrated on his domino pieces. "If you're saying that because of the switch in ballots, they won't," he said. "We left a few red ones in so there won't be any complaints." Aureliano understood the disadvantages of being in the opposition. "If I were a Liberal," he said, "I'd go to war because of those ballots." His father-in-law looked at him over his glasses.

"Come now, Aurelito," he said, "if you were a Liberal, even though you're my son-in-law, you wouldn't have seen the switching of the ballots."

What really caused indignation in the town was not the results of the elections but the fact that the soldiers had not returned the weapons. A group of women spoke with Aureliano so that he could obtain the return of their kitchen knives from his father-in-law. Don Apolinar Moscote explained to him, in strictest confidence, that the soldiers had taken the weapons off as proof that the Liberals were preparing for war. The cynicism of the remark alarmed him. He said nothing, but on a certain night when Gerineldo Márquez and Magnífico Visbal were speaking with some other friends about the incident of the knives, they asked him if he was a Liberal or a Conservative. Aureliano did not hesitate.

"If I have to be something I'll be a Liberal," he said, "because the Conservatives are tricky."

On the following day, at the urging of his friends, he went to see Dr. Alirio Noguera to be treated for a supposed pain in his liver. He did not even understand the meaning of the subterfuge. Dr. Alirio Noguera had arrived in Macondo a few years before with a medicine chest of tasteless pills and a medical motto that convinced no one: *One nail draws another.* In reality he was a charlatan. Behind his innocent façade of a doctor without prestige there was hidden a terrorist who with his short-legged boots covered the scars that five years in the stocks had left on his legs. Taken prisoner during the first federalist adventure, he managed to escape to Curaçao disguised in the garment he detested most in this world: a cassock. At the end of a prolonged exile, stirred up by the exciting news that exiles from all over the Caribbean brought to Curaçao, he set out in a smuggler's schooner and appeared in Riohacha with the bottles of pills that were nothing but refined sugar and a diploma from the University of Leipzig that he had forged himself. He wept with disappointment. The federalist fervor, which the exiles had pictured as a powder keg about to explode, had dissolved into a vague electoral illusion. Embittered by failure, yearning for a safe place where he could await old age, the false homeopath took refuge in Macondo. In the narrow bottle-crowded room that he rented on one side of the square, he lived several years off the hopelessly ill who, after having tried everything, consoled themselves with sugar pills. His instincts of an agitator remained dormant as long as Don Apolinar Moscote was a figurehead. He passed the time remembering and fighting against asthma. The approach of the elections was the thread that led him once more to the skein of subversion. He made contact with the young people in the town, who lacked political knowledge, and he embarked on a stealthy campaign of instigation. The numerous red ballots that appeared in the box and that were attributed by Don Apolinar Moscote to the curiosity that came from youth were part of his plan: he made his disciples vote in order to show them that elections were a farce. "The only effective thing," he would say, "is violence." The majority of Aureliano's friends were enthusiastic over the idea of liquidating the Conservative establishment, but no one had dared include him in the plans, not only because of his ties with the magistrate, but because of his solitary and elusive character. It was known, furthermore, that he had voted blue at his father-in-law's direction. So it was a simple matter of chance that he revealed his political sentiments, and it was purely a matter of curiosity, a caprice, that brought him to visit the doctor for the treatment of a pain that he did not have. In the den that smelled of camphorated cobwebs he found himself facing a kind of dusty iguana whose lungs whistled when he breathed. Before asking him any questions the doctor took him to the window and examined the inside of his lower eyelid. "It's not there," Aureliano said, following what they told him. He pushed the tips of his fingers into his liver and added: "Here's where I have the pain that won't let me sleep." Then Dr. Noguera closed the window with the pretext that there was too much sun, and explained to him in simple terms that it was a patriotic duty to assassinate Conservatives. For several days Aureliano carried a small bottle of pills in his shirt pocket. He would take it out every two hours, put three pills in the palm of his hand, and pop them into his mouth for them to be slowly dissolved on his tongue. Don Apolinar Moscote made fun of his faith in homeopathy, but those who were in on the plot recognized another one of their people in him. Almost all of the sons of the founders were implicated, although none of them knew concretely what action they were plotting. Nevertheless, the day the doctor revealed the secret to Aureliano, the latter elicited the whole plan of the conspiracy. Although he was convinced at that time of the urgency of liquidating the Conservative regime, the plot horrified him. Dr. Noguera had a mystique of personal assassination. His system was reduced to coordinating a series of individual actions which in one master stroke covering the whole nation would liquidate the functionaries of the regime along with their respective families, especially the children, in order to exterminate Conservatism at its roots. Don Apolinar Moscote, his wife, and his six daughters, needless to say, were on the list.

"You're no Liberal or anything else," Aureliano told him without getting excited. "You're nothing but a butcher."

"In that case," the doctor replied with equal calm, "give me back the bottle. You don't need it any more."

Only six months later did Aureliano learn that the doctor had given up on him as a man of action because he was a sentimental person with no future, with a passive character, and a definite solitary vocation. They tried to keep him surrounded, fearing that he would betray the conspiracy. Aureliano calmed them down: he would not say a word, but on the night they went to murder the Moscote family they would find him guarding the door. He showed such a convincing decision that the plan was postponed for an indefinite date. It was during those days that Úrsula asked his opinion about the marriage between Pietro Crespi and Amaranta, and he answered that these were not times to be thinking about such a thing. For a week he had been carrying an old-fashioned pistol under his shirt. He kept his eyes on his friends. In the afternoon he would go have coffee with José Arcadio and Rebeca, who had begun to put their house in order, and from seven o'clock on he would play dominoes with his father-in-law. At lunchtime he was chatting with Arcadio, who was already a huge adolescent, and he found him more and more excited over the imminence of war. In school, where Arcadio had pupils older than himself mixed in with children who were barely beginning to talk, the Liberal fever had caught on. There was talk of shooting Father Nicanor, of turning the church into a school, of instituting free love. Aureliano tried to calm down his drive. He recommended discretion and prudence to him. Deaf to his calm reasoning, to his sense of reality, Arcadio reproached him in public for his weakness of character. Aureliano waited. Finally, in the beginning of December, Úrsula burst into the workshop all upset.

"War's broken out!"

War, in fact, had broken out three months before. Martial law was in effect in the whole country. The only one who knew it immediately was Don Apolinar Moscote, but he did not give the news even to his wife while the army platoon that was to occupy the town by surprise was on its way. They entered noiselessly before dawn, with two pieces of light artillery drawn by mules, and they set up their headquarters in the school. A 6 P.M. curfew was established. A more drastic search than the previous one was undertaken, house by house, and this time they even took farm implements. They dragged out Dr. Noguera, tied him to a tree in the square, and shot him without any due process of law. Father Nicanor tried to impress the military authorities with the miracle of levitation and had his head split open by the butt of a soldier's rifle. The Liberal exaltation had been extinguished into a silent terror. Aureliano, pale, mysterious, continued playing dominoes with his father-in-law. He understood that in spite of his present title of civil and military leader of the town, Don Apolinar Moscote was once more a figurehead. The decisions were made by the army captain, who each morning collected an extraordinary levy for the defense of public order. Four soldiers under his command snatched a woman who had been bitten by a mad dog from her family and killed her with their rifle butts. One Sunday, two weeks after the occupation, Aureliano entered Gerineldo Márquez's house and with his usual terseness asked for a mug of coffee without sugar. When the two of them were alone in the kitchen, Aureliano gave his voice an authority that had never been heard before. "Get the boys ready," he said. "We're going to war." Gerineldo Márquez did not believe him.

"With what weapons?" he asked.

"With theirs," Aureliano replied.

Tuesday at midnight in a mad operation, twenty-one men under the age of thirty commanded by Aureliano Buendía, armed with table knives and sharpened tools, took the garrison by surprise, seized the weapons, and in the courtyard executed the captain and the four soldiers who had killed the woman.

That same night, while the sound of the firing squad could be heard, Arcadio was named civil and military leader of the town. The married rebels barely had time to take leave of their wives, whom they left to their own devices. They left at dawn, cheered by the people who had been liberated from the terror, to join the forces of the revolutionary general Victorio Medina, who, according to the latest reports, was on his way to Manaure. Before leaving, Aureliano brought Don Apolinar Moscote out of a closet. "Rest easy, father-in-law," he told him. "The new government guarantees on its word of honor your personal safety and that of your family." Don Apolinar Moscote had trouble identifying that conspirator in high boots and with a rifle slung over his shoulder with the person he had played dominoes with until nine in the evening.

"This is madness, Aurelito," he exclaimed.

"Not madness," Aureliano said. "War. And don't call me Aurelito any more. Now I'm Colonel Aureliano Buendía."

Colonel Aureliano Buendía organized thirty-two armed uprisings and he lost them all. He had seventeen male children by seventeen different women and they were exterminated one after the other on a single night before the oldest one had reached the age of thirty-five. He survived fourteen attempts on his life, seventy-three ambushes, and a firing squad. He lived through a dose of strychnine in his coffee that was enough to kill a horse. He refused the Order of Merit, which the President of the Republic awarded him. He rose to be Commander in Chief of the revolutionary forces, with jurisdiction and command from one border to the other, and the man most feared by the government, but he never let himself be photographed. He declined the lifetime pension offered him after the war and until old age he made his living from the little gold fishes that he manufactured in his workshop in Macondo. Although he always fought at the head of his men, the only wound that he received was the one he gave himself after signing the Treaty of Neerlandia, which put an end to almost twenty years of civil war. He shot himself in the chest with a pistol and the bullet came out through his back without damaging any vital organ. The only thing left of all that was a street that bore his name in Macondo. And yet, as he declared a few years before he died of old age, he had not expected any of that on the dawn he left with his twenty-one men to join the forces of General Victorio Medina.

"We leave Macondo in your care," was all that he said to Arcadio before leaving. "We leave it to you in good shape; try to have it in better shape when we return."

Arcadio gave a very personal interpretation to the instructions. He invented a uniform with the braid and epaulets of a marshal, inspired by the prints in one of Melquíades' books, and around his waist he buckled the saber with gold tassels that had belonged to the executed captain. He set up the two artillery pieces at the entrance to town, put uniforms on his former pupils, who had been aroused by his fiery proclamations, and let them wander through the streets armed in order to give outsiders an impression of invulnerability. It was a double-edged deception, for the government did not dare attack the place for ten months, but when it did it unleashed such a large force against it that resistance was liquidated in a half hour. From the first day of his rule Arcadio revealed his predilection for decrees. He would read as many as four a day in order to decree and institute everything that came into his head. He imposed obligatory military service for men over eighteen, declared to be public property any animals walking the streets after six in the evening, and made men who were overage wear red armbands. He sequestered Father Nicanor in the parish house under pain of execution and prohibited him from saying mass or ringing the bells unless it was for a Liberal victory. In order that no one would doubt the severity of his aims, he ordered a firing squad organized in the square and had it shoot at a scarecrow. At first no one took him seriously. They were, after all, schoolchildren playing at being grown-ups. But one night, when Arcadio went into Catarino's store, the trumpeter in the group greeted him with a fanfare that made the customers laugh and Arcadio had him shot for disrespect for the authorities. People who protested were put on bread and water with their ankles in a set of stocks that he had set up in a schoolroom. "You murderer!" Úrsula would shout at him every time she learned of some new arbitrary act. "When Aureliano finds out he's going to shoot you and I'll be the first one to be glad." But it was of no use. Arcadio continued tightening the tourniquet with unnecessary rigor until he became the cruelest ruler that Macondo had ever known. "Now let them suffer the difference," Don Apolinar Moscote said on one occasion. "This is the Liberal paradise." Arcadio found out about it. At the head of a patrol he assaulted the house, destroyed the furniture, flogged the daughters, and dragged out Don Apolinar Moscote. When Úrsula burst into the courtyard of headquarters, after having gone through the town shouting shame and brandishing with rage a pitch-covered whip, Arcadio himself was preparing to give the squad the command to fire.

"I dare you to, bastard!" Úrsula shouted.

Before Arcadio had time to react she let go with the first blow of the lash. "I dare you to, murderer!" she shouted. "And kill me too, son of an evil mother. That way I won't have the eyes to weep for the shame of having raised a monster." Whipping him without mercy, she chased him to the back of the courtyard, where Arcadio curled up like a snail in its shell. Don Apolinar Moscote was unconscious, tied to the post where previously they had had the scarecrow that had been cut to pieces by shots fired in fun. The boys in the squad scattered, fearful that Úrsula would go after them too. But she did not even look at them. She left Arcadio with his uniform torn, roaring with pain and rage, and she untied Don Apolinar Moscote and took him home. Before leaving the headquarters she released the prisoners from the stocks.

From that time on she was the one who ruled in the town. She reestablished Sunday mass, suspended the use of red armbands, and abrogated the harebrained decrees. But in spite of her strength, she still wept over her unfortunate fate. She felt so much alone that she sought the useless company of her husband, who had been forgotten under the chestnut tree. "Look what we've come to," she would tell him as the June rains threatened to knock the shelter down. "Look at the empty house, our children scattered all over the world, and the two of us alone again, the same as in the beginning." José Arcadio Buendía, sunk in an abyss of unawareness, was deaf to her lamentations. At the beginning of his madness he would announce his daily needs with urgent Latin phrases. In fleeting clear spells of lucidity, when Amaranta would bring him his meals he would tell her what bothered him most and would accept her sucking glasses and mustard plasters in a docile way. But at the time when Úrsula went to lament by his side he had lost all contact with reality. She would bathe him bit by bit as he sat on his stool while she gave him news of the family. "Aureliano went to war more than four months ago and we haven't heard anything about him," she would say, scrubbing his back with a soaped brush. "José Arcadio came back a big man, taller than you, and all covered with needlework, but he only brought shame to our house." She thought she noticed, however, that her husband would grow sad with the bad news. Then she decided to lie to him. "You won't believe what I'm going to tell you," she said as she threw ashes over his excrement in order to pick it up with the shovel. "God willed that José Arcadio and Rebeca should get married, and now they're very happy." She got to be so sincere in the deception that she ended up by consoling herself with her own lies. "Arcadio is a serious man now," she said, "and very brave, and a fine-looking young man with his uniform and saber." It was like speaking to a dead man, for José Arcadio Buendía was already beyond the reach of any worry. But she insisted. He seemed so peaceful, so indifferent to everything that she decided to release him. He did not even move from his stool. He stayed there, exposed to the sun and the rain, as if the thongs were unnecessary, for a dominion superior to any visible bond kept him tied to the trunk of the chestnut tree. Toward August, when winter began to last forever, Úrsula was finally able to give him a piece of news that sounded like the truth.

"Would you believe it that good luck is still pouring down on us?" she told him. "Amaranta and the pianola Italian are going to get married."

Amaranta and Pietro Crespi had, in fact, deepened their friendship, protected by Úrsula, who this time did not think it necessary to watch over the visits. It was a twilight engagement. The Italian would arrive at dusk, with a gardenia in his buttonhole, and he would translate Petrarch's sonnets for Amaranta. They would sit on the porch, suffocated by the oregano and the roses, he reading and she sewing lace cuffs, indifferent to the shocks and bad news of the war, until the mosquitoes made them take refuge in the parlor. Amaranta's sensibility, her discreet but enveloping tenderness had been weaving an invisible web about her fiancé, which he had to push aside materially with his pale and ringless fingers in order to leave the house at eight o'clock. They had put together a delightful album with the postcards that Pietro Crespi received from Italy. They were pictures of lovers in lonely parks, with vignettes of hearts pierced with arrows and golden ribbons held by doves. "I've been to this park in Florence," Pietro Crespi would say, going through the cards.

"A person can put out his hand and the birds will come to feed." Sometimes, over a watercolor of Venice, nostalgia would transform the smell of mud and putrefying shellfish of the canals into the warm aroma of flowers. Amaranta would sigh, laugh, and dream of a second homeland of handsome men and beautiful women who spoke a childlike language, with ancient cities of whose past grandeur only the cats among the rubble remained. After crossing the ocean in search of it, after having confused passion with the vehement stroking of Rebeca, Pietro Crespi had found love. Happiness was accompanied by prosperity. His warehouse at that time occupied almost a whole block and it was a hothouse of fantasy, with reproductions of the bell tower of Florence that told time with a concert of carillons, and music boxes from Sorrento and compacts from China that sang five-note melodies when they were opened, and all the musical instruments imaginable and all the mechanical toys that could be conceived. Bruno Crespi, his younger brother, was in charge of the store because Pietro Crespi barely had enough time to take care of the music school. Thanks to him the Street of the Turks, with its dazzling display of knickknacks, became a melodic oasis where one could forget Arcadio's arbitrary acts and the distant nightmare of the war. When Úrsula ordered the revival of Sunday mass, Pietro Crespi donated a German harmonium to the church, organized a children's chorus, and prepared a Gregorian repertory that added a note of splendor to Father Nicanor's quiet rite. No one doubted that he would make Amaranta a fortunate mate. Not pushing their feelings, letting themselves be borne along by the natural flow of their hearts, they reached a point where all that was left to do was set a wedding date. They did not encounter any obstacles. Úrsula accused herself inwardly of having twisted Rebeca's destiny with repeated postponements and she was not about to add more remorse. The rigor of the mourning for Remedios had been relegated to the background by the mortifications of the war, Aureliano's absence, Arcadio's brutality, and the expulsion of José Arcadio and Rebeca. With the imminence of the wedding, Pietro Crespi had hinted that Aureliano José, in whom he had stirred up a love that was almost filial, would be considered their oldest child. Everything made Amaranta think that she was heading toward a smooth happiness. But unlike Rebeca, she did not reveal the slightest anxiety. With the same patience with which she dyed tablecloths, sewed lace masterpieces, and embroidered needlepoint peacocks, she waited for Pietro Crespi to be unable to bear the urges of his heart and more. Her day came with the ill-fated October rains. Pietro Crespi took the sewing basket from her lap and he told her, "We'll get married next month." Amaranta did not tremble at the contact with his icy hands. She withdrew hers like a timid little animal and went back to her work.

"Don't be simple, Crespi." She smiled. "I wouldn't marry you even if I were dead."

Pietro Crespi lost control of himself. He wept shamelessly, almost breaking his fingers with desperation, but he could not break her down. "Don't waste your time," was all that Amaranta said. "If you really love me so much, don't set foot in this house again." Úrsula thought she would go mad with shame. Pietro Crespi exhausted all manner of pleas. He went through incredible extremes of humiliation. He wept one whole afternoon in Úrsula's lap and she would have sold her soul in order to comfort him. On rainy nights he could be seen prowling about the house with an umbrella, waiting for a light in Amaranta's bedroom. He was never better dressed than at that time. His august head of a tormented emperor had acquired a strange air of grandeur. He begged Amaranta's friends, the ones who sewed with her on the porch, to try to persuade her. He neglected his business. He would spend the day in the rear of the store writing wild notes, which he would send to Amaranta with flower petals and dried butterflies, and which she would return unopened. He would shut himself up for hours on end to play the zither. One night he sang. Macondo woke up in a kind of angelic stupor that was caused by a zither that deserved more than this world and a voice that led one to believe that no other person on earth could feel such love. Pietro Crespi then saw the lights go on in every window in town except that of Amaranta. On November second, All Souls' Day, his brother opened the store and found all the lamps lighted, all the music boxes opened, and all the clocks striking an interminable hour, and in the midst of that mad concert he found Pietro Crespi at the desk in the rear with his wrists cut by a razor and his hands thrust into a basin of benzoin.

Úrsula decreed that the wake would be in her house. Father Nicanor was against a religious ceremony and burial in consecrated ground. Úrsula stood up to him. "In a way that neither you nor I can understand, that man was a saint," she said. "So I am going to bury him, against your wishes, beside Melquíades' grave." She did it with the support of the whole town and with a magnificent funeral. Amaranta did not leave her bedroom. From her bed she heard Úrsula's weeping, the steps and whispers of the multitude that invaded the house, the wailing of the mourners, and then a deep silence that smelled of trampled flowers. For a long time she kept on smelling Pietro Crespi's lavender breath at dusk, but she had the strength not to succumb to delirium. Úrsula abandoned her. She did not even raise her eyes to pity her on the afternoon when Amaranta went into the kitchen and put her hand into the coals of the stove until it hurt her so much that she felt no more pain but instead smelled the pestilence of her own singed flesh. It was a stupid cure for her remorse. For several days she went about the house with her hand in a pot of egg whites, and when the burns healed it appeared as if the whites had also scarred over the sores on her heart. The only external trace that the tragedy left was the bandage of black

E*

gauze that she put on her burned hand and that she wore until her death.

Arcadio gave a rare display of generosity by decreeing official mourning for Pietro Crespi. Úrsula interpreted it as the return of the strayed lamb. But she was mistaken. She had lost Arcadio, not when he had put on his military uniform, but from the beginning. She thought she had raised him as a son, as she had raised Rebeca, with no privileges or discrimination. Nevertheless, Arcadio was a solitary and frightened child during the insomnia plague, in the midst of Úrsula's utilitarian fervor, during the delirium of José Arcadio Buendía, the hermetism of Aureliano, and the mortal rivalry between Amaranta and Rebeca. Aureliano had taught him to read and write, thinking about other things, as he would have done with a stranger. He gave him his clothing so that Visitación could take it in when it was ready to be thrown away. Arcadio suffered from shoes that were too large, from his patched pants, from his female buttocks. He never succeeded in communicating with anyone better than he did with Visitación and Cataure in their language. Melquíades was the only one who really was concerned with him as he made him listen to his incomprehensible texts and gave him lessons in the art of daguerreotype. No one imagined how much he wept in secret and the desperation with which he tried to revive Melquíades with the useless study of his papers. The school, where they paid attention to him and respected him, and then power, with his endless decrees and his glorious uniform, freed him from the weight of an old bitterness. One night in Catarino's store someone dared tell him, "You don't deserve the last name you carry." Contrary to what everyone expected, Arcadio did not have him shot.

"To my great honor," he said, "I am not a Buendía."

Those who knew the secret of his parentage thought that the answer meant that he too was aware of it, but he had really never been. Pilar Ternera, his mother, who had made his blood boil in the darkroom, was as much an irresistible obsession for him as she had been first for José Arcadio and then for Aureliano. In spite of her having lost her charms and the splendor of her laugh, he sought her out and found her by the trail of her smell of smoke. A short time before the war, one noon when she was later than usual in coming for her younger son at school, Arcadio was waiting for her in the room where he was accustomed to take his siesta and where he later set up the stocks. While the child played in the courtyard, he waited in his hammock, trembling with anxiety, knowing that Pilar Ternera would have to pass through there. She arrived. Arcadio grabbed her by the wrist and tried to pull her into the hammock. "I can't, I can't," Pilar Ternera said in horror. "You can't imagine how much I would like to make you happy, but as God is my witness I can't." Arcadio took her by the waist with his tremendous hereditary strength and he felt the world disappear with the contact of her skin. "Don't play the saint," he said. "After all, everybody knows that you're a whore." Pilar overcame the disgust that her miserable fate inspired in her.

"The children will find out," she murmured. "It will be better if you leave the bar off the door tonight."

Arcadio waited for her that night trembling with fever in his hammock. He waited without sleeping, listening to the aroused crickets in the endless hours of early morning and the implacable telling of time by the curlews, more and more convinced that he had been deceived. Suddenly, when anxiety had broken down into rage, the door opened. A few months later, facing the firing squad, Arcadio would relive the wandering steps in the classroom, the stumbling against benches, and finally the bulk of a body in the shadows of the room and the breathing of air that was pumped by a heart that was not his. He stretched out his hand and found another hand with two rings on the same finger about to go astray in the darkness. He felt the structure of the veins, the pulse of its misfortune, and felt the damp palm with a lifeline cut off at the base of the thumb by the claws of death. Then he realized that this was not the woman he was waiting for, because she did not smell of smoke but of flower lotion, and she had inflated, blind breasts with nipples like a man's, a sex as stony and round as a nut, and the chaotic tenderness of excited inexperience. She was a virgin and she had the unlikely name of Santa Sofía de la Piedad. Pilar Ternera had paid her fifty pesos, half of her life savings, to do what she was doing. Arcadio had seen her many times working in her parents' small food store but he had never taken a good look at her because she had that rare virtue of never existing completely except at the opportune moment. But from that day on he huddled like a cat in the warmth of her armpit. She would go to the school at siesta time with the consent of her parents, to whom Pilar Ternera had paid the other half of her savings. Later on, when the government troops dislodged them from the place where they had made love, they did it among the cans of lard and sacks of corn in the back of the store. About the time that Arcadio was named civil and military leader they had a daughter.

The only relatives who knew about it were José Arcadio and Rebeca, with whom Arcadio maintained close relations at that time, based not so much on kinship as on complicity. José Arcadio had put his neck into the marital yoke. Rebeca's firm character, the voracity of her stomach, her tenacious ambition absorbed the tremendous energy of her husband, who had been changed from a lazy, woman-chasing man into an enormous work animal. They kept a clean and neat house. Rebeca would open it wide at dawn and the wind from the graveyard would come in through the windows and go out through the doors to the yard and leave the whitewashed walls and furniture tanned by the saltpeter of the dead. Her hunger for earth, the *cloc-cloc* of her parents' bones, the impatience of her blood as it faced Pietro Crespi's passivity were relegated to the attic of her memory. All day long she would embroider beside the window, withdrawn from the uneasiness of the war, until the ceramic pots would begin to vibrate in the cupboard and she would get up to warm the meal, much before the appearance, first, of the mangy hounds, and then of the colossus in leggings and spurs with a double-barreled shotgun, who sometimes carried a deer on his shoulder and almost always a string of rabbits or wild ducks. One afternoon, at the beginning of his rule, Arcadio paid them a surprise visit. They had not seen him since they had left the house, but he seemed so friendly and familiar that they invited him to share the stew.

Only when they were having coffee did Arcadio reveal the motive behind his visit: he had received a complaint against José Arcadio. It was said that he had begun by plowing his own yard and had gone straight ahead into neighboring lands, knocking down fences and buildings with his oxen until he took forcible possession of the best plots of land around. On the peasants whom he had not despoiled because he was not interested in their lands, he levied a contribution which he collected every Saturday with his hunting dogs and his double-barreled shotgun. He did not deny it. He based his right on the fact that the usurped lands had been distributed by José Arcadio Buendía at the time of the founding, and he thought it possible to prove that his father had been crazy ever since that time, for he had disposed of a patrimony that really belonged to the family. It was an unnecessary allegation, because Arcadio had not come to do justice. He simply offered to set up a registry office so that José Arcadio could legalize his title to the usurped land, under the condition that he delegate to the local government the right to collect the contributions. They made an agreement. Years later, when Colonel Aureliano Buendía examined the titles to property, he found registered in his brother's name all of the land between the hill where his yard was on up to the horizon, including the cemetery, and discovered that during the eleven months of his rule, Arcadio had collected not only the money of the contributions, but had also collected fees from people for the right to bury their dead in José Arcadio's land.

It took Úrsula several months to find out what was already public knowledge because people hid it from her so as not to increase her suffering. At first she suspected it. "Arcadio is building a house," she confided with feigned pride to her husband as she tried to put a spoonful of calabash syrup into his mouth. Nevertheless, she involuntarily sighed and said, "I don't know why, but all this has a bad smell to me." Later on, when she found out that Arcadio had not only built a house but had ordered some Viennese furniture, she confirmed her suspicion that he was using public funds. "You're the shame of our family name," she shouted at him one Sunday after mass when she saw him in his new house playing cards with his officers. Arcadio paid no attention to her. Only then did Úrsula know that he had a six-month-old daughter and that Santa Sofía de la Piedad, with whom he was living outside of marriage, was pregnant again. She decided to write to Colonel Aureliano Buendía, wherever he was, to bring him up to date on the situation. But the fast-moving events of those days not only prevented her plans from being carried out, they made her regret having conceived them. The war, which until then had been only a word to designate a vague and remote circumstance, became a concrete and dramatic reality. Around the end of February an old woman with an ashen look arrived in Macondo riding a donkey loaded down with brooms. She seemed so inoffensive that the sentries let her pass without any questions as another vendor, one of the many who often arrived from the towns in the swamp. She went directly to the barracks. Arcadio received her in the place where the classroom used to be and which at that time had been transformed into a kind of rearguard encampment, with rolled hammocks hanging on hooks and mats piled up in the corners, and rifles and carbines and even hunting shotguns scattered on the floor. The old woman stiffened into a military salute before identifying herself:

"I am Colonel Gregorio Stevenson."

He brought bad news. The last centers of Liberal resistance, according to what he said, were being wiped out. Colonel Aureliano Buendía, whom he had left fighting in retreat near Riohacha, had given him a message for Arcadio. He should surrender the town without resistance on the condition that the lives and property of Liberals would be respected. Arcadio examined that strange messenger who could have been a fugitive grandmother with a look of pity.

"You have brought something in writing, naturally," he said.

"Naturally," the emissary answered, "I have brought nothing of the sort. It's easy to understand that under the present circumstances a person can't carry anything that would compromise him."

As he was speaking he reached into his bodice and took out a small gold fish. "I think that this will be sufficient," he said. Arcadio could see that indeed it was one of the little fishes made by Colonel Aureliano Buendía. But anyone could have bought it before the war or stolen it, and it had no merit as a safe-conduct pass. The messenger even went to the extreme of violating a military secret so that they would believe his identity. He revealed that he was on a mission to Curaçao, where he hoped to recruit exiles from all over the Caribbean and acquire arms and supplies sufficient to attempt a landing at the end of the year. With faith in that plan, Colonel Aureliano Buendía was not in favor of any useless sacrifices at that time. But Arcadio was inflexible. He had the prisoner put into the stocks until he could prove his identity and he resolved to defend the town to the death.

He did not have long to wait. The news of the Liberal

defeat was more and more concrete. Toward the end of March, before a dawn of premature rain, the tense calm of the previous weeks was abruptly broken by the desperate sounds of a cornet and a cannon shot that knocked down the steeple of the church. Actually, Arcadio's decision to resist was madness. He had only fifty poorly armed men with a ration of twenty cartridges apiece. But among them, his former pupils, excited by the high-sounding proclamations, the determination reigned to sacrifice their skins for a lost cause. In the midst of the tramping of boots, contradictory commands, cannon shots that made the earth tremble, wild shooting, and the senseless sound of cornets, the supposed Colonel Stevenson managed to speak to Arcadio. "Don't let me undergo the indignity of dying in the stocks in these women's clothes," he said to him. "If I have to die, let me die fighting." He succeeded in convincing him. Arcadio ordered them to give him a weapon and twenty cartridges, and he left him with five men to defend headquarters while he went off with his staff to head up the resistance. He did not get to the road to the swamp. The barricades had been broken and the defenders were openly fighting in the streets, first until they used up their ration of rifle bullets, then with pistols against rifles, and finally hand to hand. With the imminence of defeat, some women went into the street armed with sticks and kitchen knives. In that confusion Arcadio found Amaranta, who was looking for him like a madwoman, in her nightgown and with two old pistols that had belonged to José Arcadio Buendía. He gave his rifle to an officer who had been disarmed in the fight and escaped with Amaranta through a nearby street to take her home. Úrsula was in the doorway waiting, indifferent to the cannon shots that had opened up a hole in the front of the house next door. The rain was letting up, but the streets were as slippery and as smooth as melted soap, and one had to guess distances in the darkness. Arcadio left Amaranta with Úrsula and made an attempt to face two

120

soldiers who had opened up with heavy firing from the corner. The old pistols that had been kept for many years in the bureau did not work. Protecting Arcadio with her body, Úrsula tried to drag him toward the house.

"Come along in the name of God," she shouted at him. "There's been enough madness!"

The soldiers aimed at them.

"Let go of that man, ma'am," one of them shouted, "or we won't be responsible!"

Arcadio pushed Úrsula toward the house and surrendered. A short time later the shooting stopped and the bells began to toll. The resistance had been wiped out in less than half an hour. Not a single one of Arcadio's men had survived the attack, but before dying they had killed three hundred soldiers. The last stronghold was the barracks. Before being attacked, the supposed Colonel Gregorio Stevenson had freed the prisoners and ordered his men to go out and fight in the street. The extraordinary mobility and accurate aim with which he placed his twenty cartridges gave the impression that the barracks was well-defended, and the attackers blew it to pieces with cannon fire. The captain who directed the operation was startled to find the rubble deserted and a single dead man in his undershorts with an empty rifle still clutched in an arm that had been blown completely off. He had a woman's full head of hair held at the neck with a comb and on his neck a chain with a small gold fish. When he turned him over with the tip of his boot and put the light on his face, the captain was perplexed. "Jesus Christ," he exclaimed. Other officers came over.

"Look where this fellow turned up," the captain said. "It's Gregorio Stevenson."

At dawn, after a summary court-martial, Arcadio was shot against the wall of the cemetery. In the last two hours of his life he did not manage to understand why the fear that had tormented him since childhood had disappeared. Impassive, without even worrying about making a show of his recent bravery, he listened to the interminable charges of the accusation. He thought about Úrsula, who at that hour must have been under the chestnut tree having coffee with José Arcadio Buendía. He thought about his eight-month-old daughter, who still had no name, and about the child who was going to be born in August. He thought about Santa Sofía de la Piedad, whom he had left the night before salting down a deer for next day's lunch, and he missed her hair pouring over her shoulders and her eyelashes, which looked as if they were artificial. He thought about his people without sentimentality, with a strict closing of his accounts with life, beginning to understand how much he really loved the people he hated most. The president of the court-martial began his final speech when Arcadio realized that two hours had passed. "Even if the proven charges did not have merit enough," the president was saying, "the irresponsible and criminal boldness with which the accused drove his subordinates on to a useless death would be enough to deserve capital punishment." In the shattered schoolhouse where for the first time he had felt the security of power, a few feet from the room where he had come to know the uncertainty of love, Arcadio found the formality of death ridiculous. Death really did not matter to him but life did, and therefore the sensation he felt when they gave their decision was not a feeling of fear but of nostalgia. He did not speak until they asked him for his last request.

"Tell my wife," he answered in a well-modulated voice, "to give the girl the name of Úrsula." He paused and said it again: "Úrsula, like her grandmother. And tell her also that if the child that is to be born is a boy, they should name him José Arcadio, not for his uncle, but for his grandfather."

Before they took him to the execution wall Father Nicanor tried to attend him. "I have nothing to repent," Arcadio said, and he put himself under the orders of the squad after drinking a cup of black coffee. The leader of the squad, a specialist in summary executions, had a name that had much more about it than chance: Captain Roque Carnicero, which meant butcher. On the way to the cemetery, under the persistent drizzle, Arcadio saw that a radiant Wednesday was breaking out on the horizon. His nostalgia disappeared with the mist and left an immense curiosity in its place. Only when they ordered him to put his back to the wall did Arcadio see Rebeca, with wet hair and a pink flowered dress, opening wide the door. He made an effort to get her to recognize him. And Rebeca did take a casual look toward the wall and was paralyzed with stupor, barely able to react and wave good-bye to Arcadio. Arcadio answered her the same way. At that instant the smoking mouths of the rifles were aimed at him and letter by letter he heard the encyclicals that Melquíades had chanted and he heard the lost steps of Santa Sofía de la Piedad, a virgin, in the classroom, and in his nose he felt the same icy hardness that had drawn his attention in the nostrils of the corpse of Remedios. "Oh, God damn it!" he managed to think. "I forgot to say that if it was a girl they should name her Remedios." Then, all accumulated in the rip of a claw, he felt again all the terror that had tormented him in his life. The captain gave the order to fire. Arcadio barely had time to put out his chest and raise his head, not understanding where the hot liquid that burned his thighs was pouring from.

"Bastards!" he shouted. "Long live the Liberal party!"

THE WAR was over in May. Two weeks before the government made the official announcement in a high-sounding proclamation, which promised merciless punishment for those who had started the rebellion, Colonel Aureliano Buendía fell prisoner just as he was about to reach the western frontier disguised as an Indian witch doctor. Of the twenty-one men who had followed him to war, fourteen fell in combat, six were wounded, and only one accompanied him at the moment of final defeat: Colonel Gerineldo Márquez. The news of his capture was announced in Macondo with a special proclamation. "He's alive," Úrsula told her husband. "Let's pray to God for his enemies to show him clemency." After three days of weeping, one afternoon as she was stirring some sweet milk candy in the kitchen she heard her son's voice clearly in her ear. "It was Aureliano," she shouted, running toward the chestnut tree to tell her husband the news. "I don't know how the miracle took place, but he's alive and we're going to see him very soon." She took it for granted. She had the floors of the house scrubbed and changed the position of the furniture. One week later a rumor from somewhere that was not supported by any proclamation gave dramatic confirmation to the prediction. Colonel Aureliano Buendía had been condemned to death and the sentence would be carried out in Macondo as a lesson to the population. One Monday, at ten-thirty in the morning, Amaranta was dressing Aureliano José when she heard the sound of a distant troop and the blast of a cornet one second before Úrsula burst into the room with the shout: "They're bringing him now!" The troop struggled to subdue the overflowing crowd with their rifle butts. Úrsula and Amaranta ran to the corner, pushing their way through, and then they saw him. He looked like a beggar. His clothing was torn, his hair and beard were tangled, and he was barefoot. He was walking without feeling the burning dust, his hands tied behind his back with a rope that a mounted officer had attached to the head of his horse. Along with him, also ragged and defeated, they were bringing Colonel Gerineldo Márquez. They were not sad. They seemed more disturbed by the crowd that was shouting all kinds of insults at the troops.

"My son!" Úrsula shouted in the midst of the uproar, and she slapped the soldier who tried to hold her back. The officer's horse reared. Then Colonel Aureliano Buendía stopped, tremulous, avoided the arms of his mother, and fixed a stern look on her eyes.

"Go home, Mama," he said. "Get permission from the authorities to come see me in jail."

He looked at Amaranta, who stood indecisively two steps behind Úrsula, and he smiled as he asked her, "What happened to your hand?" Amaranta raised the hand with the black bandage. "A burn," she said, and took Úrsula away so that the horses would not run her down. The troop took off. A special guard surrounded the prisoners and took them to the jail at a trot.

At dusk Úrsula visited Colonel Aureliano Buendía in jail. She had tried to get permission through Don Apolinar Moscote, but he had lost all authority in the face of the military omnipotence. Father Nicanor was in bed with hepatic fever. The parents of Colonel Gerineldo Márquez, who had not been condemned to death, had tried to see him and were driven off with rifle butts. Facing the impossibility of finding anyone to intervene, convinced that her son would be shot at dawn, Úrsula wrapped up the things she wanted to bring him and went to the jail alone.

"I am the mother of Colonel Aureliano Buendía," she announced.

The sentries blocked her way. "I'm going in in any case," Úrsula warned them. "So if you have orders to shoot, start right in." She pushed one of them aside and went into the former classroom, where a group of half-dressed soldiers were oiling their weapons. An officer in a field uniform, ruddy-faced, with very thick glasses and ceremonious manners, signaled to the sentries to withdraw.

"I am the mother of Colonel Aureliano Buendía," Úrsula repeated.

"You must mean," the officer corrected her with a friendly smile, "that you are the mother of *Mister* Aureliano Buendía."

Úrsula recognized in his affected way of speaking the languid cadence of the stuck-up people from the highlands.

"As you say, *mister*," she accepted, "just as long as I can see him."

There were superior orders that prohibited visits to prisoners condemned to death, but the officer assumed the responsibility of letting her have a fifteen-minute stay. Úrsula

126

showed him what she had in the bundle: a change of clean clothing, the short boots that her son had worn at his wedding, and the sweet milk candy that she had kept for him since the day she had sensed his return. She found Colonel Aureliano Buendía in the room that was used as a cell, lying on a cot with his arms spread out because his armpits were paved with sores. They had allowed him to shave. The thick mustache with twisted ends accentuated the sharp angles of his cheekbones. He looked paler to Úrsula than when he had left, a little taller, and more solitary than ever. He knew all about the details of the house: Pietro Crespi's suicide, Arcadio's arbitrary acts and execution, the dauntlessness of José Arcadio Buendía underneath the chestnut tree. He knew that Amaranta had consecrated her virginal widowhood to the rearing of Aureliano José and that the latter was beginning to show signs of quite good judgment and that he had learned to read and write at the same time he had learned to speak. From the moment in which she entered the room Úrsula felt inhibited by the maturity of her son, by his aura of command, by the glow of authority that radiated from his skin. She was surprised that he was so well-informed. "You knew all along that I was a wizard," he joked. And he added in a serious tone, "This morning, when they brought me in, I had the impression that I had already been through all that before." In fact, while the crowd was roaring alongside him, he had been concentrating his thoughts, startled at how the town had aged. The leaves of the almond trees were broken. The houses, painted blue, then painted red, had ended up with an indefinable coloration.

"What did you expect?" Úrsula sighed. "Time passes."

"That's how it goes," Aureliano admitted, "but not so much."

In that way the long-awaited visit, for which both had prepared questions and had even anticipated answers, was once more the usual everyday conversation. When the guard announced the end of the visit, Aureliano took out a roll of sweaty papers from under the cot. They were his poetry, the poems inspired by Remedios, which he had taken with him when he left, and those he had written later on during chance pauses in the war. "Promise me that no one will read them," he said. "Light the oven with them this very night." Úrsula promised and stood up to kiss him good-bye.

"I brought you a revolver," she murmured.

Colonel Aureliano Buendía saw that the sentry could not see. "It won't do me any good," he said in a low voice, "but give it to me in case they search you on the way out." Úrsula took the revolver out of her bodice and put it under the mattress of the cot. "And don't say good-bye," he concluded with emphatic calmness. "Don't beg or bow down to anyone. Pretend that they shot me a long time ago." Úrsula bit her lip so as not to cry.

"Put some hot stones on those sores," she said.

She turned halfway around and left the room. Colonel Aureliano Buendía remained standing, thoughtful, until the door closed. Then he lay down again with his arms open. Since the beginning of adolescence, when he had begun to be aware of his premonitions, he thought that death would be announced with a definite, unequivocal, irrevocable signal, but there were only a few hours left before he would die and the signal had not come. On a certain occasion a very beautiful woman had come into his camp in Tucurinca and asked the sentries' permission to see him. They let her through because they were aware of the fanaticism of some mothers, who sent their daughters to the bedrooms of the most famous warriors, according to what they said, to improve the breed. That night Colonel Aureliano Buendía was finishing the poem about the man who is lost in the rain when the girl came into his room. He turned his back to her to put the sheet of paper into the locked drawer where he kept his poetry. And then he sensed it. He grasped the pistol in the drawer without turning his head.

"Please don't shoot," he said.

When he turned around holding his pistol, the girl had lowered hers and did not know what to do. In that way he had avoided four out of eleven traps. On the other hand, someone who was never caught entered the revolutionary headquarters one night in Manaure and stabbed to death his close friend Colonel Magnífico Visbal, to whom he had given his cot so that he could sweat out a fever. A few yards away, sleeping in a hammock in the same room, he was not aware of anything. His efforts to systematize his premonitions were useless. They would come suddenly in a wave of supernatural lucidity, like an absolute and momentaneous conviction, but they could not be grasped. On occasion they were so natural that he identified them as premonitions only after they had been fulfilled. Frequently they were nothing but ordinary bits of superstition. But when they condemned him to death and asked him to state his last wish, he did not have the least difficulty in identifying the premonition that inspired his answer:

"I ask that the sentence be carried out in Macondo," he said.

The president of the court-martial was annoyed.

"Don't be clever, Buendía," he told him. "That's just a trick to gain more time."

"If you don't fulfill it, that will be your worry," the colonel said, "but that's my last wish."

Since then the premonitions had abandoned him. The day when Úrsula visited him in jail, after a great deal of thinking he came to the conclusion that perhaps death would not be announced that time because it did not depend on chance but on the will of his executioners. He spent the night awake, tormented by the pain of his sores. A little before dawn he heard steps in the hallway. "They're coming," he said to himself, and for no reason he thought of José Arcadio Buendía, who at that moment was thinking about him under the dreary dawn of the chestnut tree. He did not feel fear or nostalgia, but an intestinal rage at the idea that this artificial death would not let him see the end of so many things that he had left unfinished. The door opened and a sentry came in with a mug of coffee. On the following day at the same hour he would still be doing what he was then, raging with the pain in his armpits, and the same thing happened. On Thursday he shared the sweet milk candy with the guards and put on his clean clothes, which were tight for him, and the patent leather boots. By Friday they had still not shot him.

Actually, they did not dare carry out the sentence. The rebelliousness of the town made the military men think that the execution of Colonel Aureliano Buendía might have serious political consequences not only in Macondo but throughout the area of the swamp, so they consulted the authorities in the capital of the province. On Saturday night, while they were waiting for an answer, Captain Roque Carnicero went with some other officers to Catarino's place. Only one woman, practically threatened, dared take him to her room. "They don't want to go to bed with a man they know is going to die," she confessed to him. "No one knows how it will come, but everybody is going around saying that the officer who shoots Colonel Aureliano Buendía and all the soldiers in the squad, one by one, will be murdered, with no escape, sooner or later, even if they hide at the ends of the earth." Captain Roque Carnicero mentioned it to the other officers and they told their superiors. On Sunday, although no one had revealed it openly, although no action on the part of the military had disturbed the tense calm of those days, the whole town knew that the officers were ready to use any manner of pretext to avoid responsibility for the execution. The official order arrived in the Monday mail: the execution was to be carried out within twenty-four hours. That night the officers put seven slips of paper into a cap, and Captain Roque Carnicero's unpeaceful fate was foreseen by his name on the prize slip. "Bad luck doesn't have any chinks in it," he said with deep bitterness. "I was born a son of a bitch and I'm going to die a son of a bitch." At five in the morning he chose the squad by lot, formed it in the courtyard, and woke up the condemned man with a premonitory phrase.

"Let's go, Buendía," he told him. "Our time has come."

"So that's what it was," the colonel replied. "I was dreaming that my sores had burst."

Rebeca Buendía got up at three in the morning when she learned that Aureliano would be shot. She stayed in the bedroom in the dark, watching the cemetery wall through the half-opened window as the bed on which she sat shook with José Arcadio's snoring. She had waited all week with the same hidden persistence with which during different times she had waited for Pietro Crespi's letters. "They won't shoot him here," José Arcadio told her. "They'll shoot him at midnight in the barracks so that no one will know who made up the squad, and they'll bury him right there." Rebeca kept on waiting. "They're stupid enough to shoot him here," she said. She was so certain that she had foreseen the way she would open the door to wave good-bye. "They won't bring him through the streets," José Arcadio insisted, "with six scared soldiers and knowing that the people are ready for anything." Indifferent to her husband's logic, Rebeca stayed by the window.

"You'll see that they're just stupid enough," she said.

On Tuesday, at five in the morning, José Arcadio had drunk his coffee and let the dogs out when Rebeca closed the window and held onto the head of the bed so as not to fall down. "There, they're bringing him," she sighed. "He's so handsome." José Arcadio looked out the window and saw him, tremulous in the light of dawn. He already had his back to the wall and his hands were on his hips because the burning knots in his armpits would not let him lower them. "A person fucks himself up so much," Colonel Aureliano Buendía said. "Fucks himself up so much just so that six weak fairies can kill him and he can't do anything about it." He repeated it with so much rage that it almost seemed to be fervor, and Captain Roque Carnicero was touched, because he thought he was praying. When the squad took aim, the rage had materialized into a viscous and bitter substance that put his tongue to sleep and made him close his eyes. Then the aluminum glow of dawn disappeared and he saw himself again in short pants, wearing a tie around his neck, and he saw his father leading him into the tent on a splendid afternoon, and he saw the ice. When he heard the shout he thought that it was the final command to the squad. He opened his eyes with a shudder of curiosity, expecting to meet the incandescent trajectory of the bullets, but he only saw Captain Roque Carnicero with his arms in the air and José Arcadio crossing the street with his fearsome shotgun ready to go off.

"Don't shoot," the captain said to José Arcadio. "You were sent by Divine Providence."

Another war began right there. Captain Roque Carnicero and his six men left with Colonel Aureliano Buendía to free the revolutionary general Victorio Medina, who had been condemned to death in Riohacha. They thought they could save time by crossing the mountains along the trail that José Arcadio Buendía had followed to found Macondo, but before a week was out they were convinced that it was an impossible undertaking. So they had to follow the dangerous route over the outcroppings with no other munitions but what the firing squad had. They would camp near the towns and one of them, with a small gold fish in his hand, would go in disguise in broad daylight to contact the dormant Liberals, who would go out hunting on the following morning and never return. When they saw Riohacha from a ridge in the mountains, General Victorio Medina had been shot. Colonel Aureliano Buendía's men proclaimed him chief of the revolutionary forces of the Caribbean coast with the rank of general. He assumed the position but refused the promotion and took the stand that he would never accept it as long as the Conservative regime was in power. At the end of three months they had succeeded in arming more than a thousand men, but they were wiped out. The survivors reached the eastern frontier. The next thing that was heard of them was that they had landed on Cabo de la Vela, coming from the smaller islands of the Antilles, and a message from the government was sent all over by telegraph and included in jubilant proclamations throughout the country announcing the death of Colonel Aureliano Buendía. But two days later a multiple telegram which almost overtook the previous one announced another uprising on the southern plains. That was how the legend of the ubiquitous Colonel Aureliano Buendía began. Simultaneous and contradictory information declared him victorious in Villanueva, defeated in Guacamayal, devoured by Motilón Indians, dead in a village in the swamp, and up in arms again in Urumita. The Liberal leaders, who at that moment were negotiating for participation in the congress, branded him an adventurer who did not represent the party. The national government placed him in the category of a bandit and put a price of five thousand pesos on his head. After sixteen defeats, Colonel Aureliano Buendía left Guajira with two thousand well-armed Indians and the garrison, which was taken by surprise as it slept, abandoned Riohacha. He established his headquarters there and proclaimed total war against the regime. The first message he received from the government was a threat to shoot Colonel Gerineldo Márquez within forty-eight hours if he did not withdraw with his forces to the eastern frontier. Colonel Roque Carnicero, who was his chief of staff then, gave him the telegram with a look of consternation, but he read it with unforeseen joy.

"How wonderful!" he exclaimed. "We have a telegraph office in Macondo now."

His reply was definitive. In three months he expected to establish his headquarters in Macondo. If he did not find Colonel Gerineldo Márquez alive at that time he would shoot out of hand all of the officers he held prisoner at that moment, starting with the generals, and he would give orders to his subordinates to do the same for the rest of the war. Three months later, when he entered Macondo in triumph, the first embrace he received on the swamp road was that of Colonel Gerineldo Márquez.

The house was full of children. Úrsula had taken in Santa Sofía de la Piedad with her older daughter and a pair of twins, who had been born five months after Arcadio had been shot. Contrary to the victim's last wishes, she baptized the girl with the name Remedios. "I'm sure that was what Arcadio meant," she alleged. "We won't call her Úrsula because a person suffers too much with that name." The twins were named José Arcadio Segundo and Aureliano Segundo. Amaranta took care of them all. She put small wooden chairs in the living room and established a nursery with other children from neighboring families. When Colonel Aureliano Buendía returned in the midst of exploding rockets and ringing bells, a children's chorus welcomed him to the house. Aureliano José, tall like his grandfather, dressed as a revolutionary officer, gave him military honors.

Not all the news was good. A year after the flight of Colonel Aureliano Buendía, José Arcadio and Rebeca went to live in the house Arcadio had built. No one knew about his intervention to halt the execution. In the new house, located on the best corner of the square, in the shade of an almond tree that was honored by three nests of redbreasts, with a large door for visitors and four windows for light, they set up a hospitable home. Rebeca's old friends, among them four of the Moscote sisters who were still single, once more took up the sessions of embroidery that had been interrupted years before on the porch with the begonias. José Arcadio continued to profit from the usurped lands, the title to which was recognized by the Conservative government. Every afternoon he could be seen returning on horseback, with his hunting dogs, and his double-barreled shotgun and a string of rabbits hanging from his saddle. One September afternoon, with the threat of a storm, he returned home earlier than usual. He greeted Rebeca in the dining room, tied the dogs up in the courtyard, hung the rabbits up in the kitchen to be salted later, and went to the bedroom to change his clothes. Rebeca later declared that when her husband went into the bedroom she was locked in the bathroom and did not hear anything. It was a difficult version to believe, but there was no other more plausible, and no one could think of any motive for Rebeca to murder the man who had made her happy. That was perhaps the only mystery that was never cleared up in Macondo. As soon as José Arcadio closed the bedroom door the sound of a pistol shot echoed through the house. A trickle of blood came out under the door, crossed the living room, went out into the street, continued on in a straight line across the uneven terraces, went down steps and climbed over curbs, passed along the Street of the Turks, turned a corner to the right and another to the left, made a right angle at the Buendía house, went in under the closed door, crossed through the parlor, hugging the walls so as not to stain the rugs, went on to the other living room, made a wide curve to avoid the dining-room table, went along the porch with the begonias, and passed without being seen under Amaranta's chair as she gave an arithmetic lesson to Aureliano José, and went through the pantry and came out in the kitchen, where Úrsula was getting ready to crack thirty-six eggs to make bread.

"Holy Mother of God!" Úrsula shouted.

She followed the thread of blood back along its course, and in search of its origin she went through the pantry, along the begonia porch where Aureliano José was chanting that three plus three is six and six plus three is nine, and she crossed the dining room and the living rooms and followed straight down the street, and she turned first to the right and then to the left to the Street of the Turks, forgetting that she was still wearing her baking apron and her house slippers, and she came out onto the square and went into the door of a house where she had never been, and she pushed open the bedroom door and was almost suffocated by the smell of burned gunpowder, and she found José Arcadio lying face down on the ground on top of the leggings he had just taken off, and she saw the starting point of the thread of blood that had already stopped flowing out of his right ear. They found no wound on his body nor could they locate the weapon. Nor was it possible to remove the smell of powder from the corpse. First they washed him three times with soap and a scrubbing brush, then they rubbed him with salt and vinegar, then with ashes and lemon, and finally they put him in a barrel of lye and let him stay for six hours. They scrubbed him so much that the arabesques of his tattooing began to fade. When they thought of the desperate measure of seasoning him with pepper, cumin seeds, and laurel leaves and boiling him for a whole day over a slow fire, he had already begun to decompose and they had to bury him hastily. They sealed him hermetically in a special coffin seven and a half feet long and four feet wide, reinforced inside with iron plates and fastened together with steel bolts, and even then the smell could be perceived on the streets through which the funeral procession passed. Father Nicanor, with his liver enlarged and tight as a drum, gave him his blessing from bed. Although in the months that followed they reinforced the grave with walls about it, between which they threw compressed ash, sawdust, and quicklime, the cemetery still smelled of powder for many years after, until the engineers from the banana company covered the grave over with a shell of concrete. As soon as they took the body out, Rebeca closed the doors of her house and buried herself alive, covered with a thick crust of disdain that no earthly temptation was ever able to break. She went out into the street on one occasion, when she was very old, with shoes the color of old silver and a hat made of tiny flowers, during the time that the Wandering Jew passed through town and brought on a heat wave that was so intense that birds broke through window screens to come to die in the bedrooms. The last time anyone saw her alive was when with one shot she killed a thief who was trying to force the door of her house. Except for Argénida, her servant and confidante, no one ever had any more contact with her after that. At one time it was discovered that she was writing letters to the Bishop, whom she claimed as a first cousin, but it was never said whether she received any reply. The town forgot about her.

In spite of his triumphal return, Colonel Aureliano Buendía was not enthusiastic over the looks of things. The government troops abandoned their positions without resistance and that aroused an illusion of victory among the Liberal population that it was not right to destroy, but the revolutionaries knew the truth, Colonel Aureliano Buendía better than any of them. Although at that moment he had more than five thousand men under his command and held two coastal states, he had the feeling of being hemmed in against the sea and caught in a situation that was so confused that when he ordered the restoration of the church steeple, which had been knocked down by army cannon fire, Father Nicanor commented from his sickbed: "This is silly; the defenders of the faith of Christ destroy the church and the Masons order it rebuilt." Looking for a loophole through which he could escape, he spent hours on end in the telegraph office conferring with the commanders of other towns, and every time he would emerge with the firmest impression that the war was at a stalemate. When news of fresh Liberal victories was received it was celebrated with jubilant proclamations, but

F

he would measure the real extent of them on the map and could see that his forces were penetrating into the jungle, defending themselves against malaria and mosquitoes, advancing in the opposite direction from reality. "We're wasting time," he would complain to his officers. "We're wasting time while the bastards in the party are begging for seats in congress." Lying awake at night, stretched out on his back in a hammock in the same room where he had awaited death, he would evoke the image of lawyers dressed in black leaving the presidential palace in the icy cold of early morning with their coat collars turned up about their ears, rubbing their hands, whispering, taking refuge in dreary early-morning cafés to speculate over what the president had meant when he said yes, or what he had meant when he said no, and even to imagine what the president was thinking when he said something quite different, as he chased away mosquitoes at a temperature of ninety-five degrees, feeling the approach of the fearsome dawn when he would have to give his men the command to jump into the sea.

One night of uncertainty, when Pilar Ternera was singing in the courtyard with the soldiers, he asked her to read the future in her cards. "Watch out for your mouth," was all that Pilar Ternera brought out after spreading and picking up the cards three times. "I don't know what it means, but the sign is very clear. Watch out for your mouth." Two days later someone gave an orderly a mug of black coffee and the orderly passed it on to someone else and that one to someone else until, hand to hand, it reached Colonel Aureliano Buendía's office. He had not asked for any coffee, but since it was there the colonel drank it. It had a dose of nux vomica strong enough to kill a horse. When they took him home he was stiff and arched and his tongue was sticking out between his teeth. Úrsula fought against death over him. After cleaning out his stomach with emetics, she wrapped him in hot blankets and fed him egg whites for two days until his harrowed body recovered its normal temperature. On the fourth day he was out of danger. Against his will, pressured by Úrsula and his officers, he stayed in bed for another week. Only then did he learn that his verses had not been burned. "I didn't want to be hasty," Úrsula explained to him. "That night when I went to light the oven I said to myself that it would be better to wait until they brought the body." In the haze of convalescence, surrounded by Remedios' dusty dolls, Colonel Aureliano Buendía brought back the decisive periods of his existence by reading his poetry. He started writing again. For many hours, balancing on the edge of the surprises of a war with no future, in rhymed verse he resolved his experience on the shores of death. Then his thoughts became so clear that he was able to examine them forward and backward. One night he asked Colonel Gerineldo Márquez:

"Tell me something, old friend: why are you fighting?"

"What other reason could there be?" Colonel Gerineldo Márquez answered. "For the great Liberal party."

"You're lucky because you know why," he answered. "As far as I'm concerned, I've come to realize only just now that I'm fighting because of pride."

"That's bad," Colonel Gerineldo Márquez said.

Colonel Aureliano Buendía was amused at his alarm. "Naturally," he said. "But in any case, it's better than not knowing why you're fighting." He looked him in the eyes and added with a smile:

"Or fighting, like you, for something that doesn't have any meaning for anyone."

His pride had prevented him from making contact with the armed groups in the interior of the country until the leaders of the party publicly rectified their declaration that he was a bandit. He knew, however, that as soon as he put those scruples aside he would break the vicious circle of the war. Convalescence gave him time to reflect. Then he succeeded in getting Úrsula to give him the rest of her buried

139

inheritance and her substantial savings. He named Colonel Gerineldo Márquez civil and military leader of Macondo and he went off to make contact with the rebel groups in the interior.

Colonel Gerineldo Márquez was not only the man closest to Colonel Aureliano Buendía, but Úrsula received him as a member of the family. Fragile, timid, with natural good manners, he was, however, better suited for war than for government. His political advisers easily entangled him in theoretical labyrinths. But he succeeded in giving Macondo the atmosphere of rural peace that Colonel Aureliano Buendía dreamed of so that he could die of old age making little gold fishes. Although he lived in his parents' house he would have lunch at Úrsula's two or three times a week. He initiated Aureliano José in the use of firearms, gave him early military instruction, and for several months took him to live in the barracks, with Úrsula's consent, so that he could become a man. Many years before, when he was still almost a child, Gerineldo Márquez had declared his love for Amaranta. At that time she was so illusioned with her lonely passion for Pietro Crespi that she laughed at him. Gerineldo Márquez waited. On a certain occasion he sent Amaranta a note from jail asking her to embroider a dozen batiste handkerchiefs with his father's initials on them. He sent her the money. A week later Amaranta brought the dozen handkerchiefs to him in jail along with the money and they spent several hours talking about the past. "When I get out of here I'm going to marry you," Gerineldo Márquez told her when she left. Amaranta laughed but she kept on thinking about him while she taught the children to read and she tried to revive her juvenile passion for Pietro Crespi. On Saturdays, visiting days for the prisoners, she would stop by the house of Gerineldo Márquez's parents and accompany them to the jail. On one of those Saturdays Úrsula was surprised to see her in the kitchen, waiting for the biscuits to come out of the oven so

140

that she could pick the best ones and wrap them in a napkin that she had embroidered for the occasion.

"Marry him," she told her. "You'll have a hard time finding another man like him."

Amaranta feigned a reaction of displeasure.

"I don't have to go around hunting for men," she answered. "I'm taking these biscuits to Gerineldo because I'm sorry that sooner or later they're going to shoot him."

She said it without thinking, but that was the time that the government had announced its threat to shoot Colonel Gerineldo Márquez if the rebel forces did not surrender Riohacha. The visits stopped. Amaranta shut herself up to weep, overwhelmed by a feeling of guilt similar to the one that had tormented her when Remedios died, as if once more her careless words had been responsible for a death. Her mother consoled her. She assured her that Colonel Aureliano Buendía would do something to prevent the execution and promised that she would take charge of attracting Gerineldo Márquez herself when the war was over. She fulfilled her promise before the imagined time. When Gerineldo Márquez returned to the house, invested with his new dignity of civil and military leader, she received him as a son, thought of delightful bits of flattery to hold him there, and prayed with all her soul that he would remember his plan to marry Amaranta. Her pleas seemed to be answered. On the days that he would have lunch at the house, Colonel Gerineldo Márquez would linger on the begonia porch playing Chinese checkers with Amaranta. Úrsula would bring them coffee and milk and biscuits and would take over the children so that they would not bother them. Amaranta was really making an effort to kindle in her heart the forgotten ashes of her youthful passion. With an anxiety that came to be intolerable, she waited for the lunch days, the afternoons of Chinese checkers, and time flew by in the company of the warrior with a nostalgic name whose fingers trembled imper-

141

ceptibly as he moved the pieces. But the day on which Colonel Gerineldo Márquez repeated his wish to marry her, she rejected him.

"I'm not going to marry anyone," she told him, "much less you. You love Aureliano so much that you want to marry me because you can't marry him."

Colonel Gerineldo Márquez was a patient man. "I'll keep on insisting," he said. "Sooner or later I'll convince you." He kept on visiting the house. Shut up in her bedroom, biting back her secret tears, Amaranta put her fingers in her ears so as not to hear the voice of the suitor as he gave Úrsula the latest war news, and in spite of the fact that she was dying to see him, she had the strength not to go out and meet him.

At that time Colonel Aureliano Buendía took the time to send a detailed account to Macondo every two weeks. But only once, almost eight months after he had left, did he write to Úrsula. A special messenger brought a sealed envelope to the house with a sheet of paper inside bearing the colonel's delicate hand: *Take good care of Papa because he is going to die.* Úrsula became alarmed. "If Aureliano says so it's because Aureliano knows," she said. And she had them help her take José Arcadio Buendía to his bedroom. Not only was he as heavy as ever, but during his prolonged stay under the chestnut tree he had developed the faculty of being able to increase his weight at will, to such a degree that seven men were unable to lift him and they had to drag him to the bed. A smell of tender mushrooms, of wood-flower fungus, of old and concentrated outdoors impregnated the air of the bedroom as it was breathed by the colossal old man weather-beaten by the sun and the rain. The next morning he was not in his bed. In spite of his undiminished strength, José Arcadio Buendía was in no condition to resist. It was all the same to him. If he went back to the chestnut tree it was not because he wanted to but because of a habit of his body. Úrsula took care of him, fed him, brought him news of Aureliano. But actually, the only person with whom he was able to have contact for a long time was Prudencio Aguilar. Almost pulverized at that time by the decrepitude of death, Prudencio Aguilar would come twice a day to chat with him. They talked about fighting cocks. They promised each other to set up a breeding farm for magnificent birds, not so much to enjoy their victories, which they would not need then, as to have something to do on the tedious Sundays of death. It was Prudencio Aguilar who cleaned him, fed him, and brought him splendid news of an unknown person called Aureliano who was a colonel in the war. When he was alone, José Arcadio Buendía consoled himself with the dream of the infinite rooms. He dreamed that he was getting out of bed, opening the door and going into an identical room with the same bed with a wrought-iron head, the same wicker chair, and the same small picture of the Virgin of Help on the back wall. From that room he would go into another that was just the same, the door of which would open into another that was just the same, the door of which would open into another one just the same, and then into another exactly alike, and so on to infinity. He liked to go from room to room, as in a gallery of parallel mirrors, until Prudencio Aguilar would touch him on the shoulder. Then he would go back from room to room, walking in reverse, going back over his trail, and he would find Prudencio Aguilar in the room of reality. But one night, two weeks after they took him to his bed, Prudencio Aguilar touched his shoulder in an intermediate room and he stayed there forever, thinking that it was the real room. On the following morning Úrsula was bringing him his breakfast when she saw a man coming along the hall. He was short and stocky, with a black suit on and a hat that was also black, enormous, pulled down to his taciturn eyes. "Good Lord," Úrsula thought, "I could have sworn it was Melquíades." It was Cataure, Visitación's brother, who had left the house fleeing from the insomnia plague and of whom there had never been any news. Visitación asked him why he had come back, and he answered her in their solemn language:

"I have come for the exequies of the king."

Then they went into José Arcadio Buendía's room, shook him as hard as they could, shouted in his ear, put a mirror in front of his nostrils, but they could not awaken him. A short time later, when the carpenter was taking measurements for the coffin, through the window they saw a light rain of tiny yellow flowers falling. They fell on the town all through the night in a silent storm, and they covered the roofs and blocked the doors and smothered the animals who slept outdoors. So many flowers fell from the sky that in the morning the streets were carpeted with a compact cushion and they had to clear them away with shovels and rakes so that the funeral procession could pass by.

Sitting· in the wicker rocking chair with her interrupted work in her lap, Amaranta watched Aureliano José, his chin covered with foam, stropping his razor to give himself his first shave. His blackheads bled and he cut his upper lip as he tried to shape a mustache of blond fuzz, and when it was all over he looked the same as before, but the laborious process gave Amaranta the feeling that she had begun to grow old at that moment.

"You look just like Aureliano when he was your age," she said. "You're a man now."

He had been for a long time, ever since that distant day when Amaranta thought he was still a child and continued getting undressed in front of him in the bathroom as she had always done, as she had been used to doing ever since Pilar

Ternera had turned him over to her to finish his upbringing. The first time that he saw her the only thing that drew his attention was the deep depression between her breasts. He was so innocent that he asked her what had happened to her and Amaranta pretended to dig into her breasts with the tips of her fingers and answered: "They gave me some terrible cuts." Some time later, when she had recovered from Pietro Crespi's suicide and would bathe with Aureliano José again, he no longer paid attention to the depression but felt a strange trembling at the sight of the splendid breasts with their brown nipples. He kept on examining her, discovering the miracle of her intimacy inch by inch, and he felt his skin tingle as he contemplated the way her skin tingled when it touched the water. Ever since he was a small child he had the custom of leaving his hammock and waking up in Amaranta's bed, because contact with her was a way of overcoming his fear of the dark. But since that day when he became aware of his own nakedness, it was not fear of the dark that drove him to crawl in under her mosquito netting but an urge to feel Amaranta's warm breathing at dawn. Early one morning during the time when she refused Colonel Gerineldo Márquez, Aureliano José awoke with the feeling that he could not breathe. He felt Amaranta's fingers searching across his stomach like warm and anxious little caterpillars. Pretending to sleep, he changed his position to make it easier, and then he felt the hand without the black bandage diving like a blind shellfish into the algae of his anxiety. Although they seemed to ignore what both of them knew and what each one knew that the other knew, from that night on they were yoked together in an inviolable complicity. Aureliano José could not get to sleep until he heard the twelve-o'clock waltz on the parlor clock, and the mature maiden whose skin was beginning to grow sad did not have a moment's rest until she felt slip in under her mosquito netting that sleepwalker whom she had raised, not thinking that he would be a palliative for

146

her solitude. Later they not only slept together, naked, exchanging exhausting caresses, but they would also chase each other into the corners of the house and shut themselves up in the bedrooms at any hour of the day in a permanent state of unrelieved excitement. They were almost discovered by Úrsula one afternoon when she went into the granary as they were starting to kiss. "Do you love your aunt a lot?" she asked Aureliano José in an innocent way. He answered that he did. "That's good of you," Úrsula concluded and finished measuring the flour for the bread and returned to the kitchen. That episode drew Amaranta out of her delirium. She realized that she had gone too far, that she was no longer playing kissing games with a child, but was floundering about in an autumnal passion, one that was dangerous and had no future, and she cut it off with one stroke. Aureliano José, who was then finishing his military training, finally woke up to reality and went to sleep in the barracks. On Saturdays he would go with the soldiers to Catarino's store. He was seeking consolation for his abrupt solitude, for his premature adolescence with women who smelled of dead flowers, whom he idealized in the darkness and changed into Amaranta by means of the anxious efforts of his imagination.

A short time later contradictory news of the war began to come in. While the government itself admitted the progress of the rebellion, the officers in Macondo had confidential reports of the imminence of a negotiated peace. Toward the first of April a special emissary identified himself to Colonel Gerineldo Márquez. He confirmed the fact to him that the leaders of the party had indeed established contact with the rebel leaders in the interior and were on the verge of arranging an armistice in exchange for three cabinet posts for the Liberals, a minority representation in the congress, and a general amnesty for rebels who laid down their arms. The emissary brought a highly confidential order from Colonel Aureliano Buendía, who was not in agreement with the terms of the armistice. Colonel Gerineldo Márquez was to choose five of his best men and prepare to leave the country with them. The order would be carried out with the strictest secrecy. One week before the agreement was announced, and in the midst of a storm of contradictory rumors, Colonel Aureliano Buendía and ten trusted officers, among them Colonel Roque Carnicero, stealthily arrived in Macondo after midnight, dismissed the garrison, buried their weapons, and destroyed their records. By dawn they had left town, along with Colonel Gerineldo Márquez and his five officers. It was such a quick and secret operation that Úrsula did not find out about it until the last moment, when someone tapped on her bedroom window and whispered, "If you want to see Colonel Aureliano Buendía, come to the door right now." Úrsula jumped out of bed and went to the door in her nightgown and she was just able to see the horsemen who were leaving town gallop off in a mute cloud of dust. Only on the following day did she discover that Aureliano José had gone with his father.

Ten days after a joint communiqué by the government and the opposition announced the end of the war, there was news of the first armed uprising of Colonel Aureliano Buendía on the western border. His small and poorly armed force was scattered in less than a week. But during that year, while Liberals and Conservatives tried to make the country believe in reconciliation, he attempted seven other revolts. One night he bombarded Riohacha from a schooner and the garrison dragged out of bed and shot the fourteen best-known Liberals in the town as a reprisal. For more than two weeks he held a customs post on the border and from there sent the nation a call to general war. Another of his expeditions was lost for three months in the jungle in a mad attempt to cross more than a thousand miles of virgin territory in order to proclaim war on the outskirts of the capital. On one occasion he was less than fifteen miles away from Macondo and was obliged by government patrols to hide in the mountains, very close to the enchanted region where his father had found the fossil of a Spanish galleon many years before.

Visitación died around that time. She had the pleasure of dying a natural death after having renounced a throne out of fear of insomnia, and her last wish was that they should dig up the wages she had saved for more than twenty years under her bed and send the money to Colonel Aureliano Buendía so that he could go on with the war. But Úrsula did not bother to dig it up because it was rumored in those days that Colonel Aureliano Buendía had been killed in a landing near the provincial capital. The official announcement—the fourth in less than two years—was considered true for almost six months because nothing further was heard of him. Suddenly, when Úrsula and Amaranta had added new mourning to the past period, unexpected news arrived. Colonel Aureliano Buendía was alive, but apparently he had stopped harassing the government of his country and had joined with the victorious federalism of other republics of the Caribbean. He would show up under different names farther and farther away from his own country. Later it would be learned that the idea that was working on him at the time was the unification of the federalist forces of Central America in order to wipe out conservative regimes from Alaska to Patagonia. The first direct news that Úrsula received from him, several years after his departure, was a wrinkled and faded letter that had arrived, passing through various hands, from Santiago, Cuba.

"We've lost him forever," Úrsula exclaimed on reading it. "If he follows this path he'll spend Christmas at the ends of the earth."

The person to whom she said it, who was the first to whom she showed the letter, was the Conservative general José Raquel Moncada, mayor of Macondo since the end of the war. "This Aureliano," General Moncada commented, "what a pity that he's not a Conservative." He really admired him.

Like many Conservative civilians, José Raquel Moncada had waged war in defense of his party and had earned the title of general on the field of battle, even though he was not a military man by profession. On the contrary, like so many of his fellow party members, he was an antimilitarist. He considered military men unprincipled loafers, ambitious plotters, experts in facing down civilians in order to prosper during times of disorder. Intelligent, pleasant, ruddy-faced, a man who liked to eat and watch cockfights, he had been at one time the most feared adversary of Colonel Aureliano Buendía. He succeeded in imposing his authority over the career officers in a wide sector along the coast. One time when he was forced by strategic circumstances to abandon a stronghold to the forces of Colonel Aureliano Buendía, he left two letters for him. In one of them, quite long, he invited him to join in a campaign to make the war more humane. The other letter was for his wife, who lived in Liberal territory, and he left it with a plea to see that it reached its destination. From then on, even in the bloodiest periods of the war, the two commanders would arrange truces to exchange prisoners. They were pauses with a certain festive atmosphere, which General Moncada took advantage of to teach Colonel Aureliano Buendía how to play chess. They became great friends. They even came to think about the possibility of coordinating the popular elements of both parties, doing away with the influence of the military men and professional politicians, and setting up a humanitarian regime that would take the best from each doctrine. When the war was over, while Colonel Aureliano Buendía was sneaking about through the narrow trails of permanent subversion, General Moncada was named magistrate of Macondo. He wore civilian clothes, replaced the soldiers with unarmed policemen, enforced the amnesty laws, and helped a few families of Liberals who had been killed in the war. He succeeded in having Macondo raised to the status of a municipality and he was therefore its

150

first mayor, and he created an atmosphere of confidence that made people think of the war as an absurd nightmare of the past. Father Nicanor, consumed by hepatic fever, was replaced by Father Coronel, whom they called "The Pup," a veteran of the first federalist war. Bruno Crespi, who was married to Amparo Moscote, and whose shop of toys and musical instruments continued to prosper, built a theater which Spanish companies included in their itineraries. It was a vast open-air hall with wooden benches, a velvet curtain with Greek masks, and three box offices in the shape of lions' heads, through whose mouths the tickets were sold. It was also about that time that the school was rebuilt. It was put under the charge of Don Melchor Escalona, an old teacher brought from the swamp, who made his lazy students walk on their knees in the lime-coated courtyard and made the students who talked in class eat hot chili, with the approval of their parents. Aureliano Segundo and José Arcadio Segundo, the willful twins of Santa Sofía de la Piedad, were the first to sit in the classroom, with their slates, their chalk, and their aluminum jugs with their names on them. Remedios, who inherited her mother's pure beauty, began to be known as Remedios the Beauty. In spite of time, of the superimposed periods of mourning, and her accumulated afflictions, Úrsula resisted growing old. Aided by Santa Sofía de la Piedad, she gave a new drive to her pastry business and in a few years not only recovered the fortune that her son had spent in the war, but she once more stuffed with pure gold the gourds buried in the bedroom. "As long as God gives me life," she would say, "there will always be money in this madhouse." That was how things were when Aureliano José deserted the federal troops in Nicaragua, signed on as a crewman on a German ship, and appeared in the kitchen of the house, sturdy as a horse, as dark and long-haired as an Indian, and with a secret determination to marry Amaranta.

When Amaranta saw him come in, even though he said

nothing she knew immediately why he had come back. At the table they did not dare look each other in the face. But two weeks after his return, in the presence of Úrsula, he set his eyes on hers and said to her, "I always thought a lot about you." Amaranta avoided him. She guarded against chance meetings. She tried not to become separated from Remedios the Beauty. She was ashamed of the blush that covered her cheeks on the day her nephew asked her how long she intended wearing the black bandage on her hand, for she interpreted it as an allusion to her virginity. When he arrived, she barred the door of her bedroom, but she heard his peaceful snoring in the next room for so many nights that she forgot about the precaution. Early one morning, almost two months after his return, she heard him come into the bedroom. Then, instead of fleeing, instead of shouting as she had thought she would, she let herself be saturated with a soft feeling of relaxation. She felt him slip in under the mosquito netting as he had done when he was a child, as he had always done, and she could not repress her cold sweat and the chattering of her teeth when she realized that he was completely naked. "Go away," she whispered, suffocating with curiosity. "Go away or I'll scream." But Aureliano José knew then what he had to do, because he was no longer a child but a barracks animal. Starting with that night the dull, inconsequential battles began again and would go on until dawn. "I'm your aunt," Amaranta murmured, spent. "It's almost as if I were your mother, not just because of my age but because the only thing I didn't do for you was nurse you." Aureliano would escape at dawn and come back early in the morning on the next day, each time more exited by the proof that she had not barred the door. He had not stopped desiring her for a single instant. He found her in the dark bedrooms of captured towns, especially in the most abject ones, and he would make her materialize in the smell of dry blood on the bandages of the wounded, in the instantaneous terror of the danger of death, at all times and in all places. He had fled from her in an attempt to wipe out her memory, not only through distance but by means of a muddled fury that his companions at arms took to be boldness, but the more her image wallowed in the dunghill of the war, the more the war resembled Amaranta. That was how he suffered in exile, looking for a way of killing her with his own death, until he heard some old man tell the tale of the man who had married his aunt, who was also his cousin, and whose son ended up being his own grandfather.

"Can a person marry his own aunt?" he asked, startled.

"He not only can do that," a soldier answered him, "but we're fighting this war against the priests so that a person can marry his own mother."

Two weeks later he deserted. He found Amaranta more withered than in his memory, more melancholy and shy, and now really turning the last corner of maturity, but more feverish than ever in the darkness of her bedroom and more challenging than ever in the aggressiveness of her resistance. "You're a brute," Amaranta would tell him as she was harried by his hounds. "You can't do that to a poor aunt unless you have a special dispensation from the Pope." Aureliano José promised to go to Rome, he promised to go across Europe on his knees to kiss the sandals of the Pontiff just so that she would lower her drawbridge.

"It's not just that," Amaranta retorted. "Any children will be born with the tail of a pig."

Aureliano José was deaf to all arguments.

"I don't care if they're born as armadillos," he begged.

Early one morning, vanquished by the unbearable pain of repressed virility, he went to Catarino's. He found a woman with flaccid breasts, affectionate and cheap, who calmed his stomach for some time. He tried to apply the treatment of disdain to Amaranta. He would see her on the porch working at the sewing machine, which she had learned to operate with admirable skill, and he would not even speak to her. Amaranta felt freed of a reef, and she herself did not understand why she started thinking again at that time about Colonel Gerineldo Márquez, why she remembered with such nostalgia the afternoons of Chinese checkers, and why she even desired him as the man in her bedroom. Aureliano José did not realize how much ground he had lost on the night he could no longer bear the farce of indifference and went back to Amaranta's room. She rejected him with an inflexible and unmistakable determination, and she barred the door of her bedroom forever.

A few months after the return of Aureliano José, an exuberant woman perfumed with jasmine appeared at the house with a boy of five. She stated that he was the son of Colonel Aureliano Buendía and that she had brought him to Úrsula to be baptized. No one doubted the origins of that nameless child: he looked exactly like the colonel at the time he was taken to see ice for the first time. The woman said that he had been born with his eyes open, looking at people with the judgment of an adult, and that she was frightened by his way of staring at things without blinking. "He's identical," Úrsula said. "The only thing missing is for him to make chairs rock by simply looking at them." They christened him Aureliano and with his mother's last name, since the law did not permit a person to bear his father's name until he had recognized him. General Moncada was the godfather. Although Amaranta insisted that he be left so that she could take over his upbringing, his mother was against it.

Úrsula at that time did not know about the custom of sending virgins to the bedrooms of soldiers in the same way that hens are turned loose with fine roosters, but in the course of that year she found out: nine more sons of Colonel Aureliano Buendía were brought to the house to be baptized. The oldest, a strange dark boy with green eyes, who was not at all like his father's family, was over ten years old. They brought children of all ages, all colors, but all males and all with a look of solitude that left no doubt as to the relationship. Only two stood out in the group. One, large for his age, made smithereens out of the flowerpots and china because his hands seemed to have the property of breaking everything they touched. The other was a blond boy with the same light eyes as his mother, whose hair had been left to grow long and curly like that of a woman. He entered the house with a great deal of familiarity, as if he had been raised there, and he went directly to a chest in Úrsula's bedroom and demanded, "I want the mechanical ballerina." Úrsula was startled. She opened the chest, searched among the ancient and dusty articles left from the days of Melquíades, and wrapped in a pair of stockings she found the mechanical ballerina that Pietro Crespi had brought to the house once and that everyone had forgotten about. In less than twelve years they baptized with the name Aureliano and the last name of the mother all the sons that the colonel had implanted up and down his theater of war: seventeen. At first Úrsula would fill their pockets with money and Amaranta tried to have them stay. But they finally limited themselves to giving them presents and serving as godmothers. "We've done our duty by baptizing them," Úrsula would say, jotting down in a ledger the name and address of the mother and the place and date of birth of the child. "Aureliano needs well-kept accounts so that he can decide things when he comes back." During lunch, commenting with General Moncada about that disconcerting proliferation, she expressed the desire for Colonel Aureliano Buendía to come back someday and gather all of his sons together in the house.

"Don't worry, dear friend," General Moncada said enigmatically. "He'll come sooner than you suspect."

What General Moncada knew and what he did not wish to reveal at lunch was that Colonel Aureliano Buendía was already on his way to head up the most prolonged, radical, and bloody rebellion of all those he had started up till then.

The situation again became as tense as it had been during

the months that preceded the first war. The cockfights, instituted by the mayor himself, were suspended. Captain Aquiles Ricardo, the commander of the garrison, took over the exercise of municipal power. The Liberals looked upon him as a provocateur. "Something terrible is going to happen," Úrsula would say to Aureliano José. "Don't go out into the street after six o'clock." The entreaties were useless. Aureliano José, just like Arcadio in other times, had ceased to belong to her. It was as if his return home, the possibility of existing without concerning himself with everyday necessities, had awakened in him the lewd and lazy leanings of his uncle José Arcadio. His passion for Amaranta had been extinguished without leaving any scars. He would drift around, playing pool, easing his solitude with occasional women, sacking the hiding places where Úrsula had forgotten her money. He ended up coming home only to change his clothes. "They're all alike," Úrsula lamented. "At first they behave very well, they're obedient and prompt and they don't seem capable of killing a fly, but as soon as their beards appear they go to ruin." Unlike Arcadio, who had never known his real origins, he found out that he was the son of Pilar Ternera, who had hung up a hammock so that he could take his siesta in her house. More than mother and son, they were accomplices in solitude. Pilar Ternera had lost the trail of all hope. Her laugh had taken on the tones of an organ, her breasts had succumbed to the tedium of endless caressing, her stomach and her thighs had been the victims of her irrevocable fate as a shared woman, but her heart grew old without bitterness. Fat, talkative, with the airs of a matron in disgrace, she renounced the sterile illusions of her cards and found peace and consolation in other people's loves. In the house where Aureliano José took his siesta, the girls from the neighborhood would receive their casual lovers. "Lend me your room, Pilar," they would simply say when they were already inside.

"Of course," Pilar would answer. And if anyone was present she would explain:

"I'm happy knowing that people are happy in bed."

She never charged for the service. She never refused the favor, just as she never refused the countless men who sought her out, even in the twilight of her maturity, without giving her money or love and only occasionally pleasure. Her five daughters, who inherited a burning seed, had been lost on the byways of life since adolescence. Of the two sons she managed to raise, one died fighting in the forces of Colonel Aureliano Buendía and the other was wounded and captured at the age of fourteen when he tried to steal a crate of chickens in a town in the swamp. In a certain way, Aureliano José was the tall, dark man who had been promised her for half a century by the king of hearts, and like all men sent by the cards he reached her heart when he was already stamped with the mark of death. She saw it in the cards.

"Don't go out tonight," she told him. "Stay and sleep here because Carmelita Montiel is getting tired of asking me to put her in your room."

Aureliano José did not catch the deep feeling of begging that was in the offer.

"Tell her to wait for me at midnight," he said.

He went to the theater, where a Spanish company was putting on *The Dagger of the Fox*, which was really Zorrilla's play with the title changed by order of Captain Aquiles Ricardo, because the Liberals called the Conservatives Goths. Only when he handed in his ticket at the door did Aureliano José realize that Captain Aquiles Ricardo and two soldiers armed with rifles were searching the audience.

"Be careful, captain," Aureliano José warned him. "The man hasn't been born yet who can lay hands on me." The captain tried to search him forcibly and Aureliano José, who was unarmed, began to run. The soldiers disobeyed the order to shoot. "He's a Buendía," one of them explained. Blind with

157

rage, the captain then snatched away the rifle, stepped into the center of the street, and took aim.

"Cowards!" he shouted. "I only wish it was Colonel Aureliano Buendía."

Carmelita Montiel, a twenty-year-old virgin, had just bathed in orange-blossom water and was strewing rosemary leaves on Pilar Ternera's bed when the shot rang out. Aureliano José had been destined to find with her the happiness that Amaranta had denied him, to have seven children, and to die in her arms of old age, but the bullet that entered his back and shattered his chest had been directed by a wrong interpretation of the cards. Captain Aquiles Ricardo, who was really the one destined to die that night, did indeed die, four hours before Aureliano José. As soon as the shot was heard he was brought down by two simultaneous bullets whose origin was never established and a shout of many voices shook the night.

"Long live the Liberal party! Long live Colonel Aureliano Buendía!"

At twelve o'clock, when Aureliano José had bled to death and Carmelita Montiel found that the cards showing her future were blank, more than four hundred men had filed past the theater and discharged their revolvers into the abandoned body of Captain Aquiles Ricardo. A patrol had to use a wheelbarrow to carry the body, which was heavy with lead and fell apart like a water-soaked loaf of bread.

Annoyed by the outrages of the regular army, General José Raquel Moncada used his political influence, put on his uniform again, and assumed the civil and military leadership of Macondo. He did not expect, however, that his conciliatory attitude would be able to prevent the inevitable. The news in September was contradictory. While the government announced that it was maintaining control throughout the country, the Liberals were receiving secret news of armed uprisings in the interior. The regime would not admit a state of war until it was proclaimed in a decree that had followed a court-martial which had condemned Colonel Aureliano Buendía to death in absentia. The first unit that captured him was ordered to carry the sentence out. "This means he's come back," Úrsula said joyfully to General Moncada. But he himself knew nothing about it.

Actually, Colonel Aureliano Buendía had been in the country for more than a month. He was preceded by conflicting rumors, supposed to be in the most distant places at the same time, and even General Moncada did not believe in his return until it was officially announced that he had seized two states on the coast. "Congratulations, dear friend," he told Úrsula, showing her the telegram. "You'll soon have him here." Úrsula was worried then for the first time. "And what will you do?" she asked. General Moncada had asked himself that same question many times.

"The same as he, my friend," he answered. "I'll do my duty."

At dawn on the first of October Colonel Aureliano Buendía attacked Macondo with a thousand well-armed men and the garrison received orders to resist to the end. At noon, while General Moncada was lunching with Úrsula, a rebel cannon shot that echoed in the whole town blew the front of the municipal treasury to dust. "They're as well armed as we are," General Moncada sighed, "but besides that they're fighting because they want to." At two o'clock in the afternoon, while the earth trembled with the artillery fire from both sides, he took leave of Úrsula with the certainty that he was fighting a losing battle.

"I pray to God that you won't have Aureliano in the house tonight," he said. "If it does happen that way, give him an embrace for me, because I don't expect ever to see him again."

That night he was captured when he tried to escape from Macondo after writing a long letter to Colonel Aureliano

Buendía in which he reminded him of their common aim to humanize the war and he wished him a final victory over the corruption of the militarists and the ambitions of the politicians in both parties. On the following day Colonel Aureliano Buendía had lunch with him in Úrsula's house, where he was being held until a revolutionary court-martial decided his fate. It was a friendly gathering. But while the adversaries forgot the war to remember things of the past, Úrsula had the gloomy feeling that her son was an intruder. She had felt it ever since she saw him come in protected by a noisy military retinue, which turned the bedrooms inside out until they were convinced there was no danger. Colonel Aureliano Buendía not only accepted it but he gave strict orders that no one should come closer than ten feet, not even Úrsula, while the members of his escort finished placing guards about the house. He was wearing an ordinary denim uniform with no insignia of any kind and high boots with spurs that were caked with mud and dried blood. On his waist he wore a holster with the flap open and his hand, which was always on the butt of the pistol, revealed the same watchful and resolute tension as his look. His head, with deep recessions in the hairline now, seemed to have been baked in a slow oven. His face, tanned by the salt of the Caribbean, had acquired a metallic hardness. He was preserved against imminent old age by a vitality that had something to do with the coldness of his insides. He was taller than when he had left, paler and bonier, and he showed the first symptoms of resistance to nostalgia. "Good Lord," Úrsula said to herself. "Now he looks like a man capable of anything." He was. The Aztec shawl that he brought Amaranta, the remembrances he spoke of at lunch, the funny stories he told were simple leftovers from his humor of a different time. As soon as the order to bury the dead in a common grave was carried out, he assigned Colonel Roque Carnicero the mission of setting up courts-martial and he went ahead with the exhausting task of imposing radical reforms which would not leave a stone of the re-established Conservative regime in place. "We have to get ahead of the politicians in the party," he said to his aides. "When they open their eyes to reality they'll find accomplished facts." It was then that he decided to review the titles to land that went back a hundred years and he discovered the legalized outrages of his brother José Arcadio. He annulled the registrations with a stroke of the pen. As a last gesture of courtesy, he left his affairs for an hour and visited Rebeca to bring her up to date on what he was determined to do.

In the shadows of her house, the solitary widow who at one time had been the confidante of his repressed loves and whose persistence had saved his life was a specter out of the past. Encased in black down to her knuckles, with her heart turned to ash, she scarcely knew anything about the war. Colonel Aureliano Buendía had the impression that the phosphorescence of her bones was showing through her skin and that she moved in an atmosphere of Saint Elmo's fire, in a stagnant air where one could still note a hidden smell of gunpowder. He began by advising her to moderate the rigor of her mourning, to ventilate the house, to forgive the world for the death of José Arcadio. But Rebeca was already beyond any vanity. After searching for it uselessly in the taste of earth, in the perfumed letters from Pietro Crespi, in the tempestuous bed of her husband, she had found peace in that house where memories materialized through the strength of implacable evocation and walked like human beings through the cloistered rooms. Leaning back in her wicker rocking chair, looking at Colonel Aureliano Buendía as if he were the one who looked like a ghost out of the past, Rebeca was not even upset by the news that the lands usurped by José Arcadio would be returned to their rightful owners.

"Whatever you decide will be done, Aureliano," she sighed. "I always thought and now I have the proof that you're a renegade."

The revision of the deeds took place at the same time as the summary courts-martial presided over by Colonel Gerineldo Márquez, which ended with the execution of all officers of the regular army who had been taken prisoner by the revolutionaries. The last court-martial was that of José Raquel Moncada. Úrsula intervened. "His government was the best we've ever had in Macondo," she told Colonel Aureliano Buendía. "I don't have to tell you anything about his good heart, about his affection for us, because you know better than anyone." Colonel Aureliano Buendía gave her a disapproving look.

"I can't take over the job of administering justice," he replied. "If you have something to say, tell it to the court-martial."

Úrsula not only did that, she also brought all of the mothers of the revolutionary officers who lived in Macondo to testify. One by one the old women who had been founders of the town, several of whom had taken part in the daring crossing of the mountains, praised the virtues of General Moncada. Úrsula was the last in line. Her gloomy dignity, the weight of her name, the convincing vehemence of her declaration made the scale of justice hesitate for a moment. "You have taken this horrible game very seriously and you have done well because you are doing your duty," she told the members of the court. "But don't forget that as long as God gives us life we will still be mothers and no matter how revolutionary you may be, we have the right to pull down your pants and give you a whipping at the first sign of disrespect." The court retired to deliberate as those words still echoed in the school that had been turned into a barracks. At midnight General José Raquel Moncada was sentenced to death. Colonel Aureliano Buendía, in spite of the violent recriminations of Úrsula, refused to commute the sentence. A short while before dawn he visited the condemned man in the room used as a cell.

"Remember, old friend," he told him. "I'm not shooting you. It's the revolution that's shooting you."

General Moncada did not even get up from the cot when he saw him come in.

"Go to hell, friend," he answered.

Until that moment, ever since his return, Colonel Aureliano Buendía had not given himself the opportunity to see him with his heart. He was startled to see how much he had aged, how his hands shook, and the rather punctilious conformity with which he awaited death, and then he felt a great disgust with himself, which he mingled with the beginnings of pity.

"You know better than I," he said, "that all courts-martial are farces and that you're really paying for the crimes of other people, because this time we're going to win the war at any price. Wouldn't you have done the same in my place?"

General Moncada got up to clean his thick horn-rimmed glasses on his shirttail. "Probably," he said. "But what worries me is not your shooting me, because after all, for people like us it's a natural death." He laid his glasses on the bed and took off his watch and chain. "What worries me," he went on, "is that out of so much hatred for the military, out of fighting them so much and thinking about them so much, you've ended up as bad as they are. And no ideal in life is worth that much baseness." He took off his wedding ring and the medal of the Virgin of Help and put them alongside his glasses and watch.

"At this rate," he concluded, "you'll not only be the most despotic and bloody dictator in our history, but you'll shoot my dear friend Úrsula in an attempt to pacify your conscience."

Colonel Aureliano Buendía stood there impassively. General Moncada then gave him the glasses, medal, watch, and ring and he changed his tone.

"But I didn't send for you to scold you," he said. "I wanted to ask you the favor of sending these things to my wife."

Colonel Aureliano Buendía put them in his pockets.

"Is she still in Manaure?"

"She's still in Manaure," General Moncada confirmed, "in the same house behind the church where you sent the letter."

"I'll be glad to, José Raquel," Colonel Aureliano Buendía said.

When he went out into the blue air of the mist his face grew damp as on some other dawn in the past and only then did he realize that he had ordered the sentence to be carried out in the courtyard and not at the cemetery wall. The firing squad, drawn up opposite the door, paid him the honors of a head of state.

"They can bring him out now," he ordered.

COLONEL GERINELDO MÁRQUEZ was the first to perceive the emptiness of the war. In his position as civil and military leader of Macondo he would have telegraphic conversations twice a week with Colonel Aureliano Buendía. At first those exchanges would determine the course of a flesh-and-blood war, the perfectly defined outlines of which told them at any moment the exact spot where it was and the prediction of its future direction. Although he never let himself be pulled into the area of confidences, not even by his closest friends, Colonel Aureliano Buendía still had at that time the familiar tone that made it possible to identify him at the other end of the wire. Many times he would prolong the talks beyond the expected limit and let them drift into comments of a domestic nature. Little by little, however, and as the war became more intense and widespread, his image was fading away into a universe of unreality. The characteristics of his speech were more and more uncertain, and they came together and combined to form words that were gradually losing all meaning. Colonel Gerineldo Márquez limited himself then to just listening, burdened by the impression that he was in telegraphic contact with a stranger from another world.

"I understand, Aureliano," he would conclude on the key. "Long live the Liberal party!"

He finally lost all contact with the war. What in other times had been a real activity, an irresistible passion of his youth, became a remote point of reference for him: an emptiness. His only refuge was Amaranta's sewing room. He would visit her every afternoon. He liked to watch her hands as she curled frothy petticoat cloth in the machine that was kept in motion by Remedios the Beauty. They spent many hours without speaking, content with their reciprocal company, but while Amaranta was inwardly pleased in keeping the fire of his devotion alive, he was unaware of the secret designs of that indecipherable heart. When the news of his return reached her, Amaranta had been smothered by anxiety. But when she saw him enter the house in the middle of Colonel Aureliano Buendía's noisy escort and she saw how he had been mistreated by the rigors of exile, made old by age and oblivion, dirty with sweat and dust, smelling like a herd, ugly, with his left arm in a sling, she felt faint with disillusionment. "My God," she thought. "This wasn't the person I was waiting for." On the following day, however, he came back to the house shaved and clean, with his mustache perfumed with lavender water and without the bloody sling. He brought her a prayerbook bound in mother-of-pearl.

"How strange men are," she said, because she could not think of anything else to say. "They spend their lives fighting against priests and then give prayerbooks as gifts."

From that time on, even during the most critical days of the war, he visited her every afternoon. Many times, when Remedios the Beauty was not present, it was he who turned the wheel on the sewing machine. Amaranta felt upset by the perseverance, the loyalty, the submissiveness of that man who was invested with so much authority and who nevertheless took off his sidearms in the living room so that he could go into the sewing room without weapons. But for four years he kept repeating his love and she would always find a way to reject him without hurting him, for even though she had not succeeded in loving him she could no longer live without him. Remedios the Beauty, who seemed indifferent to everything and who was thought to be mentally retarded, was not insensitive to so much devotion and she intervened in Colonel Gerineldo Márquez's favor. Amaranta suddenly discovered that the girl she had raised, who was just entering adolescence, was already the most beautiful creature that had even been seen in Macondo. She felt reborn in her heart the rancor that she had felt in other days for Rebeca, and begging God not to impel her into the extreme state of wishing her dead, she banished her from the sewing room. It was around that time that Colonel Gerineldo Márquez began to feel the boredom of the war. He summoned his reserves of persuasion, his broad and repressed tenderness, ready to give up for Amaranta a glory that had cost him the sacrifice of his best years. But he could not succeed in convincing her. One August afternoon, overcome by the unbearable weight of her own obstinacy, Amaranta locked herself in her bedroom to weep over her solitude unto death after giving her final answer to her tenacious suitor:

"Let's forget about each other forever," she told him. "We're too old for this sort of thing now."

Colonel Gerineldo Márquez had a telegraphic call from Colonel Aureliano Buendía that afternoon. It was a routine conversation which was not going to bring about any break in the stagnant war. At the end, Colonel Gerineldo Márquez looked at the desolate streets, the crystal water on the almond trees, and he found himself lost in solitude.

"Aureliano," he said sadly on the key, "it's raining in Macondo."

There was a long silence on the line. Suddenly the apparatus jumped with the pitiless letters from Colonel Aureliano Buendía.

"Don't be a jackass, Gerineldo," the signals said. "It's natural for it to be raining in August."

They had not seen each other for such a long time that Colonel Gerineldo Márquez was upset by the aggressiveness of the reaction. Two months later, however, when Colonel Aureliano Buendía returned to Macondo, his upset was changed to stupefaction. Even Úrsula was surprised at how much he had changed. He came with no noise, no escort, wrapped in a cloak in spite of the heat, and with three mistresses, whom he installed in the same house, where he spent most of his time lying in a hammock. He scarcely read the telegraphic dispatches that reported routine operations. On one occasion Colonel Gerineldo Márquez asked him for instructions for the evacuation of a spot on the border where there was a danger that the conflict would become an international affair.

"Don't bother me with trifles," he ordered him. "Consult Divine Providence."

It was perhaps the most critical moment of the war. The Liberal landowners, who had supported the revolution in the beginning, had made secret alliances with the Conservative landowners in order to stop the revision of property titles. The politicians who supplied funds for the war from exile had publicly repudiated the drastic aims of Colonel Aureliano Buendía, but even that withdrawal of authorization did not seem to bother him. He had not returned to reading his poetry, which filled more than five volumes and lay forgotten at the bottom of his trunk. At night or at siesta time he would call one of his women to his hammock and obtain a rudimentary satisfaction from her, and then he would sleep like a stone that was not concerned by the slightest indication of worry. Only he knew at that time that his confused heart was condemned to uncertainty forever. At first, intoxicated by the glory of his return, by his remarkable victories, he had peeped into the abyss of greatness. He took pleasure in keeping by his right hand the Duke of Marlborough, his great teacher in the art of war, whose attire of skins and tiger claws aroused the respect of adults and the awe of children. It was then that he decided that no human being, not even Úrsula, could come closer to him than ten feet. In the center of the chalk circle that his aides would draw wherever he stopped, and which only he could enter, he would decide with brief orders that had no appeal the fate of the world. The first time that he was in Manaure after the shooting of General Moncada, he hastened to fulfill his victim's last wish and the widow took the glasses, the medal, the watch, and the ring, but she would not let him in the door.

"You can't come in, colonel," she told him. "You may be in command of your war, but I'm in command of my house."

Colonel Aureliano Buendía did not show any sign of anger, but his spirit only calmed down when his bodyguard had sacked the widow's house and reduced it to ashes. "Watch out for your heart, Aureliano," Colonel Gerineldo Márquez would say to him then. "You're rotting alive." About that time he called together a second assembly of the principal rebel commanders. He found all types: idealists, ambitious people, adventurers, those with social resentments, even common criminals. There was even a former Conservative functionary who had taken refuge in the revolt to escape a judgment for misappropriation of funds. Many of them did not even know why they were fighting. In the midst of that

G

motley crowd, whose differences of values were on the verge of causing an internal explosion, one gloomy authority stood out: General Teófilo Vargas. He was a full-blooded Indian, untamed, illiterate, and endowed with quiet wiles and a messianic vocation that aroused a demented fanaticism in his men. Colonel Aureliano Buendía called the meeting with the aim of unifying the rebel command against the maneuvers of the politicians. General Teófilo Vargas came forward with his intentions: in a few hours he shattered the coalition of better-qualified commanders and took charge of the main command. "He's a wild beast worth watching," Colonel Aurelliano Buendía told his officers. "That man is more dangerous to us than the Minister of War." Then a very young captain who had always been outstanding for his timidity raised a cautious index finger.

"It's quite simple, colonel," he proposed. "He has to be killed."

Colonel Aureliano Buendía was not alarmed by the coldness of the proposition but by the way in which, by a fraction of a second, it had anticipated his own thoughts.

"Don't expect me to give an order like that," he said.

He did not give it, as a matter of fact. But two weeks later General Teófilo Vargas was cut to bits by machetes in an ambush and Colonel Aureliano Buendía assumed the main command. The same night that his authority was recognized by all the rebel commands, he woke up in a fright, calling for a blanket. An inner coldness which shattered his bones and tortured him even in the heat of the sun would not let him sleep for several months, until it became a habit. The intoxication of power began to break apart under waves of discomfort. Searching for a cure against the chill, he had the young officer who had proposed the murder of General Teófilo Vargas shot. His orders were being carried out even before they were given, even before he thought of them, and they always went much beyond what he would have dared have them do. Lost in the solitude of his immense power, he began to lose direction. He was bothered by the people who cheered him in neighboring villages, and he imagined that they were the same cheers they gave the enemy. Everywhere he met adolescents who looked at him with his own eyes, who spoke to him with his own voice, who greeted him with the same mistrust with which he greeted them, and who said they were his sons. He felt scattered about, multiplied, and more solitary than ever. He was convinced that his own officers were lying to him. He fought with the Duke of Marlborough. "The best friend a person has," he would say at that time, "is one who has just died." He was weary of the uncertainty, of the vicious circle of that eternal war that always found him in the same place, but always older, wearier, even more in the position of not knowing why, or how, or even when. There was always someone outside of the chalk circle. Someone who needed money, someone who had a son with whooping cough, or someone who wanted to go off and sleep forever because he could not stand the shit taste of the war in his mouth and who, nevertheless, stood at attention to inform him: "Everything normal, colonel." And normality was precisely the most fearful part of that infinite war: nothing ever happened. Alone, abandoned by his premonitions, fleeing the chill that was to accompany him until death, he sought a last refuge in Macondo in the warmth of his oldest memories. His indolence was so serious that when they announced the arrival of a commission from his party that was authorized to discuss the stalemate of the war, he rolled over in his hammock without completely waking up.

"Take them to the whores," he said.

They were six lawyers in frock coats and top hats who endured the violent November sun with stiff stoicism. Úrsula put them up in her house. They spent the greater part of the day closeted in the bedroom in hermetic conferences and at dusk they asked for an escort and some accordion players and took over Catarino's store. "Leave them alone," Colonel Aureliano Buendía ordered. "After all, I know what they want." At the beginning of December the long-awaited interview, which many had foreseen as an interminable argument, was resolved in less than an hour.

In the hot parlor, beside the specter of the pianola shrouded in a white sheet, Colonel Aureliano Buendía did not sit down that time inside the chalk circle that his aides had drawn. He sat in a chair between his political advisers and, wrapped in his woolen blanket, he listened in silence to the brief proposals of the emissaries. They asked first that he renounce the revision of property titles in order to get back the support of the Liberal landowners. They asked, secondly, that he renounce the fight against clerical influence in order to obtain the support of the Catholic masses. They asked, finally, that he renounce the aim of equal rights for natural and illegitimate children in order to preserve the integrity of the home.

"That means," Colonel Aureliano Buendía said, smiling when the reading was over, "that all we're fighting for is power."

"They're tactical changes," one of the delegates replied. "Right now the main thing is to broaden the popular base of the war. Then we'll have another look."

One of Colonel Aureliano Buendía's political advisers hastened to intervene.

"It's a contradiction," he said. "If these changes are good, it means that the Conservative regime is good. If we succeed in broadening the popular base of the war with them, as you people say, it means that the regime has a broad popular base. It means, in short, that for almost twenty years we've been fighting against the sentiments of the nation."

He was going to go on, but Colonel Aureliano Buendía stopped him with a signal. "Don't waste your time, doctor," he said. "The important thing is that from now on we'll be fighting only for power." Still smiling, he took the documents the delegates gave him and made ready to sign them.

"Since that's the way it is," he concluded, "we have no objection to accepting."

His men looked at one another in consternation.

"Excuse me, colonel," Colonel Gerineldo Márquez said softly, "but this is a betrayal."

Colonel Aureliano Buendía held the inked pen in the air and discharged the whole weight of his authority on him.

"Surrender your weapons," he ordered.

Colonel Gerineldo Márquez stood up and put his sidearms on the table.

"Report to the barracks," Colonel Aureliano Buendía ordered him. "Put yourself at the disposition of the revolutionary court."

Then he signed. the declaration and gave the sheets of paper to the emissaries, saying to them:

"Here are your papers, gentlemen. I hope you can get some advantage out of them."

Two days later, Colonel Gerineldo Márquez, accused of high treason, was condemned to death. Lying in his hammock, Colonel Aureliano Buendía was insensible to the pleas for clemency. On the eve of the execution, disobeying the orders not to bother him, Úrsula visited him in his bedroom. Encased in black, invested with a rare solemnity, she stood during the three minutes of the interview. "I know that you're going to shoot Gerineldo," she said calmly, "and that I can't do anything to stop it. But I give you one warning: as soon as I see his body I swear to you by the bones of my father and mother, by the memory of José Arcadio Buendía, I swear to you before God that I will drag you out from wherever you're hiding and kill you with my own two hands." Before leaving the room, without waiting for any reply, she concluded:

"It's the same as if you'd been born with the tail of a pig."

During that interminable night, while Colonel Gerineldo Márquez thought about his dead afternoons in Amaranta's sewing room, Colonel Aureliano Buendía scratched for many hours trying to break the hard shell of his solitude. His only happy moments, since that remote afternoon when his father had taken him to see ice, had taken place in his silver workshop where he passed the time putting little gold fishes together. He had had to start thirty-two wars and had had to violate all of his pacts with death and wallow like a hog in the dungheap of glory in order to discover the privileges of simplicity almost forty years late.

At dawn, worn out by the tormented vigil, he appeared in the cell an hour before the execution. "The farce is over, old friend," he said to Colonel Gerineldo Márquez. "Let's get out of here before the mosquitoes in here execute you." Colonel Gerineldo Márquez could not repress the disdain that was inspired in him by that attitude.

"No, Aureliano," he replied. "I'd rather be dead than see you changed into a bloody tyrant."

"You won't see me," Colonel Aureliano Buendía said. "Put on your shoes and help me get this shitty war over with."

When he said it he did not know that it was easier to start a war than to end one. It took him almost a year of fierce and bloody effort to force the government to propose conditions of peace favorable to the rebels and another year to convince his own partisans of the convenience of accepting them. He went to inconceivable extremes of cruelty to put down the rebellion of his own officers, who resisted and called for victory, and he finally relied on enemy forces to make them submit.

He was never a greater soldier than at that time. The certainty that he was finally fighting for his own liberation and not for abstract ideals, for slogans that politicians could twist left and right according to the circumstances, filled him with an ardent enthusiasm. Colonel Gerineldo Márquez, who fought for defeat with as much conviction and loyalty as he had previously fought for victory, reproached him for his useless temerity. "Don't worry," he would say, smiling. "Dying is much more difficult than one imagines." In his case it was true. The certainty that his day was assigned gave him a mysterious immunity, an immortality for a fixed period that made him invulnerable to the risks of war and in the end permitted him to win a defeat that was much more difficult, much more bloody and costly than victory.

In almost twenty years of war, Colonel Aureliano Buendía had been at his house many times, but the state of urgency with which he always arrived, the military retinue that accompanied him everywhere, the aura of legend that glowed about his presence and of which even Úrsula was aware, changed him into a stranger in the end. The last time that he was in Macondo and took a house for his three concubines, he was seen in his own house only on two or three occasions when he had the time to accept an invitation to dine. Remedios the Beauty and the twins, born during the middle of the war, scarcely knew him. Amaranta could not reconcile her image of the brother who had spent his adolescence making little gold fishes with that of the mythical warrior who had placed a distance of ten feet between himself and the rest of humanity. But when the approach of the armistice became known and they thought that he would return changed back into a human being, delivered at last for the hearts of his own people, the family feelings, dormant for such a long time, were reborn stronger than ever.

"We'll finally have a man in the house again," Úrsula said.

Amaranta was the first to suspect that they had lost him forever. One week before the armistice, when he entered the house without an escort, preceded by two barefoot orderlies who deposited on the porch the saddle from the mule and the trunk of poetry, all that was left of his former imperial baggage, she saw him pass by the sewing room and she called to him. Colonel Aureliano Buendía had trouble recognizing her.

"It's Amaranta," she said good-humoredly, happy at his return, and she showed him the hand with the black bandage. "Look."

Colonel Aureliano Buendía smiled at her the same way as when he had first seen her with the bandage on that remote morning when he had come back to Macondo condemned to death.

"How awful," he said, "the way time passes!"

The regular army had to protect the house. He arrived amid insults, spat upon, accused of having accelerated the war in order to sell it for a better price. He was trembling with fever and cold and his armpits were studded with sores again. Six months before, when she had heard talk about the armistice, Úrsula had opened up and swept out the bridal chamber and had burned myrrh in the corners, thinking that he would come back ready to grow old slowly among Remedios' musty dolls. But actually, during the last two years he had paid his final dues to life, including growing old. When he passed by the silver shop, which Úrsula had prepared with special diligence, he did not even notice that the keys were in the lock. He did not notice the minute, tearing destruction that time had wreaked on the house and that, after such a prolonged absence, would have looked like a disaster to any man who had kept his memories alive. He was not pained by the peeling of the whitewash on the walls or the dirty, cottony cobwebs in the corners or the dust on the begonias or the veins left on the beams by the termites or the moss on the hinges or any of the insidious traps that nostalgia offered him. He sat down on the porch, wrapped in his blanket and with his boots still on, as if only waiting for it to clear, and he spent the whole afternoon watching it rain on the begonias. Úrsula understood then that they would not have him home for long. "If it's not the war," she thought, "it can only be death." It was a supposition that was so neat, so convincing that she identified it as a premonition.

That night, at dinner, the supposed Aureliano Segundo broke his bread with his right hand and drank his soup with his left. His twin brother, the supposed José Arcadio Segundo, broke his bread with his left hand and drank his soup with his right. So precise was their coordination that they did not look like two brothers sitting opposite each other but like a trick with mirrors. The spectacle that the twins had invented when they became aware that they were equal was repeated in honor of the new arrival. But Colonel Aureliano Buendía did not notice it. He seemed so alien to everything that he did not even notice Remedios the Beauty as she passed by naked on her way to her bedroom. Úrsula was the only one who dared disturb his abstraction.

"If you have to go away again," she said halfway through dinner, "at least try to remember how we were tonight."

Then Colonel Aureliano Buendía realized, without surprise, that Úrsula was the only human being who had succeeded in penetrating his misery, and for the first time in many years he looked her in the face. Her skin was leathery, her teeth decayed, her hair faded and colorless, and her look frightened. He compared her with the oldest memory that he had of her, the afternoon when he had the premonition that a pot of boiling soup was going to fall off the table, and he found her broken to pieces. In an instant he discovered the scratches, the welts, the sores, the ulcers, and the scars that had been left on her by more than half a century of daily life, and he saw that those damages did not even arouse a feeling of pity in him. Then he made one last effort to search in his heart for the place where his affection had rotted away and he

G*

could not find it. On another occasion, he felt at least a confused sense of shame when he found the smell of Úrsula on his own skin, and more than once he felt her thoughts interfering with his. But all of that had been wiped out by the war. Even Remedios, his wife, at that moment was a hazy image of someone who might have been his daughter. The countless women he had known on the desert of love and who had spread his seed all along the coast had left no trace in his feelings. Most of them had come into his room in the dark and had left before dawn, and on the following day they were nothing but a touch of fatigue in his bodily memory. The only affection that prevailed against time and the war was that which he had felt for his brother José Arcadio when they both were children, and it was not based on love but on complicity.

"I'm sorry," he excused himself from Úrsula's request. "It's just that the war has done away with everything."

During the following days he busied himself destroying all trace of his passage through the world. He stripped the silver shop until all that were left were impersonal objects, he gave his clothes away to the orderlies, and he buried his weapons in the courtyard with the same feeling of penance with which his father had buried the spear that had killed Prudencio Aguilar. He kept only one pistol with one bullet in it. Úrsula did not intervene. The only time she dissuaded him was when he was about to destroy the daguerreotype of Remedios that was kept in the parlor lighted by an eternal lamp. "That picture stopped belonging to you a long time ago," she told him. "It's a family relic." On the eve of the armistice, when no single object that would let him be remembered was left in the house, he took the trunk of poetry to the bakery when Santa Sofía de la Piedad was making ready to light the oven.

"Light it with this," he told her, handing her the first roll of yellowish papers. "It will burn better because they're very old things."

Santa Sofía de la Piedad, the silent one, the condescending one, the one who never contradicted anyone, not even her own children, had the impression that it was a forbidden act.

"They're important papers," she said.

"Nothing of the sort," the colonel said. "They're things that a person writes to himself."

"In that case," she said, "you burn them, colonel."

He not only did that, but he broke up the trunk with a hatchet and threw the pieces into the fire. Hours before, Pilar Ternera had come to visit him. After so many years of not seeing her, Colonel Aureliano Buendía was startled at how old and fat she had become and how much she had lost of the splendor of her laugh, but he was also startled at the depths she had reached in her reading of the cards. "Watch out for your mouth," she told him, and he wondered whether the other time she had told him that during the height of his glory it had not been a surprisingly anticipated vision of his fate. A short time later, when his personal physician finished removing his sores, he asked him, without showing any particular interest, where the exact location of his heart was. The doctor listened with his stethoscope and then painted a circle on his chest with a piece of cotton dipped in iodine.

The Tuesday of the armistice dawned warm and rainy. Colonel Aureliano Buendía appeared in the kitchen before five o'clock and had his usual black coffee without sugar. "You came into the world on a day like this," Úrsula told him. "Everybody was amazed at your open eyes." He did not pay any attention because he was listening to the forming of the troops, the sound of the cornets, and the voices of command that were shattering the dawn. Even though after so many years of war they should have sounded familiar to him, this time he felt the same weakness in his knees and the same tingling in his skin that he had felt in his youth in the presence of a naked woman. He thought confusedly, finally captive in a trap of nostalgia, that perhaps if he had married her he would have been a man without war and without glory, a nameless artisan, a happy animal. That tardy shudder which had not figured in his forethought made his breakfast bitter. At seven in the morning, when Colonel Gerineldo Márquez came to fetch him, in the company of a group of rebel officers, he found him more taciturn than ever, more pensive and solitary. Úrsula tried to throw a new wrap over his shoulders. "What will the government think," she told him. "They'll figure that you've surrendered because you didn't have anything left to buy a cloak with." But he would not accept it. When he was at the door, he let her put an old felt hat of José Arcadio Buendía's on his head.

"Aureliano," Úrsula said to him then, "promise me that if you find that it's a bad hour for you there that you'll think of your mother."

He gave her a distant smile, raising his hand with all his fingers extended, and without saying a word he left the house and faced the shouts, insults, and blasphemies that would follow him until he left the town. Úrsula put the bar on the door, having decided not to take it down for the rest of her life. "We'll rot in here," she thought. "We'll turn to ashes in this house without men, but we won't give this miserable town the pleasure of seeing us weep." She spent the whole morning looking for a memory of her son in the most hidden corners, but she could find none.

The ceremony took place fifteen miles from Macondo in the shade of a gigantic ceiba tree around which the town of Neerlandia would be founded later. The delegates from the government and the party and the commission of the rebels who were laying down their arms were served by a noisy group of novices in white habits who looked like a flock of doves that had been frightened by the rain. Colonel Aureliano Buendía arrived on a muddy mule. He had not shaved, more tormented by the pain of the sores than by the great failure of his dreams, for he had reached the end of all hope, beyond glory and the nostalgia of glory. In accordance with his arrangements there was no music, no fireworks, no pealing bells, no shouts of victory, or any other manifestation that might alter the mournful character of the armistice. An itinerant photographer who took the only picture of him that could have been preserved was forced to smash his plates without developing them.

The ceremony lasted only the time necessary to sign the documents. Around the rustic table placed in the center of a patched circus tent where the delegates sat were the last officers who were faithful to Colonel Aureliano Buendía. Before taking the signatures, the personal delegate of the president of the republic tried to read the act of surrender aloud, but Colonel Aureliano Buendía was against it. "Let's not waste time on formalities," he said and prepared to sign the papers without reading them. One of his officers then broke the soporific silence of the tent.

"Colonel," he said, "please do us the favor of not being the first to sign."

Colonel Aureliano Buendía acceded. When the documents went all around the table, in the midst of a silence that was so pure that one could have deciphered the signatures from the scratching of the pen on the paper, the first line was still blank. Colonel Aureliano Buendía prepared to fill it.

"Colonel," another of his officers said, "there's still time for everything to come out right."

Without changing his expression, Colonel Aureliano Buendía signed the first copy. He had not finished signing the last one when a rebel colonel appeared in the doorway leading a mule carrying two chests. In spite of his extreme youth he had a dry look and a patient expression. He was the treasurer of the revolution in the Macondo region. He had made a difficult journey of six days, pulling along the mule, who was dying of hunger, in order to arrive at the armistice on time. With an exasperating parsimony he took down the chests, opened them, and placed on the table, one by one, seventy-two gold bricks. Everyone had forgotten about the existence of that fortune. In the disorder of the past year, when the central command fell apart and the revolution degenerated into a bloody rivalry of leaders, it was impossible to determine any responsibility. The gold of the revolution, melted into blocks that were then covered with baked clay, was beyond all control. Colonel Aureliano Buendía had the seventy-two gold bricks included in the inventory of surrender and closed the ceremony without allowing any speeches. The filthy adolescent stood opposite him, looking into his eyes with his own calm, syrup-colored eyes.

"Something else?" Colonel Aureliano Buendía asked him.

The young colonel tightened his mouth.

"The receipt," he said.

Colonel Aureliano Buendía wrote it out in his own hand. Then he had a glass of lemonade and a piece of biscuit that the novices were passing around and retired to a field tent which had been prepared for him in case he wished to rest. There he took off his shirt, sat on the edge of the cot, and at three-fifteen in the afternoon took his pistol and shot himself in the iodine circle that his personal physician had painted on his chest. At that moment in Macondo Úrsula took the cover off the pot of milk on the stove, wondering why it was taking so long to boil, and found it full of worms.

"They've killed Aureliano," she exclaimed.

She looked toward the courtyard, obeying a habit of her solitude, and then she saw José Arcadio Buendía, soaking wet and sad in the rain and much older than when he had died. "They shot him in the back," Úrsula said more precisely, "and no one was charitable enough to close his eyes." At dusk through her tears she saw the swift and luminous disks that crossed the sky like an exhalation and she thought that it was a signal of death. She was still under the chestnut tree, sobbing at her husband's knees, when they brought in Colonel

Aureliano Buendía, wrapped in a blanket that was stiff with dry blood and with his eyes open in rage.

He was out of danger. The bullet had followed such a neat path that the doctor was able to put a cord soaked in iodine in through the chest and withdraw it from the back. "That was my masterpiece," he said with satisfaction. "It was the only point where a bullet could pass through without harming any vital organ." Colonel Aureliano Buendía saw himself surrounded by charitable novices who intoned desperate psalms for the repose of his soul and then he was sorry that he had not shot himself in the roof of the mouth as he had considered doing if only to mock the prediction of Pilar Ternera.

"If I still had the authority," he told the doctor, "I'd have you shot out of hand. Not for having saved my life but for having made a fool of me."

The failure of his death brought back his lost prestige in a few hours. The same people who invented the story that he had sold the war for a room with walls made of gold bricks defined the attempt at suicide as an act of honor and proclaimed him a martyr. Then, when he rejected the Order of Merit awarded him by the president of the republic, even his most bitter enemies filed through the room asking him to withdraw recognition of the armistice and to start a new war. The house was filled with gifts meant as amends. Impressed finally by the massive support of his former comrades in arms, Colonel Aureliano Buendía did not put aside the possibility of pleasing them. On the contrary, at a certain moment he seemed so enthusiastic with the idea of a new war that Colonel Gerineldo Márquez thought that he was only waiting for a pretext to proclaim it. The pretext was offered, in fact, when the president of the republic refused to award any military pensions to former combatants, Liberal or Conservative, until each case was examined by a special commission and the award approved by the congress. "That's an outrage," thundered Colonel Aureliano Buendía. "They'll die of old age waiting for the mail to come." For the first time he left the rocker that Úrsula had bought for his convalescence, and, walking about the bedroom, he dictated a strong message to the president of the republic. In that telegram, which was never made public, he denounced the first violation of the Treaty of Neerlandia and threatened to proclaim war to the death if the assignment of pensions was not resolved within two weeks. His attitude was so just that it allowed him to hope even for the support of former Conservative combatants. But the only reply from the government was the reinforcement of the military guard that had been placed at the door of his house with the pretext of protecting him, and the prohibition of all types of visits. Similar methods were adopted all through the country with other leaders who bore watching. It was an operation that was so timely, drastic, and effective that two months after the armistice, when Colonel Aureliano Buendía had recovered, his most dedicated conspirators were dead or exiled or had been assimilated forever into public administration.

Colonel Aureliano Buendía left his room in December and it was sufficient for him to look at the porch in order not to think about war again. With a vitality that seemed impossible at her age, Úrsula had rejuvenated the house again. "Now they're going to see who I am," she said when she saw that her son was going to live. "There won't be a better, more open house in all the world than this madhouse." She had it washed and painted, changed the furniture, restored the garden and planted new flowers, and opened doors and windows so that the dazzling light of summer would penetrate even into the bedrooms. She decreed an end to the numerous superimposed periods of mourning and she herself exchanged her rigorous old gowns for youthful clothing. The music of the pianola again made the house merry. When she heard it, Amaranta thought of Pietro Crespi, his evening gardenia,

184

and his smell of lavender, and in the depths of her withered heart a clean rancor flourished, purified by time. One afternoon when she was trying to put the parlor in order, Úrsula asked for the help of the soldiers who were guarding the house. The young commander of the guard gave them permission. Little by little, Úrsula began assigning them new chores. She invited them to eat, gave them clothing and shoes, and taught them how to read and write. When the government withdrew the guard, one of them continued living in the house and was in her service for many years. On New Year's Day, driven mad by rebuffs from Remedios the Beauty, the young commander of the guard was found dead under her window.

YEARS LATER on his deathbed Aureliano Segundo
would remember the rainy afternoon in June when he went
into the bedroom to meet his first son. Even though the child
was languid and weepy, with no mark of a Buendía, he did
not have to think twice about naming him.

"We'll call him José Arcadio," he said.

Fernanda del Carpio, the beautiful woman he had married
the year before, agreed. Úrsula, on the other hand, could not
conceal a vague feeling of doubt. Throughout the long history of the family the insistent repetition of names had made
her draw some conclusions that seemed to be certain. While
the Aurelianos were withdrawn, but with lucid minds, the
José Arcadios were impulsive and enterprising, but they were

186

marked with a tragic sign. The only cases that were impossible to classify were those of José Arcadio Segundo and Aureliano Segundo. They were so much alike and so mischievous during childhood that not even Santa Sofía de la Piedad could tell them apart. On the day of their christening Amaranta put bracelets on them with their respective names and dressed them in different colored clothing marked with each one's initials, but when they began to go to school they decided to exchange clothing and bracelets and call each other by opposite names. The teacher, Melchor Escalona, used to knowing José Arcadio Segundo by his green shirt, went out of his mind when he discovered that the latter was wearing Aureliano Segundo's bracelet and that the other one said, nevertheless, that his name was Aureliano Segundo in spite of the fact that he was wearing the white shirt and the bracelet with José Arcadio Segundo's name. From then on he was never sure who was who. Even when they grew up and life made them different, Úrsula still wondered if they themselves might not have made a mistake in some moment of their intricate game of confusion and had become changed forever. Until the beginning of adolescence they were two synchronized machines. They would wake up at the same time, have the urge to go to the bathroom at the same time, suffer the same upsets in health, and they even dreamed about the same things. In the house, where it was thought that they coordinated their actions with a simple desire to confuse, no one realized what really was happening until one day when Santa Sofía de la Piedad gave one of them a glass of lemonade and as soon as he tasted it the other one said that it needed sugar. Santa Sofía de la Piedad, who had indeed forgotten to put sugar in the lemonade, told Úrsula about it. "That's what they're all like," she said without surprise, "crazy from birth." In time things became less disordered. The one who came out of the game of confusion with the name of Aureliano Segundo grew to monumental size like his grandfathers, and the one who kept the name of José Arcadio Segundo grew to be bony like the colonel, and the only thing they had in common was the family's solitary air. Perhaps it was that crossing of stature, names, and character that made Úrsula suspect that they had been shuffled like a deck of cards since childhood.

The decisive difference was revealed in the midst of the war, when José Arcadio Segundo asked Colonel Gerineldo Márquez to let him see an execution. Against Úrsula's better judgment his wishes were satisfied. Aureliano Segundo, on the other hand, shuddered at the mere idea of witnessing an execution. He preferred to stay home. At the age of twelve he asked Úrsula what was in the locked room. "Papers," she answered. "Melquíades' books and the strange things that he wrote in his last years." Instead of calming him, the answer increased his curiosity. He demanded so much, promised with such insistence that he would not mistreat the things, that Úrsula gave him the keys. No one had gone into the room again since they had taken Melquíades' body out and had put on the door a padlock whose parts had become fused together with rust. But when Aureliano Segundo opened the windows a familiar light entered that seemed accustomed to lighting the room every day and there was not the slightest trace of dust or cobwebs, with everything swept and clean, better swept and cleaner than on the day of the burial, and the ink had not dried up in the inkwell nor had oxidation diminished the shine of the metals nor had the embers gone out under the water pipe where José Arcadio Buendía had vaporized mercury. On the shelves were the books bound in a cardboard-like material, pale, like tanned human skin, and the manuscripts were intact. In spite of the room's having been shut up for many years, the air seemed fresher than in the rest of the house. Everything was so recent that several weeks later, when Úrsula went into the room with a pail of water and a brush to wash the floor, there was nothing for her to do. Aureliano Segundo was deep in the reading of a book. Although it had no cover and the title did not appear anywhere, the boy enjoyed the story of a woman who sat at a table and ate nothing but kernels of rice, which she picked up with a pin, and the story of the fisherman who borrowed a weight for his net from a neighbor and when he gave him a fish in payment later it had a diamond in its stomach, and the one about the lamp that fulfilled wishes and about flying carpets. Surprised, he asked Úrsula if all that was true and she answered him that it was, that many years ago the gypsies had brought magic lamps and flying mats to Macondo.

"What's happening," she sighed, "is that the world is slowly coming to an end and those things don't come here any more."

When he finished the book, in which many of the stories had no endings because there were pages missing, Aureliano Segundo set about deciphering the manuscripts. It was impossible. The letters looked like clothes hung out to dry on a line and they looked more like musical notation than writing. One hot noontime, while he was poring over the manuscripts, he sensed that he was not alone in the room. Against the light from the window, sitting with his hands on his knees, was Melquíades. He was under forty years of age. He was wearing the same old-fashioned vest and the hat that looked like a raven's wings, and across his pale temples there flowed the grease from his hair that had been melted by the heat, just as Aureliano and José Arcadio had seen him when they were children. Aureliano Segundo recognized him at once, because that hereditary memory had been transmitted from generation to generation and had come to him through the memory of his grandfather.

"Hello," Aureliano Segundo said.

"Hello, young man," said Melquíades.

From then on, for several years, they saw each other almost every afternoon. Melquíades talked to him about the world, tried to infuse him with his old wisdom, but he refused to translate the manuscripts. "No one must know their meaning until he has reached one hundred years of age," he explained. Aureliano kept those meetings secret forever. On one occasion he felt that his private world had fallen apart because Úrsula came in when Melquíades was in the room. But she did not see him.

"Who were you talking to?" she asked him.

"Nobody," Aureliano Segundo said.

"That's what your great-grandfather did," Úrsula said. "He used to talk to himself too."

José Arcadio Segundo, in the meantime, had satisfied his wish to see a shooting. For the rest of his life he would remember the livid flash of the six simultaneous shots and the echo of the discharge as it broke against the hills and the sad smile and perplexed eyes of the man being shot, who stood erect while his shirt became soaked with blood, and who was still smiling even when they untied him from the post and put him in a box filled with quicklime. "He's alive," he thought. "They're going to bury him alive." It made such an impression on him that from then on he detested military practices and war, not because of the executions but because of the horrifying custom of burying the victims alive. No one knew then exactly when he began to ring the bells in the church tower and assist Father Antonio Isabel, the successor to "The Pup," at mass, and take care of the fighting cocks in the courtyard of the parish house. When Colonel Gerineldo Márquez found out he scolded him strongly for learning occupations repudiated by the Liberals. "The fact is," he answered, "I think I've turned out to be a Conservative." He believed it as if it had been determined by fate. Colonel Gerineldo Márquez, scandalized, told Úrsula about it.

"It's better that way," she approved. "Let's hope that he becomes a priest so that God will finally come into this house."

190

It was soon discovered that Father Antonio Isabel was preparing him for his first communion. He was teaching him the catechism as he shaved the necks of his roosters. He explained to him with simple examples, as he put the brooding hens into their nests, how it had occurred to God on the second day of creation that chickens would be formed inside of an egg. From that time on the parish priest began to show the signs of senility that would lead him to say years later that the devil had probably won his rebellion against God, and that he was the one who sat on the heavenly throne, without revealing his true identity in order to trap the unwary. Warmed up by the persistence of his mentor, in a few months José Arcadio Segundo came to be as adept in theological tricks used to confuse the devil as he was skilled in the tricks of the cockpit. Amaranta made him a linen suit with a collar and tie, bought him a pair of white shoes, and engraved his name in gilt letters on the ribbon of the candle. Two nights before the first communion, Father Antonio Isabel closeted himself with him in the sacristy to hear his confession with the help of a dictionary of sins. It was such a long list that the aged priest, used to going to bed at six o'clock, fell asleep in his chair before it was over. The interrogation was a revelation for José Arcadio Segundo. It did not surprise him that the priest asked him if he had done bad things with women, and he honestly answered no, but he was upset with the question as to whether he had done them with animals. The first Friday in May he received communion, tortured by curiosity. Later on he asked Petronio, the sickly sexton who lived in the belfry and who, according to what they said, fed himself on bats, about it, and Petronio answered him: "There are some corrupt Christians who do their business with female donkeys." José Arcadio Segundo still showed so much curiosity and asked so many questions that Petronio lost his patience.

"I go Tuesday nights," he confessed. "If you promise not to tell anyone I'll take you next Tuesday."

Indeed, on the following Tuesday Petronio came down out of the tower with a wooden stool which until then no one had known the use of, and he took José Arcadio Segundo to a nearby pasture. The boy became so taken with those nocturnal raids that it was a long time before he was seen at Catarino's. He became a cockfight man. "Take those creatures somewhere else," Úrsula ordered him the first time she saw him come in with his fine fighting birds. "Roosters have already brought too much bitterness to this house for you to bring us any more." José Arcadio Segundo took them away without any argument, but he continued breeding them at the house of Pilar Ternera, his grandmother, who gave him everything he needed in exchange for having him in her house. He soon displayed in the cockpit the wisdom that Father Antonio Isabel had given him, and he made enough money not only to enrich his brood but also to look for a man's satisfactions. Úrsula compared him with his brother at that time and could not understand how the twins, who looked like the same person in childhood, had ended up so differently. Her perplexity did not last very long, for quite soon Aureliano Segundo began to show signs of laziness and dissipation. While he was shut up in Melquíades' room he was drawn into himself, the way Colonel Aureliano Buendía had been in his youth. But a short time after the Treaty of Neerlandia, a piece of chance took him out of his withdrawn self and made him face the reality of the world. A young woman who was selling numbers for the raffle of an accordion greeted him with a great deal of familiarity. Aureliano Segundo was not surprised, for he was frequently confused with his brother. But he did not clear up the mistake, not even when the girl tried to soften his heart with sobs, and she ended taking him to her room. She liked him so much from that first meeting that she fixed things so that he would win the accordion in the raffle. At the end of two weeks Aureliano Segundo realized that the woman had been going to bed alternately with him and his brother, thinking that they were the same man, and instead of making things clear, he arranged to prolong the situation. He did not return to Melquíades' room. He would spend his afternoons in the courtyard, learning to play the accordion by ear over the protests of Úrsula, who at that time had forbidden music in the house because of the mourning and who, in addition, despised the accordion as an instrument worthy only of the vagabond heirs of Francisco the Man. Nevertheless, Aureliano Segundo became a virtuoso on the accordion and he still was after he had married and had children and was one of the most respected men in Macondo.

For almost two months he shared the woman with his brother. He would watch him, mix up his plans, and when he was sure that José Arcadio Segundo was not going to visit their common mistress that night, he would go and sleep with her. One morning he found that he was sick. Two days later he found his brother clinging to a beam in the bathroom, soaked in sweat and with tears pouring down, and then he understood. His brother confessed to him that the woman had sent him away because he had given her what she called a low-life sickness. He also told him how Pilar Ternera had tried to cure him. Aureliano Segundo submitted secretly to the burning baths of permanganate and to diuretic waters, and both were cured separately after three months of secret suffering. José Arcadio Segundo did not see the woman again. Aureliano Segundo obtained her pardon and stayed with her until his death.

Her name was Petra Cotes. She had arrived in Macondo in the middle of the war with a chance husband who lived off raffles, and when the man died she kept up the business. She was a clean young mulatto woman with yellow almond-shaped eyes that gave her face the ferocity of a panther, but she had a generous heart and a magnificent vocation for love. When Úrsula realized that José Arcadio Segundo was a cockfight man and that Aureliano Segundo played the accordion at his concubine's noisy parties, she thought she would go mad with the combination. It was as if the defects of the family and none of the virtues had been concentrated in both. Then she decided that no one again would be called Aureliano or José Arcadio. Yet when Aureliano Segundo had his first son she did not dare go against his will.

"All right," Úrsula said, "but on one condition: I will bring him up."

Although she was already a hundred years old and on the point of going blind from cataracts, she still had her physical dynamism, her integrity of character, and her mental balance intact. No one would be better able than she to shape the virtuous man who would restore the prestige of the family, a man who would never have heard talk of war, fighting cocks, bad women, or wild undertakings, four calamities that, according to what Úrsula thought, had determined the downfall of their line. "This one will be a priest," she promised solemnly. "And if God gives me life he'll be Pope someday." They all laughed when they heard her, not only in the bedroom but all through the house, where Aureliano Segundo's rowdy friends were gathered. The war, relegated to the attic of bad memories, was momentarily recalled with the popping of champagne bottles.

"To the health of the Pope," Aureliano Segundo toasted.

The guests toasted in a chorus. Then the man of the house played the accordion, fireworks were set off, and drums celebrated the event throughout the town. At dawn the guests, soaked in champagne, sacrificed six cows and put them in the street at the disposal of the crowd. No one was scandalized. Since Aureliano Segundo had taken charge of the house those festivities were a common thing, even when there was no motive as proper as the birth of a Pope. In a few years, without effort, simply by luck, he had accumulated one of the largest fortunes in the swamp thanks to the supernatural

194

proliferation of his animals. His mares would bear triplets, his hens laid twice a day, and his hogs fattened with such speed that no one could explain such disorderly fecundity except through the use of black magic. "Save something now," Úrsula would tell her wild great-grandson. "This luck is not going to last all your life." But Aureliano Segundo paid no attention to her. The more he opened champagne to soak his friends, the more wildly his animals gave birth and the more he was convinced that his lucky star was not a matter of his conduct but an influence of Petra Cotes, his concubine, whose love had the virtue of exasperating nature. So convinced was he that this was the origin of his fortune that he never kept Petra Cotes far away from his breeding grounds and even when he married and had children he continued living with her with the consent of Fernanda. Solid, monumental like his grandfathers, but with a joie de vivre and an irresistible good humor that they did not have, Aureliano Segundo scarcely had time to look after his animals. All he had to do was to take Petra Cotes to his breeding grounds and have her ride across his land in order to have every animal marked with his brand succumb to the irremediable plague of proliferation.

Like all the good things that occurred in his long life, that tremendous fortune had its origins in chance. Until the end of the wars Petra Cotes continued to support herself with the returns from her raffles and Aureliano Segundo was able to sack Úrsula's savings from time to time. They were a frivolous couple, with no other worries except going to bed every night, even on forbidden days, and frolicking there until dawn. "That woman has been your ruination," Úrsula would shout at her great-grandson when she saw him coming into the house like a sleepwalker. "She's got you so bewitched that one of these days I'm going to see you twisting around with colic and with a toad in your belly." José Arcadio Segundo, who took a long time to discover that he had been supplanted, was unable to understand his brother's passion. He remembered Petra Cotes as an ordinary woman, rather lazy in bed, and completely lacking in any resources for lovemaking. Deaf to Úrsula's clamor and the teasing of his brother, Aureliano Segundo only thought at that time of finding a trade that would allow him to maintain a house for Petra Cotes, and to die with her, on top of her and underneath her, during a night of feverish license. When Colonel Aureliano Buendía opened up his workshop again, seduced at last by the peaceful charms of old age, Aureliano Segundo thought that it would be good business to devote himself to the manufacture of little gold fishes. He spent many hours in the hot room watching how the hard sheets of metal, worked by the colonel with the inconceivable patience of disillusionment, were slowly being converted into golden scales. The work seemed so laborious to him and the thought of Petra Cotes was so persistent and pressing that after three weeks he disappeared from the workshop. It was during that time that it occurred to Petra Cotes to raffle off rabbits. They reproduced and grew up so fast that there was barely time to sell the tickets for the raffle. At first Aureliano Segundo did not notice the alarming proportions of the proliferation. But one night, when nobody in town wanted to hear about the rabbit raffle any more, he heard a noise by the courtyard door. "Don't get worried," Petra Cotes said. "It's only the rabbits." They could not sleep, tormented by the uproar of the animals. At dawn Aureliano Segundo opened the door and saw the courtyard paved with rabbits, blue in the glow of dawn. Petra Cotes, dying with laughter, could not resist the temptation of teasing him.

"Those are the ones who were born last night," she said.

"Oh my God!" he said. "Why don't you raffle off cows?"

A few days later, in an attempt to clean out her courtyard, Petra Cotes exchanged the rabbits for a cow, who two months later gave birth to triplets. That was how things began. Overnight Aureliano Segundo became the owner of land and livestock and he barely had time to enlarge his overflowing barns and pigpens. It was a delirious prosperity that even made him laugh, and he could not help doing crazy things to release his good humor. "Cease, cows, life is short," he would shout. Úrsula wondered what entanglements he had got into, whether he might be stealing, whether he had become a rustler, and every time she saw him uncorking champagne just for the pleasure of pouring the foam over his head, she would shout at him and scold him for the waste. It annoyed him so much that one day when he awoke in a merry mood, Aureliano Segundo appeared with a chest full of money, a can of paste, and a brush, and singing at the top of his lungs the old songs of Francisco the Man, he papered the house inside and out and from top to bottom with one-peso banknotes. The old mansion, painted white since the time they had brought the pianola, took on the strange look of a mosque. In the midst of the excitement of the family, the scandalization of Úrsula, the joy of the people cramming the street to watch that apotheosis of squandering, Aureliano Segundo finished by papering the house from the front to the kitchen, including bathrooms and bedrooms, and threw the leftover bills into the courtyard.

"Now," he said in a final way, "I hope that nobody in this house ever talks to me about money again."

That was what happened. Úrsula had the bills taken down, stuck to great cakes of whitewash, and the house was painted white again. "Dear Lord," she begged, "make us poor again the way we were when we founded this town so that you will not collect for this squandering in the other life." Her prayers were answered in reverse. One of the workmen removing the bills bumped into an enormous plaster statue of Saint Joseph that someone had left in the house during the last years of the war and the hollow figure broke to pieces on the floor. It had been stuffed with gold coins. No one could remember who had brought that life-size saint. "Three men brought it," Amaranta explained. "They asked us to keep it until the rains were over and I told them to put it there in the corner where nobody would bump into it, and there they put it, very carefully, and there it's been ever since because they never came back for it." Later on, Úrsula had put candles on it and had prostrated herself before it, not suspecting that instead of a saint she was adoring almost four hundred pounds of gold. The tardy evidence of her involuntary paganism made her even more upset. She spat on the spectacular pile of coins, put them in three canvas sacks, and buried them in a secret place, hoping that sooner or later the three unknown men would come to reclaim them. Much later, during the difficult years of her decrepitude, Úrsula would intervene in the conversations of the many travelers who came by the house at that time and ask them if they had left a plaster Saint Joseph there during the war to be taken care of until the rains passed.

Things like that, which gave Úrsula such consternation, were commonplace in those days. Macondo was swamped in a miraculous prosperity. The adobe houses of the founders had been replaced by brick buildings with wooden blinds and cement floors which made the suffocating heat of two o'clock in the afternoon more bearable. All that remained at that time of José Arcadio Buendía's ancient village were the dusty almond trees, destined to resist the most arduous of circumstances, and the river of clear water whose prehistoric stones had been pulverized by the frantic hammers of José Arcadio Segundo when he set about opening the channel in order to establish a boat line. It was a mad dream, comparable to those of his great-grandfather, for the rocky riverbed and the numerous rapids prevented navigation from Macondo to the sea. But José Arcadio Segundo, in an unforeseen burst of temerity, stubbornly kept on with the project. Until then he had shown no sign of imagination. Except for his precarious adventure with Petra Cotes, he had never known a woman. Úrsula had considered him the quietest example the family had ever produced in all its history, incapable of standing out even as a handler of fighting cocks, when Colonel Aureliano Buendía told him the story of the Spanish galleon aground eight miles from the sea, the carbonized frame of which he had seen himself during the war. The story, which for so many years had seemed fantastic to so many people, was a revelation for José Arcadio Segundo. He auctioned off his roosters to the highest bidder, recruited men, bought tools, and set about the awesome task of breaking stones, digging canals, clearing away rapids, and even harnessing waterfalls. "I know all of this by heart," Úrsula would shout. "It's as if time had turned around and we were back at the beginning." When he thought that the river was navigable, José Arcadio Segundo gave his brother a detailed account of his plans and the latter gave him the money he needed for the enterprise. He disappeared for a long time. It had been said that his plan to buy a boat was nothing but a trick to make off with his brother's money, when the news spread that a strange craft was approaching the town. The inhabitants of Macondo, who no longer remembered the colossal undertakings of José Arcadio Buendía, ran to the riverbank and saw with eyes popping in disbelief the arrival of the first and last boat ever to dock in the town. It was nothing but a log raft drawn by thick ropes pulled by twenty men who walked along the bank. In the prow, with a glow of satisfaction in his eyes, José Arcadio Segundo was directing the arduous maneuver. There arrived with him a rich group of splendid matrons who were protecting themselves from the burning sun with gaudy parasols, and wore on their shoulders fine silk kerchiefs, with colored creams on their faces and natural flowers in their hair and golden serpents on their arms and diamonds in their teeth. The log raft was the only vessel that José Arcadio Segundo was able to bring to Macondo, and only once, but he never recognized the failure of his enterprise, but proclaimed his deed as a victory of will power. He gave a scrupulous accounting to his brother and very soon plunged back into the routine of cockfights. The only thing that remained of that unfortunate venture was the breath of renovation that the matrons from France brought, as their magnificent arts transformed traditional methods of love and their sense of social well-being abolished Catarino's antiquated place and turned the street into a bazaar of Japanese lanterns and nostalgic hand organs. They were the promoters of the bloody carnival that plunged Macondo into delirium for three days and whose only lasting consequence was having given Aureliano Segundo the opportunity to meet Fernanda del Carpio.

Remedios the Beauty was proclaimed queen. Úrsula, who shuddered at the disquieting beauty of her great-granddaughter, could not prevent the choice. Until then she had succeeded in keeping her off the streets unless it was to go to mass with Amaranta, but she made her cover her face with a black shawl. The most impious men, those who would disguise themselves as priests to say sacrilegious masses in Catarino's store, would go to church with an aim to see, if only for an instant, the face of Remedios the Beauty, whose legendary good looks were spoken of with alarming excitement throughout the swamp. It was a long time before they were able to do so, and it would have been better for them if they never had, because most of them never recovered their peaceful habits of sleep. The man who made it possible, a foreigner, lost his serenity forever, became involved in the sloughs of abjection and misery, and years later was cut to pieces by a train after he had fallen asleep on the tracks. From the moment he was seen in the church, wearing a green velvet suit and an embroidered vest, no one doubted that he came from far away, perhaps from some distant city outside of the country, attracted by the magical fascination of

Remedios the Beauty. He was so handsome, so elegant and dignified, with such presence, that Pietro Crespi would have been a mere fop beside him, and many women whispered with spiteful smiles that he was the one who really should have worn the shawl. He did not speak to anyone in Macondo. He appeared at dawn on Sunday like a prince in a fairy tale, riding a horse with silver stirrups and a velvet blanket, and he left town after mass.

The power of his presence was such that from the first time he was seen in the church everybody took it for granted that a silent and tense duel had been established between him and Remedios the Beauty, a secret pact, an irrevocable challenge that would end not only in love but also in death. On the sixth Sunday the gentleman appeared with a yellow rose in his hand. He heard mass standing, as he always did, and at the end he stepped in front of Remedios the Beauty and offered her the solitary rose. She took it with a natural gesture, as if she had been prepared for that homage, and then she uncovered her face and gave her thanks with a smile. That was all she did. Not only for the gentleman, but for all the men who had the unfortunate privilege of seeing her, that was an eternal instant.

From then on the gentleman had a band of musicians play beside the window of Remedios the Beauty, sometimes until dawn. Aureliano Segundo was the only one who felt a cordial compassion for him and he tried to break his perseverance. "Don't waste your time any more," he told him one night. "The women in this house are worse than mules." He offered him his friendship, invited him to bathe in champagne, tried to make him understand that the females of his family had insides made of flint, but he could not weaken his obstinacy. Exasperated by the interminable nights of music, Colonel Aureliano Buendía threatened to cure his affliction with a few pistol shots. Nothing made him desist except his own lamentable state of demoralization. From a well-dressed and

H

neat individual he became filthy and ragged. It was rumored that he had abandoned power and fortune in his distant nation, although his origins were actually never known. He became argumentative, a barroom brawler, and he would wake up rolling in his own filth in Catarino's store. The saddest part of his drama was that Remedios the Beauty did not notice him, not even when he appeared in church dressed like a prince. She accepted the yellow rose without the least bit of malice, amused, rather, by the extravagance of the act, and she lifted her shawl to see his face better, not to show hers.

Actually, Remedios the Beauty was not a creature of this world. Until she was well along in puberty Santa Sofía de la Piedad had to bathe and dress her, and even when she could take care of herself it was necessary to keep an eye on her so that she would not paint little animals on the walls with a stick daubed in her own excrement. She reached twenty without knowing how to read or write, unable to use the silver at the table, wandering naked through the house because her nature rejected all manner of convention. When the young commander of the guard declared his love for her, she rejected him simply because his frivolity startled her. "See how simple he is," she told Amaranta. "He says that he's dying because of me, as if I were a bad case of colic." When, indeed, they found him dead beside her window, Remedios the Beauty confirmed her first impression.

"You see," she commented. "He was a complete simpleton."

It seemed as if some penetrating lucidity permitted her to see the reality of things beyond any formalism. That at least was the point of view of Colonel Aureliano Buendía, for whom Remedios the Beauty was in no way mentally retarded, as was generally believed, but quite the opposite. "It's as if she's come back from twenty years of war," he would say. Úrsula, for her part, thanked God for having awarded the family with a creature of exceptional purity, but at the same time she was disturbed by her beauty, for it seemed a contradictory virtue to her, a diabolical trap at the center of her innocence. It was for that reason that she decided to keep her away from the world, to protect her from all earthly temptation, not knowing that Remedios the Beauty, even from the time when she was in her mother's womb, was safe from any contagion. It never entered her head that they would elect her beauty queen of the carnival pandemonium. But Aureliano Segundo, excited at the caprice of disguising himself as a tiger, brought Father Antonio Isabel to the house in order to convince Úrsula that the carnival was not a pagan feast, as she said, but a Catholic tradition. Finally convinced, even though reluctantly, she consented to the coronation.

The news that Remedios Buendía was going to be the sovereign ruler of the festival went beyond the limits of the swamp in a few hours, reached distant places where the prestige of her beauty was not known, and it aroused the anxiety of those who still thought of her last name as a symbol of subversion. The anxiety was baseless. If anyone had become harmless at that time it was the aging and disillusioned Colonel Aureliano Buendía, who was slowly losing all contact with the reality of the nation. Enclosed in his workshop, his only relationship with the rest of the world was his business in little gold fishes. One of the soldiers who had guarded his house during the first days of peace would go sell them in the villages of the swamp and return loaded down with coins and news. That the Conservative government, he would say, with the backing of the Liberals, was reforming the calendar so that every president could remain in power for a hundred years. That the concordat with the Holy See had finally been signed and a cardinal had come from Rome with a crown of diamonds and a throne of solid gold, and that the Liberal ministers had had their pictures taken on their knees in the act of kissing his ring. That the leading lady of a Spanish company passing through the capital had been kidnapped by a band of masked highwaymen and on the following Sunday she had danced in the nude at the summer house of the president of the republic. "Don't talk to me about politics," the colonel would tell him. "Our business is selling little fishes." The rumor that he did not want to hear anything about the situation in the country because he was growing rich in his workshop made Úrsula laugh when it reached her ears. With her terrible practical sense she could not understand the colonel's business as he exchanged little fishes for gold coins and then converted the coins into little fishes, and so on, with the result that he had to work all the harder with the more he sold in order to satisfy an exasperating vicious circle. Actually, what interested him was not the business but the work. He needed so much concentration to link scales, fit minute rubies into the eyes, laminate gills, and put on fins that there was not the smallest empty moment left for him to fill with his disillusionment of the war. So absorbing was the attention required by the delicacy of his artistry that in a short time he had aged more than during all the years of the war, and his position had twisted his spine and the close work had used up his eyesight, but the implacable concentration awarded him with a peace of the spirit. The last time he was seen to take an interest in some matter related to the war was when a group of veterans from both parties sought his support for the approval of lifetime pensions, which had always been promised and were always about to be put into effect. "Forget about it," he told them. "You can see how I refuse my pension in order to get rid of the torture of waiting for it until the day I died." At first Colonel Gerineldo Márquez would visit him at dusk and they would both sit in the street door and talk about the past. But Amaranta could not bear the memories that that man, whose baldness had plunged him into the abyss of premature old age, aroused in her, and she would torment him with snide remarks until he did not come back except on special occasions and he finally disappeared, extinguished by paralysis. Taciturn, silent, insensible to the new breath of vitality that was shaking the house, Colonel Aureliano Buendía could understand only that the secret of a good old age is simply an honorable pact with solitude. He would get up at five in the morning after a light sleep, have his eternal mug of bitter coffee in the kitchen, shut himself up all day in the workshop, and at four in the afternoon he would go along the porch dragging a stool, not even noticing the fire of the rose bushes or the brightness of the hour or the persistence of Amaranta, whose melancholy made the noise of a boiling pot, which was perfectly perceptible at dusk, and he would sit in the street door as long as the mosquitoes would allow him to. Someone dared to disturb his solitude once.

"How are you, Colonel?" he asked in passing.

"Right here," he answered. "Waiting for my funeral procession to pass."

So that the anxiety caused by the public reappearance of his family name, having to do with the coronation of Remedios the Beauty, was baseless. Many people did not think that way, however. Innocent of the tragedy that threatened it, the town poured into the main square in a noisy explosion of merriment. The carnival had reached its highest level of madness and Aureliano Segundo had satisfied at last his dream of dressing up like a tiger and was walking along the wild throng, hoarse from so much roaring, when on the swamp road a parade of several people appeared carrying in a gilded litter the most fascinating woman that imagination could conceive. For a moment the inhabitants of Macondo took off their masks in order to get a better look at the dazzling creature with a crown of emeralds and an ermine cape, who seemed invested with legitimate authority, and was not merely a sovereign of bangles and crepe paper. There were many people who had sufficient insight to suspect that it was a question of provocation. But Aureliano Segundo immediately conquered his perplexity and declared the new arrivals to be guests of honor, and with the wisdom of Solomon he seated Remedios the Beauty and the intruding queen on the same dais. Until midnight the strangers, disguised as bedouins, took part in the delirium and even enriched it with sumptuous fireworks and acrobatic skills that made one think of the art of the gypsies. Suddenly, during the paroxysm of the celebration, someone broke the delicate balance.

"Long live the Liberal party!" he shouted. "Long live Colonel Aureliano Buendía!"

The rifle shots drowned out the splendor of the fireworks and the cries of terror drowned out the music and joy turned into panic. Many years later there were those who still insisted that the royal guard of the intruding queen was a squad of regular army soldiers who were concealing government-issue rifles under their rich Moorish robes. The government denied the charge in a special proclamation and promised a complete investigation of the bloody episode. But the truth never came to light and the version always prevailed that the royal guard, without provocation of any kind, took up combat positions upon a signal from their commander and opened fire without pity on the crowd. When calm was restored, not one of the false bedouins remained in town and there were many dead and wounded lying on the square: nine clowns, four Columbines, seventeen playing-card kings, one devil, three minstrels, two peers of France, and three Japanese empresses. In the confusion of the panic José Arcadio Segundo managed to rescue Remedios the Beauty and Aureliano Segundo carried the intruding queen to the house in his arms, her dress torn and the ermine cape stained with blood. Her name was Fernanda del Carpio. She had been chosen as the most beautiful of the five thousand most beautiful women in the land and they had brought her to Macondo with the promise of naming her Queen of Madagascar. Úrsula took care of her as if she were her own daughter. The town, instead of doubting her innocence, pitied her candor. Six months after the massacre, when the wounded had recovered and the last flowers on the mass grave had withered, Aureliano Segundo went to fetch her from the distant city where she lived with her father and he married her in Macondo with a noisy celebration that lasted twenty days.

THE MARRIAGE was on the point of breaking up after two months because Aureliano Segundo, in an attempt to placate Petra Cotes, had a picture taken of her dressed as the Queen of Madagascar. When Fernanda found out about it she repacked her bridal trunks and left Macondo without saying good-bye. Aureliano Segundo caught up with her on the swamp road. After much pleading and promises of reform he succeeded in getting her to come home and he abandoned his concubine.

Petra Cotes, aware of her strength, showed no signs of worry. She had made a man of him. While he was still a child she had drawn him out of Melquíades' room, his head full of fantastic ideas and lacking any contact with reality, and she had given him a place in the world. Nature had made him reserved and withdrawn, with tendencies toward solitary meditation, and she had molded an opposite character in him, one that was vital, expansive, open, and she had injected him with a joy for living and a pleasure in spending and celebrating until she had converted him, inside and out, into the man she had dreamed of for herself ever since adolescence. Then he married, as all sons marry sooner or later. He did not dare tell her the news. He assumed an attitude that was quite childish under the circumstances, feigning anger and imaginary resentment so that Petra Cotes would be the one who would bring about the break. One day, when Aureliano Segundo reproached her unjustly, she eluded the trap and put things in their proper place.

"What it all means," she said, "is that you want to marry the queen."

Aureliano Segundo, ashamed, pretended an attack of rage, said that he was misunderstood and abused, and did not visit her again. Petra Cotes, without losing her poise of a wild beast in repose for a single instant, heard the music and the fireworks from the wedding, the wild bustle of the celebration as if all of it were nothing but some new piece of mischief on the part of Aureliano Segundo. Those who pitied her fate were calmed with a smile. "Don't worry," she told them. "Queens run errands for me." To a neighbor woman who brought her a set of candles so that she could light up the picture of her lost lover with them, she said with an enigmatic security:

"The only candle that will make him come is always lighted."

Just as she had foreseen, Aureliano Segundo went back to her house as soon as the honeymoon was over. He brought his usual old friends, a traveling photographer, and the gown and ermine cape soiled with blood that Fernanda had worn during the carnival. In the heat of the merriment that broke

H*

out that evening, he had Petra Cotes dress up as queen, crowned her absolute and lifetime ruler of Madagascar, and handed out copies of the picture to his friends. She not only went along with the game, but she felt sorry for him inside, thinking that he must have been very frightened to have conceived of that extravagant means of reconciliation. At seven in the evening, still dressed as the queen, she received him in bed. He had been married scarcely two months, but she realized at once that things were not going well in the nuptial bed, and she had the delicious pleasure of vengeance fulfilled. Two days later, however, when he did not dare return but sent an intermediary to arrange the terms of the separation, she understood that she was going to need more patience than she had foreseen because he seemed ready to sacrifice himself for the sake of appearances. Nor did she get upset that time. Once again she made things easy with a submission that confirmed the generalized belief that she was a poor devil, and the only souvenir she kept of Aureliano Segundo was a pair of patent leather boots, which, according to what he himself had said, were the ones he wanted to wear in his coffin. She kept them wrapped in cloth in the bottom of a trunk and made ready to feed on memories, waiting without despair.

"He has to come sooner or later," she told herself, "even if it's just to put on those boots."

She did not have to wait as long as she had imagined. Actually, Aureliano Segundo understood from the night of his wedding that he would return to the house of Petra Cotes much sooner than when he would have to put on the patent leather boots: Fernanda was a woman who was lost in the world. She had been born and raised in a city six hundred miles away, a gloomy city where on ghostly nights the coaches of the viceroys still rattled through the cobbled streets. Thirty-two belfries tolled a dirge at six in the afternoon. In the manor house, which was paved with tomblike slabs, the sun was never seen. The air had died in the cypresses in the courtyard, in the pale trappings of the bedrooms, in the dripping archways of the garden of perennials. Until puberty Fernanda had no news of the world except for the melancholy piano lessons taken in some neighboring house by someone who for years and years had the drive not to take a siesta. In the room of her sick mother, green and yellow under the powdery light from the windowpanes, she would listen to the methodical, stubborn, heartless scales and think that that music was in the world while she was being consumed as she wove funeral wreaths. Her mother, perspiring with five-o'clock fever, spoke to her of the splendor of the past. When she was a little girl, on one moonlit night Fernanda saw a beautiful woman dressed in white crossing the garden toward the chapel. What bothered her most about that fleeting vision was that she felt it was exactly like her, as if she had seen herself twenty years in advance. "It was your great-grandmother the queen," her mother told her during a truce in her coughing. "She died of some bad vapors while she was cutting a string of bulbs." Many years later, when she began to feel she was the equal of her great-grandmother, Fernanda doubted her childhood vision, but her mother scolded her disbelief.

"We are immensely rich and powerful," she told her. "One day you will be a queen."

She believed it, even though they were sitting at the long table with a linen tablecloth and silver service to have a cup of watered chocolate and a sweet bun. Until the day of her wedding she dreamed about a legendary kingdom, in spite of the fact that her father, Don Fernando, had to mortgage the house in order to buy her trousseau. It was not innocence or delusions of grandeur. That was how they had brought her up. Since she had had the use of reason she remembered having done her duty in a gold pot with the family crest on it. She left the house for the first time at the age of twelve in a coach and horses that had to travel only two blocks to take her to the convent. Her classmates were surprised that she sat apart from them in a chair with a very high back and that she would not even mingle with them during recess. "She's different," the nuns would explain. "She's going to be a queen." Her schoolmates believed this because she was already the most beautiful, distinguished, and discreet girl they had ever seen. At the end of eight years, after having learned to write Latin poetry, play the clavichord, talk about falconry with gentlemen and apologetics with archbishops, discuss affairs of state with foreign rulers and affairs of God with the Pope, she returned to her parents' home to weave funeral wreaths. She found it despoiled. All that was left was the furniture that was absolutely necessary, the silver candelabra and table service, for the everyday utensils had been sold one by one to underwrite the costs of her education. Her mother had succumbed to five-o'clock fever. Her father, Don Fernando, dressed in black with a stiff collar and a gold watch chain, would give her a silver coin on Mondays for the household expenses, and the funeral wreaths finished the week before would be taken away. He spent most of his time shut up in his study and the few times that he went out he would return to recite the rosary with her. She had intimate friendships with no one. She had never heard mention of the wars that were bleeding the country. She continued her piano lessons at three in the afternoon. She had even begun to lose the illusion of being a queen when two peremptory raps of the knocker sounded at the door and she opened it to a well-groomed military officer with ceremonious manners who had a scar on his cheek and a gold medal on his chest. He closeted himself with her father in the study. Two hours later her father came to get her in the sewing room. "Get your things together," he told her. "You have to take a long trip." That was how they took her to Macondo. In one single day, with a brutal slap, life threw on top of her the whole weight of a reality that her parents had kept hidden from her for many years. When she returned home she shut herself up in her room to weep, indifferent to Don Fernando's pleas and explanations as he tried to erase the scars of that strange joke. She had sworn to herself never to leave her bedroom until she died when Aureliano Segundo came to get her. It was an act of impossible fate, because in the confusion of her indignation, in the fury of her shame, she had lied to him so that he would never know her real identity. The only real clues that Aureliano Segundo had when he left to look for her were her unmistakable highland accent and her trade as a weaver of funeral wreaths. He searched for her without cease. With the fierce temerity with which José Arcadio Buendía had crossed the mountains to found Macondo, with the blind pride with which Colonel Aureliano Buendía had undertaken his fruitless wars, with the mad tenacity with which Úrsula watched over the survival of the line, Aureliano Segundo looked for Fernanda, without a single moment of respite. When he asked where they sold funeral wreaths they took him from house to house so that he could choose the best ones. When he asked for the most beautiful woman who had ever been seen on this earth, all the women brought him their daughters. He became lost in misty byways, in times reserved for oblivion, in labyrinths of disappointment. He crossed a yellow plain where the echo repeated one's thoughts and where anxiety brought on premonitory mirages. After sterile weeks he came to an unknown city where all the bells were tolling a dirge. Although he had never seen them and no one had ever described them to him he immediately recognized the walls eaten away by bone salt, the broken-down wooden balconies gutted by fungus, and nailed to the outside door, almost erased by rain, the saddest cardboard sign in the world: *Funeral Wreaths for Sale*. From that moment until the icy morning when Fernanda left her house under the care of the Mother Superior there was barely enough time for the

nuns to sew her trousseau and in six trunks put the candelabra, the silver service, and the gold chamberpot, along with
the countless and useless remains of a family catastrophe that
had been two centuries late in its fulfillment. Don Fernando
declined the invitation to go along. He promised to go later
when he had cleared up his affairs, and from the moment
when he gave his daughter his blessing he shut himself up in
his study again to write out the announcements with mournful sketches and the family coat of arms, which would be the
first human contact that Fernanda and her father would have
had in all their lives. That was the real date of her birth for
her. For Aureliano Segundo it was almost simultaneously the
beginning and the end of happiness.

Fernanda carried a delicate calendar with small golden
keys on which her spiritual adviser had marked in purple ink
the dates of venereal abstinence. Not counting Holy Week,
Sundays, holy days of obligation, first Fridays, retreats, sacrifices, and cyclical impediments, her effective year was reduced
to forty-two days that were spread out through a web of
purple crosses. Aureliano Segundo, convinced that time
would break up that hostile network, prolonged the wedding
celebration beyond the expected time. Tired of throwing out
so many empty brandy and champagne bottles so that they
would not clutter up the house and at the same time intrigued by the fact that the newlyweds slept at different times
and in separate rooms while the fireworks and music and the
slaughtering of cattle went on, Úrsula remembered her own
experience and wondered whether Fernanda might have a
chastity belt too which would sooner or later provoke jokes in
the town and give rise to a tragedy. But Fernanda confessed
to her that she was just letting two weeks go by before allowing the first contact with her husband. Indeed, when the
period was over, she opened her bedroom with a resignation
worthy of an expiatory victim and Aureliano Segundo saw
the most beautiful woman on earth, with her glorious eyes of

214

a frightened animal and her long, copper-colored hair spread out across the pillow. He was so fascinated with that vision that it took him a moment to realize that Fernanda was wearing a white nightgown that reached down to her ankles, with long sleeves and with a large, round buttonhole, delicately trimmed, at the level of her lower stomach. Aureliano Segundo could not suppress an explosion of laughter.

"That's the most obscene thing I've ever seen in my life," he shouted with a laugh that rang through the house. "I married a Sister of Charity."

A month later, unsuccessful in getting his wife to take off her nightgown, he had the picture taken of Petra Cotes dressed as a queen. Later on, when he succeeded in getting Fernanda to come back home, she gave in to his urges in the fever of reconciliation, but she could not give him the repose he had dreamed about when he went to fetch her in the city with the thirty-two belfries. Aureliano Segundo found only a deep feeling of desolation in her. One night, a short time before their first child was born, Fernanda realized that her husband had returned in secret to the bed of Petra Cotes.

"That's what happened," he admitted. And he explained in a tone of prostrated resignation: "I had to do it so that the animals would keep on breeding."

He needed a little time to convince her about such a strange expedient, but when he finally did so by means of proofs that seemed irrefutable, the only promise that Fernanda demanded from him was that he should not be surprised by death in his concubine's bed. In that way the three of them continued living without bothering each other. Aureliano Segundo, punctual and loving with both of them, Petra Cotes, strutting because of the reconciliation, and Fernanda, pretending that she did not know the truth.

The pact did not succeed, however, in incorporating Fernanda into the family. Úrsula insisted in vain that she take off the woolen ruff which she would have on when she got up from making love and which made the neighbors whisper. She could not convince her to use the bathroom or the night lavatory and sell the gold chamberpot to Colonel Aureliano Buendía so that he could convert it into little fishes. Amaranta felt so uncomfortable with her defective diction and her habit of using euphemisms to designate everything that she would always speak gibberish in front of her.

"Thifisif," she would say, "ifisif onefos ofosif thofosif whosufu cantantant statantand thefesef smufumellu ofosif therisir owfisown shifisifit."

One day, irritated by the mockery, Fernanda wanted to know what Amaranta was saying, and she did not use euphemisms in answering her.

"I was saying," she told her, "that you're one of those people who mix up their ass and their ashes."

From that time on they did not speak to each other again. When circumstances demanded it they would send notes. In spite of the visible hostility of the family, Fernanda did not give up her drive to impose the customs of her ancestors. She put an end to the custom of eating in the kitchen and whenever anyone was hungry, and she imposed the obligation of doing it at regular hours at the large table in the dining room, covered with a linen cloth and with silver candlesticks and table service. The solemnity of an act which Úrsula had considered the most simple one of daily life created a tense atmosphere against which the silent José Arcadio Segundo rebelled before anyone else. But the custom was imposed, the same as that of reciting the rosary before dinner, and it drew the attention of the neighbors, who soon spread the rumor that the Buendías did not sit down to the table like other mortals but had changed the act of eating into a kind of high mass. Even Úrsula's superstitions, with origins that came more from an inspiration of the moment than from tradition, came into conflict with those of Fernanda, who had inherited them from her parents and kept them defined and catalogued for every occasion. As long as Úrsula had full use of her faculties some of the old customs survived and the life of the family kept some quality of her impulsiveness, but when she lost her sight and the weight of her years relegated her to a corner, the circle of rigidity begun by Fernanda from the moment she arrived finally closed completely and no one but she determined the destiny of the family. The business in pastries and small candy animals that Santa Sofía de la Piedad had kept up because of Úrsula's wishes was considered an unworthy activity by Fernanda and she lost no time in putting a stop to it. The doors of the house, wide open from dawn until bedtime, were closed during siesta time under the pretext that the sun heated up the bedrooms and in the end they were closed for good. The aloe branch and loaf of bread that had been hanging over the door since the days of the founding were replaced by a niche with the Sacred Heart of Jesus. Colonel Aureliano Buendía became aware somehow of those changes and foresaw their consequences. "We're becoming people of quality," he protested. "At this rate we'll end up fighting against the Conservative regime again, but this time to install a king in its place." Fernanda very tactfully tried not to cross his path. Within herself she was bothered by his independent spirit, his resistance to all kinds of social rigidity. She was exasperated by his mugs of coffee at five in the morning, the disorder of his workshop, his frayed blanket, and his custom of sitting in the street door at dusk. But she had to tolerate that one loose piece in the family machinery because she was sure that the old colonel was an animal who had been tamed by the years and by disappointment and who, in a burst of senile rebellion, was quite capable of uprooting the foundations of the house. When her husband decided to give their first son the name of his great-grandfather, she did not dare oppose him because she had been there only a year. But when the first daughter was born she expressed her unreserved determination to name her

Renata after her mother. Úrsula had decided to call her Remedios. After a tense argument, in which Aureliano Segundo acted as the laughing go-between, they baptized her with the name Renata Remedios, but Fernanda went on calling her just Renata while her husband's family and everyone in town called her Meme, a diminutive of Remedios.

At first Fernanda did not talk about her family, but in time she began to idealize her father. She spoke of him at the table as an exceptional being who had renounced all forms of vanity and was on his way to becoming a saint. Aureliano Segundo, startled at that unbridled glorification of his father-in-law, could not resist the temptation to make small jokes behind his wife's back. The rest of the family followed his example. Even Úrsula, who was extremely careful to preserve family harmony and who suffered in secret from the domestic friction, once allowed herself the liberty of saying that her little great-great-grandson had his pontifical future assured because he was "the grandson of a saint and the son of a queen and a rustler." In spite of that conspiracy of smiles, the children became accustomed to think of their grandfather as a legendary being who wrote them pious verses in his letters and every Christmas sent them a box of gifts that barely fitted through the outside door. Actually they were the last remains of his lordly inheritance. They used them to build an altar of life-size saints in the children's bedroom, saints with glass eyes that gave them a disquietingly lifelike look, whose artistically embroidered clothing was better than that worn by any inhabitant of Macondo. Little by little the funereal splendor of the ancient and icy mansion was being transformed into the splendor of the House of Buendía. "They've already sent us the whole family cemetery," Aureliano Segundo commented one day. "All we need now are the weeping willows and the tombstones." Although nothing ever arrived in the boxes that the children could play with, they would spend all year waiting for December because, after all, the antique and always unpredictable gifts were something new in the house. On the tenth Christmas, when little José Arcadio was getting ready to go to the seminary, the enormous box from their grandfather arrived earlier than usual, nailed tight and protected with pitch, and addressed in the usual Gothic letters to the Very Distinguished Lady Doña Fernanda del Carpio de Buendía. While she read the letter in her room, the children hastened to open the box. Aided as was customary by Aureliano Segundo, they broke the seals, opened the cover, took out the protective sawdust, and found inside a long lead chest closed by copper bolts. Aureliano Segundo took out the eight bolts as the children watched impatiently, and he barely had time to give a cry and push the children aside when he raised the lead cover and saw Don Fernando, dressed in black and with a crucifix on his chest, his skin broken out in pestilential sores and cooking slowly in a frothy stew with bubbles like live pearls.

A short time after the birth of their daughter, the unexpected jubilee for Colonel Aureliano Buendía, ordered by the government to celebrate another anniversary of the Treaty of Neerlandia, was announced. It was a decision so out of line with official policy that the colonel spoke out violently against it and rejected the homage. "It's the first time I've ever heard of the word 'jubilee,'" he said. "But whatever it means, it has to be a trick." The small goldsmith's shop was filled with emissaries. Much older and more solemn, the lawyers in dark suits who in other days had flapped about the colonel like crows had returned. When he saw them appear, the same as the other time, when they came to put a stop to the war, he could not bear the cynicism of their praise. He ordered them to leave him in peace, insisting that he was not a hero of the nation as they said but an artisan without memories whose only dream was to die of fatigue in the oblivion and misery of his little gold fishes. What made him most indignant was the word that the president of the republic himself planned to be present at the ceremonies in Macondo in order to decorate him with the Order of Merit. Colonel Aureliano Buendía had him told, word for word, that he was eagerly awaiting that tardy but deserved occasion in order to take a shot at him, not as payment for the arbitrary acts and anachronisms of his regime, but for his lack of respect for an old man who had not done anyone any harm. Such was the vehemence with which he made the threat that the president of the republic canceled his trip at the last moment and sent the decoration with a personal representative. Colonel Gerineldo Márquez, besieged by pressures of all kinds, left his bed of a paralytic in order to persuade his former companion in arms. When the latter saw the rocking chair carried by four men appear and saw the friend who had shared his victories and defeats since youth sitting in it among some large pillows, he did not have a single doubt but that he was making that effort in order to express his solidarity. But when he discovered the real motive for his visit he had them take him out of the workshop.

"Now I'm convinced too late," he told him, "that I would have done you a great favor if I'd let them shoot you."

So the jubilee was celebrated without the attendance of any members of the family. Chance had it that it also coincided with carnival week, but no one could get the stubborn idea out of Colonel Aureliano Buendía's head that the coincidence had been foreseen by the government in order to heighten the cruelty of the mockery. From his lonely workshop he could hear the martial music, the artillery salutes, the tolling of the Te Deum, and a few phrases of the speeches delivered in front of the house as they named the street after him. His eyes grew moist with indignation, with angry impotence, and for the first time since his defeat it pained him not to have the strength of youth so that he could begin a bloody war that would wipe out the last vestiges of the Conservative regime. The echoes of the homage had not died down when Úrsula knocked at the workshop door.

"Don't bother me," he said. "I'm busy."

"Open up," Úrsula insisted in a normal voice. "This has nothing to do with the celebration."

Then Colonel Aureliano Buendía took down the bar and saw at the door seventeen men of the most varied appearance, of all types and colors, but all with a solitary air that would have been enough to identify them anywhere on earth. They were his sons. Without any previous agreement, without knowing each other, they had arrived from the most distant corners of the coast, captivated by the talk of the jubilee. They all bore with pride the name Aureliano and the last name of their mothers. The three days that they stayed in the house, to the satisfaction of Úrsula and the scandal of Fernanda, were like a state of war. Amaranta searched among old papers for the ledger where Úrsula had written down the names and birth and baptism dates of all of them, and beside the space for each one she added his present address. That list could well have served as a recapitulation of twenty years of war. From it the nocturnal itinerary of the colonel from the dawn he left Macondo at the head of twenty-one men on his way to a fanciful rebellion until he returned for the last time wrapped in a blanket stiff with blood could have been reconstructed. Aureliano Segundo did not let the chance go by to regale his cousins with a thunderous champagne and accordion party that was interpreted as a tardy adjustment of accounts with the carnival, which went awry because of the jubilee. They smashed half of the dishes, they destroyed the rose bushes as they chased a bull they were trying to hog-tie, they killed the hens by shooting at them, they made Amaranta dance the sad waltzes of Pietro Crespi, they got Remedios the Beauty to put on a pair of men's pants and climb a greased pole, and in the dining room they turned loose a pig daubed with lard, which prostrated Fernanda, but no one regretted the destruction because the house shook with a healthy earthquake. Colonel Aureliano Buendía who at first received them with mistrust and even doubted the parentage of some, was amused by their wildness, and before they left he gave each one a little gold fish. Even the withdrawn José Arcadio Segundo offered them an afternoon of cockfights, which was at the point of ending in tragedy because several of the Aurelianos were so expert in matters of the cockpit that they spotted Father Antonio Isabel's tricks at once. Aureliano Segundo, who saw the limitless prospect of wild times offered by those mad relatives, decided that they should all stay and work for him. The only one who accepted was Aureliano Triste, a big mulatto with the drive and explorer's spirit of his grandfather. He had already tested his fortune in half the world and it did not matter to him where he stayed. The others, even though they were unmarried, considered their destinies established. They were all skillful craftsmen, the men of their houses, peace-loving people. The Ash Wednesday before they went back to scatter out along the coast, Amaranta got them to put on Sunday clothes and accompany her to church. More amused than devout, they let themselves be led to the altar rail where Father Antonio Isabel made the sign of the cross in ashes on them. Back at the house, when the youngest tried to clean his forehead, he discovered that the mark was indelible and so were those of his brothers. They tried soap and water, earth and a scrubbing brush, and lastly a pumice stone and lye, but they could not remove the crosses. On the other hand, Amaranta and the others who had gone to mass took it off without any trouble. "It's better that way," Úrsula stated as she said good-bye to them. "From now on everyone will know who you are." They went off in a troop, preceded by a band of musicians and shooting off fireworks, and they left behind in the town an impression that the Buendía line had enough seed for many centuries. Aureliano Triste, with the cross of ashes on his forehead, set up on the edge of town the ice factory that José Arcadio Buendía had dreamed of in his inventive delirium.

Some months after his arrival, when he was already well-known and well-liked, Aureliano Triste went about looking for a house so that he could send for his mother and an unmarried sister (who was not the colonel's daughter), and he became interested in the run-down big house that looked abandoned on a corner of the square. He asked who owned it. Someone told him that it did not belong to anyone, that in former times a solitary widow who fed on earth and white-wash from the walls had lived there, and that in her last years she was seen only twice on the street with a hat of tiny artificial flowers and shoes the color of old silver when she crossed the square to the post office to mail a letter to the Bishop. They told him that her only companion was a pitiless servant woman who killed dogs and cats and any animal that got into the house and threw their corpses into the middle of the street in order to annoy people with the rotten stench. So much time had passed since the sun had mummified the empty skin of the last animal that everybody took it for granted that the lady of the house and the maid had died long before the wars were over, and that if the house was still standing it was because in recent years there had not been a rough winter or destructive wind. The hinges had crumbled with rust, the doors were held up only by clouds of cobwebs, the windows were soldered shut by dampness, and the floor was broken by grass and wildflowers and in the cracks lizards and all manner of vermin had their nests, all of which seemed to confirm the notion that there had not been a human being there for at least half a century. The impulsive Aureliano Triste did not need such proof to proceed. He pushed on the main door with his shoulder and the worm-eaten wooden frame fell down noiselessly amid a dull cataclysm of dust and termite nests. Aureliano Triste stood on the threshold waiting for the dust to clear and then he saw in the center of the room the squalid woman, still dressed in clothing of the past century, with a few yellow threads on her bald head, and with two large eyes, still beautiful, in which the last stars of hope had gone out, and the skin of her face was wrinkled by the aridity of solitude. Shaken by that vision from another world, Aureliano Triste barely noticed that the woman was aiming an antiquated pistol at him.

"I beg your pardon," he murmured.

She remained motionless in the center of the room filled with knickknacks, examining inch by inch the giant with square shoulders and with a tattoo of ashes on his forehead, and through the haze of dust she saw him in the haze of other times with a double-barreled shotgun on his shoulder and a string of rabbits in his hand.

"For the love of God," she said in a low voice, "it's not right for them to come to me with that memory now."

"I want to rent the house," Aureliano Triste said.

The woman then raised the pistol, aiming with a firm wrist at the cross of ashes, and she held the trigger with a determination against which there was no appeal.

"Get out," she ordered.

That night at dinner Aureliano Triste told the family about the episode and Úrsula wept with consternation. "Holy God!" she exclaimed, clutching her head with her hands. "She's still alive!" Time, wars, the countless everyday disasters had made her forget about Rebeca. The only one who had not lost for a single minute the awareness that she was alive and rotting in her wormhole was the implacable and aging Amaranta. She thought of her at dawn, when the ice of her heart awakened her in her solitary bed, and she thought of her when she soaped her withered breasts and her lean stomach, and when she put on the white stiff-starched petticoats and corsets of old age, and when she changed the black bandage of terrible expiation on her hand. Always, at every moment, asleep and awake, during the most sublime and most abject moments, Amaranta thought about Rebeca, because solitude had made a selection in her memory and had burned the dimming piles of nostalgic waste that life had accumulated in her heart, and had purified, magnified, and eternalized the others, the most bitter ones. Remedios the Beauty knew about Rebeca's existence from her. Every time they passed the run-down house she would tell her about an unpleasant incident, a tale of hate, trying in that way to make her extended rancor be shared by her niece and consequently prolonged beyond death, but her plan did not work because Remedios was immune to any kind of passionate feelings and much less to those of others. Úrsula, on the other hand, who had suffered through a process opposite to Amaranta's, recalled Rebeca with a memory free of impurities, for the image of the pitiful child brought to the house with the bag containing her parents' bones prevailed over the offense that had made her unworthy to be connected to the family tree any longer. Aureliano Segundo decided that they would have to bring her to the house and take care of her, but his good intentions were frustrated by the firm intransigence of Rebeca, who had needed many years of suffering and misery in order to attain the privileges of solitude and who was not disposed to renounce them in exchange for an old age disturbed by the false attractions of charity.

In February, when the sixteen sons of Colonel Aureliano Buendía returned, still marked with the cross of ashes, Aureliano Triste spoke to them about Rebeca in the tumult of the celebration and in half a day they restored the appearance of the house, changing doors and windows, painting the front with gay colors, bracing walls and pouring fresh cement on the floor, but they could not get any authorization to continue the work inside. Rebeca did not even come to the door. She let them finish the mad restoration, then calculated what it had cost and sent Argénida, her old servant who was still with her, to them with a handful of coins that had been withdrawn from circulation after the last war and that Rebeca thought were still worth something. It was then that they saw to what a fantastic point her separation from the world had arrived and they understood that it would be impossible to rescue her from her stubborn enclosure while she still had a breath of life in her.

On the second visit by the sons of Colonel Aureliano Buendía to Macondo, another of them, Aureliano Centeno, stayed on to work with Aureliano Triste. He was one of the first who had been brought to the house for baptism and Úrsula and Amaranta remembered him very well because in a few hours he had destroyed every breakable object that passed through his hands. Time had moderated his early impulse for growth and he was a man of average height marked by smallpox scars, but his amazing power for manual destruction remained intact. He broke so many plates, even without touching them, that Fernanda decided to buy him a set of pewterware before he did away with the last pieces of her expensive china, and even the resistant metal plates were soon dented and twisted. But to make up for that irremediable power, which was exasperating even for him, he had a cordiality that won the immediate confidence of others and a stupendous capacity for work. In a short time he had increased the production of ice to such a degree that it was too much for the local market and Aureliano Triste had to think about the possibility of expanding the business to other towns in the swamp. It was then that he thought of the decisive step, not only for the modernization of his business but to link the town with the rest of the world.

"We have to bring in the railroad," he said.

That was the first time that the word had ever been heard in Macondo. Looking at the sketch that Aureliano Triste drew on the table and that was a direct descendent of the plans with which José Arcadio Buendía had illustrated his project for solar warfare, Úrsula confirmed her impression that time was going in a circle. But unlike his forebear, Aureliano Triste did not lose any sleep or appetite nor did he torment anyone with crises of ill humor, but he considered the most harebrained of projects as immediate possibilities, made rational calculations about costs and dates, and brought them off without any intermediate exasperation. If Aureliano Segundo had something of his great-grandfather in him and lacked something of Colonel Aureliano Buendía, it was an absolute indifference to mockery, and he gave the money to bring the railroad with the same lighthearted air with which he had given it for his brother's absurd navigation project. Aureliano Triste consulted the calendar and left the following Wednesday, planning to return after the rains had passed. There was no more news of him. Aureliano Centeno, overwhelmed by the abundance of the factory, had already begun to experiment with the production of ice with a base of fruit juices instead of water, and without knowing it or thinking about it, he conceived the essential fundamentals for the invention of sherbet. In that way he planned to diversify the production of an enterprise he considered his own, because his brother showed no signs of returning after the rains had passed and a whole summer had gone by with no news of him. At the start of another winter, however, a woman who was washing clothes in the river during the hottest time of the day ran screaming down the main street in an alarming state of commotion.

"It's coming," she finally explained. "Something frightful, like a kitchen dragging a village behind it."

At that moment the town was shaken by a whistle with a fearful echo and a loud, panting respiration. During the previous weeks they had seen the gangs who were laying ties and tracks and no one paid attention to them because they thought it was some new trick of the gypsies, coming back with whistles and tambourines and their age-old and discredited song and dance about the qualities of some concoction put together by journeyman geniuses of Jerusalem. But when they recovered from the noise of the whistles and the snorting, all the inhabitants ran out into the street and saw Aureliano Triste waving from the locomotive, and in a trance they saw the flower-bedecked train which was arriving for the first time eight months late. The innocent yellow train that was to bring so many ambiguities and certainties, so many pleasant and unpleasant moments, so many changes, calamities, and feelings of nostalgia to Macondo.

DAZZLED BY SO MANY and such marvelous inventions, the people of Macondo did not know where their amazement began. They stayed up all night looking at the pale electric bulbs fed by the plant that Aureliano Triste had brought back when the train made its second trip, and it took time and effort for them to grow accustomed to its obsessive *toom-toom*. They became indignant over the living images that the prosperous merchant Bruno Crespi projected in the theater with the lion-head ticket windows, for a character who had died and was buried in one film and for whose misfortune tears of affliction had been shed would reappear alive and transformed into an Arab in the next one. The audience, who paid two cents apiece to share the difficulties of the actors, would not tolerate that outlandish fraud and they broke up the seats. The mayor, at the urging of Bruno Crespi, explained in a proclamation that the cinema was a machine of illusions that did not merit the emotional outbursts of the audience. With that discouraging explanation many felt that they had been the victims of some new and showy gypsy business and they decided not to return to the movies, considering that they already had too many troubles of their own to weep over the acted-out misfortunes of imaginary beings. Something similar happened with the cylinder phonographs that the merry matrons from France brought with them as a substitute for the antiquated hand organs and that for a time had serious effects on the livelihood of the band of musicians. At first curiosity increased the clientele on the forbidden street and there was even word of respectable ladies who disguised themselves as workers in order to observe the novelty of the phonograph from first hand, but from so much and such close observation they soon reached the conclusion that it was not an enchanted mill as everyone had thought and as the matrons had said, but a mechanical trick that could not be compared with something so moving, so human, and so full of everyday truth as a band of musicians. It was such a serious disappointment that when phonographs became so popular that there was one in every house they were not considered objects for amusement for adults but as something good for children to take apart. On the other hand, when someone from the town had the opportunity to test the crude reality of the telephone installed in the railroad station, which was thought to be a rudimentary version of the phonograph because of its crank, even the most incredulous were upset. It was as if God had decided to put to the test every capacity for surprise and was keeping the inhabitants of Macondo in a permanent alternation between excitement and disappointment, doubt and revelation, to such an extreme that no one knew for certain where the limits of reality lay. It was an intricate stew of truths and mirages that convulsed the ghost of José Arcadio Buendía under the chestnut tree with impatience and made him wander all through the house even in broad daylight. Ever since the railroad had been officially inaugurated and had begun to arrive with regularity on Wednesdays at eleven o'clock and the primitive wooden station with a desk, a telephone, and a ticket window had been built, on the streets of Macondo men and women were seen who had adopted everyday and normal customs and manners but who really looked like people out of a circus. In a town that had chafed under the tricks of the gypsies there was no future for those ambulatory acrobats of commerce who with equal effrontery offered a whistling kettle and a daily regime that would assure the salvation of the soul on the seventh day; but from those who let themselves be convinced out of fatigue and the ones who were always unwary, they reaped stupendous benefits. Among those theatrical creatures, wearing riding breeches and leggings, a pith helmet and steel-rimmed glasses, with topaz eyes and the skin of a thin rooster, there arrived in Macondo on one of so many Wednesdays the chubby and smiling Mr. Herbert, who ate at the house.

No one had noticed him at the table until the first bunch of bananas had been eaten. Aureliano Segundo had come across him by chance as he protested in broken Spanish because there were no rooms at the Hotel Jacob, and as he frequently did with strangers, he took him home. He was in the captive-balloon business, which had taken him halfway around the world with excellent profits, but he had not succeeded in taking anyone up in Macondo because they considered that invention backward after having seen and tried the gypsies' flying carpets. He was leaving, therefore, on the next train. When they brought to the table the tiger-striped bunch of bananas that they were accustomed to hang in the dining room during lunch, he picked the first piece of fruit without great enthusiasm. But he kept on eating as he spoke, tasting, chewing, more with the distraction of a wise man than with the delight of a good eater, and when he finished the first bunch he asked them to bring him another. Then he took a small case with optical instruments out of the toolbox that he always carried with him. With the suspicious attention of a diamond merchant he examined the banana meticulously, dissecting it with a special scalpel, weighing the pieces on a pharmacist's scale, and calculating its breadth with a gunsmith's calipers. Then he took a series of instruments out of the chest with which he measured the temperature, the level of humidity in the atmosphere, and the intensity of the light. It was such an intriguing ceremony that no one could eat in peace as everybody waited for Mr. Herbert to pass a final and revealing judgment, but he did not say anything that allowed anyone to guess his intentions.

On the days that followed he was seen with a net and a small basket, hunting butterflies on the outskirts of town. On Wednesday a group of engineers, agronomists, hydrologists, topographers, and surveyors arrived who for several weeks explored the places where Mr. Herbert had hunted his butterflies. Later on Mr. Jack Brown arrived in an extra coach that had been coupled onto the yellow train and that was silver-plated all over, with seats of episcopal velvet, and a roof of blue glass. Also arriving on the special car, fluttering around Mr. Brown, were the solemn lawyers dressed in black who in different times had followed Colonel Aureliano Buendía everywhere, and that led the people to think that the agronomists, hydrologists, topographers, and surveyors, like Mr. Herbert with his captive balloons and his colored butterflies and Mr. Brown with his mausoleum on wheels and his ferocious German shepherd dogs, had something to do with the war. There was not much time to think about it, however, because the suspicious inhabitants of Macondo barely began to wonder what the devil was going on when the town had already become transformed into an encampment of wooden houses with zinc roofs inhabited by foreigners who arrived on the train from halfway around the world, riding not only on the seats and platforms but even on the roof of the coaches. The gringos, who later on brought their languid wives in muslin dresses and large veiled hats, built a separate town across the railroad tracks with streets lined with palm trees, houses with screened windows, small white tables on the terraces, and fans mounted on the ceilings, and extensive blue lawns with peacocks and quails. The section was surrounded by a metal fence topped with a band of electrified chicken wire which during the cool summer mornings would be black with roasted swallows. No one knew yet what they were after, or whether they were actually nothing but philanthropists, and they had already caused a colossal disturbance, much more than that of the old gypsies, but less transitory and understandable. Endowed with means that had been reserved for Divine Providence in former times, they changed the pattern of the rains, accelerated the cycle of harvests, and moved the river from where it had always been and put it with its white stones and icy currents on the other side of the town, behind the cemetery. It was at that time that they built a fortress of reinforced concrete over the faded tomb of José Arcadio, so that the corpse's smell of powder would not contaminate the waters. For the foreigners who arrived without love they converted the street of the loving matrons from France into a more extensive village than it had been, and on one glorious Wednesday they brought in a trainload of strange whores, Babylonish women skilled in age-old methods and in possession of all manner of unguents and devices to stimulate the unaroused, to give courage to the timid, to satiate the voracious, to exalt the modest man, to teach a lesson to repeaters, and to correct solitary people. The Street of the Turks, enriched by well-lit stores with products from abroad, displacing the old bazaars with their bright colors, overflowed on Saturday nights with the crowds of adventurers

I

who bumped into each other among gambling tables, shooting galleries, the alley where the future was guessed and dreams interpreted, and tables of fried food and drinks, and on Sunday mornings there were scattered on the ground bodies that were sometimes those of happy drunkards and more often those of onlookers felled by shots, fists, knives, and bottles during the brawls. It was such a tumultuous and intemperate invasion that during the first days it was impossible to walk through the streets because of the furniture and trunks, and the noise of the carpentry of those who were building their houses in any vacant lot without asking anyone's permission, and the scandalous behavior of couples who hung their hammocks between the almond trees and made love under the netting in broad daylight and in view of everyone. The only serene corner had been established by peaceful West Indian Negroes, who built a marginal street with wooden houses on piles where they would sit in the doors at dusk singing melancholy hymns in their disordered gabble. So many changes took place in such a short time that eight months after Mr. Herbert's visit the old inhabitants had a hard time recognizing their own town.

"Look at the mess we've got ourselves into," Colonel Aureliano Buendía said at that time, "just because we invited a gringo to eat some bananas."

Aureliano Segundo, on the other hand, could not contain his happiness over the avalanche of foreigners. The house was suddenly filled with unknown guests, with invincible and worldly carousers, and it became necessary to add bedrooms off the courtyard, widen the dining room, and exchange the old table for one that held sixteen people, with new china and silver, and even then they had to eat lunch in shifts. Fernanda had to swallow her scruples and treat guests of the worst sort like kings as they muddied the porch with their boots, urinated in the garden, laid their mats down anywhere to take their siesta, and spoke without regard for the sensitivi-

234

ties of ladies or the proper behavior of gentlemen. Amaranta was so scandalized with the plebeian invasion that she went back to eating in the kitchen as in olden days. Colonel Aureliano Buendía, convinced that the majority of those who came into his workshop to greet him were not doing it because of sympathy or regard but out of the curiosity to meet a historical relic, a museum fossil, decided to shut himself in by barring the door and he was not seen any more except on very rare occasions when he would sit at the street door. Úrsula, on the other hand, even during the days when she was already dragging her feet and walking about groping along the walls, felt a juvenile excitement as the time for the arrival of the train approached. "We have to prepare some meat and fish," she would order the four cooks, who hastened to have everything ready under the imperturbable direction of Santa Sofía de la Piedad. "We have to prepare everything," she insisted, "because we never know what these strangers like to eat." The train arrived during the hottest time of day. At lunchtime the house shook with the bustle of a marketplace, and the perspiring guests—who did not even know who their hosts were—trooped in to occupy the best places at the table, while the cooks bumped into each other with enormous kettles of soup, pots of meat, large gourds filled with vegetables, and troughs of rice, and passed around the contents of barrels of lemonade with inexhaustible ladles. The disorder was such that Fernanda was troubled by the idea that many were eating twice and on more than one occasion she was about to burst out with a vegetable hawker's insults because someone at the table in confusion asked her for the check. More than a year had gone by since Mr. Herbert's visit and the only thing that was known was that the gringos were planning to plant banana trees in the enchanted region that José Arcadio Buendía and his men had crossed in search of the route to the great inventions. Two other sons of Colonel Aureliano Buendía, with the cross of ashes on their foreheads, arrived, drawn by that great volcanic belch, and they justified their determination with a phrase that may have explained everybody's reasons.

"We came," they said, "because everyone is coming."

Remedios the Beauty was the only one who was immune to the banana plague. She was becalmed in a magnificent adolescence, more and more impenetrable to formality, more and more indifferent to malice and suspicion, happy in her own world of simple realities. She did not understand why women complicated their lives with corsets and petticoats, so she sewed herself a coarse cassock that she simply put over her and without further difficulties resolved the problem of dress, without taking away the feeling of being naked, which according to her lights was the only decent way to be when at home. They bothered her so much to cut the rain of hair that already reached to her thighs and to make rolls with combs and braids with red ribbons that she simply shaved her head and used the hair to make wigs for the saints. The startling thing about her simplifying instinct was that the more she did away with fashion in a search for comfort and the more she passed over conventions as she obeyed spontaneity, the more disturbing her incredible beauty became and the more provocative she became to men. When the sons of Colonel Aureliano Buendía were in Macondo for the first time, Úrsula remembered that in their veins they bore the same blood as her great-granddaughter and she shuddered with a forgotten fright. "Keep your eyes wide open," she warned her. "With any of them your children will come out with the tail of a pig." The girl paid such little attention to the warning that she dressed up as a man and rolled around in the sand in order to climb the greased pole, and she was at the point of bringing on a tragedy among the seventeen cousins, who were driven mad by the unbearable spectacle. That was why none of them slept at the house when they visited the town and the four who had stayed lived in rented rooms at Úrsula's insistence. Remedios the Beauty, however, would have died laughing if she had known about that precaution. Until her last moment on earth she was unaware that her irreparable fate as a disturbing woman was a daily disaster. Every time she appeared in the dining room, against Úrsula's orders, she caused a panic of exasperation among the outsiders. It was all too evident that she was completely naked underneath her crude nightshirt and no one could understand that her shaved and perfect skull was not some kind of challenge, and that the boldness with which she uncovered her thighs to cool off was not a criminal provocation, nor was her pleasure when she sucked her fingers after eating. What no member of the family ever knew was that the strangers did not take long to realize that Remedios the Beauty gave off a breath of perturbation, a tormenting breeze that was still perceptible several hours after she had passed by. Men expert in the disturbances of love, experienced all over the world, stated that they had never suffered an anxiety similar to the one produced by the natural smell of Remedios the Beauty. On the porch with the begonias, in the parlor, in any place in the house, it was possible to point out the exact place where she had been and the time that had passed since she had left it. It was a definite, unmistakable trace that no one in the family could distinguish because it had been incorporated into the daily odors for a long time, but it was one that the outsiders identified immediately. They were the only ones, therefore, who understood how the young commander of the guard had died of love and how a gentleman from a faraway land had been plunged into desperation. Unaware of the restless circle in which she moved, of the unbearable state of intimate calamity that she provoked as she passed by, Remedios the Beauty treated the men without the least bit of malice and in the end upset them with her innocent complaisance. When Úrsula succeeded in imposing the command that she eat with Amaranta in the kitchen so that the outsiders would not see her, she felt more comfortable, because, after all, she was beyond all discipline. In reality, it made no difference to her where she ate, and not at regular hours but according to the whims of her appetite. Sometimes she would get up to have lunch at three in the morning, sleep all day long, and she spent several months with her timetable all in disarray until some casual incident would bring her back into the order of things. When things were going better she would get up at eleven o'clock in the morning and shut herself up until two o'clock, completely nude, in the bathroom, killing scorpions as she came out of her dense and prolonged sleep. Then she would throw water from the cistern over herself with a gourd. It was an act so prolonged, so meticulous, so rich in ceremonial aspects that one who did not know her well would have thought that she was given over to the deserved adoration of her own body. For her, however, that solitary rite lacked all sensuality and was simply a way of passing the time until she was hungry. One day, as she began to bathe herself, a stranger lifted a tile from the roof and was breathless at the tremendous spectacle of her nudity. She saw his desolate eyes through the broken tiles and had no reaction of shame but rather one of alarm.

"Be careful," she exclaimed. "You'll fall."

"I just wanted to see you," the foreigner murmured.

"Oh, all right," she said. "But be careful, those tiles are rotten."

The stranger's face had a pained expression of stupor and he seemed to be battling silently against his primary instincts so as not to break up the mirage. Remedios the Beauty thought that he was suffering from the fear that the tiles would break and she bathed herself more quickly than usual so that the man would not be in danger. While she was pouring water from the cistern she told him that the roof was in that state because she thought that the bed of leaves had been rotted by the rain and that was what was filling the bathroom

238

with scorpions. The stranger thought that her small talk was a way of covering her complaisance, so that when she began to soap herself he gave into temptation and went a step further.

"Let me soap you," he murmured.

"Thank you for your good intentions," she said, "but my two hands are quite enough."

"Even if it's just your back," the foreigner begged.

"That would be silly," she said. "People never soap their backs."

Then, while she was drying herself, the stranger begged her, with his eyes full of tears, to marry him. She answered him sincerely that she would never marry a man who was so simple that he had wasted almost an hour and even went without lunch just to see a woman taking a bath. Finally, when she put on her cassock, the man could not bear the proof that, indeed, she was not wearing anything underneath, as everyone had suspected, and he felt himself marked forever with the white-hot iron of that secret. Then he took two more tiles off in order to drop down into the bathroom.

"It's very high," she warned him in fright. "You'll kill yourself!"

The rotten tiles broke with a noise of disaster and the man barely had time to let out a cry of terror as he cracked his skull and was killed outright on the cement floor. The foreigners who heard the noise in the dining room and hastened to remove the body noticed the suffocating odor of Remedios the Beauty on his skin. It was so deep in his body that the cracks in his skull did not give off blood but an amber-colored oil that was impregnated with that secret perfume, and then they understood that the smell of Remedios the Beauty kept on torturing men beyond death, right down to the dust of their bones. Nevertheless, they did not relate that horrible accident to the other two men who had died because of Remedios the Beauty. A victim was still needed before the outsiders and many of the old inhabitants of Macondo would credit the legend that Remedios Buendía did not give off a breath of love but a fatal emanation. The occasion for the proof of it came some months later on one afternoon when Remedios the Beauty went with a group of girl friends to look at the new plantings. For the girls of Macondo that novel game was reason for laughter and surprises, frights and jokes, and at night they would talk about their walk as if it had been an experience in a dream. Such was the prestige of that silence that Úrsula did not have the heart to take the fun away from Remedios the Beauty, and she let her go one afternoon, providing that she wore a hat and a decent dress. As soon as the group of friends went into the plantings the air became impregnated with a fatal fragrance. The men who were working along the rows felt possessed by a strange fascination, menaced by some invisible danger, and many succumbed to a terrible desire to weep. Remedios the Beauty and her startled friends managed to take refuge in a nearby house just as they were about to be assaulted by a pack of ferocious males. A short time later they were rescued by the four Aurelianos, whose crosses of ash inspired a sacred respect, as if they were caste marks, stamps of invulnerability. Remedios the Beauty did not tell anyone that one of the men, taking advantage of the tumult, had managed to attack her stomach with a hand that was more like the claw of an eagle clinging to the edge of a precipice. She faced the attacker in a kind of instantaneous flash and saw the disconsolate eyes, which remained stamped on her heart like the hot coals of pity. That night the man boasted of his audacity and swaggered over his good luck on the Street of the Turks a few minutes before the kick of a horse crushed his chest and a crowd of outsiders saw him die in the middle of the street, drowned in his own bloody vomiting.

The supposition that Remedios the Beauty possessed powers of death was then borne out by four irrefutable events.

Although some men who were easy with their words said that it was worth sacrificing one's life for a night of love with such an arousing woman, the truth was that no one made any effort to do so. Perhaps, not only to attain her but also to conjure away her dangers, all that was needed was a feeling as primitive and as simple as that of love, but that was the only thing that did not occur to anyone. Úrsula did not worry about her any more. On another occasion, when she had not yet given up the idea of saving her for the world, she had tried to get her interested in basic domestic affairs. "Men demand much more than you think," she would tell her enigmatically. "There's a lot of cooking, a lot of sweeping, a lot of suffering over little things beyond what you think." She was deceiving herself within, trying to train her for domestic happiness because she was convinced that once his passion was satisfied there would not be a man on the face of the earth capable of tolerating even for a day a negligence that was beyond all understanding. The birth of the latest José Arcadio and her unshakable will to bring him up to be Pope finally caused her to cease worrying about her great-granddaughter. She abandoned her to her fate, trusting that sooner or later a miracle would take place and that in this world of everything there would also be a man with enough sloth to put up with her. For a long time already Amaranta had given up trying to make her into a useful woman. Since those forgotten afternoons when her niece barely had enough interest to turn the crank on the sewing machine, she had reached the conclusion that she was simpleminded. "We're going to have to raffle you off," she would tell her, perplexed at the fact that men's words would not penetrate her. Later on, when Úrsula insisted that Remedios the Beauty go to mass with her face covered with a shawl, Amaranta thought that a mysterious recourse like that would turn out to be so provoking that soon a man would come who would be intrigued enough to search out patiently for the weak point of her heart. But

1*

when she saw the stupid way in which she rejected a pre-
tender who for many reasons was more desirable than a
prince, she gave up all hope. Fernanda did not even make
any attempt to understand her. When she saw Remedios the
Beauty dressed as a queen at the bloody carnival she thought
that she was an extraordinary creature. But when she saw her
eating with her hands, incapable of giving an answer that was
not a miracle of simplemindedness, the only thing that she
lamented was the fact that the idiots in the family lived so
long. In spite of the fact that Colonel Aureliano Buendía kept
on believing and repeating that Remedios the Beauty was in
reality the most lucid being that he had ever known and that
she showed it at every moment with her startling ability to
put things over on everyone, they let her go her own way.
Remedios the Beauty stayed there wandering through the
desert of solitude, bearing no cross on her back, maturing in
her dreams without nightmares, her interminable baths, her
unscheduled meals, her deep and prolonged silences that had
no memory until one afternoon in March, when Fernanda
wanted to fold her brabant sheets in the garden and asked the
women in the house for help. She had just begun when
Amaranta noticed that Remedios the Beauty was covered all
over by an intense paleness.

"Don't you feel well?" she asked her.

Remedios the Beauty, who was clutching the sheet by the
other end, gave a pitying smile.

"Quite the opposite," she said, "I never felt better."

She had just finished saying it when Fernanda felt a delicate
wind of light pull the sheets out of her hands and open them
up wide. Amaranta felt a mysterious trembling in the lace on
her petticoats and she tried to grasp the sheet so that she
would not fall down at the instant in which Remedios the
Beauty began to rise. Úrsula, almost blind at the time, was
the only person who was sufficiently calm to identify the
nature of that determined wind and she left the sheets to the

mercy of the light as she watched Remedios the Beauty waving good-bye in the midst of the flapping sheets that rose up with her, abandoning with her the environment of beetles and dahlias and passing through the air with her as four o'clock in the afternoon came to an end, and they were lost forever with her in the upper atmosphere where not even the highest-flying birds of memory could reach her.

The outsiders, of course, thought that Remedios the Beauty had finally succumbed to her irrevocable fate of a queen bee and that her family was trying to save her honor with that tale of levitation. Fernanda, burning with envy, finally accepted the miracle, and for a long time she kept on praying to God to send her back her sheets. Most people believed in the miracle and they even lighted candles and celebrated novenas. Perhaps there might have been talk of nothing else for a long time if the barbarous extermination of the Aurelianos had not replaced amazement with horror. Although he had never thought of it as an omen, Colonel Aureliano Buendía had foreseen the tragic end of his sons in a certain way. When Aureliano Serrador and Aureliano Arcaya, the two who arrived during the tumult, expressed a wish to stay in Macondo, their father tried to dissuade them. He could not understand what they were going to do in a town that had been transformed into a dangerous place overnight. But Aureliano Centeno and Aureliano Triste, backed by Aureliano Segundo, gave them work in their businesses. Colonel Aureliano Buendía had reasons that were still very confused and were against that determination. When he saw Mr. Brown in the first automobile to reach Macondo—an orange convertible with a horn that frightened the dogs with its bark—the old soldier grew indignant with the servile excitement of the people and he realized that something had changed in the makeup of the men since the days when they would leave their wives and children and toss a shotgun on their shoulders to go off to war. The local authorities, after the armistice of Neerlandia, were mayors without initiative, decorative judges picked from among the peaceful and tired Conservatives of Macondo. "This is a regime of wretches," Colonel Aureliano Buendía would comment when he saw the barefoot policemen armed with wooden clubs pass. "We fought all those wars and all of it just so that we didn't have to paint our houses blue." When the banana company arrived, however, the local functionaries were replaced by dictatorial foreigners whom Mr. Brown brought to live in the electrified chicken yard so that they could enjoy, as he explained it, the dignity that their status warranted and so that they would not suffer from the heat and the mosquitoes and the countless discomforts and privations of the town. The old policemen were replaced by hired assassins with machetes. Shut up in his workshop, Colonel Aureliano Buendía thought about those changes and for the first time in his quiet years of solitude he was tormented by the definite certainty that it had been a mistake not to have continued the war to its final conclusion. During that time a brother of the forgotten Colonel Magnífico Visbal was taking his seven-year-old grandson to get a soft drink at one of the pushcarts on the square and because the child accidentally bumped into a corporal of police and spilled the drink on his uniform, the barbarian cut him to pieces with his machete, and with one stroke he cut off the head of the grandfather as he tried to stop him. The whole town saw the decapitated man pass by as a group of men carried him to his house, with a woman dragging the head along by its hair, and the bloody sack with the pieces of the child.

For Colonel Aureliano Buendía it meant the limits of atonement. He suddenly found himself suffering from the same indignation that he had felt in his youth over the body of the woman who had been beaten to death because she had been bitten by a rabid dog. He looked at the groups of bystanders in front of the house and with his old stentorian voice, restored by a deep disgust with himself, he unloaded upon them the burden of hate that he could no longer bear in his heart.

"One of these days," he shouted, "I'm going to arm my boys so we can get rid of these shitty gringos!"

During the course of that week, at different places along the coast, his seventeen sons were hunted down like rabbits by invisible criminals who aimed at the center of their crosses of ash. Aureliano Triste was leaving the house with his mother at seven in the evening when a rifle shot came out of the darkness and perforated his forehead. Aureliano Centeno was found in the hammock that he was accustomed to hang up in the factory with an icepick between his eyebrows driven in up to the handle. Aureliano Serrador had left his girl friend at her parents' house after having taken her to the movies and was returning through the well-lighted Street of the Turks when someone in the crowd who was never identified fired a revolver shot which knocked him over into a caldron of boiling lard. A few minutes later someone knocked at the door of the room where Aureliano Arcaya was shut up with a woman and shouted to him: "Hurry up, they're killing your brothers." The woman who was with him said later that Aureliano Arcaya jumped out of bed and opened the door and was greeted with the discharge of a Mauser that split his head open. On that night of death, while the house was preparing to hold a wake for the four corpses, Fernanda ran through the town like a madwoman looking for Aureliano Segundo, whom Petra Cotes had locked up in a closet, thinking that the order of extermination included all who bore the colonel's name. She would not let him out until the fourth day, when the telegrams received from different places along the coast made it clear that the fury of the invisible enemy was directed only at the brothers marked with the crosses of ash. Amaranta fetched the ledger where she had written down the facts about her nephews and as the telegrams arrived she drew lines through the names until only that of the eldest remained. They remembered him very well because of the contrast between his dark skin and his green eyes. His name was Aureliano Amador and he was a carpenter, living in a village hidden in the foothills. After waiting two weeks for the telegram telling of his death, Aureliano Segundo sent a messenger to him in order to warn him, thinking that he might not know about the threat that hung over him. The emissary returned with the news that Aureliano Amador was safe. The night of the extermination two men had gone to get him at his house and had shot at him with their revolvers but they had missed the cross of ashes. Aureliano Amador had been able to leap over the wall of the courtyard and was lost in the labyrinth of the mountains, which he knew like the back of his hand thanks to the friendship he maintained with the Indians, from whom he bought wood. Nothing more was heard of him.

Those were dark days for Colonel Aureliano Buendía. The president of the republic sent him a telegram of condolence in which he promised an exhaustive investigation and paid homage to the dead men. At his command, the mayor appeared at the services with four funeral wreaths, which he tried to place on the coffins, but the colonel ordered him into the street. After the burial he drew up and personally submitted to the president of the republic a violent telegram, which the telegrapher refused to send. Then he enriched it with terms of singular aggressiveness, put it in an envelope, and mailed it. As had happened with the death of his wife, as had happened to him so many times during the war with the deaths of his best friends, he did not have a feeling of sorrow but a blind and directionless rage, a broad feeling of impotence. He even accused Father Antonio Isabel of complicity for having marked his sons with indelible ashes so that they could be identified by their enemies. The decrepit priest, who could no longer string ideas together and who was beginning to startle his parishioners with the wild interpretations he gave from the pulpit, appeared one afternoon at the house with the goblet in which he had prepared the ashes that Wednesday and he tried to anoint the whole family with them to show that they could be washed off with water. But the horror of the misfortune had penetrated so deeply that not even Fernanda would let him experiment on her and never again was a Buendía seen to kneel at the altar rail on Ash Wednesday.

Colonel Aureliano Buendía did not recover his calm for a long time. He abandoned the manufacture of little fishes, ate with great difficulty, and wandered all through the house as if walking in his sleep, dragging his blanket and chewing on his quiet rage. At the end of three months his hair was ashen, his old waxed mustache poured down beside his colorless lips, but, on the other hand, his eyes were once more the burning coals that had startled those who had seen him born and that in other days had made chairs rock with a simple glance. In the fury of his torment he tried futilely to rouse the omens that had guided his youth along dangerous paths into the desolate wasteland of glory. He was lost, astray in a strange house where nothing and no one now stirred in him the slightest vestige of affection. Once he opened Melquíades' room, looking for the traces of a past from before the war, and he found only rubble, trash, piles of waste accumulated over all the years of abandonment. Between the covers of the books that no one had ever read again, in the old parchments damaged by dampness, a livid flower had prospered, and in the air that had been the purest and brightest in the house an unbearable smell of rotten memories floated. One morning he found Úrsula weeping under the chestnut tree at the knees of her dead husband. Colonel Aureliano Buendía was the only inhabitant of the house who still did not see the powerful old man who had been beaten down by half a century in the open air. "Say hello to your father," Úrsula told him. He stopped for an instant in front of the chestnut tree and once again he saw that the empty space before him did not arouse an affection either.

"What does he say?" he asked.

"He's very sad," Úrsula answered, "because he thinks that you're going to die."

"Tell him," the colonel said, smiling, "that a person doesn't die when he should but when he can."

The omen of the dead father stirred up the last remnant of pride that was left in his heart, but he confused it with a sudden gust of strength. It was for that reason that he hounded Úrsula to tell him where in the courtyard the gold coins that they had found inside the plaster Saint Joseph were buried. "You'll never know," she told him with a firmness inspired by an old lesson. "One day," she added, "the owner of that fortune will appear and only he can dig it up." No one knew why a man who had always been so generous had begun to covet money with such anxiety, and not the modest amounts that would have been enough to resolve an emergency, but a fortune of such mad size that the mere mention of it left Aureliano Segundo awash in amazement. His old fellow party members, to whom he went asking for help, hid so as not to receive him. It was around that time that he was heard to say: "The only difference today between Liberals and Conservatives is that the Liberals go to mass at five o'clock and the Conservatives at eight." Nevertheless, he insisted with such perseverence, begged in such a way, broke his code of dignity to such a degree, that with a little help from here and a little more from there, sneaking about everywhere, with a slippery diligence and a pitiless perseverance, he managed to put together in eight months more money than Úrsula had buried. Then he visited the ailing Colonel Gerineldo Márquez so that he would help him start the total war.

At a certain time Colonel Gerineldo Márquez was really

the only one who could have pulled, even from his paralytic's chair, the musty strings of rebellion. After the armistice of Neerlandia, while Colonel Aureliano Buendía took refuge with his little gold fishes, he kept in touch with the rebel officers who had been faithful to him until the defeat. With them he waged the sad war of daily humiliation, of entreaties and petitions, of come-back-tomorrow, of any-time-now, of we're-studying-your-case-with-the-proper-attention; the war hopelessly lost against the many yours-most-trulys who should have signed and would never sign the lifetime pensions. The other war, the bloody one of twenty years, did not cause them as much damage as the corrosive war of eternal postponements. Even Colonel Gerineldo Márquez, who escaped three attempts on his life, survived five wounds, and emerged unscathed from innumerable battles, succumbed to that atrocious siege of waiting and sank into the miserable defeat of old age, thinking of Amaranta among the diamond-shaped patches of light in a borrowed house. The last veterans of whom he had word had appeared photographed in a newspaper with their faces shamelessly raised beside an anonymous president of the republic who gave them buttons with his likeness on them to wear in their lapels and returned to them a flag soiled with blood and gunpowder so that they could place it on their coffins. The others, more honorable, were still waiting for a letter in the shadow of public charity, dying of hunger, living through rage, rotting of old age amid the exquisite shit of glory. So that when Colonel Aureliano Buendía invited him to start a mortal conflagration that would wipe out all vestiges of a regime of corruption and scandal backed by the foreign invader, Colonel Gerineldo Márquez could not hold back a shudder of compassion.

"Oh, Aureliano," he sighed. "I already knew that you were old, but now I realize that you're a lot older than you look."

In the bewilderment of her last years, Úrsula had had very little free time to attend to the papal education of José Arcadio, and the time came for him to get ready to leave for the seminary right away. Meme, his sister, dividing her time between Fernanda's rigidity and Amaranta's bitterness, at almost the same moment reached the age set for her to be sent to the nuns' school, where they would make a virtuoso on the clavichord of her. Úrsula felt tormented by grave doubts concerning the effectiveness of the methods with which she had molded the spirit of the languid apprentice Supreme Pontiff, but she did not put the blame on her staggering old age or the dark clouds that barely permitted her to make out the shape of things, but on something that she herself could not really define and that she conceived confusedly as a progressive breakdown of time. "The years nowadays don't pass the way the old ones used to," she would say, feeling that everyday reality was slipping through her hands. In the past, she thought, children took a long time to grow up. All one had to do was remember all the time needed for José Arcadio, the elder, to go away with the gypsies and all that happened before he came back painted like a snake and talking like an astronomer, and the things that happened in the house before Amaranta and Arcadio forgot the language of the Indians and learned Spanish. One had to see only the days of sun and dew that poor José Arcadio Buendía went through under the chestnut tree and all the time needed to mourn his death before they brought in a dying Colonel Aureliano Buendía, who after so much war and so much suffering from it was still not fifty years of age. In other times, after spending the whole day making candy animals, she had more than enough time for the children, to see from the whites of their eyes that they needed a dose of castor oil. Now, however, when she had nothing to do and would go about with José Arcadio riding on her hip from dawn to dusk, this bad kind of time compelled her to leave things half done. The truth was that Úrsula resisted growing old even when she had already lost count of her age and she was a bother on all sides as she tried to meddle in everything and as she annoyed strangers with her questions as to whether they had left a plaster Saint Joseph to be kept until the rains were over during the days of the war. No one knew exactly when she had begun to lose her sight. Even in her later years, when she could no longer get out of bed, it seemed that she was simply defeated by decrepitude, but no one discovered that she was blind. She had noticed it before the birth of José Arcadio. At first she thought it was a matter of a passing debility and she secretly took marrow syrup and put honey on her eyes, but quite soon she began to realize that she was irrevocably sinking into the darkness, to a point where she never had a clear notion of the invention of the electric light, for when they put in the first bulbs she was only able to perceive the glow. She did not tell anyone about it because it would have been a public recognition of her uselessness. She concentrated on a silent schooling in the distances of things and people's voices, so that she would still be able to see with her memory what the shadows of her cataracts no longer allowed her to. Later on she was to discover the unforeseen help of odors, which were defined in the shadows with a strength that was much more convincing than that of bulk and color, and which saved her finally from the shame of admitting defeat. In the darkness of the room she was able to thread a needle and sew a buttonhole and she knew when the milk was about to boil. She knew with so much certainty the location of everything that she herself forgot that she was blind at times. On one occasion Fernanda had the whole house upset because she had lost her wedding ring, and Úrsula found it on a shelf in the children's bedroom. Quite simply, while the others were going carelessly all about, she watched them with her four senses so that they never took her by surprise, and after some time she discovered that every member of the family, without realizing it, repeated the same path every day, the same actions, and almost repeated the same words at the same hour. Only when they deviated from meticulous routine did they run the risk of losing something. So when she heard Fernanda all upset because she had lost her ring, Úrsula remembered that the only thing different that she had done that day was to put the mattresses out in the sun because Meme had found a bedbug the night before. Since the children had been present at the fumigation, Úrsula figured that Fernanda had put the ring in the only place where they could not reach it: the shelf. Fernanda, on the other hand, looked for it in vain along the paths of her everyday itinerary without knowing that the search for lost things is hindered by routine habits and that is why it is so difficult to find them.

The rearing of José Arcadio helped Úrsula in the exhausting task of keeping herself up to date on the smallest changes in the house. When she realized that Amaranta was dressing the saints in the bedroom she pretended to show the boy the differences in the colors.

"Let's see," she would tell him. "Tell me what color the Archangel Raphael is wearing."

In that way the child gave her the information that was denied her by her eyes, and long before he went away to the seminary Úrsula could already distinguish the different colors of the saints' clothing by the texture. Sometimes unforeseen accidents would happen. One afternoon when Amaranta was embroidering on the porch with the begonias Úrsula bumped into her.

"For heaven's sake," Amaranta protested, "watch where you're going."

"It's your fault," Úrsula said. "You're not sitting where you're supposed to."

She was sure of it. But that day she began to realize something that no one had noticed and it was that with the passage of the year the sun imperceptibly changed position and those who sat on the porch had to change their position little by little without being aware of it. From then on Úrsula had only to remember the date in order to know exactly where Amaranta was sitting. Even though the trembling of her hands was more and more noticeable and the weight of her feet was too much for her, her small figure was never seen in so many places at the same time. She was almost as diligent as when she had the whole weight of the house on her shoulders. Nevertheless, in the impenetrable solitude of decrepitude she had such clairvoyance as she examined the most insignificant happenings in the family that for the first time she saw clearly the truths that her busy life in former times had prevented her from seeing. Around the time they were preparing José Arcadio for the seminary she had already made a detailed recapitulation of life in the house since the founding of Macondo and had completely changed the opinion that she had aways held of her descendants. She realized that Colonel Aureliano Buendía had not lost his love for the family because he had been hardened by the war, as she had thought before, but that he had never loved anyone, not even his wife Remedios or the countless one-night women who had passed through his life, and much less his sons. She sensed that he had fought so many wars not out of idealism, as everyone had thought, nor had he renounced a certain victory because of fatigue, as everyone had thought, but that he had won and lost for the same reason, pure and sinful pride. She reached the conclusion that the son for whom she would have given her life was simply a man incapable of love. One night when she was carrying him in her belly she heard him weeping. It was such a definite lament that José Arcadio Buendía woke up beside her and was happy with the idea that his son was going to be a ventriloquist. Other people predicted that he would be a prophet. She, on the other hand, shuddered from the certainty that the deep moan was a first indication of the fearful pig tail and she begged God to let the child die in her womb. But the lucidity of her old age allowed her to see, and she said so many times, that the cries of children in their mothers' wombs are not announcements of ventriloquism or a faculty for prophecy but an unmistakable sign of an incapacity for love. The lowering of the image of her son brought out in her all at once all of the compassion that she owed him. Amaranta, however, whose hardness of heart frightened her, whose concentrated bitterness made her bitter, suddenly became clear to her in the final analysis as the most tender woman who had ever existed, and she understood with pitying clarity that the unjust tortures to which she had submitted Pietro Crespi had not been dictated by a desire for vengeance, as everyone had thought, nor had the slow martyrdom with which she had frustrated the life of Colonel Gerineldo Márquez been determined by the gall of her bitterness, as everyone had thought, but that both actions had been a mortal struggle between a measureless love and an invincible cowardice, and that the irrational fear that Amaranta had always had of her own tormented heart had triumphed in the end. It was during that time that Úrsula began to speak Rebeca's name, bringing back the memory of her with an old love that was exalted by tardy repentance and a sudden admiration, coming to understand that only she, Rebeca, the one who had never fed of her milk but only of the earth of the land and the whiteness of the walls, the one who did not carry the blood of her veins in hers but the unknown blood of the strangers whose bones were still *cloc*ing in their grave. Rebeca, the one with an impatient heart, the one with a fierce womb, was the only one who had the unbridled courage that Úrsula had wanted for her line.

"Rebeca," she would say, feeling along the walls, "how unfair we've been to you!"

In the house they simply thought that her mind was wandering, especially since the time she had begun walking about with her right arm raised like the Archangel Gabriel. Fernanda, however, realized that there was a sun of clairvoyance in the shadows of that wandering, for Úrsula could say without hestitation how much money had been spent in the house during the previous year. Amaranta had a similar idea one day as her mother was stirring a pot of soup in the kitchen and said all at once without knowing that they were listening to her that the corn grinder they had bought from the first gypsies and that had disappeared during the time before José Arcadio had taken his sixty-five trips around the world was still in Pilar Ternera's house. Also almost a hundred years old, but fit and agile in spite of her inconceivable fatness, which frightened children as her laughter had frightened the doves in other times, Pilar Ternera was not surprised that Úrsula was correct because her own experience was beginning to tell her that an alert old age can be more keen than the cards.

Nevertheless, when Úrsula realized that she had not had enough time to consolidate the vocation of José Arcadio, she let herself be disturbed by consternation. She began to make mistakes, trying to see with her eyes the things that intuition allowed her to see with greater clarity. One morning she poured the contents of an inkwell over the boy's head thinking that it was rose water. She stumbled so much in her insistence in taking part in everything that she felt herself upset by gusts of bad humor and she tried to get rid of the shadows that were beginning to wrap her in a straitjacket of cobwebs. It was then that it occurred to her that her clumsiness was not the first victory of decrepitude and darkness but a sentence passed by time. She thought that previously, when God did not make the same traps out of the months and years that the Turks used when they measured a yard of percale, things were different. Now children not only grew faster, but even feelings developed in a different way. No sooner had Remedios the Beauty ascended to heaven in body and soul than the inconsiderate Fernanda was going about mumbling to herself because her sheets had been carried off. The bodies of the Aurelianos were no sooner cold in their graves than Aureliano Segundo had the house lighted up again, filled with drunkards playing the accordion and dousing themselves in champagne, as if dogs and not Christians had died, and as if that madhouse which had cost her so many headaches and so many candy animals was destined to become a trash heap of perdition. Remembering those things as she prepared José Arcadio's trunk, Úrsula wondered if it was not preferable to lie down once and for all in her grave and let them throw the earth over her, and she asked God, without fear, if he really believed that people were made of iron in order to bear so many troubles and mortifications; and asking over and over she was stirring up her own confusion and she felt irrepressible desires to let herself go and scamper about like a foreigner and allow herself at last an instant of rebellion, that instant yearned for so many times and so many times postponed, putting her resignation aside and shitting on everything once and for all and drawing out of her heart the infinite stacks of bad words that she had been forced to swallow over a century of conformity.

"Shit!" she shouted.

Amaranta, who was starting to put the clothes into the trunk, thought that she had been bitten by a scorpion.

"Where is it?" she asked in alarm.

"What?"

"The bug!" Amaranta said.

Úrsula put a finger on her heart.

"Here," she said.

On Thursday, at two in the afternoon, José Arcadio left for the seminary. Úrsula would remember him always as she said good-bye to him, languid and serious, without shedding a tear, as she had taught him, sweltering in the heat in the green corduroy suit with copper buttons and a starched bow around his neck. He left the dining room impregnated with the penetrating fragrance of rose water that she had sprinkled on his head so that she could follow his tracks through the house. While the farewell lunch was going on, the family concealed its nervousness with festive expressions and they celebrated with exaggerated enthusiasm the remarks that Father Antonio Isabel made. But when they took out the trunk bound in velvet and with silver corners, it was as if they had taken a coffin out of the house. The only one who refused to take part in the farewell was Colonel Aureliano Buendía.

"That's all we need," he muttered. "A Pope!"

Three months later Aureliano Segundo and Fernanda took Meme to school and came back with a clavichord, which took the place of the pianola. It was around that time that Amaranta started sewing her own shroud. The banana fever had calmed down. The old inhabitants of Macondo found themselves surrounded by newcomers and working hard to cling to their precarious resources of times gone by, but comforted in any case by the sense that they had survived a shipwreck. In the house they still had guests for lunch and the old routine was never really set up again until the banana company left years later. Nevertheless, there were radical changes in the traditional sense of hospitality because at that time it was Fernanda who imposed her rules. With Úrsula relegated to the shadows and with Amaranta absorbed in the work of her winding cloth, the former apprentice queen had the freedom to choose the guests and impose on them the rigid norms that her parents had taught her. Her severity made the house a redoubt of old customs in a town convulsed by the vulgarity with which the outsiders squandered their easy fortunes. For her, with no further questions asked, proper people were those who had nothing to do with the banana company. Even José Arcadio Segundo, her brother-in-law, was the victim of her discriminatory jealousy because during the excitement of the first days he gave up his stupendous fighting cocks again and took a job as foreman with the banana company.

"He won't ever come into this house again," Fernanda said, "as long as he carries the rash of the foreigners."

Such was the narrowness imposed in the house that Aureliano Segundo felt more comfortable at Petra Cotes's. First, with the pretext of taking the burden off his wife, he transferred his parties. Then, with the pretext that the animals were losing their fertility, he transferred his barns and stables. Finally, with the pretext that it was cooler in his concubine's house, he transferred the small office in which he handled his business. When Fernanda realized that she was a widow whose husband had still not died, it was already too late for things to return to their former state. Aureliano

Segundo barely ate at home and the only appearances he put in, such as to sleep with his wife, were not enough to convince anyone. One night, out of carelessness, morning found him in Petra Cotes's bed. Fernanda, contrary to expectations, did not reproach him in the least or give the slightest sigh of resentment, but on the same day she sent two trunks with his clothing to the house of his concubine. She sent them in broad daylight and with instructions that they be carried through the middle of the street so that everyone could see them, thinking that her straying husband would be unable to bear the shame and would return to the fold with his head hung low. But that heroic gesture was just one more proof of how poorly Fernanda knew not only the character of her husband but the character of a community that had nothing to do with that of her parents, for everyone who saw the trunks pass by said that it was the natural culmination of a story whose intimacies were known to everyone, and Aureliano Segundo celebrated the freedom he had received with a party that lasted for three days. To the greater disadvantage of his wife, as she was entering into a sad maturity with her somber long dresses, her old-fashioned medals, and her out-of-place pride, the concubine seemed to be bursting with a second youth, clothed in gaudy dresses of natural silk and with her eyes tiger-striped with a glow of vindication. Aureliano Segundo gave himself over to her again with the fury of adolescence, as before, when Petra Cotes had not loved him for himself but because she had him mixed up with his twin brother and as she slept with both of them at the same time she thought that God had given her the good fortune of having a man who could make love like two. The restored passion was so pressing that on more than one occasion they would look each other in the eyes as they were getting ready to eat and without saying anything they would cover their plates and go into the bedroom dying of hunger and of love. Inspired by the things he had seen on his furtive visits to the

French matrons, Aureliano Segundo bought Petra Cotes a bed with an archepiscopal canopy, put velvet curtains on the windows, and covered the ceiling and the walls of the bedroom with large rock-crystal mirrors. At the same time he was more of a carouser and spendthrift than ever. On the train, which arrived every day at eleven o'clock, he would receive cases and more cases of champagne and brandy. On the way back from the station he would drag the improvised *cumbiamba* along in full view of all the people on the way, natives or outsiders, acquaintances or people yet to be known, without distinctions of any kind. Even the slippery Mr. Brown, who talked only in a strange tongue, let himself be seduced by the tempting signs that Aureliano Segundo made him and several times he got dead drunk in Petra Cotes's house and he even made the fierce German shepherd dogs that went everywhere with him dance to some Texas songs that he himself mumbled in one way or another to the accompaniment of the accordion.

"Cease, cows," Aureliano Segundo shouted at the height of the party. "Cease, because life is short."

He never looked better, nor had he been loved more, nor had the breeding of his animals been wilder. There was a slaughtering of so many cows, pigs, and chickens for the endless parties that the ground in the courtyard turned black and muddy with so much blood. It was an eternal execution ground of bones and innards, a mud pit of leftovers, and they had to keep exploding dynamite bombs all the time so that the buzzards would not pluck out the guests' eyes. Aureliano Segundo grew fat, purple-colored, turtle-shaped, because of an appetite comparable only to that of José Arcadio when he came back from traveling around the world. The prestige of his outlandish voracity, of his immense capacity as a spendthrift, of his unprecedented hospitality went beyond the borders of the swamp and attracted the best-qualified gluttons from all along the coast. Fabulous eaters arrived from everywhere to take part in the irrational tourneys of capacity and resistance that were organized in the house of Petra Cotes. Aureliano Segundo was the unconquered eater until the luckless Saturday when Camila Sagastume appeared, a totemic female known all through the land by the good name of "The Elephant." The duel lasted until dawn on Tuesday. During the first twenty-four hours, having dispatched a dinner of veal, with cassava, yams, and fried bananas, and a case and a half of champagne in addition, Aureliano Segundo was sure of victory. He seemed more enthusiastic, more vital than his imperturbable adversary, who possessed a style that was obviously more professional, but at the same time less emotional for the large crowd that filled the house. While Aureliano Segundo ate with great bites, overcome by the anxiety of victory, The Elephant was slicing her meat with the art of a surgeon and eating it unhurriedly and even with a certain pleasure. She was gigantic and sturdy, but over her colossal form a tenderness of femininity prevailed and she had a face that was so beautiful, hands so fine and well cared for, and such an irresistible personal charm that when Aureliano Segundo saw her enter the house he commented in a low voice that he would have preferred to have the tourney in bed and not at the table. Later on, when he saw her consume a side of veal without breaking a single rule of good table manners, he commented seriously that that delicate, fascinating, and insatiable proboscidian was in a certain way the ideal woman. He was not mistaken. The reputation of a bone crusher that had preceded The Elephant had no basis. She was not a beef cruncher or a bearded lady from a Greek circus, as had been said, but the director of a school of voice. She had learned to eat when she was already the respectable mother of a family, looking for a way for her children to eat better and not by means of any artificial stimulation of their appetites but through the absolute tranquillity of their spirits. Her theory, demonstrated in practice, was based on the principle that a person who had all matters of conscience in perfect shape should be able to eat until overcome by fatigue. And it was for moral reasons and sporting interest that she left her school and her home to compete with a man whose fame as a great, unprincipled eater had spread throughout the country. From the first moment she saw him she saw that Aureliano Segundo would lose not his stomach but his character. At the end of the first night, while The Elephant was boldly going on, Aureliano Segundo was wearing himself out with a great deal of talking and laughing. They slept four hours. On awakening each one had the juice of forty oranges, eight quarts of coffee, and thirty raw eggs. On the second morning, after many hours without sleep and having put away two pigs, a bunch of bananas, and four cases of champagne, The Elephant suspected that Aureliano Segundo had unknowingly discovered the same method as hers, but by the absurd route of total irresponsibility. He was, therefore, more dangerous than she had thought. Nevertheless, when Petra Cotes brought two roast turkeys to the table, Aureliano Segundo was a step away from being stuffed.

"If you can't, don't eat any more," The Elephant said to him. "Let's call it a tie."

She said it from her heart, understanding that she could not eat another mouthful either, out of remorse for bringing on the death of her adversary. But Aureliano Segundo interpreted it as another challenge and he filled himself with turkey beyond his incredible capacity. He lost consciousness. He fell face down into the plate filled with bones, frothing at the mouth like a dog, and drowning in moans of agony. He felt, in the midst of the darkness, that they were throwing him from the top of a tower into a bottomless pit and in a last flash of consciousness he realized that at the end of that endless fall death was waiting for him.

"Take me to Fernanda," he managed to say.

His friends left him at the house thinking that they had

helped him fulfill his promise to his wife not to die in his concubine's bed. Petra Cotes had shined his patent leather boots that he wanted to wear in his coffin, and she was already looking for someone to take them when they came to tell her that Aureliano Segundo was out of danger. He did recover, indeed, in less than a week, and two weeks later he was celebrating the fact of his survival with unprecedented festivities. He continued living at Petra Cotes's but he would visit Fernanda every day and sometimes he would stay to eat with the family, as if fate had reversed the situation and had made him the husband of his concubine and the lover of his wife.

It was a rest for Fernanda. During the boredom of her abandonment her only distractions were the clavichord lessons at siesta time and the letters from her children. In the detailed messages that she sent them every two weeks there was not a single line of truth. She hid her troubles from them. She hid from them the sadness of a house which, in spite of the light on the begonias, in spite of the heaviness at two in the afternoon, in spite of the frequent waves of festivals that came in from the street, was more and more like the colonial mansion of her parents. Fernanda would wander alone among the three living ghosts and the dead ghost of José Arcadio Buendía, who at times would come to sit down with an inquisitive attention in the half-light of the parlor while she was playing the clavichord. Colonel Aureliano Buendía was a shadow. Since the last time that he had gone out into the street to propose a war without any future to Colonel Gerineldo Márquez, he left the workshop only to urinate under the chestnut tree. He did not receive any visits except that of the barber every three weeks. He fed on anything that Úrsula brought him once a day, and even though he kept on making little gold fishes with the same passion as before, he stopped selling them when he found out that people were buying them not as pieces of jewelry but as historic relics. He made a bonfire in the courtyard of the dolls of

Remedios which had decorated their bedroom since their wedding. The watchful Úrsula realized what her son was doing but she could not stop him.

"You have a heart of stone," she told him.

"It's not a question of a heart," he said. "The room's getting full of moths."

Amaranta was weaving her shroud. Fernanda did not understand why she would write occasional letters to Meme and even send her gifts and on the other hand did not even want to hear about José Arcadio. "They'll die without knowing why," Amaranta answered when she was asked through Úrsula, and that answer planted an enigma in Fernanda's heart that she was never able to clarify. Tall, broad-shouldered, proud, always dressed in abundant petticoats with lace and an air of distinction that resisted the years and bad memories, Amaranta seemed to carry the cross of ashes of virginity on her forehead. In reality she carried it on her hand in the black bandage, which she did not take off even to sleep and which she washed and ironed herself. Her life was spent in weaving her shroud. It might have been said that she wove during the day and unwove during the night, and not with any hope of defeating solitude in that way, but, quite the contrary, in order to nurture it.

The greatest worry that Fernanda had during her years of abandonment was that Meme would come to spend her first vacation and not find Aureliano Segundo at home. His congestion had put an end to that fear. When Meme returned, her parents had made an agreement that not only would the girl think that Aureliano Segundo was still a domesticated husband but also that she would not notice the sadness of the house. Every year for two months Aureliano Segundo played his role of an exemplary husband and he organized parties with ice cream and cookies which the gay and lively schoolgirl enhanced with the clavichord. It was obvious from then on that she had inherited very little of her mother's charac-

264

ter. She seemed more of a second version of Amaranta when the latter had not known bitterness and was arousing the house with her dance steps at the age of twelve or fourteen before her secret passion for Pietro Crespi was to twist the direction of her heart in the end. But unlike Amaranta, unlike all of them, Meme still did not reveal the solitary fate of the family and she seemed entirely in conformity with the world, even when she would shut herself up in the parlor at two in the afternoon to practice the clavichord with an inflexible discipline. It was obvious that she liked the house, that she spent the whole year dreaming about the excitement of the young people her arrival brought around, and that she was not far removed from the festive vocation and hospitable excesses of her father. The first sign of that calamitous inheritance was revealed on her third vacation, when Meme appeared at the house with four nuns and sixty-eight classmates whom she had invited to spend a week with her family on her own initiative and without any previous warning.

"How awful!" Fernanda lamented. "This child is as much of a barbarian as her father!"

It was necessary to borrow beds and hammocks from the neighbors, to set up nine shifts at the table, to fix hours for bathing, and to borrow forty stools so that the girls in blue uniforms with masculine buttons would not spend the whole day running from one place to another. The visit was a failure because the noisy schoolgirls would scarcely finish breakfast before they had to start taking turns for lunch and then for dinner, and for the whole week they were able to take only one walk through the plantations. At nightfall the nuns were exhausted, unable to move, give another order, and still the troop of tireless adolescents was in the courtyard singing school songs out of tune. One day they were on the point of trampling Úrsula, who made an effort to be useful precisely where she was most in the way. On another day the nuns got all excited because Colonel Aureliano Buendía had urinated under the chestnut tree without being concerned that the schoolgirls were in the courtyard. Amaranta was on the point of causing panic because one of the nuns went into the kitchen as she was salting the soup and the only thing that occurred to her to say was to ask what those handfuls of white powder were.

"Arsenic," Amaranta answered.

The night of their arrival the students carried on in such a way, trying to go to the bathroom before they went to bed, that at one o'clock in the morning the last ones were still going in. Fernanda then bought seventy-two chamberpots but she only managed to change the nocturnal problem into a morning one, because from dawn on there was a long line of girls, each with her pot in her hand, waiting for her turn to wash it. Although some of them suffered fevers and several of them were infected by mosquito bites, most of them showed an unbreakable resistance as they faced the most troublesome difficulties, and even at the time of the greatest heat they would scamper through the garden. When they finally left, the flowers were destroyed, the furniture broken, and the walls covered with drawings and writing, but Fernanda pardoned them for all of the damage because of her relief at their leaving. She returned the borrowed beds and stools and kept the seventy-two chamberpots in Melquíades' room. The locked room, about which the spiritual life of the house revolved in former times, was known from that time on as the "chamberpot room." For Colonel Aureliano Buendía it was the most appropriate name, because while the rest of the family was still amazed by the fact that Melquíades' room was immune to dust and destruction, he saw it turned into a dunghill. In any case, it did not seem to bother him who was correct, and if he found out about the fate of the room it was because Fernanda kept passing by and disturbing his work for a whole afternoon as she put away the chamberpots.

During those days José Arcadio Segundo reappeared in the

house. He went along the porch without greeting anyone and he shut himself up in the workshop to talk to the colonel. In spite of the fact that she could not see him, Úrsula analyzed the clicking of his foreman's boots and was surprised at the unbridgeable distance that separated him from the family, even from the twin brother with whom he had played ingenious games of confusion in childhood and with whom he no longer had any traits in common. He was linear, solemn, and had a pensive air and the sadness of a Saracen and a mournful glow on his face that was the color of autumn. He was the one who most resembled his mother, Santa Sofía de la Piedad. Úrsula reproached herself for the habit of forgetting about him when she spoke about the family, but when she sensed him in the house again and noticed that the colonel let him into the workshop during working hours, she re-examined her old memories and confirmed the belief that at some moment in childhood he had changed places with his twin brother, because it was he and not the other one who should have been called Aureliano. No one knew the details of his life. At one time it was discovered that he had no fixed abode, that he raised fighting cocks at Pilar Ternera's house and that sometimes he would stay there to sleep but that he almost always spent the night in the rooms of the French matrons. He drifted about, with no ties of affection, with no ambitions, like a wandering star in Úrsula's planetary system.

In reality, José Arcadio Segundo was not a member of the family, nor would he ever be of any other since that distant dawn when Colonel Gerineldo Márquez took him to the barracks, not so that he could see an execution, but so that for the rest of his life he would never forget the sad and somewhat mocking smile of the man being shot. That was not only his oldest memory, but the only one he had of his childhood. The other one, that of an old man with an old-fashioned vest and a hat with a brim like a crow's wings who told him marvelous things framed in a dazzling window, he was unable to place in any period. It was an uncertain memory, entirely devoid of lessons or nostalgia, the opposite of the memory of the executed man, which had really set the direction of his life and would return to his memory clearer and clearer as he grew older, as if the passage of time were bringing him closer to it. Úrsula tried to use José Arcadio Segundo to get Colonel Aureliano Buendía to give up his imprisonment. "Get him to go to the movies," she said to him. "Even if he doesn't like the picture, at least he'll breathe a little fresh air." But it did not take her long to realize that he was as insensible to her begging as the colonel would have been, and that they were armored by the same impermeability of affection. Although she never knew, nor did anyone know, what they spoke about in their prolonged sessions shut up in the workshop, she understood that they were probably the only members of the family who seemed drawn together by some affinity.

The truth is that not even José Arcadio Segundo would have been able to draw the colonel out of his confinement. The invasion of schoolgirls had lowered the limits of his patience. With the pretext that his wedding bedroom was at the mercy of the moths in spite of the destruction of Remedios' appetizing dolls, he hung a hammock in the workshop and then he would leave it only to go into the courtyard to take care of his necessities. Úrsula was unable to string together even a trivial conversation with him. She knew that he did not look at the dishes of food but would put them at one end of his workbench while he finished a little fish and it did not matter to him if the soup curdled or if the meat got cold. He grew harder and harder ever since Colonel Gerineldo Márquez refused to back him up in a senile war. He locked himself up inside himself and the family finally thought of him as if he were dead. No other human reaction was seen in him until one October eleventh, when he went to the street door to watch a circus parade. For Colonel Aureliano Buendía it had been a day just like all of those of his last years. At five o'clock in the morning the noise of the toads and crickets outside the wall woke him up. The drizzle had persisted since Saturday and there was no necessity for him to hear their tiny whispering among the leaves of the garden because he would have felt the cold in his bones in any case. He was, as always, wrapped in his woolen blanket and wearing his crude cotton long drawers, which he still wore for comfort, even though because of their musty, old-fashioned style he called them his "Goth drawers." He put on his tight pants but did not button them up, nor did he put the gold button into his shirt collar as he always did, because he planned to take a bath. Then he put the blanket over his head like a cowl, brushed his dripping mustache with his fingers, and went to urinate in the courtyard. There was still so much time left for the sun to come out that José Arcadio Buendía was still dozing under the shelter of palm fronds that had been rotted by the rain. He did not see him, as he had never seen him, nor did he hear the incomprehensible phrase that the ghost of his father addressed to him as he awakened, startled by the stream of hot urine that splattered his shoes. He put the bath off for later, not because of the cold and the dampness, but because of the oppressive October mist. On his way back to the workshop he noticed the odor of the wick that Santa Sofía de la Piedad was using to light the stoves, and he waited in the kitchen for the coffee to boil so that he could take along his mug without sugar. Santa Sofía de la Piedad asked him, as on every morning, what day of the week it was, and he answered that it was Tuesday, October eleventh. Watching the glow of the fire as it gilded the persistent woman who neither then nor in any instant of her life seemed to exist completely, he suddenly remembered that on one October eleventh in the middle of the war he had awakened with the brutal certainty that the woman with whom he had slept was dead. She really

was and he could not forget the date because she had asked
him an hour before what day it was. In spite of the memory
he did not have an awareness this time either of to what
degree his omens had abandoned him and while the coffee
was boiling he kept on thinking out of pure curiosity but
without the slightest risk of nostalgia about the woman whose
name he had never known and whose face he had not seen
because she had stumbled to his hammock in the dark. Nevertheless, in the emptiness of so many women who came into
his life in the same way, he did not remember that she was
the one who in the delirium of that first meeting was on the
point of foundering in her own tears and scarcely an hour
before her death had sworn to love him until she died. He
did not think about her again or about any of the others after
he went into the workshop with the steaming cup, and he
lighted the lamp in order to count the little gold fishes, which
he kept in a tin pail. There were seventeen of them. Since he
had decided not to sell any, he kept on making two fishes a
day and when he finished twenty-five he would melt them
down and start all over again. He worked all morning, absorbed, without thinking about anything, without realizing
that at ten o'clock the rain had grown stronger and someone
ran past the workshop shouting to close the doors before the
house was flooded, and without thinking even about himself
until Úrsula came in with his lunch and turned out the
light.

"What a rain!" Úrsula said.

"October," he said.

When he said it he did not raise his eyes from the first little
fish of the day because he was putting in the rubies for the
eyes. Only when he finished it and put it with the others in
the pail did he begin to drink the soup. Then, very slowly, he
ate the piece of meat roasted with onions, the white rice, and
the slices of fried bananas all on the same plate together. His
appetite did not change under either the best or the harshest

of circumstances. After lunch he felt the drowsiness of inactivity. Because of a kind of scientific superstition he never worked, or read, or bathed, or made love until two hours of digestion had gone by, and it was such a deep-rooted belief that several times he held up military operations so as not to submit the troops to the risks of indigestion. So he lay down in the hammock, removing the wax from his ears with a penknife, and in a few minutes he was asleep. He dreamed that he was going into an empty house with white walls and that he was upset by the burden of being the first human being to enter it. In the dream he remembered that he had dreamed the same thing the night before and on many nights over the past years and he knew that the image would be erased from his memory when he awakened because that recurrent dream had the quality of not being remembered except within the dream itself. A moment later, indeed, when the barber knocked at the workshop door, Colonel Aureliano Buendía awoke with the impression that he had fallen asleep involuntarily for a few seconds and that he had not had time to dream anything.

"Not today," he told the barber. "We'll make it on Friday."

He had a three-day beard speckled with white hairs, but he did not think it necessary to shave because on Friday he was going to have his hair cut and it could all be done at the same time. The sticky sweat of the unwanted siesta aroused the scars of the sores in his armpits. The sky had cleared but the sun had not come out. Colonel Aureliano Buendía released a sonorous belch which brought back the acidity of the soup to his palate and which was like a command from his organism to throw his blanket over his shoulders and go to the toilet. He stayed there longer than was necessary, crouched over the dense fermentation that was coming out of the wooden box until habit told him that it was time to start work again. During the time he lingered he remembered again that it was

Tuesday and that José Arcadio Segundo had not come to the workshop because it was payday on the banana company farms. That recollection, as all of those of the past few years, led him to think about the war without his realizing it. He remembered that Colonel Gerineldo Márquez had once promised to get him a horse with a white star on its face and that he had never spoken about it again. Then he went on toward scattered episodes but he brought them back without any judgment because since he could not think about anything else, he had learned to think coldly so that inescapable memories would not touch any feeling. On his way back to the workshop, seeing that the air was beginning to dry out, he decided that it was a good time to take a bath, but Amaranta had got there ahead of him. So he started on the second little fish of the day. He was putting a hook on the tail when the sun came out with such strength that the light creaked like a fishing boat. The air, which had been washed by the three-day drizzle, was filled with flying ants. Then he came to the realization that he felt like urinating and he had been putting it off until he had finished fixing the little fish. He went out into the courtyard at ten minutes after four, when he heard the distant brass instruments, the beating of the bass drum, and the shouting of the children, and for the first time since his youth he knowingly fell into a trap of nostalgia and relived that prodigious afternoon of the gypsies when his father took him to see ice. Santa Sofía de la Piedad dropped what she was doing in the kitchen and ran to the door.

"It's the circus," she shouted.

Instead of going to the chestnut tree, Colonel Aureliano Buendía also went to the street door and mingled with the bystanders who were watching the parade. He saw a woman dressed in gold sitting on the head of an elephant. He saw a sad dromedary. He saw a bear dressed like a Dutch girl keeping time to the music with a soup spoon and a pan. He saw the clowns doing cartwheels at the end of the parade and once more he saw the face of his miserable solitude when everything had passed by and there was nothing but the bright expanse of the street and the air full of flying ants with a few onlookers peering into the precipice of uncertainty. Then he went to the chestnut tree, thinking about the circus, and while he urinated he tried to keep on thinking about the circus, but he could no longer find the memory. He pulled his head in between his shoulders like a baby chick and remained motionless with his forehead against the trunk of the chestnut tree. The family did not find him until the following day at eleven o'clock in the morning when Santa Sofía de la Piedad went to throw out the garbage in back and her attention was attracted by the descending vultures.

K*

MEME'S LAST VACATIONS coincided with the period of mourning for Colonel Aureliano Buendía. The shuttered house was no place for parties. They spoke in whispers, ate in silence, recited the rosary three times a day, and even clavichord practice during the heat of siesta time had a funereal echo. In spite of her secret hostility toward the colonel, it was Fernanda who imposed the rigor of that mourning, impressed by the solemnity with which the government exalted the memory of its dead enemy. Aureliano Segundo, as was his custom, came back to sleep in the house during his daughter's vacation and Fernanda must have done something to regain her privileges as his legitimate wife because the following year Meme found a newborn little sister who against the wishes of her mother had been baptized with the name Amaranta Úrsula.

Meme had finished her course of study. The diploma that certified her as a concert clavichordist was ratified by the virtuosity with which she executed popular melodies of the seventeenth century at the gathering organized to celebrate the completion of her studies and with which the period of mourning came to an end. More than her art, the guests admired her duality. Her frivolous and even slightly infantile character did not seem up to any serious activity, but when she sat down at the clavichord she became a different girl, one whose unforeseen maturity gave her the air of an adult. That was how she had always been. She really did not have any definite vocation, but she had earned the highest grades by means of an inflexible discipline simply in order not to annoy her mother. They could have imposed on her an apprenticeship in any other field and the results would have been the same. Since she had been very small she had been troubled by Fernanda's strictness, her custom of deciding in favor of extremes; and she would have been capable of a much more difficult sacrifice than the clavichord lessons merely not to run up against her intransigence. During the graduation ceremonies she had the impression that the parchment with Gothic letters and illuminated capitals was freeing her from a compromise that she had accepted not so much out of obedience as out of convenience, and she thought that from then on not even the insistent Fernanda would worry any more about an instrument that even the nuns looked upon as a museum fossil. During the first years she thought that her calculations were mistaken because after she had put half the town to sleep, not only in the parlor but also at all charitable functions, school ceremonies, and patriotic celebrations that took place in Macondo, her mother still invited to the house every newcomer whom she thought capable of appreciating her daughter's virtues. Only after the death of Amaranta, when the family shut itself up again in a period of mourning, was Meme able to lock the clavichord and forget the key in some dresser drawer without Fernanda's being annoyed on finding out when and through whose fault it had been lost. Meme bore up under the exhibitions with the same stoicism that she had dedicated to her apprenticeship. It was the price of her freedom. Fernanda was so pleased with her docility and so proud of the admiration that her art inspired that she was never against the house being full of girl friends, her spending the afternoon in the groves, and going to the movies with Aureliano Segundo or some trusted lady as long as the film was approved by Father Antonio Isabel from the pulpit. During those moments of relaxation Meme's real tastes were revealed. Her happiness lay at the other extreme from discipline, in noisy parties, in gossip about lovers, in prolonged sessions with her girl friends, where they learned to smoke and talked about male business, and where they once got their hands on some cane liquor and ended up naked, measuring and comparing the parts of their bodies. Meme would never forget that night when she arrived home chewing licorice lozenges, and without noticing their consternation, sat down at the table where Fernanda and Amaranta were eating dinner without saying a word to each other. She had spent two tremendous hours in the bedroom of a girl friend, weeping with laughter and fear, and beyond all crises she had found the rare feeling of bravery that she needed in order to run away from school and tell her mother in one way or another that she could use the clavichord as an enema. Sitting at the head of the table, drinking a chicken broth that landed in her stomach like an elixir of resurrection, Meme then saw Fernanda and Amaranta wrapped in an accusatory halo of reality. She had to make a great effort not to throw at them their prissiness, their poverty of spirit, their delusions of grandeur. From the time of her second vacation she had known that her father was living at home only in order to keep up appearances, and knowing Fernanda as she did and having arranged later to meet Petra Cotes, she thought that her father was right. She also would have preferred being the daughter of the concubine. In the haziness of the alcohol Meme thought with pleasure about the scandal that would have taken place if she were to express her thoughts at that moment, and the intimate satisfaction of her roguishness was so intense that Fernanda noticed it.

"What's the matter?" she asked.

"Nothing," Meme answered. "I was only now discovering how much I loved you both."

Amaranta was startled by the obvious burden of hate that the declaration carried. But Fernanda felt so moved that she thought she would go mad when Meme awoke at midnight with her head splitting with pain and drowning in vomited gall. She gave her a vial of castor oil, put compresses on her stomach and ice cubes on her head, and she made her stay in bed for five days and follow the diet ordered by the new and outlandish French doctor, who after examining her for more than two hours reached the foggy conclusion that she had an ailment peculiar to women. Having lost her courage, in a miserable state of demoralization, Meme had no other recourse but to bear up under it. Úrsula, completely blind by then but still active and lucid, was the only one who guessed the exact diagnosis. "As far as I can see," she thought, "that's the same thing that happens to drunken people." But she not only rejected the idea, she reproached herself for the frivolity of her thought. Aureliano Segundo felt a twinge of conscience when he saw Meme's state of prostration and he promised himself to take better care of her in the future. That was how the relationship of jolly comradeship was born between father and daughter, which freed him for a time from the bitter solitude of his revels and freed her from Fernanda's watchful eye without the necessity of provoking the domestic crisis that seemed inevitable by then. At that time Aureliano Segundo postponed any appointments in order to be with Meme, to take her to the movies or the circus, and he spent the greater part of his idle time with her. In recent times his annoyance with the absurd obesity that prevented him from tying his shoes and his abusive satisfaction with all manner of appetites had begun to sour his character. The discovery of his daughter restored his former joviality and the pleasure of being with her was slowly leading him away from dissipation. Meme was entering a fruitful age. She was not beautiful, as Amaranta had never been, but on the other hand she was pleasant, uncomplicated, and she had the virtue of making a good impression on people from the first moment. She had a modern spirit that wounded the antiquated sobriety and poorly disguised miserly heart of Fernanda, and that, on the other hand, Aureliano Segundo took pleasure in developing. It was he who resolved to take her out of the bedroom she had occupied since childhood, where the fearful eyes of the saints still fed her adolescent terrors, and he furnished for her a room with a royal bed, a large dressing table, and velvet curtains, not realizing that he was producing a second version of Petra Cotes's room. He was so lavish with Meme that he did not even know how much money he gave her because she herself would take it out of his pockets, and he kept abreast of every kind of new beauty aid that arrived in the commissary of the banana company. Meme's room became filled with pumice-stone cushions to polish her nails with, hair curlers, toothbrushes, drops to make her eyes languid, and so many and such new cosmetics and artifacts of beauty that every time Fernanda went into the room she was scandalized by the idea that her daughter's dressing table must have been the same as those of the French matrons. Nevertheless, Fernanda divided her time in those days between little Amaranta Úrsula, who was mischievous and sickly, and a touching correspondence with the invisible physicians. So that when she noticed the complicity between father and daughter the only promise she extracted from Aureliano Segundo was that he would never take Meme to

Petra Cotes's house. It was a meaningless demand because the concubine was so annoyed with the comradeship between her lover and his daughter that she did not want anything to do with her, Petra was tormented by an unknown fear, as if instinct were telling her that Meme, by just wanting it, could succeed in what Fernanda had been unable to do: deprive her of a love that by then she considered assured until death. For the first time Aureliano Segundo had to tolerate the harsh expressions and the violent tirades of his concubine, and he was even afraid that his wandering trunks would make the return journey to his wife's house. That did not happen. No one knew a man better than Petra Cotes knew her lover and she knew that the trunks would remain where they had been sent because if Aureliano Segundo detested anything it was complicating his life with modifications and changes. So the trunks stayed where they were and Petra Cotes set about reconquering the husband by sharpening the only weapons that his daughter could not use on him. It too was an unnecessary effort because Meme had no desire to intervene in her father's affairs and if she had, it would certainly have been in favor of the concubine. She had no time to bother anybody. She herself swept her room and made her bed, as the nuns had taught her. In the morning she took care of her clothes, sewing on the porch or using Amaranta's old pedal machine. While the others were taking their siestas she would practice the clavichord for two hours, knowing that the daily sacrifice would keep Fernanda calm. For the same reason she continued giving concerts at church fairs and school parties, even though the requests were less and less frequent. At nightfall she would fix herself up, put on one of her simple dresses and her stiff high shoes, and if she had nothing to do with her father she would go to the homes of her girl friends, where she would stay until dinnertime. It was rare that Aureliano Segundo would not call for her then to take her to the movies.

Among Meme's friends there were three young American girls who broke through the electrified chicken fence barrier and made friends with girls from Macondo. One of them was Patricia Brown. Grateful for the hospitality of Aureliano Segundo, Mr. Brown opened the doors of his house to Meme and invited her to the Saturday dances, which were the only ones where gringos and natives mingled. When Fernanda found out about it she forgot about Amaranta Úrsula and the invisible doctors for a moment and became very melodramatic. "Just think," she said to Meme, "what the colonel must be thinking in his grave." She sought, of course, the backing of Úrsula. But the blind old woman, contrary to what everyone expected, saw nothing reproachable in Meme's going to the dances and making friends with American girls her own age as long as she kept her strict habits and was not converted to the Protestant religion. Meme sensed the thought of her great-great-grandmother very well and the day after the dances she would get up earlier than usual to go to mass. Fernanda's opposition lasted until the day when Meme broke down her resistance with the news that the Americans wanted to hear her play the clavichord. The instrument was taken out of the house again and carried to Mr. Brown's, where the young concert artist really did receive very sincere applause and the most enthusiastic congratulations. From then on she was invited not only to the dances but also to the Sunday swim parties in the pool and to lunch once a week. Meme learned to swim like a professional, to play tennis, and to eat Virginia ham with slices of pineapple. Among dances, swimming, and tennis she soon found herself getting involved in the English language. Aureliano Segundo was so enthusiastic over the progress of his daughter that from a traveling salesman he bought a six-volume English encyclopedia with many color prints which Meme read in her spare time. The reading occupied the attention that she had formerly given to gossip about sweethearts and the experimental retreats that she would go through with her girl friends, not because it was imposed as discipline but because she had lost all interest by then in talking about mysteries that were in the public domain. She looked back on the drunken episode as an infantile adventure and it seemed so funny to her that she told Aureliano Segundo about it and he thought it was more amusing than she did. "If your mother only knew," he told her, doubling up with laughter, as he always said when he told her something in confidence. He had made her promise that she would let him know about her first love affair with the same confidence, and Meme told him that she liked a redheaded American boy who had come to spend his vacation with his parents. "What do you know," Aureliano Segundo said, laughing. "If your mother only knew." But Meme also told him that the boy had gone back to his country and had disappeared from sight. The maturity of her judgment ensured peace in the family. Aureliano Segundo then devoted more time to Petra Cotes, and although his body and soul no longer permitted him the debauches of days gone by, he lost no chance to arrange them and to dig out the accordion, which by then had some keys held in place by shoelaces. At home, Amaranta was weaving her interminable shroud and Úrsula dragged about in her decrepitude through the depths of the shadows where the only thing that was still visible was the ghost of José Arcadio Buendía under the chestnut tree. Fernanda consolidated her authority. Her monthly letters to her son José Arcadio at that time did not carry a string of lies and she hid from him only her correspondence with the invisible doctors, who had diagnosed a benign tumor in her large intestine and were preparing her for a telepathic operation.

It might have been said that peace and happiness reigned for a long time in the tired mansion of the Buendías if it had not been for the sudden death of Amaranta, which caused a new uproar. It was an unexpected event. Although she was old and isolated from everyone, she still looked firm and upright and with the health of a rock that she had always had. No one knew her thoughts since the afternoon on which she had given Colonel Gerineldo Márquez his final rejection and shut herself up to weep. She was not seen to cry during the ascension to heaven of Remedios the Beauty or over the extermination of the Aurelianos or the death of Colonel Aureliano Buendía, who was the person she loved most in this world, although she showed it only when they found his body under the chestnut tree. She helped pick up the body. She dressed him in his soldier's uniform, shaved him, combed his hair, and waxed his mustache better than he had ever done in his days of glory. No one thought that there was any love in that act because they were accustomed to the familiarity of Amaranta with the rites of death. Fernanda was scandalized that she did not understand the relationship of Catholicism with life but only its relationship with death, as if it were not a religion but a compendium of funeral conventions. Amaranta was too wrapped up in the eggplant patch of her memories to understand those subtle apologetics. She had reached old age with all of her nostalgias intact. When she listened to the waltzes of Pietro Crespi she felt the same desire to weep that she had had in adolescence, as if time and harsh lessons had meant nothing. The rolls of music that she herself had thrown into the trash with the pretext that they had rotted from dampness kept spinning and playing in her memory. She had tried to sink them into the swampy passion that she allowed herself with her nephew Aureliano José, and she tried to take refuge in the calm and virile protection of Colonel Gerineldo Márquez, but she had not been able to overcome them, not even with the most desperate act of her old age when she would bathe the small José Arcadio three years before he was sent to the seminary and caress him not as a grandmother would have done with a grandchild, but as a woman would have done with a man, as it was said that the French matrons did and as she had wanted to do with Pietro Crespi at the age of twelve, fourteen, when she saw him in his dancing tights and with the magic wand with which he kept time to the metronome. At times it pained her to have let that outpouring of misery follow its course, and at times it made her so angry that she would prick her fingers with the needles, but what pained her most and enraged her most and made her most bitter was the fragrant and wormy guava grove of love that was dragging her toward death. Just as Colonel Aureliano Buendía thought about his war, unable to avoid it, so Amaranta thought about Rebeca. But while her brother had managed to sterilize his memories, she had only managed to make hers more scalding. The only thing that she asked of God for many years was that he would not visit on her the punishment of dying before Rebeca. Every time she passed by her house and noted the progress of destruction she took comfort in the idea that God was listening to her. One afternoon, when she was sewing on the porch, she was assailed by the certainty that she would be sitting in that place, in the same position, and under the same light when they brought her the news of Rebeca's death. She sat down to wait for it, as one waits for a letter, and the fact was that at one time she would pull off buttons to sew them on again so that inactivity would not make the wait longer and more anxious. No one in the house realized that at that time Amaranta was sewing a fine shroud for Rebeca. Later on, when Aureliano Triste told how he had seen her, changed into an apparition with leathery skin and a few golden threads on her skull, Amaranta was not surprised because the specter described was exactly what she had been imagining for some time. She had decided to restore Rebeca's corpse, to disguise with paraffin the damage to her face and make a wig for her from the hair of the saints. She would manufacture a beautiful corpse, with the linen shroud and a plush-lined coffin with purple trim, and she would put it at the disposition of the worms with splendid funeral ceremonies. She worked out the plan with such hatred that it made her tremble to think about the scheme, which she would have carried out in exactly the same way if it had been done out of love, but she would not allow herself to become upset by the confusion and went on perfecting the details so minutely that she came to be more than a specialist and was a virtuoso in the rites of death. The only thing that she did not keep in mind in her fearsome plan was that in spite of her pleas to God she might die before Rebeca. That was, in fact, what happened. At the final moment, however, Amaranta did not feel frustrated, but, on the contrary, free of all bitterness because death had awarded her the privilege of announcing itself several years ahead of time. She saw it on one burning afternoon sewing with her on the porch a short time after Meme had left for school. She saw it because it was a woman dressed in blue with long hair, with a sort of antiquated look, and with a certain resemblance to Pilar Ternera during the time when she had helped with the chores in the kitchen. Fernanda was present several times and did not see her, in spite of the fact that she was so real, so human, and on one occasion asked of Amaranta the favor of threading a needle. Death did not tell her when she was going to die or whether her hour was assigned before that of Rebeca, but ordered her to begin sewing her own shroud on the next sixth of April. She was authorized to make it as complicated and as fine as she wanted, but just as honestly executed as Rebeca's, and she was told that she would die without pain, fear, or bitterness at dusk on the day that she finished it. Trying to waste the most time possible, Amaranta ordered some rough flax and spun the thread herself. She did it so carefully that the work alone took four years. Then she started the sewing. As she got closer to the unavoidable end she began to understand that only a miracle would allow her to prolong the work past Rebeca's death, but the very concentration gave her the calmness that she needed to accept the idea of frustration. It was then that she

284

understood the vicious circle of Colonel Aureliano Buendía's little gold fishes. The world was reduced to the surface of her skin and her inner self was safe from all bitterness. It pained her not to have had that revelation many years before when it would have still been possible to purify memories and reconstruct the universe under a new light and evoke without trembling Pietro Crespi's smell of lavender at dusk and rescue Rebeca from her slough of misery, not out of hatred or out of love but because of the measureless understanding of solitude. The hatred that she noticed one night in Meme's words did not upset her because it was directed at her, but she felt the repetition of another adolescence that seemed as clean as hers must have seemed and that, however, was already tainted with rancor. But by then her acceptance of her fate was so deep that she was not even upset by the certainty that all possibilities of rectification were closed to her. Her only objective was to finish the shroud. Instead of slowing it down with useless detail as she had done in the beginning, she speeded up the work. One week before she calculated that she would take the last stitch on the night of February 4, and without revealing the motives, she suggested to Meme that she move up a clavichord concert that she had arranged for the day after, but the girl paid no attention to her. Amaranta then looked for a way to delay for forty-eight hours, and she even thought that death was giving her her way because on the night of February fourth a storm caused a breakdown at the power plant. But on the following day, at eight in the morning, she took the last stitch in the most beautiful piece of work that any woman had ever finished, and she announced without the least bit of dramatics that she was going to die at dusk. She not only told the family but the whole town, because Amaranta had conceived of the idea that she could make up for a life of meanness with one last favor to the world, and she thought that no one was in a better position to take letters to the dead.

The news that Amaranta Buendía was sailing at dusk carrying the mail of death spread throughout Macondo before noon, and at three in the afternoon there was a whole carton full of letters in the parlor. Those who did not want to write gave Amaranta verbal messages, which she wrote down in a notebook with the name and the date of death of the recipient. "Don't worry," she told the senders. "The first thing I'll do when I get there is to ask for him and give him your message." It was farcical. Amaranta did not show any upset or the slightest sign of grief, and she even looked a bit rejuvenated by a duty accomplished. She was as straight and as slim as ever. If it had not been for her hardened cheekbones and a few missing teeth, she would have looked much younger than she really was. She herself arranged for them to put the letters in a box sealed with pitch and told them to place it in her grave in a way best to protect it from the dampness. In the morning she had a carpenter call who took her measurements for the coffin as she stood in the parlor, as if it were for a new dress. She showed such vigor in her last hours that Fernanda thought she was making fun of everyone. Úrsula, with the experience that Buendías died without any illness, did not doubt at all that Amaranta had received an omen of death, but in any case she was tormented by the fear that with the business of the letters and the anxiety of the senders for them to arrive quickly they would bury her alive in their confusion. So she set about clearing out the house, arguing with the intruders as she shouted at them, and by four in the afternoon she was successful. At that time Amaranta had finished dividing her things among the poor and had left on the severe coffin of unfinished boards only the change of clothing and the simple cloth slippers that she would wear in death. She did not neglect that precaution because she remembered that when Colonel Aureliano Buendía died they had to buy a pair of new shoes for him because all he had left were the bedroom slippers that he wore in the workshop. A little before five Aureliano Segundo came to fetch Meme for the concert and was surprised that the house was prepared for the funeral. If anyone seemed alive at that moment it was the serene Amaranta, who had even had enough time to cut her corns. Aureliano Segundo and Meme took leave of her with mocking farewells and promised her that on the following Saturday they would have a big resurrection party. Drawn by the public talk that Amaranta Buendía was receiving letters for the dead, Father Antonio Isabel arrived at five o'clock for the last rites and he had to wait for more than fifteen minutes for the recipient to come out of her bath. When he saw her appear in a madapollam nightshirt and with her hair loose over her shoulders, the decrepit parish priest thought that it was a trick and sent the altar boy away. He thought, however, that he would take advantage of the occasion to have Amaranta confess after twenty years of reticence. Amaranta answered simply that she did not need spiritual help of any kind because her conscience was clean. Fernanda was scandalized. Without caring that people could hear her she asked herself aloud what horrible sin Amaranta had committed to make her prefer an impious death to the shame of a confession. Thereupon Amaranta lay down and made Úrsula give public testimony as to her virginity.

"Let no one have any illusions," she shouted so that Fernanda would hear her. "Amaranta Buendía is leaving this world just as she came into it."

She did not get up again. Lying on cushions, as if she really were ill, she braided her long hair and rolled it about her ears as death had told her it should be on her bier. Then she asked Úrsula for a mirror and for the first time in more than forty years she saw her face, devastated by age and martyrdom, and she was surprised at how much she resembled the mental image that she had of herself. Úrsula understood by the silence in the bedroom that it had begun to grow dark.

"Say good-bye to Fernanda," she begged her. "One minute of reconciliation is worth more than a whole life of friendship."

"It's of no use now," Amaranta replied.

Meme could not help thinking about her when they turned on the lights on the improvised stage and she began the second part of the program. In the middle of the piece someone whispered the news in her ear and the session stopped. When he arrived home, Aureliano Segundo had to push his way through the crowd to see the corpse of the aged virgin, ugly and discolored, with the black bandage on her hand and wrapped in the magnificent shroud. She was laid out in the parlor beside the box of letters.

Úrsula did not get up again after the nine nights of mourning for Amaranta, Santa Sofía de la Piedad took care of her. She took her meals to her bedroom and annatto water for her to wash in and she kept her up to date on everything that happened in Macondo. Aureliano Segundo visited her frequently and he brought her clothing which she would place beside the bed along with the things most indispensable for daily life, so that in a short time she had built up a world within reach of her hand. She managed to arouse a great love in little Amaranta Úrsula, who was just like her, and whom she taught how to read. Her lucidity, the ability to be sufficient unto herself made one think that she was naturally conquered by the weight of her hundred years, but even though it was obvious that she was having trouble seeing, no one suspected that she was totally blind. She had so much time at her disposal then and so much interior silence to watch over the life of the house that she was the first to notice Meme's silent tribulation.

"Come here," she told her. "Now that we're alone, confess to this poor old woman what's bothering you."

Meme avoided the conversation with a short laugh. Úrsula did not insist, but she ended up confirming her suspicions when Meme did not come back to visit her. She knew that she was getting up earlier than usual, that she did not have a moment's rest as she waited for the time for her to go out, that she spent whole nights walking back and forth in the adjoining bedroom, and that the fluttering of a butterfly would bother her. On one occasion she said that she was going to see Aureliano Segundo and Úrsula was surprised that Fernanda's imagination was so limited when her husband came to the house looking for his daughter. It was too obvious that Meme was involved in secret matters, in pressing matters, in repressed anxieties long before the night that Fernanda upset the house because she caught her kissing a man in the movies.

Meme was so wrapped up in herself at that time that she accused Úrsula of having told on her. Actually, she told on herself. For a long time she had been leaving a trail that would have awakened the most drowsy person and it took Fernanda so long to discover it because she too was befogged, by her relationship with the invisible doctors. Even so she finally noticed the deep silences, the sudden outbursts, the changes in mood, and the contradictions of her daughter. She set about on a disguised but implacable vigilance. She let her go out with her girl friends as always, she helped her get dressed for the Saturday parties, and she never asked an embarrassing question that might arouse her. She already had a great deal of proof that Meme was doing different things from what she said, and yet she would give no indication of her suspicions, hoping for the right moment. One night Meme said that she was going to the movies with her father. A short time later Fernanda heard the fireworks of the debauch and the unmistakable accordion of Aureliano Segundo from the direction of Petra Cotes's place. Then she got dressed, went to the movie theater, and in the darkness of the seats she recognized her daughter. The upsetting feeling of certainty stopped her from seeing the man she was kissing, but she managed to hear his tremulous voice in the midst of the deafening shouts and laughter of the audience. "I'm sorry, love," she heard him say, and she took Meme out of the place without saying a word to her, put her through the shame of parading her along the noisy Street of the Turks, and locked her up in her bedroom.

On the following day at six in the afternoon, Fernanda recognized the voice of the man who came to call on her. He was young, sallow, with dark and melancholy eyes which would not have startled her so much if she had known the gypsies, and a dreamy air that to any woman with a heart less rigid would have been enough to make her understand her daughter's motives. He was wearing a shabby linen suit with shoes that showed the desperate defense of superimposed patches of white zinc, and in his hand he was carrying a straw hat he had bought the Saturday before. In all of his life he could never have been as frightened as at that moment, but he had a dignity and presence that spared him from humiliation and a genuine elegance that was defeated only by tarnished hands and nails that had been shattered by rough work. Fernanda, however, needed only one look to guess his status of mechanic. She saw that he was wearing his one Sunday suit and that underneath his shirt he bore the rash of the banana company. She would not let him speak. She would not even let him come through the door, which a moment later she had to close because the house was filled with yellow butterflies.

"Go away," she told him. "You've got no reason to come calling on any decent person."

His name was Mauricio Babilonia. He had been born and raised in Macondo and he was an apprentice mechanic in the banana company garage. Meme had met him by chance one afternoon when she went with Patricia Brown to get a car to take a drive through the groves. Since the chauffeur was sick they assigned him to take them and Meme was finally able to satisfy her desire to sit next to the driver and see what he did. Unlike the regular chauffeur, Mauricio Babilonia gave her a practical lesson. That was during the time that Meme was beginning to frequent Mr. Brown's house and it was still considered improper for a lady to drive a car. So she was satisfied with the technical information and she did not see Mauricio Babilonia again for several months. Later on she would remember that during the drive her attention had been called to his masculine beauty, except for the coarseness of his hands, but that afterward she had mentioned to Patricia Brown that she had been bothered by his rather proud sense of security. The first Saturday that she went to the movies with her father she saw Mauricio Babilonia again, with his linen suit, sitting a few seats away from them, and she noticed that he was not paying much attention to the film in order to turn around and look at her. Meme was bothered by the vulgarity of that. Afterward Mauricio Babilonia came over to say hello to Aureliano Segundo and only then did Meme find out that they knew each other because he had worked in Aureliano Triste's early power plant and he treated her father with the air of an employee. That fact relieved the dislike that his pride had caused in her. They had never been alone together nor had they spoken except in way of greeting, the night when she dreamed that he was saving her from a shipwreck and she did not feel gratitude but rage. It was as if she had given him the opportunity he was waiting for, since Meme yearned for just the opposite, not only with Mauricio Babilonia but with any other man who was interested in her. Therefore she was so indignant after the dream that instead of hating him, she felt an irresistible urge to see him. The anxiety became more intense during the course of the week and on Saturday it was so pressing that she had to make a great effort for Mauricio Babilonia not to notice that when he greeted her in the movies her heart was in her mouth. Dazed by a confused feeling of pleasure and rage, she gave him her hand for the first time and only then did Mauricio Babilonia let himself shake hers. Meme managed to repent her impulse in a fraction of a second, but the repentance changed immediately into a cruel satisfaction on seeing that his hand too was sweaty and cold. That night she realized that she would not have a moment of rest until she showed Mauricio Babilonia the uselessness of his aspiration and she spent the week turning that anxiety about in her mind. She resorted to all kinds of useless tricks so that Patricia Brown would go get the car with her. Finally she made use of the American redhead who was spending his vacation in Macondo at that time and with the pretext of learning about new models of cars she had him take her to the garage. From the moment she saw him Meme let herself be deceived by herself and believed that what was really going on was that she could not bear the desire to be alone with Mauricio Babilonia, and she was made indignant by the certainty that he understood that when he saw her arrive.

"I came to see the new models," Meme said.

"That's a fine excuse," he said.

Meme realized that he was burning in the heat of his pride, and she desperately looked for a way to humiliate him. But he would not give her any time. "Don't get upset," he said to her in a low voice. "It's not the first time that a woman has gone crazy over a man." She felt so defeated that she left the garage without seeing the new models and she spent the night turning over in bed and weeping with indignation. The American redhead, who was really beginning to interest her, looked like a baby in diapers. It was then that she realized that the yellow butterflies preceded the appearances of Mauricio Babilonia. She had seen them before, especially over the garage, and she had thought that they were drawn by the smell of paint. Once she had seen them fluttering about her head before she went into the movies. But when Mauricio Babilonia began to pursue her like a ghost that only she could identify in the crowd, she understood that the butterflies had something to do with him. Mauricio Babilonia was always in the audience at the concerts, at the movies, at high mass, and she did not have to see him to know that he was

there, because the butterflies were always there. Once Aureliano Segundo became so impatient with the suffocating fluttering that she felt the impulse to confide her secret to him,
as she had promised, but instinct told her that he would
laugh as usual and say: "What would your mother say if she
found out?" One morning, while she was pruning the roses,
Fernanda let out a cry of fright and had Meme taken away
from the spot where she was, which was the same place in the
garden where Remedios the Beauty had gone up to heaven.
She had thought for an instant that the miracle was going to
be repeated with her daughter, because she had been bothered by a sudden flapping of wings. It was the butterflies.
Meme saw them as if they had suddenly been born out of the
light and her heart gave a turn. At that moment Mauricio
Babilonia came in with a package that, according to what he
said, was a present from Patricia Brown. Meme swallowed
her blush, absorbed her tribulation, and even managed a
natural smile as she asked him the favor of leaving it on the
railing because her hands were dirty from the garden. The
only thing that Fernanda noted in the man whom a few
months later she was to expel from the house without remembering where she had seen him was the bilious texture
of his skin.

"He's a very strange man," Fernanda said. "You can see in
his face that he's going to die."

Meme thought that her mother had been impressed by the
butterflies. When they finished pruning the rose bushes she
washed her hands and took the package to her bedroom to
open it. It was a kind of Chinese toy, made up of five con-
centric boxes, and in the last one there was a card laboriously
inscribed by someone who could barely write: *We'll get together Saturday at the movies.* Meme felt with an aftershock
that the box had been on the railing for a long time within
reach of Fernanda's curiosity, and although she was flattered
by the audacity and ingenuity of Mauricio Babilonia, she was

moved by his innocence in expecting that she would keep the date. Meme knew at that time that Aureliano Segundo had an appointment on Saturday night. Nevertheless, the fire of anxiety burned her so much during the course of the week that on Saturday she convinced her father to leave her alone in the theater and come back for her after the show. A nocturnal butterfly fluttered about her head while the lights were on. And then it happened. When the lights went out, Mauricio Babilonia sat down beside her. Meme felt herself splashing in a bog of hesitation from which she could only be rescued, as had occurred in her dreams, by that man smelling of grease whom she could barely see in the shadows.

"If you hadn't come," he said, "you never would have seen me again."

Meme felt the weight of his hand on her knee and she knew that they were both arriving at the other side of abandonment at that instant.

"What shocks me about you," she said, smiling, "is that you always say exactly what you shouldn't be saying."

She lost her mind over him. She could not sleep and she lost her appetite and sank so deeply into solitude that even her father became an annoyance. She worked out an intricate web of false dates to throw Fernanda off the track, lost sight of her girl friends, leaped over conventions to be with Mauricio Babilonia at any time and at any place. At first his crudeness bothered her. The first time that they were alone on the deserted fields behind the garage he pulled her mercilessly into an animal state that left her exhausted. It took her a time to realize that it was also a form of tenderness and it was then that she lost her calm and lived only for him, upset by the desire to sink into his stupefying odor of grease washed off by lye. A short time before the death of Amaranta she suddenly stumbled into an open space of lucidity within the madness and she trembled before the uncertainty of the future. Then she heard about a woman who made predic-

294

tions from cards and went to see her in secret. It was Pilar Ternera. As soon as Pilar saw her come in she was aware of Meme's hidden motives. "Sit down," she told her. "I don't need cards to tell the future of a Buendía." Meme did not know and never would that the centenarian witch was her great-grandmother. Nor would she have believed it after the aggressive realism with which she revealed to her that the anxiety of falling in love could not find repose except in bed. It was the same point of view as Mauricio Babilonia's, but Meme resisted believing it because underneath it all she imagined that it had been inspired by the poor judgment of a mechanic. She thought then that love on one side was defeating love on the other, because it was characteristic of men to deny hunger once their appetites were satisfied. Pilar Ternera not only cleared up that mistake, she also offered the old canopied bed where she had conceived Arcadio, Meme's grandfather, and where afterward she conceived Aureliano José. She also taught her how to avoid an unwanted conception by means of the evaporation of mustard plasters and gave her recipes for potions that in cases of trouble could expel "even the remorse of conscience." That interview instilled in Meme the same feeling of bravery that she had felt on the drunken evening. Amaranta's death, however, obliged her to postpone the decision. While the nine nights lasted she did not once leave the side of Mauricio Babilonia, who mingled with the crowd that invaded the house. Then came the long period of mourning and the obligatory withdrawal and they separated for a time. Those were days of such inner agitation, such irrepressible anxiety, and so many repressed urges that on the first evening that Meme was able to get out she went straight to Pilar Ternera's. She surrendered to Mauricio Babilonia without resistance, without shyness, without formalities, and with a vocation that was so fluid and an intuition that was so wise that a more suspicious man than hers would have confused them with obvious experience. They made love twice a week for more than three months, protected by the innocent complicity of Aureliano Segundo, who believed without suspicion in his daughter's alibis simply in order to set her free from her mother's rigidity.

On the night that Fernanda surprised them in the movies Aureliano Segundo felt weighted down by the burden of his conscience and he visited Meme in the bedroom where Fernanda kept her locked up, trusting that she would reveal to him the confidences that she owed him. But Meme denied everything. She was so sure of herself, so anchored in her solitude that Aureliano Segundo had the impression that no link existed between them anymore, that the comradeship and the complicity were nothing but an illusion of the past. He thought of speaking to Mauricio Babilonia, thinking that his authority as his former boss would make him desist from his plans, but Petra Cotes convinced him that it was a woman's business, so he was left floating in a limbo of indecision, barely sustained by the hope that the confinement would put an end to his daughter's troubles.

Meme showed no signs of affliction. On the contrary, from the next room Úrsula perceived the peaceful rhythm of her sleep, the serenity of her tasks, the order of her meals, and the good health of her digestion. The only thing that intrigued Úrsula after almost two months of punishment was that Meme did not take a bath in the morning like everyone else, but at seven in the evening. Once she thought of warning her about the scorpions, but Meme was so distant, convinced that she had given her away, that she preferred not to disturb her with the impertinences of a great-great-grandmother. The yellow butterflies would invade the house at dusk. Every night on her way back from her bath Meme would find a desperate Fernanda killing butterflies with an insecticide bomb. "This is terrible," she would say. "All my life they told me that butterflies at night bring bad luck." One night, while Meme was in the bathroom, Fernanda went into her bedroom by chance and there were so many butterflies that she could scarcely breathe. She grabbed for the nearest piece of cloth to shoo them away and her heart froze with terror as she connected her daughter's evening baths with the mustard plasters that rolled onto the floor. She did not wait for an opportune moment as she had the first time. On the following day she invited the new mayor to lunch. Like her, he had come down from the highlands, and she asked him to station a guard in the backyard because she had the impression that hens were being stolen. That night the guard brought down Mauricio Babilonia as he was lifting up the tiles to get into the bathroom where Meme was waiting for him, naked and trembling with love among the scorpions and butterflies as she had done almost every night for the past few months. A bullet lodged in his spinal column reduced him to his bed for the rest of his life. He died of old age in solitude, without a moan, without a protest, without a single moment of betrayal, tormented by memories and by the yellow butterflies, who did not give him a moment's peace, and ostracized as a chicken thief.

L

THE EVENTS that would deal Macondo its fatal blow were just showing themselves when they brought Meme Buendía's son home. The public situation was so uncertain then that no one had sufficient spirit to become involved with private scandals, so that Fernanda was able to count on an atmosphere that enabled her to keep the child hidden as if he had never existed. She had to take him in because the circumstances under which they brought him made rejection impossible. She had to tolerate him against her will for the rest of her life because at the moment of truth she lacked the courage to go through with her inner determination to drown him in the bathroom cistern. She locked him up in Colonel Aureliano Buendía's old workshop. She succeeded in convincing Santa Sofía de la Piedad that she had found him floating in a basket. Úrsula would die without ever knowing his origin. Little Amaranta Úrsula, who went into the workshop once when Fernanda was feeding the child, also believed the version of the floating basket. Aureliano Segundo, having broken finally with his wife because of the irrational way in which she handled Meme's tragedy, did not know of the existence of his grandson until three years after they brought him home, when the child escaped from captivity through an oversight on Fernanda's part and appeared on the porch for a fraction of a second, naked, with matted hair, and with an impressive sex organ that was like a turkey's wattles, as if he were not a human child but the encyclopedia definition of a cannibal.

Fernanda had not counted on that nasty trick of her incorrigible fate. The child was like the return of a shame that she had thought exiled by her from the house forever. As soon as they carried off Mauricio Babilonia with his shattered spinal column, Fernanda had worked out the most minute details of a plan destined to wipe out all traces of the burden. Without consulting her husband, she packed her bags, put the three changes of clothing that her daughter would need into a small suitcase, and went to get her in her bedroom a half hour before the train arrived.

"Let's go, Renata," she told her.

She gave no explanation. Meme, for her part, did not expect or want any. She not only did not know where they were going, but it would have been the same to her if they had been taking her to the slaughterhouse. She had not spoken again nor would she do so for the rest of her life from the time that she heard the shot in the backyard and the simultaneous cry of pain from Mauricio Babilonia. When her mother ordered her out of the bedroom she did not comb her hair or wash her face and she got into the train as if she were walking in her sleep, not even noticing the yellow butterflies that were still accompanying her. Fernanda never found out, nor did she take the trouble to, whether that stony silence was a determination of her will or whether she had become mute because of the impact of the tragedy. Meme barely took notice of the journey through the formerly enchanted region. She did not see the shady, endless banana groves on both sides of the tracks. She did not see the white houses of the gringos or their gardens, dried out by dust and heat, or the women in shorts and blue-striped shirts playing cards on the terraces. She did not see the oxcarts on the dusty roads loaded down with bunches of bananas. She did not see the girls diving into the transparent rivers like tarpons, leaving the passengers on the train with the bitterness of their splendid breasts, or the miserable huts of the workers all huddled together where Mauricio Babilonia's yellow butterflies fluttered about, and in the doorways of which there were green and squalid children sitting on their pots, and pregnant women who shouted insults at the train. That fleeting vision, which had been a celebration for her when she came home from school, passed through Meme's heart without a quiver. She did not look out of the window, not even when the burning dampness of the groves ended and the train went through a poppy-laden plain where the carbonized skeleton of the Spanish galleon still sat and then came out into the clear air alongside the frothy, dirty sea where almost a century before José Arcadio Buendía's illusions had met defeat.

At five o'clock in the afternoon, when they had come to the last station in the swamp, she got out of the train because Fernanda made her. They got into a small carriage that looked like an enormous bat, drawn by an asthmatic horse, and they went through the desolate city in the endless streets of which, split by saltiness, there was the sound of a piano lesson just like the one that Fernanda heard during the siestas of her adolescence. They went on board a riverboat, the wooden wheel of which had a sound of conflagration, and whose rusted metal plates reverberated like the mouth of an oven. Meme shut herself up in her cabin. Twice a day Fernanda left a plate of food by her bed and twice a day she took it away intact, not because Meme had resolved to die of hunger, but because even the smell of food was repugnant to her and her stomach rejected even water. Not even she herself knew that her fertility had outwitted the mustard vapors, just as Fernanda did not know until almost a year later, when they brought the child. In the suffocating cabin, maddened by the vibration of the metal plates and the unbearable stench of the mud stirred up by the paddle wheel, Meme lost track of the days. Much time had passed when she saw the last yellow butterfly destroyed in the blades of the fan and she admitted as an irremediable truth that Mauricio Babilonia had died. She did not let herself be defeated by resignation, however. She kept on thinking about him during the arduous muleback crossing of the hallucinating plateau where Aureliano Segundo had become lost when he was looking for the most beautiful woman who had ever appeared on the face of the earth, and when they went over the mountains along Indian trails and entered the gloomy city in whose stone alleys the funereal bronze bells of thirty-two churches tolled. That night they slept in the abandoned colonial mansion on boards that Fernanda laid on the floor of a room invaded by weeds, wrapped in the shreds of curtains that they pulled off the windows and that fell to pieces with every turn of the body. Meme knew where they were because in the fright of her insomnia she saw pass by the gentleman dressed in black whom they delivered to the house inside a lead box on one distant Christmas Eve. On the following day, after mass, Fernanda took her to a somber building that Meme recognized immediately from her mother's stories of the convent where they had raised her to be a queen, and then she understood that they had come to the end of the journey. While Fernanda was speaking to someone in the office next door,

Meme remained in a parlor checkered with large oil paintings of colonial archbishops, still wearing an etamine dress with small black flowers and stiff high shoes which were swollen by the cold of the uplands. She was standing in the center of the parlor thinking about Mauricio Babilonia under the yellow stream of light from the stained glass windows when a very beautiful novice came out of the office carrying her suitcase with the three changes of clothing. As she passed Meme she took her hand without stopping.

"Come, Renata," she said to her.

Meme took her hand and let herself be led. The last time that Fernanda saw her, trying to keep up with the novice, the iron grating of the cloister had just closed behind her. She was still thinking about Mauricio Babilonia, his smell of grease, and his halo of butterflies, and she would keep on thinking about him for all the days of her life until the remote autumn morning when she died of old age, with her name changed and her head shaved and without ever having spoken a word, in a gloomy hospital in Cracow.

Fernanda returned to Macondo on a train protected by armed police. During the trip she noticed the tension of the passengers, the military preparations in the towns along the line, and an atmosphere rarefied by the certainty that something serious was going to happen, but she had no information until she reached Macondo and they told her that José Arcadio Segundo was inciting the workers of the banana company to strike. "That's all we need," Fernanda said to herself. "An anarchist in the family." The strike broke out two weeks later and it did not have the dramatic consequences that had been feared. The workers demanded that they not be obliged to cut and load bananas on Sundays, and the position seemed so just that even Father Antonio Isabel interceded in its favor because he found it in accordance with the laws of God. That victory, along with other actions that were initiated during the following months, drew the colorless José Arcadio Segundo out of his anonymity, for people had been accustomed to say that he was only good for filling up the town with French whores. With the same impulsive decision with which he had auctioned off his fighting cocks in order to organize a harebrained boat business, he gave up his position as foreman in the banana company and took the side of the workers. Quite soon he was pointed out as the agent of an international conspiracy against public order. One night, during the course of a week darkened by somber rumors, he miraculously escaped four revolver shots taken at him by an unknown party as he was leaving a secret meeting. The atmosphere of the following months was so tense that even Úrsula perceived it in her dark corner, and she had the impression that once more she was living through the dangerous times when her son Aureliano carried the homeopathic pills of subversion in his pocket. She tried to speak to José Arcadio Segundo, to let him know about that precedent, but Aureliano Segundo told her that since the night of the attempt on his life no one knew his whereabouts.

"Just like Aureliano," Úrsula exclaimed. "It's as if the world were repeating itself."

Fernanda was immune to the uncertainty of those days. She had no contact with the outside world since the violent altercation she had had with her husband over her having decided Meme's fate without his consent. Aureliano Segundo was prepared to rescue his daughter with the help of the police if necessary, but Fernanda showed him some papers that were proof that she had entered the convent of her own free will. Meme had indeed signed once she was already behind the iron grating and she did it with the same indifference with which she had allowed herself to be led away. Underneath it all, Aureliano Segundo did not believe in the legitimacy of the proof, just as he never believed that Mauricio Babilonia had gone into the yard to steal chickens, but both expedients served to ease his conscience, and thus he could go back without remorse under the shadow of Petra Cotes, where he revived his noisy revelry and unlimited gourmandizing. Foreign to the restlessness of the town, deaf to Úrsula's quiet predictions, Fernanda gave the last turn to the screw of her preconceived plan. She wrote a long letter to her son José Arcadio, who was then about to take his first orders, and in it she told him that his sister Renata had expired in the peace of the Lord and as a consequence of the black vomit. Then she put Amaranta Úrsula under the care of Santa Sofía de la Piedad and dedicated herself to organizing her correspondence with the invisible doctors, which had been upset by Meme's trouble. The first thing that she did was to set a definite date for the postponed telepathic operation. But the invisible doctors answered her that it was not wise so long as the state of social agitation continued in Macondo. She was so urgent and so poorly informed that she explained to them in another letter that there was no such state of agitation and that everything was the result of the lunacy of a brother-in-law of hers who was fiddling around at that time in that labor union nonsense just as he had been involved with cockfighting and riverboats before. They were still not in agreement on the hot Wednesday when an aged nun knocked at the door bearing a small basket on her arm. When she opened the door Santa Sofía de la Piedad thought that it was a gift and tried to take the small basket that was covered with a lovely lace wrap. But the nun stopped her because she had instructions to give it personally and with the strictest secrecy to Doña Fernanda del Carpio de Buendía. It was Meme's son. Fernanda's former spiritual director explained to her in a letter that he had been born two months before and that they had taken the privilege of baptizing him Aureliano, for his grandfather, because his mother would not open her lips to tell them her wishes. Fernanda rose up inside against that trick of fate, but she had sufficient strength to hide it in front of the nun.

"We'll tell them that we found him floating in the basket," she said, smiling.

"No one will believe it," the nun said.

"If they believe it in the Bible," Fernanda replied, "I don't see why they shouldn't believe it from me."

The nun lunched at the house while she waited for the train back, and in accordance with the discretion they asked of her, she did not mention the child again, but Fernanda viewed her as an undesirable witness of her shame and lamented the fact that they had abandoned the medieval custom of hanging a messenger who bore bad news. It was then that she decided to drown the child in the cistern as soon as the nun left, but her heart was not strong enough and she preferred to wait patiently until the infinite goodness of God would free her from the annoyance.

The new Aureliano was a year old when the tension of the people broke with no forewarning. José Arcadio Segundo and other union leaders who had remained underground until then suddenly appeared one weekend and organized demonstrations in towns throughout the banana region. The police merely maintained public order. But on Monday night the leaders were taken from their homes and sent to jail in the capital of the province with two-pound irons on their legs. Taken among them were José Arcadio Segundo and Lorenzo Gavilán, a colonel in the Mexican revolution, exiled in Macondo, who said that he had been witness to the heroism of his comrade Artemio Cruz. They were set free, however, within three months because of the fact that the government and the banana company could not reach an agreement as to who should feed them in jail. The protests of the workers this time were based on the lack of sanitary facilities in their living quarters, the nonexistence of medical services, and terrible working conditions. They stated, furthermore, that they were not being paid in real money but in scrip, which was good only to buy Virginia ham in the company

L*

commissaries. José Arcadio Segundo was put in jail because he revealed that the scrip system was a way for the company to finance its fruit ships, which without the commissary merchandise would have to return empty from New Orleans to the banana ports. The other complaints were common knowledge. The company physicians did not examine the sick but had them line up behind one another in the dispensaries and a nurse would put a pill the color of copper sulfate on their tongues, whether they had malaria, gonorrhea, or constipation. It was a cure that was so common that children would stand in line several times and instead of swallowing the pills would take them home to use as bingo markers. The company workers were crowded together in miserable barracks. The engineers, instead of putting in toilets, had a portable latrine for every fifty people brought to the camps at Christmas time and they held public demonstrations of how to use them so that they would last longer. The decrepit lawyers dressed in black who during other times had beseiged Colonel Aureliano Buendía and who now were controlled by the banana company dismissed those demands with decisions that seemed like acts of magic. When the workers drew up a list of unanimous petitions, a long time passed before they were able to notify the banana company officially. As soon as he found out about the agreement, Mr. Brown hitched his luxurious glassed-in coach to the train and disappeared from Macondo along with the more prominent representatives of his company. Nonetheless, some workers found one of them the following Saturday in a brothel and they made him sign a copy of the sheet with the demands while he was naked with the women who had helped to entrap him. The mournful lawyers showed in court that that man had nothing to do with the company and in order that no one doubt their arguments they had him jailed as an impostor. Later on, Mr. Brown was surprised traveling incognito in a third-class coach and they made him sign another copy of the demands. On the following day he appeared before the judges with his hair dyed black and speaking flawless Spanish. The lawyers showed that the man was not Mr. Jack Brown, the superintendent of the banana company, born in Prattville, Alabama, but a harmless vendor of medicinal plants, born in Macondo and baptized there with the name of Dagoberto Fonseca. A while later, faced with a new attempt by the workers, the lawyers publicly exhibited Mr. Brown's death certificate, attested to by consuls and foreign ministers, which bore witness that on June ninth last he had been run over by a fire engine in Chicago. Tired of that hermeneutical delirium, the workers turned away from the authorities in Macondo and brought their complaints up to the higher courts. It was there that the sleight-of-hand lawyers proved that the demands lacked all validity for the simple reason that the banana company did not have, never had had, and never would have any workers in its service because they were all hired on a temporary and occasional basis. So that the fable of the Virginia ham was nonsense, the same as that of the miraculous pills and the Yuletide toilets, and by a decision of the court it was established and set down in solemn decrees that the workers did not exist.

The great strike broke out. Cultivation stopped halfway, the fruit rotted on the trees and the hundred-twenty-car trains remained on the sidings. The idle workers overflowed the towns. The Street of the Turks echoed with a Saturday that lasted for several days and in the poolroom at the Hotel Jacob they had to arrange twenty-four-hour shifts. That was where José Arcadio Segundo was on the day it was announced that the army had been assigned to re-establish public order. Although he was not a man given to omens, the news was like an announcement of death that he had been waiting for ever since that distant morning when Colonel Gerineldo Márquez had let him see an execution. The bad omen did not change his solemnity, however. He took the shot he had planned and it was good. A short time later the drumbeats, the shrill of the bugle, the shouting and running of the people told him that not only had the game of pool come to an end, but also the silent and solitary game that he had been playing with himself ever since that dawn execution. Then he went out into the street and saw them. There were three regiments, whose march in time to a galley drum made the earth tremble. Their snorting of a many-headed dragon filled the glow of noon with a pestilential vapor. They were short, stocky, and brutelike. They perspired with the sweat of a horse and had a smell of suntanned hide and the taciturn and impenetrable perseverance of men from the uplands. Although it took them over an hour to pass by, one might have thought that they were only a few squads marching in a circle, because they were all identical, sons of the same bitch, and with the same stolidity they all bore the weight of their packs and canteens, the shame of their rifles with fixed bayonets, and the chancre of blind obedience and a sense of honor. Úrsula heard them pass from her bed in the shadows and she made a cross with her fingers. Santa Sofía de la Piedad existed for an instant, leaning over the embroidered tablecloth that she had just ironed, and she thought of her son, José Arcadio Segundo, who without changing expression watched the last soldiers pass by the door of the Hotel Jacob.

Martial law enabled the army to assume the functions of arbitrator in the controversy, but no effort at conciliation was made. As soon as they appeared in Macondo, the soldiers put aside their rifles and cut and loaded the bananas and started the trains running. The workers, who had been content to wait until then, went into the woods with no other weapons but their working machetes and they began to sabotage the sabotage. They burned plantations and commissaries, tore up tracks to impede the passage of the trains that began to open their path with machine-gun fire, and they cut telegraph and

308

telephone wires. The irrigation ditches were stained with blood. Mr. Brown, who was alive in the electrified chicken coop, was taken out of Macondo with his family and those of his fellow countrymen and brought to a safe place under the protection of the army. The situation was threatening to lead to a bloody and unequal civil war when the authorities called upon the workers to gather in Macondo. The summons announced that the civil and military leader of the province would arrive on the following Friday ready to intercede in the conflict.

José Arcadio Segundo was in the crowd that had gathered at the station on Friday since early in the morning. He had taken part in a meeting of union leaders and had been commissioned, along with Colonel Gavilán, to mingle in the crowd and orient it according to how things went. He did not feel well and a salty paste was beginning to collect on his palate when he noticed that the army had set up machine-gun emplacements around the small square and that the wired city of the banana company was protected by artillery pieces. Around twelve o'clock, waiting for a train that was not arriving, more than three thousand people, workers, women, and children, had spilled out of the open space in front of the station and were pressing into the neighboring streets, which the army had closed off with rows of machine guns. At that time it all seemed more like a jubilant fair than a waiting crowd. They had brought over the fritter and drink stands from the Street of the Turks and the people were in good spirits as they bore the tedium of waiting and the scorching sun. A short time before three o'clock the rumor spread that the official train would not arrive until the following day. The crowd let out a sigh of disappointment. An army lieutenant then climbed up onto the roof of the station where there were four machine-gun emplacements aiming at the crowd and called for silence. Next to José Arcadio Segundo there was a barefooted woman, very fat, with two children between the ages of four and seven. She was carrying the smaller one and she asked José Arcadio Segundo, without knowing him, if he would lift up the other one so that he could hear better. José Arcadio Segundo put the child on his shoulders. Many years later that child would still tell, to the disbelief of all, that he had seen the lieutenant reading Decree No. 4 of the civil and military leader of the province through an old phonograph horn. It had been signed by General Carlos Cortes Vargas and his secretary, Major Enrique García Isaza, and in three articles of eighty words he declared the strikers to be a "bunch of hoodlums" and he authorized the army to shoot to kill.

After the decree was read, in the midst of a deafening hoot of protest, a captain took the place of the lieutenant on the roof of the station and with the horn he signaled that he wanted to speak. The crowd was quiet again.

"Ladies and gentlemen," the captain said in a low voice that was slow and a little tired, "you have five minutes to withdraw."

The redoubled hooting and shouting drowned out the bugle call that announced the start of the count. No one moved.

"Five minutes have passed," the captain said in the same tone. "One more minute and we'll open fire."

José Arcadio Segundo, sweating ice, lowered the child and gave him to the woman. "Those bastards might just shoot," she murmured. José Arcadio Segundo did not have time to speak because at that instant he recognized the hoarse voice of Colonel Gavilán echoing the words of the woman with a shout. Intoxicated by the tension, by the miraculous depth of the silence, and furthermore convinced that nothing could move that crowd held tight in a fascination with death, José Arcadio Segundo raised himself up over the heads in front of him and for the first time in his life he raised his voice.

"You bastards!" he shouted. "Take the extra minute and stick it up your ass!"

After his shout something happened that did not bring on fright but a kind of hallucination. The captain gave the order to fire and fourteen machine guns answered at once. But it all seemed like a farce. It was as if the machine guns had been loaded with caps, because their panting rattle could be heard and their incandescent spitting could be seen, but not the slightest reaction was perceived, not a cry, not even a sigh among the compact crowd that seemed petrified by an instantaneous invulnerability. Suddenly, on one side of the station, a cry of death tore open the enchantment: "Aaaagh, Mother." A seismic voice, a volcanic breath, the roar of a cataclysm broke out in the center of the crowd with a great potential of expansion. José Arcadio Segundo barely had time to pick up the child while the mother with the other one was swallowed up by the crowd that swirled about in panic.

Many years later that child would still tell, in spite of people thinking that he was a crazy old man, how José Arcadio Segundo had lifted him over his head and hauled him, almost in the air, as if floating on the terror of the crowd, toward a nearby street. The child's privileged position allowed him to see at that moment that the wild mass was starting to get to the corner and the row of machine guns opened fire. Several voices shouted at the same time:

"Get down! Get down!"

The people in front had already done so, swept down by the wave of bullets. The survivors, instead of getting down, tried to go back to the small square, and the panic became a dragon's tail as one compact wave ran against another which was moving in the opposite direction, toward the other dragon's tail in the street across the way, where the machine guns were also firing without cease. They were penned in, swirling about in a gigantic whirlwind that little by little was being reduced to its epicenter as the edges were systematically being cut off all around like an onion being peeled by the insatiable and methodical shears of the machine guns. The child saw a woman kneeling with her arms in the shape of a cross in an open space, mysteriously free of the stampede. José Arcadio Segundo put him up there at the moment he fell with his face bathed in blood, before the colossal troop wiped out the empty space, the kneeling woman, the light of the high, drought-stricken sky, and the whorish world where Úrsula Iguarán had sold so many little candy animals.

When José Arcadio Segundo came to he was lying face up in the darkness. He realized that he was riding on an endless and silent train and that his head was caked with dry blood and that all his bones ached. He felt an intolerable desire to sleep. Prepared to sleep for many hours, safe from the terror and the horror, he made himself comfortable on the side that pained him less, and only then did he discover that he was lying against dead people. There was no free space in the car except for an aisle in the middle. Several hours must have passed since the massacre because the corpses had the same temperature as plaster in autumn and the same consistency of petrified foam that it had, and those who had put them in the car had had time to pile them up in the same way in which they transported bunches of bananas. Trying to flee from the nightmare, José Arcadio Segundo dragged himself from one car to another in the direction in which the train was heading, and in the flashes of light that broke through the wooden slats as they went through sleeping towns he saw the man corpses, woman corpses, child corpses who would be thrown into the sea like rejected bananas. He recognized only a woman who sold drinks in the square and Colonel Gavilán, who still held wrapped in his hand the belt with a buckle of Morelia silver with which he had tried to open his way through the panic. When he got to the first car he jumped into the darkness and lay beside the tracks until the train had passed. It was the longest one he had ever seen, with almost two hundred freight cars and a locomotive at either end and a third one in the middle. It had no lights, not even the red and green running lights, and it slipped off with a nocturnal and stealthy velocity. On top of the cars there could be seen the dark shapes of the soldiers with their emplaced machine guns.

After midnight a torrential cloudburst came up. José Arcadio Segundo did not know where it was that he had jumped off, but he knew that by going in the opposite direction to that of the train he would reach Macondo. After walking for more than three hours, soaked to the skin, with a terrible headache, he was able to make out the first houses in the light of dawn. Attracted by the smell of coffee, he went into a kitchen where a woman with a child in her arms was leaning over the stove.

"Hello," he said, exhausted. "I'm José Arcadio Segundo Buendía."

He pronounced his whole name, letter by letter, in order to convince her that he was alive. He was wise in doing so, because the woman had thought that he was an apparition as she saw the dirty, shadowy figure with his head and clothing dirty with blood and touched with the solemnity of death come through the door. She recognized him. She brought him a blanket so that he could wrap himself up while his clothes dried by the fire, she warmed some water to wash his wound, which was only a flesh wound, and she gave him a clean diaper to bandage his head. Then she gave him a mug of coffee without sugar as she had been told the Buendías drank it, and she spread his clothing out near the fire.

José Arcadio Segundo did not speak until he had finished drinking his coffee.

"There must have been three thousand of them," he murmured.

"What?"

"The dead," he clarified. "It must have been all of the people who were at the station."

The woman measured him with a pitying look. "There

haven't been any dead here," she said. "Since the time of your uncle, the colonel, nothing has happened in Macondo." In the three kitchens where José Arcadio Segundo stopped before reaching home they told him the same thing: "There weren't any dead." He went through the small square by the station and he saw the fritter stands piled one on top of the other and he could find no trace of the massacre. The streets were deserted under the persistent rain and the houses locked up with no trace of life inside. The only human note was the first tolling of the bells for mass. He knocked at the door at Colonel Gavilán's house. A pregnant woman whom he had seen several times closed the door in his face. "He left," she said, frightened. "He went back to his own country." The main entrance to the wire chicken coop was guarded as always by two local policemen who looked as if they were made of stone under the rain, with raincoats and rubber boots. On their marginal street the West Indian Negroes were singing their Saturday psalms. José Arcadio Segundo jumped over the courtyard wall and entered the house through the kitchen. Santa Sofía de la Piedad barely raised her voice. "Don't let Fernanda see you," she said. "She's just getting up." As if she were fulfilling an implicit pact, she took her son to the "chamberpot room," arranged Melquíades' broken-down cot for him, and at two in the afternoon, while Fernanda was taking her siesta, she passed a plate of food in to him through the window.

Aureliano Segundo had slept at home because the rain had caught him there and at three in the afternoon he was still waiting for it to clear. Informed in secret by Santa Sofía de la Piedad, he visited his brother in Melquíades' room at that time. He did not believe the version of the massacre or the nightmare trip of the train loaded with corpses traveling toward the sea either. The night before he had read an extraordinary proclamation to the nation which said that the workers had left the station and had returned home in peaceful groups. The proclamation also stated that the union leaders, with great patriotic spirit, had reduced their demands to two points: a reform of medical services and the building of latrines in the living quarters. It was stated later that when the military authorities obtained the agreement with the workers, they hastened to tell Mr. Brown and he not only accepted the new conditions but offered to pay for three days of public festivities to celebrate the end of the conflict. Except that when the military asked him on what date they could announce the signing of the agreement, he looked out the window at the sky crossed with lightning flashes and made a profound gesture of doubt.

"When the rain stops," he said. "As long as the rain lasts we're suspending all activities."

It had not rained for three months and there had been a drought. But when Mr. Brown announced his decision a torrential downpour spread over the whole banana region. It was the one that caught José Arcadio Segundo on his way to Macondo. A week later it was still raining. The official version, repeated a thousand times and mangled out all over the country by every means of communication the government found at hand, was finally accepted: there were no dead, the satisfied workers had gone back to their families, and the banana company was suspending all activity until the rains stopped. Martial law continued with an eye to the necessity of taking emergency measures for the public disaster of the endless downpour, but the troops were confined to quarters. During the day the soldiers walked through the torrents in the streets with their pant legs rolled up, playing with boats with the children. At night, after taps, they knocked doors down with their rifle butts, hauled suspects out of their beds, and took them off on trips from which there was no return. The search for and extermination of the hoodlums, murderers, arsonists, and rebels of Decree No. 4 was still going on, but the military denied it even to the relatives of the victims who crowded the commandants' offices in search of news. "You must have been dreaming," the officers insisted. "Nothing has happened in Macondo, nothing has ever happened, and nothing ever will happen. This is a happy town." In that way they were finally able to wipe out the union leaders.

The only survivor was José Arcadio Segundo. One February night the unmistakable blows of rifle butts were heard at the door. Aureliano Segundo, who was still waiting for it to clear, opened the door to six soldiers under the command of an officer. Soaking from the rain, without saying a word, they searched the house room by room, closet by closet, from parlor to pantry. Úrsula woke up when they turned on the light in her room and she did not breathe while the search went on but held her fingers in the shape of a cross, pointing them to where the soldiers were moving about. Santa Sofía de la Piedad managed to warn José Arcadio Segundo, who was sleeping in Melquíades' room, but he could see that it was too late to try to escape. So Santa Sofía de la Piedad locked the door again and he put on his shirt and his shoes and sat down on the cot to wait for them. At that moment they were searching the gold workshop. The officer made them open the padlock and with a quick sweep of his lantern he saw the workbench and the glass cupboard with bottles of acid and instruments that were still where their owner had left them and he seemed to understand that no one lived in that room. He wisely asked Aureliano Segundo if he was a silversmith, however, and the latter explained to him that it had been Colonel Aureliano Buendía's workshop. "Oho," the officer said, turned on the lights, and ordered such a minute search that they did not miss the eighteen little gold fishes that had not been melted down and that were hidden behind the bottles in their tin can. The officer examined them one by one on the workbench and then he turned human. "I'd like to take one, if I may," he said. "At one time they were a mark of subversion, but now they're relics." He was young, almost an adolescent, with no sign of timidity and with a natural pleasant manner that had not shown itself until then. Aureliano Segundo gave him the little fish. The officer put it in his shirt pocket with a childlike glow in his eyes and he put the others back in the can and set it back where it had been.

"It's a wonderful memento," he said. "Colonel Aureliano Buendía was one of our greatest men."

Nevertheless, that surge of humanity did not alter his professional conduct. At Melquíades' room, which was locked up again with the padlock, Santa Sofía de la Piedad tried one last hope. "No one has lived in that room for a century," she said. The officer had it opened and flashed the beam of the lantern over it, and Aureliano Segundo and Santa Sofía de la Piedad saw the Arab eyes of José Arcadio Segundo at the moment when the ray of light passed over his face and they understood that it was the end of one anxiety and the beginning of another which would find relief only in resignation. But the officer continued examining the room with the lantern and showed no sign of interest until he discovered the seventy-two chamberpots piled up in the cupboards. Then he turned on the light. José Arcadio Segundo was sitting on the edge of the cot, ready to go, more solemn and pensive than ever. In the background were the shelves with the shredded books, the rolls of parchment, and the clean and orderly worktable with the ink still fresh in the inkwells. There was the same pureness in the air, the same clarity, the same respite from dust and destruction that Aureliano Segundo had known in childhood and that only Colonel Aureliano Buendía could not perceive. But the officer was only interested in the chamberpots.

"How many people live in this house?" he asked.

"Five."

The officer obviously did not understand. He paused with his glance on the space where Aureliano Segundo and Santa

Sofía de la Piedad were still seeing José Arcadio Segundo and the latter also realized that the soldier was looking at him without seeing him. Then he turned out the light and closed the door. When he spoke to the soldiers, Aureliano Segundo understood that the young officer had seen the room with the same eyes as Colonel Aureliano Buendía.

"It's obvious that no one has been in that room for at least a hundred years," the officer said to the soldiers. "There must even be snakes in there."

When the door closed, José Arcadio Segundo was sure that the war was over. Years before Colonel Aureliano Buendía had spoken to him about the fascination of war and had tried to show it to him with countless examples drawn from his own experience. He had believed him. But the night when the soldiers looked at him without seeing him while he thought about the tension of the past few months, the misery of jail, the panic at the station, and the train loaded with dead people, José Arcadio Segundo reached the conclusion that Colonel Aureliano Buendía was nothing but a faker or an imbecile. He could not understand why he had needed so many words to explain what he felt in war because one was enough: fear. In Melquíades' room, on the other hand, protected by the supernatural light, by the sound of the rain, by the feeling of being invisible, he found the repose that he had not had for one single instant during his previous life, and the only fear that remained was that they would bury him alive. He told Santa Sofía de la Piedad about it when she brought him his daily meals and she promised to struggle to stay alive even beyond her natural forces in order to make sure that they would bury him dead. Free from all fear, José Arcadio Segundo dedicated himself then to peruse the manuscripts of Melquíades many times, and with so much more pleasure when he could not understand them. He became accustomed to the sound of the rain, which after two months had become another form of silence, and the only thing that disturbed his solitude was the coming and going of Santa Sofía de la Piedad. He asked her, therefore, to leave the meals on the windowsill and padlock the door. The rest of the family forgot about him, including Fernanda, who did not mind leaving him there when she found that the soldiers had seen him without recognizing him. After six months of enclosure, since the soldiers had left Macondo Aureliano Segundo removed the padlock, looking for someone he could talk to until the rain stopped. As soon as he opened the door he felt the pestilential attack of the chamberpots, which were placed on the floor and all of which had been used several times. José Arcadio Segundo, devoured by baldness, indifferent to the air that had been sharpened by the nauseating vapors, was still reading and rereading the unintelligible parchments. He was illuminated by a seraphic glow. He scarcely raised his eyes when he heard the door open, but that look was enough for his brother to see repeated in it the irreparable fate of his great-grandfather.

"There were more than three thousand of them," was all that José Arcadio Segundo said. "I'm sure now that they were everybody who had been at the station."

It RAINED for four years, eleven months, and two days. There were periods of drizzle during which everyone put on his full dress and a convalescent look to celebrate the clearing, but people soon grew accustomed to interpret the pauses as a sign of redoubled rain. The sky crumbled into a set of destructive storms and out of the north came hurricanes that scattered roofs about and knocked down walls and uprooted every last plant of the banana groves. Just as during the insomnia plague, as Úrsula came to remember during those days, the calamity itself inspired defenses against boredom. Aureliano Segundo was one of those who worked hardest not to be conquered by idleness. He had gone home for some minor matter on the night that Mr. Brown unleashed the storm, and Fernanda tried to help him with a half-blown-out umbrella that she found in a closet. "I don't need it," he said. "I'll stay until it clears." That was not, of course, an ironclad promise, but he would accomplish it literally. Since his clothes were at Petra Cotes's, every three days he would take off what he had on and wait in his shorts until they were washed. In order not to become bored, he dedicated himself to the task of repairing the many things that needed fixing in the house. He adjusted hinges, oiled locks, screwed knockers tight, and planed doorjambs. For several months he was seen wandering about with a toolbox that the gypsies must have left behind in José Arcadio Buendía's days, and no one knew whether because of the involuntary exercise, the winter tedium, or the imposed abstinence, but his belly was deflating little by little like a wineskin and his face of a beatific tortoise was becoming less bloodshot and his double chin less prominent until he became less pachydermic all over and was able to tie his own shoes again. Watching him putting in latches and repairing clocks, Fernanda wondered whether or not he too might be falling into the vice of building so that he could take apart like Colonel Aureliano Buendía and his little gold fishes, Amaranta and her shroud and her buttons, José Arcadio and the parchments, and Úrsula and her memories. But that was not the case. The worst part was that the rain was affecting everything and the driest of machines would have flowers popping out among their gears if they were not oiled every three days, and the threads in brocades rusted, and wet clothing would break out in a rash of saffron-colored moss. The air was so damp that fish could have come in through the doors and swum out the windows, floating through the atmosphere in the rooms. One morning Úrsula woke up feeling that she was reaching her end in a placid swoon and she had already asked them to take her to Father Antonio Isabel, even if it had to be on a stretcher, when Santa Sofía de la Piedad discovered that her back was paved with leeches. She took them off one by one, crushing them with a firebrand before they bled her to death. It was necessary to dig canals to get the water out of the house and rid it of the frogs and snails so that they could dry the floors and take the bricks from under the bedposts and walk in shoes once more. Occupied with the many small details that called for his attention, Aureliano Segundo did not realize that he was getting old until one afternoon when he found himself contemplating the premature dusk from a rocking chair and thinking about Petra Cotes without quivering. There would have been no problem in going back to Fernanda's insipid love, because her beauty had become solemn with age, but the rain had spared him from all emergencies of passion and had filled him with the spongy serenity of a lack of appetite. He amused himself thinking about the things that he could have done in other times with that rain which had already lasted a year. He had been one of the first to bring zinc sheets to Macondo, much earlier than their popularization by the banana company, simply to roof Petra Cotes's bedroom with them and to take pleasure in the feeling of deep intimacy that the sprinkling of the rain produced at that time. But even those wild memories of his mad youth left him unmoved, just as during his last debauch he had exhausted his quota of salaciousness and all he had left was the marvelous gift of being able to remember it without bitterness or repentance. It might have been thought that the deluge had given him the opportunity to sit and reflect and that the business of the pliers and the oilcan had awakened in him the tardy yearning of so many useful trades that he might have followed in his life and did not; but neither case was true, because the temptation of a sedentary domesticity that was besieging him was not the result of any rediscovery or moral lesson. It came from much farther off, unearthed by the rain's pitchfork from the days when in Melquíades' room he would read the prodigious fables about flying carpets and whales that fed on entire ships and their crews. It was during those days that in a moment of carelessness little Aureliano appeared on the porch and his grandfather recognized the secret of his identity. He cut his hair, dressed him, taught him not to be afraid of people, and very soon it was evident that he was a legitimate Aureliano Buendía, with his high cheekbones, his startled look, and his solitary air. It was a relief for Fernanda. For some time she had measured the extent of her pridefulness, but she could not find any way to remedy it because the more she thought of solutions the less rational they seemed to her. If she had known that Aureliano Segundo was going to take things the way he did, with the fine pleasure of a grandfather, she would not have taken so many turns or got so mixed up, but would have freed herself from mortification the year before. Amaranta Úrsula, who already had her second teeth, thought of her nephew as a scurrying toy who was a consolation for the tedium of the rain. Aureliano Segundo remembered then the English encyclopedia that no one had since touched in Meme's old room. He began to show the children the pictures, especially those of animals, and later on the maps and photographs of remote countries and famous people. Since he did not know any English and could identify only the most famous cities and people, he would invent names and legends to satisfy the children's insatiable curiosity.

Fernanda really believed that her husband was waiting for it to clear to return to his concubine. During the first months of the rain she was afraid that he would try to slip into her bedroom and that she would have to undergo the shame of revealing to him that she was incapable of reconciliation since the birth of Amaranta Úrsula. That was the reason for her anxious correspondence with the invisible doctors, interrupted by frequent disasters of the mail. During the first months when it was learned that the trains were jumping their tracks in the rain, a letter from the invisible doctors told her that hers were not arriving. Later on, when contact with the unknown correspondents was broken, she had seriously thought of putting on the tiger mask that her husband had worn in the bloody carnival and having herself examined under a fictitious name by the banana company doctors. But one of the many people who regularly brought unpleasant news of the deluge had told her that the company was dismantling its dispensaries to move them to where it was not raining. Then she gave up hope. She resigned herself to waiting until the rain stopped and the mail service was back to normal, and in the meantime she sought relief from her secret ailments with recourse to her imagination, because she would rather have died than put herself in the hands of the only doctor left in Macondo, the extravagant Frenchman who ate grass like a donkey. She drew close to Úrsula, trusting that she would know of some palliative for her attacks. But her twisted habit of not calling things by their names made her put first things last and use "expelled" for "gave birth" and "burning" for "flow" so that it would all be less shameful, with the result that Úrsula reached the reasonable conclusion that her trouble was intestinal rather than uterine, and she advised her to take a dose of calomel on an empty stomach. If it had not been for that suffering, which would have had nothing shameful about it for someone who did not suffer as well from shamefulness, and if it had not been for the loss of the letters, the rain would not have bothered Fernanda, because, after all, her whole life had been spent as if it had been raining. She did not change her schedule or modify her ritual. When the table was still raised up on bricks and the chairs put on planks so that those at the table would not get their feet wet, she still served with linen tablecloths and fine chinaware and with lighted candles, because she felt that the calamities should not be used as a pretext for any relaxation in customs. No one went out into the street any more. If it had depended on Fernanda, they would never have done so, not only since it started raining but since long before that, because she felt that doors had been invented to stay closed and that curiosity for what was going on in the street was a matter for harlots. Yet she was the first one to look out when they were told that the funeral procession for Colonel Gerineldo Márquez was passing by, and even though she only watched it through the half-opened window it left her in such a state of affliction that for a long time she repented of her weakness.

She could not have conceived of a more desolate cortege. They had put the coffin in an oxcart over which they built a canopy of banana leaves, but the pressure of the rain was so intense and the streets so muddy that with every step the wheels got stuck and the covering was on the verge of falling apart. The streams of sad water that fell on the coffin were soaking the flag that had been placed on top, which was actually the flag stained with blood and gunpowder that had been rejected by more honorable veterans. On the coffin they had also placed the saber with tassels of silver and copper, the same one that Colonel Gerineldo Márquez used to hang on the coat rack in order to go into Amaranta's sewing room unarmed. Behind the cart, some barefoot and all of them with their pants rolled up, splashing in the mud were the last survivors of the surrender at Neerlandia, carrying a drover's staff in one hand and in the other a wreath of paper flowers that had become discolored in the rain. They appeared like an unreal vision along the street which still bore the name of Colonel Aureliano Buendía, and they all looked at the house as they passed and turned the corner at the square, where they had to ask for help to move the cart, which was stuck. Úrsula had herself carried to the door by Santa Sofía de la Piedad. She followed the difficulties of the procession with such attention that no one doubted that she was seeing it, especially because her raised hand of an archangelic messenger was moving with the swaying of the cart.

"Good-bye, Gerineldo, my son," she shouted. "Say hello

to my people and tell them I'll see them when it stops raining."

Aureliano Segundo helped her back to bed and with the same informality with which he always treated her, he asked her the meaning of her farewell.

"It's true," she said. "I'm only waiting for the rain to stop in order to die."

The condition of the streets alarmed Aureliano Segundo. He finally became worried about the state of his animals and he threw an oilcloth over his head and went to Petra Cotes's house. He found her in the courtyard, in the water up to her waist, trying to float the corpse of a horse. Aureliano Segundo helped her with a lever, and the enormous swollen body gave a turn like a bell and was dragged away by the torrent of liquid mud. Since the rain began, all that Petra Cotes had done was to clear her courtyard of dead animals. During the first weeks she sent messages to Aureliano Segundo for him to take urgent measures and he had answered that there was no rush, that the situation was not alarming, that there would be plenty of time to think about something when it cleared. She sent him word that the horse pastures were being flooded, that the cattle were fleeing to high ground, where there was nothing to eat and where they were at the mercy of jaguars and sickness. "There's nothing to be done," Aureliano Segundo answered her. "Others will be born when it clears." Petra Cotes had seen them die in clusters and she was able to butcher only those stuck in the mud. She saw with quiet impotence how the deluge was pitilessly exterminating a fortune that at one time was considered the largest and most solid in Macondo, and of which nothing remained but pestilence. When Aureliano Segundo decided to go see what was going on, he found only the corpse of the horse and a squalid mule in the ruins of the stable. Petra Cotes watched him arrive without surprise, joy, or resentment, and she only allowed herself an ironic smile.

"It's about time!" she said.

She had aged, all skin and bones, and her tapered eyes of a carnivorous animal had become sad and tame from looking at the rain so much. Aureliano Segundo stayed at her house more than three months, not because he felt better there than in that of his family, but because he needed all that time to make the decision to throw the piece of oilcloth back over his head. "There's no rush," he said, as he had said in the other house. "Let's hope that it clears in the next few hours." During the course of the first week he became accustomed to the inroads that time and the rain had made in the health of his concubine, and little by little he was seeing her as she had been before, remembering her jubilant excesses and the delirious fertility that her love provoked in the animals, and partly through love, partly through interest, one night during the second week he awoke her with urgent caresses. Petra Cotes did not react. "Go back to sleep," she murmured. "These aren't times for things like that." Aureliano Segundo saw himself in the mirrors on the ceiling, saw Petra Cotes's spinal column like a row of spools strung together along a cluster of withered nerves, and he saw that she was right, not because of the times but because of themselves, who were no longer up to those things.

Aureliano Segundo returned home with his trunks, convinced that not only Úrsula but all the inhabitants of Macondo were waiting for it to clear in order to die. He had seen them as he passed by, sitting in their parlors with an absorbed look and folded arms, feeling unbroken time pass, relentless time, because it was useless to divide it into months and years, and the days into hours, when one could do nothing but contemplate the rain. The children greeted Aureliano Segundo with excitement because he was playing the asthmatic accordion for them again. But the concerts did not attract their attention as much as the sessions with the encyclopedia, and once more they got together in Meme's room,

327

where Aureliano Segundo's imagination changed a dirigible into a flying elephant who was looking for a place to sleep among the clouds. On one occasion he came across a man on horseback who in spite of his strange outfit had a familiar look, and after examining him closely he came to the conclusion that it was a picture of Colonel Aureliano Buendía. He showed it to Fernanda and she also admitted the resemblance of the horseman not only to the colonel but to everybody in the family, although he was actually a Tartar warrior. Time passed in that way with the Colossus of Rhodes and snake charmers until his wife told him that there were only three pounds of dried meat and a sack of rice left in the pantry.

"And what do you want me to do about it?" he asked.

"I don't know," Fernanda answered. "That's men's business."

"Well," Aureliano Segundo said, "something will be done when it clears."

He was more interested in the encyclopedia than in the domestic problem, even when he had to content himself with a scrap of meat and a little rice for lunch. "It's impossible to do anything now," he would say. "It can't rain for the rest of our lives." And while the urgencies of the pantry grew greater, Fernanda's indignation also grew, until her eventual protests, her infrequent outbursts came forth in an uncontained, unchained torrent that began one morning like the monotonous drone of a guitar and as the day advanced rose in pitch, richer and more splendid. Aureliano Segundo was not aware of the singsong until the following day after breakfast when he felt himself being bothered by a buzzing that was by then more fluid and louder than the sound of the rain, and it was Fernanda, who was walking throughout the house complaining that they had raised her to be a queen only to have her end up as a servant in a madhouse, with a lazy, idolatrous, libertine husband who lay on his back waiting for bread to rain down from heaven while she was straining her kidneys trying to keep afloat a home held together with pins where there was so much to do, so much to bear up under and repair from the time God gave his morning sunlight until it was time to go to bed that when she got there her eyes were full of ground glass, and yet no one ever said to her, "Good morning, Fernanda, did you sleep well?" Nor had they asked her, even out of courtesy, why she was so pale or why she awoke with purple rings under her eyes in spite of the fact that she expected it, of course, from a family that had always considered her a nuisance, an old rag, a booby painted on the wall, and who were always going around saying things against her behind her back, calling her churchmouse, calling her Pharisee, calling her crafty, and even Amaranta, may she rest in peace, had said aloud that she was one of those people who could not tell their rectums from their ashes, God have mercy, such words, and she had tolerated everything with resignation because of the Holy Father, but she had not been able to tolerate it any more when that evil José Arcadio Segundo said that the damnation of the family had come when it opened its doors to a stuck-up highlander, just imagine, a bossy highlander, Lord save us, a highland daughter of evil spit of the same stripe as the highlanders the government sent to kill workers, you tell me, and he was referring to no one but her, the godchild of the Duke of Alba, a lady of such lineage that she made the liver of presidents' wives quiver, a noble dame of fine blood like her, who had the right to sign eleven peninsular names and who was the only mortal creature in that town full of bastards who did not feel all confused at the sight of sixteen pieces of silverware, so that her adulterous husband could die of laughter afterward and say that so many knives and forks and spoons were not meant for a human being but for a centipede, and the only one who could tell with her eyes closed when the white wine was served and on what side and in which glass and when the

M

red wine and on what side and in which glass, and not like that peasant of an Amaranta, may she rest in peace, who thought that white wine was served in the daytime and red wine at night, and the only one on the whole coast who could take pride in the fact that she took care of her bodily needs only in golden chamberpots, so that Colonel Aureliano Buendía, may he rest in peace, could have the effrontery to ask her with his Masonic ill humor where she had received that privilege and whether she did not shit shit but shat sweet basil, just imagine, with those very words, and so that Renata, her own daughter, who through an oversight had seen her stool in the bedroom, had answered that even if the pot was all gold and with a coat of arms, what was inside was pure shit, physical shit, and worse even than any other kind because it was stuck-up highland shit, just imagine, her own daughter, so that she never had any illusions about the rest of the family, but in any case she had the right to expect a little more consideration from her husband because, for better or for worse, he was her consecrated spouse, her helpmate, her legal despoiler, who took upon himself of his own free and sovereign will the grave responsibility of taking her away from her paternal home, where she never wanted for or suffered from anything, where she wove funeral wreaths as a pastime, since her godfather had sent a letter with his signature and the stamp of his ring on the sealing wax simply to say that the hands of his goddaughter were not meant for tasks of this world except to play the clavichord, and, nevertheless, her insane husband had taken her from her home with all manner of admonitions and warnings and had brought her to that frying pan of hell where a person could not breathe because of the heat, and before she had completed her Pentecostal fast he had gone off with his wandering trunks and his wastrel's accordion to loaf in adultery with a wretch of whom it was only enough to see her behind, well, that's been said, to see her wiggle her mare's behind in order to guess that she was a, that she was a, just the opposite of her, who was a lady in a palace or a pigsty, at the table or in bed, a lady of breeding, God-fearing, obeying His laws and submissive to His wishes, and with whom he could not perform, naturally, the acrobatics and trampish antics that he did with the other one, who, of course, was ready for anything, like the French matrons, and even worse, if one considers well, because they at least had the honesty to put a red light at their door, swinishness like that, just imagine, and that was all that was needed by the only and beloved daughter of Doña Renata Argote and Don Fernando del Carpio, and especially the latter, an upright man, a fine Christian, a Knight of the Order of the Holy Sepulcher, those who receive direct from God the privilege of remaining intact in their graves with their skin smooth like the cheeks of a bride and their eyes alive and clear like emeralds.

"That's not true," Aureliano Segundo interrupted her. "He was already beginning to smell when they brought him here."

He had the patience to listen to her for a whole day until he caught her in a slip. Fernanda did not pay him any mind, but she lowered her voice. That night at dinner the exasperating buzzing of the singsong had conquered the sound of the rain. Aureliano Segundo ate very little, with his head down, and he went to his room early. At breakfast on the following day Fernanda was trembling, with a look of not having slept well, and she seemed completely exhausted by her rancor. Nevertheless, when her husband asked if it was not possible to have a soft-boiled egg, she did not answer simply that they had run out of eggs the week before, but she worked up a violent diatribe against men who spent their time contemplating their navels and then had the gall to ask for larks' livers at the table. Aureliano Segundo took the children to look at the encyclopedia, as always, and Fernanda pretended to straighten out Meme's room just so that he

331

could listen to her muttering, of course, that it certainly took cheek for him to tell the poor innocents that there was a picture of Colonel Aureliano Buendía in the encyclopedia. During the afternoon, while the children were having their nap, Aureliano Segundo sat on the porch and Fernanda pursued him even there, provoking him, tormenting him, hovering about him with her implacable horsefly buzzing, saying that, of course, while there was nothing to eat except stones, her husband was sitting there like a sultan of Persia watching it rain, because that was all he was, a slob, a sponge, a good-for-nothing, softer than cotton batting, used to living off women and convinced that he had married Jonah's wife, who was so content with the story of the whale. Aureliano Segundo listened to her for more than two hours, impassive, as if he were deaf. He did not interrupt her until late in the afternoon, when he could no longer bear the echo of the bass drum that was tormenting his head.

"Please shut up," he begged.

Fernanda, quite the contrary, raised her pitch. "I don't have any reason to shut up," she said. "Anyone who doesn't want to listen to me can go someplace else." Then Aureliano Segundo lost control. He stood up unhurriedly, as if he only intended to stretch, and with a perfectly regulated and methodical fury he grabbed the pots with the begonias one after the other, those with the ferns, the oregano, and one after the other he smashed them onto the floor. Fernanda was frightened because until then she had really not had a clear indication of the tremendous inner force of her singsong, but it was too late for any attempt at rectification. Intoxicated by the uncontained torrent of relief, Aureliano Segundo broke the glass on the china closet and piece by piece, without hurrying, he took out the chinaware and shattered it on the floor. Systematically, serenely, in the same parsimonious way in which he had papered the house with banknotes, he then set about smashing the Bohemian crystal ware against the walls, the hand-painted vases, the pictures of maidens in flower-laden boats, the mirrors in their gilded frames, everything that was breakable, from parlor to pantry, and he finished with the large earthen jar in the kitchen, which exploded in the middle of the courtyard with a hollow boom. Then he washed his hands, threw the oilcloth over himself, and before midnight he returned with a few strings of dried meat, several bags of rice, corn with weevils, and some emaciated bunches of bananas. From then on there was no more lack of food.

Amaranta Úrsula and little Aureliano would remember the rains as a happy time. In spite of Fernanda's strictness, they would splash in the puddles in the courtyard, catch lizards and dissect them, and pretend that they were poisoning the soup with dust from butterfly wings when Santa Sofía de la Piedad was not looking. Úrsula was their most amusing plaything. They looked upon her as a big, broken-down doll that they carried back and forth from one corner to another wrapped in colored cloth and with her face painted with soot and annatto, and once they were on the point of plucking out her eyes with the pruning shears as they had done with the frogs. Nothing gave them as much excitement as the wanderings of her mind. Something, indeed, must have happened to her mind during the third year of the rain, for she was gradually losing her sense of reality and confusing present time with remote periods in her life to the point where, on one occasion, she spent three days weeping deeply over the death of Petronila Iguarán, her great-grandmother, buried for over a century. She sank into such an insane state of confusion that she thought little Aureliano was her son the colonel during the time he was taken to see ice, and that the José Arcadio who was at that time in the seminary was her firstborn who had gone off with the gypsies. She spoke so much about the family that the children learned to make up imaginary visits with beings who had not only been dead for a long time, but who had existed at different times. Sitting on the bed, her hair covered with ashes and her face wrapped in a red kerchief, Úrsula was happy in the midst of the unreal relatives whom the children described in all detail, as if they had really known them. Úrsula would converse with her forebears about events that took place before her own existence, enjoying the news they gave her, and she would weep with them over deaths that were much more recent than the guests themselves. The children did not take long to notice that in the course of those ghostly visits Úrsula would always ask a question destined to establish the one who had brought a life-size plaster Saint Joseph to the house to be kept until the rains stopped. It was in that way that Aureliano Segundo remembered the fortune buried in some place that only Úrsula knew, but the questions and astute maneuvering that occurred to him were of no use because in the labyrinth of her madness she seemed to preserve enough of a margin of lucidity to keep the secret which she would reveal only to the one who could prove that he was the real owner of the buried gold. She was so skillful and strict that when Aureliano Segundo instructed one of his carousing companions to pass himself off as the owner of the fortune, she got him all caught up in a minute interrogation sown with subtle traps.

Convinced that Úrsula would carry the secret to her grave, Aureliano Segundo hired a crew of diggers under the pretext that they were making some drainage canals in the courtyard and the backyard, and he himself took soundings in the earth with iron bars and all manner of metal-detectors without finding anything that resembled gold in three months of exhaustive exploration. Later on he went to Pilar Ternera with the hope that the cards would see more than the diggers, but she began by explaining that any attempt would be useless unless Úrsula cut the cards. On the other hand, she confirmed the existence of the treasure with the precision of its consisting of seven thousand two hundred fourteen coins buried in three canvas sacks reinforced with copper wire within a circle with a radius of three hundred eighty-eight feet with Úrsula's bed as the center, but she warned that it would not be found until it stopped raining and the suns of three consecutive Junes had changed the piles of mud into dust. The profusion and meticulous vagueness of the information seemed to Aureliano Segundo so similar to the tales of spiritualists that he kept on with his enterprise in spite of the fact that they were in August and they would have to wait at least three years in order to satisfy the conditions of the prediction. The first thing that startled him, even though it increased his confusion at the same time, was the fact that it was precisely three hundred eighty-eight feet from Úrsula's bed to the backyard wall. Fernanda feared that he was as crazy as his twin brother when she saw him taking the measurements, and even more when he told the digging crew to make the ditches three feet deeper. Overcome by an exploratory delirium comparable only to that of his great-grandfather when he was searching for the route of inventions, Aureliano Segundo lost the last layers of fat that he had left and the old resemblance to his twin brother was becoming accentuated again, not only because of his slim figure, but also because of the distant air and the withdrawn attitude. He no longer bothered with the children. He ate at odd hours, muddied from head to toe, and he did so in a corner of the kitchen, barely answering the occasional questions asked by Santa Sofía de la Piedad. Seeing him work that way, as she had never dreamed him capable of doing, Fernanda thought that his stubbornness was diligence, his greed abnegation, and his thickheadedness perseverance, and her insides tightened with remorse over the virulence with which she had attacked his idleness. But Aureliano Segundo was in no mood for merciful reconciliations at that time. Sunk up to his neck in a morass of dead branches and rotting flowers, he flung the dirt of the garden all about after having finished with the courtyard and the backyard, and he excavated so deeply under the foundations of the east wing of the house that one night they woke up in terror at what seemed to be an earthquake, as much because of the trembling as the fearful underground creaking. Three of the rooms were collapsing and a frightening crack had opened up from the porch to Fernanda's room. Aureliano Segundo did not give up the search because of that. Even when his last hopes had been extinguished and the only thing that seemed to make any sense was what the cards had predicted, he reinforced the jagged foundation, repaired the crack with mortar, and continued on the side to the west. He was still there on the second week of the following June when the rain began to abate and the clouds began to lift and it was obvious from one moment to the next that it was going to clear. That was what happened. One Friday at two in the afternoon the world lighted up with a crazy crimson sun as harsh as brick dust and almost as cool as water, and it did not rain again for ten years.

Macondo was in ruins. In the swampy streets there were the remains of furniture, animal skeletons covered with red lilies, the last memories of the hordes of newcomers who had fled Macondo as wildly as they had arrived. The houses that had been built with such haste during the banana fever had been abandoned. The banana company tore down its installations. All that remained of the former wired-in city were the ruins. The wooden houses, the cool terraces for breezy card-playing afternoons, seemed to have been blown away in an anticipation of the prophetic wind that years later would wipe Macondo off the face of the earth. The only human trace left by that voracious blast was a glove belonging to Patricia Brown in an automobile smothered in wild pansies. The enchanted region explored by José Arcadio Buendía in the days of the founding, where later on the banana plantations flourished, was a bog of rotting roots, on the horizon of which one could manage to see the silent foam of the sea.

Aureliano Segundo went through a crisis of affliction on the first Sunday that he put on dry clothes and went out to renew his acquaintance with the town. The survivors of the catastrophe, the same ones who had been living in Macondo before it had been struck by the banana company hurricane, were sitting in the middle of the street enjoying their first sunshine. They still had the green of the algae on their skin and the musty smell of a corner that had been stamped on them by the rain, but in their hearts they seemed happy to have recovered the town in which they had been born. The Street of the Turks was again what it had been earlier, in the days when the Arabs with slippers and rings in their ears were going about the world swapping knickknacks for macaws and had found in Macondo a good bend in the road where they could find respite from their age-old lot as wanderers. Having crossed through to the other side of the rain, the merchandise in the booths was falling apart, the cloths spread over the doors were splotched with mold, the counters undermined by termites, the walls eaten away by dampness, but the Arabs of the third generation were sitting in the same place and in the same position as their fathers and grandfathers, taciturn, dauntless, invulnerable to time and disaster, as alive or as dead as they had been after the insomnia plague and Colonel Aureliano Buendía's thirty-two wars. Their strength of spirit in the face of the ruins of the gaming tables, the fritter stands, the shooting galleries, and the alley where they interpreted dreams and predicted the future made Aureliano Segundo ask them with his usual informality what mysterious resources they had relied upon so as not to have gone awash in the storm, what the devil they had done so as not to drown, and one after the other, from door to door, they returned a crafty smile and a dreamy look, and without any previous consultation they all gave the same answer:

"Swimming."

Petra Cotes was perhaps the only native who had an Arab

M*

337

heart. She had seen the final destruction of her stables, her barns dragged off by the storm, but she had managed to keep her house standing. During the second year she had sent pressing messages to Aureliano Segundo and he had answered that he did not know when he would go back to her house, but that in any case he would bring along a box of gold coins to pave the bedroom floor with. At that time she had dug deep into her heart, searching for the strength that would allow her to survive the misfortune, and she had discovered a reflective and just rage with which she had sworn to restore the fortune squandered by her lover and then wiped out by the deluge. It was such an unbreakable decision that Aureliano Segundo went back to her house eight months after the last message and found her green, disheveled, with sunken eyelids and skin spangled with mange, but she was writing out numbers on small pieces of paper to make a raffle. Aureliano Segundo was astonished, and he was so dirty and so solemn that Petra Cotes almost believed that the one who had come to see her was not the lover of all her life but his twin brother.

"You're crazy," he told her. "Unless you plan to raffle off bones."

Then she told him to look in the bedroom and Aureliano Segundo saw the mule. Its skin was clinging to its bones like that of its mistress, but it was just as alive and resolute as she. Petra Cotes had fed it with her wrath, and when there was no more hay or corn or roots, she had given it shelter in her own bedroom and fed it on the percale sheets, the Persian rugs, the plush bedspreads, the velvet drapes, and the canopy embroidered with gold thread and silk tassels on the episcopal bed.

Úrsula HAD to make a great effort to fulfill her promise to die when it cleared. The waves of lucidity that were so scarce during the rains became more frequent after August, when an arid wind began to blow and suffocated the rose bushes and petrified the piles of mud, and ended up scattering over Macondo the burning dust that covered the rusted zinc roofs and the age-old almond trees forever. Úrsula cried in lamentation when she discovered that for more than three years she had been a plaything for the children. She washed her painted face, took off the strips of brightly colored cloth, the dried lizards and frogs, and the rosaries and old Arab necklaces that they had hung all over her body, and for the first time since the death of Amaranta she got up out of bed without anybody's help to join in the family life once more. The spirit of her invincible heart guided her through the shadows. Those who noticed her stumbling and who bumped into the archangelic arm she kept raised at head level thought that she was having trouble with her body, but they still did not think she was blind. She did not need to see to realize that the flower beds, cultivated with such care since the first rebuilding, had been destroyed by the rain and ruined by Aureliano Segundo's excavations, and that the walls and the cement of the floors were cracked, the furniture mushy and discolored, the doors off their hinges, and the family menaced by a spirit of resignation and despair that was inconceivable in her time. Feeling her way along through the empty bedrooms she perceived the continuous rumble of the termites as they carved the wood, the snipping of the moths in the clothes closets, and the devastating noise of the enormous red ants that had prospered during the deluge and were undermining the foundations of the house. One day she opened the trunk with the saints and had to ask Santa Sofía de la Piedad to get off her body the cockroaches that jumped out and that had already turned the clothing to dust. "A person can't live in neglect like this," she said. "If we go on like this we'll be devoured by animals." From then on she did not have a moment of repose. Up before dawn, she would use anybody available, even the children. She put the few articles of clothing that were still usable out into the sun, she drove the cockroaches off with powerful insecticide attacks, she scratched out the veins that the termites had made on doors and windows and asphyxiated the ants in their anthills with quicklime. The fever of restoration finally brought her to the forgotten rooms. She cleared out the rubble and cobwebs in the room where José Arcadio Buendía had lost his wits looking for the philosopher's stone, she put the silver shop which had been upset by the soldiers in order, and lastly she asked for the keys to Melquíades' room to see what state it was in. Faithful to the wishes of José Arcadio Segundo, who had

340

forbidden anyone to come in unless there was a clear indication that he had died, Santa Sofía de la Piedad tried all kinds of subterfuges to throw Úrsula off the track. But so inflexible was her determination not to surrender even the most remote corner of the house to the insects that she knocked down every obstacle in her path, and after three days of insistence she succeeded in getting them to open the door for her. She had to hold on to the doorjamb so that the stench would not knock her over, but she needed only two seconds to remember that the schoolgirls' seventy-two chamberpots were in there and that on one of the rainy nights a patrol of soldiers had searched the house looking for José Arcadio Segundo and had been unable to find him.

"Lord save us!" she exclaimed, as if she could see everything. "So much trouble teaching you good manners and you end up living like a pig."

José Arcadio Segundo was still reading over the parchments. The only thing visible in the intricate tangle of hair was the teeth striped with green slime and his motionless eyes. When he recognized his great-grandmother's voice he turned his head toward the door, tried to smile, and without knowing it repeated an old phrase of Úrsula's.

"What did you expect?" he murmured. "Time passes."

"That's how it goes," Úrsula said, "but not so much."

When she said it she realized that she was giving the same reply that Colonel Aureliano Buendía had given in his death cell, and once again she shuddered with the evidence that time was not passing, as she had just admitted, but that it was turning in a circle. But even then she did not give resignation a chance. She scolded José Arcadio Segundo as if he were a child and insisted that he take a bath and shave and lend a hand in fixing up the house. The simple idea of abandoning the room that had given him peace terrified José Arcadio Segundo. He shouted that there was no human power capable of making him go out because he did not want

341

to see the train with two hundred cars loaded with dead people which left Macondo every day at dusk on its way to the sea. "They were all of those who were at the station," he shouted. "Three thousand four hundred eight." Only then did Úrsula realize that he was in a world of shadows more impenetrable than hers, as unreachable and solitary as that of his great-grandfather. She left him in the room, but she succeeded in getting them to leave the padlock off, clean it every day, throw the chamberpots away except for one, and to keep José Arcadio Segundo as clean and presentable as his great-grandfather had been during his long captivity under the chestnut tree. At first Fernanda interpreted that bustle as an attack of senile madness and it was difficult for her to suppress her exasperation. But about that time José Arcadio told her that he planned to come to Macondo from Rome before taking his final vows, and the good news filled her with such enthusiasm that from morning to night she would be seen watering the flowers four times a day so that her son would not have a bad impression of the house. It was that same incentive which induced her to speed up her correspondence with the invisible doctors and to replace the pots of ferns and oregano and the begonias on the porch even before Úrsula found out that they had been destroyed by Aureliano Segundo's exterminating fury. Later on she sold the silver service and bought ceramic dishes, pewter bowls and soup spoons, and alpaca tablecloths, and with them brought poverty to the cupboards that had been accustomed to India Company chinaware and Bohemian crystal. Úrsula always tried to go a step beyond. "Open the windows and the doors," she shouted. "Cook some meat and fish, buy the largest turtles around, let strangers come and spread their mats in the corners and urinate in the rose bushes and sit down to eat as many times as they want, and belch and rant and muddy everything with their boots, and let them do whatever they want to us, because that's the only way to drive off ruin." But it was a vain illusion. She was too old then and living on borrowed time to repeat the miracle of the little candy animals, and none of her descendants had inherited her strength. The house stayed closed on Fernanda's orders.

Aureliano Segundo, who had taken his trunks back to the house of Petra Cotes, barely had enough means to see that the family did not starve to death. With the raffling of the mule, Petra Cotes and he bought some more animals with which they managed to set up a primitive lottery business. Aureliano Segundo would go from house to house selling the tickets that he himself painted with colored ink to make them more attractive and convincing, and perhaps he did not realize that many people bought them out of gratitude and most of them out of pity. Nevertheless, even the most pitying purchaser was getting a chance to win a pig for twenty cents or a calf for thirty-two, and they became so hopeful that on Tuesday nights Petra Cotes's courtyard overflowed with people waiting for the moment when a child picked at random drew the winning number from a bag. It did not take long to become a weekly fair, for at dusk food and drink stands would be set up in the courtyard and many of those who were favored would slaughter the animals they had won right there on the condition that someone else supply the liquor and music, so that without having wanted to, Aureliano Segundo suddenly found himself playing the accordion again and participating in modest tourneys of voracity. Those humble replicas of the revelry of former times served to show Aureliano Segundo himself how much his spirits had declined and to what a degree his skill as a masterful carouser had dried up. He was a changed man. The two hundred forty pounds that he had attained during the days when he had been challenged by The Elephant had been reduced to one hundred fifty-six; the glowing and bloated tortoise face had turned into that of an iguana, and he was always on the verge of boredom and fatigue. For Petra Cotes, however, he had never been a better man than at that time, perhaps because the pity that he inspired was mixed with love, and because of the feeling of solidarity that misery aroused in both of them. The broken-down bed ceased to be the scene of wild activities and was changed into an intimate refuge. Freed of the repetitious mirrors, which had been auctioned off to buy animals for the lottery, and from the lewd damasks and velvets, which the mule had eaten, they would stay up very late with the innocence of two sleepless grandparents, taking advantage of the time to draw up accounts and put away pennies which they formerly wasted just for the sake of it. Sometimes the cock's crow would find them piling and unpiling coins, taking a bit away from here to put there, so that this bunch would be enough to keep Fernanda happy and that would be for Amaranta Úrsula's shoes, and that other one for Santa Sofía de la Piedad, who had not had a new dress since the time of all the noise, and this to order the coffin if Úrsula died, and this for the coffee which was going up a cent a pound in price every three months, and this for the sugar which sweetened less every day, and this for the lumber which was still wet from the rains, and this other one for the paper and the colored ink to make tickets with, and what was left over to pay off the winner of the April calf whose hide they had miraculously saved when it came down with a symptomatic carbuncle just when all of the numbers in the raffle had already been sold. Those rites of poverty were so pure that they nearly always set aside the largest share for Fernanda, and they did not do so out of remorse or charity, but because her well-being was more important to them than their own. What was really happening to them, although neither of them realized it, was that they both thought of Fernanda as the daughter that they would have liked to have and never did, to the point where on a certain occasion they resigned themselves to eating crumbs for three days so that she

344

could buy a Dutch tablecloth. Nevertheless, no matter how much they killed themselves with work, no matter how much money they eked out, and no matter how many schemes they thought of, their guardian angels were asleep with fatigue while they put in coins and took them out trying to get just enough to live with. During the waking hours when the accounts were bad, they wondered what had happened in the world for the animals not to breed with the same drive as before, why money slipped through their fingers, and why people who a short time before had burned rolls of bills in the carousing considered it highway robbery to charge twelve cents for a raffle of six hens. Aureliano Segundo thought without saying so that the evil was not in the world but in some hidden place in the mysterious heart of Petra Cotes, where something had happened during the deluge that had turned the animals sterile and made money scarce. Intrigued by that enigma, he dug so deeply into her sentiments that in search of interest he found love, because by trying to make her love him he ended up falling in love with her. Petra Cotes, for her part, loved him more and more as she felt his love increasing, and that was how in the ripeness of autumn she began to believe once more in the youthful superstition that poverty was the servitude of love. Both looked back then on the wild revelry, the gaudy wealth, and the unbridled fornication as an annoyance and they lamented that it had cost them so much of their lives to find the paradise of shared solitude. Madly in love after so many years of sterile complicity, they enjoyed the miracle of loving each other as much at the table as in bed, and they grew to be so happy that even when they were two worn-out old people they kept on blooming like little children and playing together like dogs.

The raffles never got very far. At first Aureliano Segundo would spend three days of the week shut up in what had been his rancher's office drawing ticket after ticket, painting with a fair skill a red cow, a green pig, or a group of blue hens, according to the animal being raffled, and he would sketch out a good imitation of printed numbers and the name that Petra Cotes thought good to call the business: *Divine Providence Raffles*. But with time he felt so tired after drawing up to two thousand tickets a week that he had the animals, the name, and the numbers put on rubber stamps, and then the work was reduced to moistening them on pads of different colors. In his last years it occurred to him to substitute riddles for the numbers so that the prize could be shared by all of those who guessed it, but the system turned out to be so complicated and was open to so much suspicion that he gave it up after the second attempt.

Aureliano Segundo was so busy trying to maintain the prestige of his raffles that he barely had time to see the children. Fernanda put Amaranta Úrsula in a small private school where they admitted only six girls, but she refused to allow Aureliano to go to public school. She considered that she had already relented too much in letting him leave the room. Besides, the schools in those days accepted only the legitimate offspring of Catholic marriages and on the birth certificate that had been pinned to Aureliano's clothing when they brought him to the house he was registered as a foundling. So he remained shut in at the mercy of Santa Sofía de la Piedad's loving eyes and Úrsula's mental quirks, learning in the narrow world of the house whatever his grandmothers explained to him. He was delicate, thin, with a curiosity that unnerved the adults, but unlike the inquisitive and sometimes clairvoyant look that the colonel had at his age, his look was blinking and somewhat distracted. While Amaranta Úrsula was in kindergarten, he would hunt earthworms and torture insects in the garden. But once when Fernanda caught him putting scorpions in a box to put in Úrsula's bed, she locked him up in Meme's old room, where he spent his solitary hours looking through the pictures in the encyclopedia. Úrsula found him there one afternoon when she was going about sprinkling the house with distilled water and a bunch of nettles, and in spite of the fact that she had been with him many times she asked him who he was.

"I'm Aureliano Buendía," he said.

"That's right," she replied. "And now it's time for you to start learning how to be a silversmith."

She had confused him with her son again, because the hot wind that came after the deluge and had brought occasional waves of lucidity to Úrsula's brain had passed. She never got her reason back. When she went into the bedroom she found Petronila Iguarán there with the bothersome crinolines and the beaded jacket that she put on for formal visits, and she found Tranquilina María Miniata Alacoque Buendía, her grandmother, fanning herself with a peacock feather in her invalid's rocking chair, and her great-grandfather Aureliano Arcadio Buendía, with his imitation dolman of the viceregal guard, and Aureliano Iguarán, her father, who had invented a prayer to make the worms shrivel up and drop off cows, and her timid mother, and her cousin with the pig's tail, and José Arcadio Buendía, and her dead sons, all sitting in chairs lined up against the wall as if it were a wake and not a visit. She was tying a colorful string of chatter together, commenting on things from many separate places and many different times, so that when Amaranta Úrsula returned from school and Aureliano grew tired of the encyclopedia, they would find her sitting on her bed talking to herself and lost in a labyrinth of dead people. "Fire!" she shouted once in terror and for an instant panic spread through the house, but what she was telling about was the burning of a barn that she had witnessed when she was four years old. She finally mixed up the past with the present in such a way that in the two or three waves of lucidity that she had before she died, no one knew for certain whether she was speaking about what she felt or what she remembered. Little by little she was shrink-

347

ing, turning into a fetus, becoming mummified in life to the point that in her last months she was a cherry raisin lost inside of her nightgown, and the arm that she always kept raised looked like the paw of a marimonda monkey. She was motionless for several days, and Santa Sofía de la Piedad had to shake her to convince herself that she was alive and sat her on her lap to feed her a few spoonfuls of sugar water. She looked like a newborn old woman. Amaranta Úrsula and Aureliano would take her in and out of the bedroom, they would lay her on the altar to see if she was any larger than the Christ child, and one afternoon they hid her in a closet in the pantry where the rats could have eaten her. One Palm Sunday they went into the bedroom while Fernanda was in church and carried Úrsula out by the neck and ankles.

"Poor great-great-grandmother," Amaranta Úrsula said. "She died of old age."

Úrsula was startled.

"I'm alive!" she said.

"You can see," Amaranta Úrsula said, suppressing her laughter, "that she's not even breathing."

"I'm talking!" Úrsula shouted.

"She can't even talk," Aureliano said. "She died like a little cricket."

Then Úrsula gave in to the evidence. "My God," she exclaimed in a low voice. "So this is what it's like to be dead." She started an endless, stumbling, deep prayer that lasted more than two days, and that by Tuesday had degenerated into a hodgepodge of requests to God and bits of practical advice to stop the red ants from bringing the house down, to keep the lamp burning by Remedios' daguerreotype, and never to let any Buendía marry a person of the same blood because their children would be born with the tail of a pig. Aureliano Segundo tried to take advantage of her delirium to get her to tell him where the gold was buried, but his entreaties were useless once more. "When the owner appears,"

Úrsula said, "God will illuminate him so that he will find it." Santa Sofía de la Piedad had the certainty that they would find her dead from one moment to the next, because she noticed during those days a certain confusion in nature: the roses smelled like goosefoot, a pod of chick peas fell down and the beans lay on the ground in a perfect geometrical pattern in the shape of a starfish, and one night she saw a row of luminous orange disks pass across the sky.

They found her dead on the morning of Good Friday. The last time that they had helped her calculate her age, during the time of the banana company, she had estimated it as between one hundred fifteen and one hundred twenty-two. They buried her in a coffin that was not much larger than the basket in which Aureliano had arrived, and very few people were at the funeral, partly because there were not many left who remembered her, and partly because it was so hot that noon that the birds in their confusion were running into walls like clay pigeons and breaking through screens to die in the bedrooms.

At first they thought it was a plague. Housewives were exhausted from sweeping away so many dead birds, especially at siesta time, and the men dumped them into the river by the cartload. On Easter Sunday the hundred-year-old Father Antonio Isabel stated from the pulpit that the death of the birds was due to the evil influence of the Wandering Jew, whom he himself had seen the night before. He described him as a cross between a billy goat and a female heretic, an infernal beast whose breath scorched the air and whose look brought on the birth of monsters in newlywed women. There were not many who paid attention to his apocalyptic talk, for the town was convinced that the priest was rambling because of his age. But one woman woke everybody up at dawn on Wednesday because she found the tracks of a biped with a cloven hoof. They were so clear and unmistakable that those who went to look at them had no doubt about the existence of a fearsome creature similar to the one described by the parish priest and they got together to set traps in their court-yards. That was how they managed to capture it. Two weeks after Úrsula's death, Petra Cotes and Aureliano Segundo woke up frightened by the especially loud bellowing of a calf that was coming from nearby. When they got there a group of men were already pulling the monster off the sharpened stakes they had set in the bottom of a pit covered with dry leaves, and it stopped lowing. It was as heavy as an ox in spite of the fact that it was no taller than a young steer, and a green and greasy liquid flowed from its wounds. Its body was covered with rough hair, plagued with small ticks, and the skin was hardened with the scales of a remora fish, but unlike the priest's description, its human parts were more like those of a sickly angel than of a man, for its hands were tense and agile, its eyes large and gloomy, and on its shoulderblades it had the scarred-over and calloused stumps of powerful wings which must have been chopped off by a woodsman's ax. They hung it to an almond tree in the square by its ankles so that everyone could see it, and when it began to rot they burned it in a bonfire, for they could not determine whether its bastard nature was that of an animal to be thrown into the river or a human being to be buried. It was never established whether it had really caused the death of the birds, but the newly married women did not bear the predicted monsters, nor did the intensity of the heat decrease.

Rebeca died at the end of that year. Argénida, her lifelong servant, asked the authorities for help to knock down the door to the bedroom where her mistress had been locked in for three days, and they found her on her solitary bed, curled up like a shrimp, with her head bald from ringworm and her finger in her mouth. Aureliano Segundo took charge of the funeral and tried to restore the house in order to sell it, but the destruction was so far advanced in it that the walls became scaly as soon as they were painted and there was not enough mortar to stop the weeds from cracking the floors and the ivy from rotting the beams.

That was how everything went after the deluge. The indolence of the people was in contrast to the voracity of oblivion, which little by little was undermining memories in a pitiless way, to such an extreme that at that time, on another anniversary of the Treaty of Neerlandia, some emissaries from the president of the republic arrived in Macondo to award at last the decoration rejected several times by Colonel Aureliano Buendía, and they spent a whole afternoon looking for someone who could tell them where they could find one of his descendants. Aureliano Segundo was tempted to accept it, thinking that it was a medal of solid gold, but Petra Cotes convinced him that it was not proper when the emissaries already had some proclamations and speeches ready for the ceremony. It was also around that time that the gypsies returned, the last heirs to Melquíades' science, and they found the town so defeated and its inhabitants so removed from the rest of the world that once more they went through the houses dragging magnetized ingots as if that really were the Babylonian wise men's latest discovery, and once again they concentrated the sun's rays with the giant magnifying glass, and there was no lack of people standing open-mouthed watching kettles fall and pots roll and who paid fifty cents to be startled as a gypsy woman put in her false teeth and took them out again. A broken-down yellow train that neither brought anyone in nor took anyone out and that scarcely paused at the deserted station was the only thing that was left of the long train to which Mr. Brown would couple his glass-topped coach with the episcopal lounging chairs and of the fruit trains with one hundred twenty cars which took a whole afternoon to pass by. The ecclesiastical delegates who had come to investigate the report of the strange death of the birds and the sacrifice of the Wandering Jew found Father Antonio Isabel playing blind man's buff with the children, and thinking that his report was the product of a hallucination, they took him off to an asylum. A short time later they sent Father Augusto Ángel, a crusader of the new breed, intransigent, audacious, daring, who personally rang the bells several times a day so that the people's spirits would not get drowsy, and who went from house to house waking up the sleepers to go to mass, but before a year was out he too was conquered by the negligence that one breathed in with the air, by the hot dust that made everything old and clogged up, and by the drowsiness caused by lunchtime meatballs in the unbearable heat of siesta time.

With Úrsula's death the house again fell into a neglect from which it could not be rescued even by a will as resolute and vigorous as that of Amaranta Úrsula, who many years later, being a happy, modern woman without prejudices, with her feet on the ground, opened doors and windows in order to drive away the ruin, restored the garden, exterminated the red ants who were already walking across the porch in broad daylight, and tried in vain to reawaken the forgotten spirit of hospitality. Fernanda's cloistered passion built an impenetrable dike against Úrsula's torrential hundred years. Not only did she refuse to open doors when the arid wind passed through, but she had the windows nailed shut with boards in the shape of a cross, obeying the paternal order of being buried alive. The expensive correspondence with the invisible doctors ended in failure. After numerous postponements, she shut herself up in her room on the date and hour agreed upon, covered only by a white sheet and with her head pointed north, and at one o'clock in the morning she felt that they were covering her head with a handkerchief soaked in a glacial liquid. When she woke up the sun was shining in the window and she had a barbarous stitch in the shape of an arc that began at her crotch and ended at her sternum. But before she could complete the prescribed rest she received a disturbed letter from the invisible doctors, who said they had inspected her for six hours without finding anything that corresponded to the symptoms so many times and so scrupulously described by her. Actually, her pernicious habit of not calling things by their names had brought about a new confusion, for the only thing that the telepathic surgeons had found was a drop in the uterus which could be corrected by the use of a pessary. The disillusioned Fernanda tried to obtain more precise information, but the unknown correspondents did not answer her letters any more. She felt so defeated by the weight of an unknown word that she decided to put shame behind her and ask what a pessary was, and only then did she discover that the French doctor had hanged himself to a beam three months earlier and had been buried against the wishes of the townspeople by a former companion in arms of Colonel Aureliano Buendía. Then she confided in her son José Arcadio and the latter sent her the pessaries from Rome along with a pamphlet explaining their use, which she flushed down the toilet after committing it to memory so that no one would learn the nature of her troubles. It was a useless precaution because the only people who lived in the house scarcely paid any attention to her. Santa Sofía de la Piedad was wandering about in her solitary old age, cooking the little that they ate and almost completely dedicated to the care of José Arcadio Segundo. Amaranta Úrsula, who had inherited certain attractions of Remedios the Beauty, spent the time that she had formerly wasted tormenting Úrsula at her schoolwork, and she began to show good judgment and a dedication to study that brought back to Aureliano Segundo the high hopes that Meme had inspired in him. He had promised her to send her to finish her studies in Brussels, in accord with a custom established during the time of the banana company, and that illusion had brought him to attempt to revive the lands devastated by the deluge. The few times that he appeared at the house were for Amaranta Úrsula, because with time he had become a stranger to

Fernanda and little Aureliano was becoming withdrawn as he approached puberty. Aureliano Segundo had faith that Fernanda's heart would soften with old age so that the child could join in the life of a town where no one certainly would make any effort to speculate suspiciously about his origins. But Aureliano himself seemed to prefer the cloister of solitude and he did not show the least desire to know the world that began at the street door of the house. When Úrsula had the door of Melquíades' room opened he began to linger about it, peeping through the half-opened door, and no one knew at what moment he became close to José Arcadio Segundo in a link of mutual affection. Aureliano Segundo discovered that friendship a long time after it had begun, when he heard the child talking about the killing at the station. It happened once when someone at the table complained about the ruin into which the town had sunk when the banana company had abandoned it, and Aureliano contradicted him with maturity and with the vision of a grown person. His point of view, contrary to the general interpretation, was that Macondo had been a prosperous place and well on its way until it was disordered and corrupted and suppressed by the banana company, whose engineers brought on the deluge as a pretext to avoid promises made to the workers. Speaking with such good sense that to Fernanda he was like a sacrilegious parody of Jesus among the wise men, the child described with precise and convincing details how the army had machine-gunned more than three thousand workers penned up by the station and how they loaded the bodies onto a two-hundred-car train and threw them into the sea. Convinced as most people were by the official version that nothing had happened, Fernanda was scandalized with the idea that the child had inherited the anarchist ideas of Colonel Aureliano Buendía and told him to be quiet. Aureliano Segundo, on the other hand, recognized his twin brother's version. Actually, in spite of the fact that everyone considered him mad, José Arcadio Segundo was at that time the most lucid inhabitant of the house. He taught little Aureliano how to read and write, initiated him in the study of the parchments, and he inculcated him with such a personal interpretation of what the banana company had meant to Macondo that many years later, when Aureliano became part of the world, one would have thought that he was telling a hallucinated version, because it was radically opposed to the false one that historians had created and consecrated in the schoolbooks. In the small isolated room where the arid air never penetrated, nor the dust, nor the heat, both had the atavistic vision of an old man, his back to the window, wearing a hat with a brim like the wings of a crow who spoke about the world many years before they had been born. Both described at the same time how it was always March there and always Monday, and then they understood that José Arcadio Buendía was not as crazy as the family said, but that he was the only one who had enough lucidity to sense the truth of the fact that time also stumbled and had accidents and could therefore splinter and leave an eternalized fragment in a room. José Arcadio Segundo had managed, furthermore, to classify the cryptic letters of the parchments. He was certain that they corresponded to an alphabet of forty-seven to fifty-three characters, which when separated looked like scratching and scribbling, and which in the fine hand of Melquíades looked like pieces of clothing put out to dry on a line. Aureliano remembered having seen a similar table in the English encyclopedia, so he brought it to the room to compare it with that of José Arcadio Segundo. They were indeed the same.

Around the time of the riddle lottery, Aureliano Segundo began waking up with a knot in his throat, as if he were repressing a desire to weep. Petra Cotes interpreted it as one more of so many upsets brought on by the bad situation, and every morning for over a year she would touch his palate with a dash of honey and give him some radish syrup. When the knot in his throat became so oppressive that it was difficult for him to breathe, Aureliano Segundo visited Pilar Ternera to see if she knew of some herb that would give him relief. The dauntless grandmother, who had reached a hundred years of age managing a small, clandestine brothel, did not trust therapeutic superstitions, so she turned the matter over to her cards. She saw the queen of diamonds with her throat wounded by the steel of the jack of spades, and she deduced that Fernanda was trying to get her husband back home by means of the discredited method of sticking pins into his picture but that she had brought on an internal tumor because of her clumsy knowledge of the black arts. Since Aureliano Segundo had no other pictures except those of his wedding and the copies were all in the family album, he kept searching all through the house when his wife was not looking, and finally, in the bottom of the dresser, he came across a half-dozen pessaries in their original boxes. Thinking that the small red rubber rings were objects of witchcraft he put them in his pocket so that Pilar Ternera could have a look at them. She could not determine their nature, but they looked so suspicious to her that in any case she burned them in a bonfire she built in the courtyard. In order to conjure away Fernanda's alleged curse, she told Aureliano Segundo that he should soak a broody hen and bury her alive under the chestnut tree, and he did it with such good faith that when he finished hiding the turned-up earth with dried leaves he already felt that he was breathing better. For her part, Fernanda interpreted the disappearance as a reprisal by the invisible doctors and she sewed a pocket of casing to the inside of her camisole where she kept the new pessaries that her son sent her.

Six months after he had buried the hen, Aureliano Segundo woke up at midnight with an attack of coughing and the feeling that he was being strangled within by the claws of a crab. It was then that he understood that for all of the magical pessaries that he destroyed and all the conjuring hens that he soaked, the single and sad piece of truth was that he was dying. He did not tell anyone. Tormented by the fear of dying without having sent Amaranta Úrsula to Brussels, he worked as he had never done, and instead of one he made three weekly raffles. From very early in the morning he could be seen going through the town, even in the most outlying and miserable sections, trying to sell tickets with an anxiety that could only be conceivable in a dying man. "Here's Divine Providence," he hawked. "Don't let it get away, because it only comes every hundred years." He made pitiful efforts to appear gay, pleasant, talkative, but it was enough to see his sweat and paleness to know that his heart was not in it. Sometimes he would go to vacant lots, where no one could see him, and sit down to rest from the claws that were tearing him apart inside. Even at midnight he would be in the red-light district trying to console with predictions of good luck the lonely women who were weeping beside their phonographs. "This number hasn't come up in four months," he told them, showing them the tickets. "Don't let it get away, life is shorter than you think." They finally lost respect for him, made fun of him, and in his last months they no longer called him Don Aureliano, as they had always done, but they called him Mr. Divine Providence right to his face. His voice was becoming filled with wrong notes. It was getting out of tune, and it finally diminished into the growl of a dog, but he still had the drive to see that there should be no diminishing of the hope people brought to Petra Cotes's courtyard. As he lost his voice, however, and realized that in a short time he would be unable to bear the pain, he began to understand that it was not through raffled pigs and goats that his daughter would get to Brussels, so he conceived the idea of organizing the fabulous raffle of the lands destroyed by the deluge, which could easily be restored by a person with the money to do so. It was such a spectacular undertaking that the mayor himself lent his aid by announcing it in a proclamation, and associations were formed to buy tickets at one hundred pesos apiece and they were sold out in less than a week. The night of the raffle the winners held a huge celebration, comparable only to those of the good days of the banana company, and Aureliano Segundo, for the last time, played the forgotten songs of Francisco the Man on the accordion, but he could no longer sing them.

Two months later Amaranta Úrsula went to Brussels. Aureliano Segundo gave her not only the money from the special raffle, but also what he had managed to put aside over the previous months and what little he had received from the sale of the pianola, the clavichord, and other junk that had fallen into disrepair. According to his calculations, that sum would be enough for her studies, so that all that was lacking was the price of her fare back home. Fernanda was against the trip until the last moment, scandalized by the idea that Brussels was so close to Paris and its perdition, but she calmed down with the letter that Father Ángel gave her addressed to a boardinghouse run by nuns for Catholic young ladies where Amaranta Úrsula promised to stay until her studies were completed. Furthermore, the parish priest arranged for her to travel under the care of a group of Franciscan nuns who were going to Toledo, where they hoped to find dependable people to accompany her to Belgium. While the urgent correspondence that made the coordination possible went forward, Aureliano Segundo, aided by Petra Cotes, prepared Amaranta Úrsula's baggage. The night on which they were packing one of Fernanda's bridal trunks, the things were so well organized that the schoolgirl knew by heart which were the suits and cloth slippers she would wear crossing the Atlantic and the blue cloth coat with copper buttons and the cordovan shoes she would wear when she landed. She also knew how to walk so as not to fall into the water as she went

358

up the gangplank, that at no time was she to leave the company of the nuns or leave her cabin except to eat, and that for no reason was she to answer the questions asked by people of any sex while they were at sea. She carried a small bottle with drops for seasickness and a notebook written by Father Ángel in his own hand containing six prayers to be used against storms. Fernanda made her a canvas belt to keep her money in, and she would not have to take it off even to sleep. She tried to give her the chamberpot, washed out with lye and disinfected with alcohol, but Amaranta Úrsula refused it for fear that her schoolmates would make fun of her. A few months later, at the hour of his death, Aureliano Segundo would remember her as he had seen her for the last time as she tried unsuccessfully to lower the window of the second-class coach to hear Fernanda's last piece of advice. She was wearing a pink silk dress with a corsage of artificial pansies pinned to her left shoulder, her cordovan shoes, with buckles and low heels, and sateen stockings held up at the thighs with elastic garters. Her body was slim, her hair loose and long, and she had the lively eyes that Úrsula had had at her age and the way in which she said good-bye, without crying but without smiling either, revealed the same strength of character. Walking beside the coach as it picked up speed and holding Fernanda by the arm so that she would not stumble, Aureliano scarcely had time to wave at his daughter as she threw him a kiss with the tips of her fingers. The couple stood motionless under the scorching sun, looking at the train as it merged with the black strip of the horizon, linking arms for the first time since the day of their wedding.

On the ninth of August, before they received the first letter from Brussels, José Arcadio Segundo was speaking to Aureliano in Melquíades' room and, without realizing it, he said:

"Always remember that they were more than three thousand and that they were thrown into the sea."

Then he fell back on the parchments and died with his eyes open. At that same instant, in Fernanda's bed, his twin brother came to the end of the prolonged and terrible martyrdom of the steel crabs that were eating his throat away. One week previously he had returned home, without any voice, unable to breathe, and almost skin and bones, with his wandering trunks and his wastrel's accordion, to fulfill the promise of dying beside his wife. Petra Cotes helped him pack his clothes and bade him farewell without shedding a tear, but she forgot to give him the patent leather shoes that he wanted to wear in his coffin. So when she heard that he had died, she dressed in black, wrapped the shoes up in a newspaper, and asked Fernanda for permission to see the body. Fernanda would not let her through the door.

"Put yourself in my place," Petra Cotes begged. "Imagine how much I must have loved him to put up with this humiliation."

"There is no humiliation that a concubine does not deserve," Fernanda replied. "So wait until another one of your men dies and put the shoes on him."

In fulfillment of her promise, Santa Sofía de la Piedad cut the throat of José Arcadio Segundo's corpse with a kitchen knife to be sure that they would not bury him alive. The bodies were placed in identical coffins, and then it could be seen that once more in death they had become as identical as they had been until adolescence. Aureliano Segundo's old carousing comrades laid on his casket a wreath that had a purple ribbon with the words: *Cease, cows, life is short.* Fernanda was so indignant with such irreverence that she had the wreath thrown onto the trash heap. In the tumult of the last moment, the sad drunkards who carried them out of the house got the coffins mixed up and buried them in the wrong graves.

Aᴜʀᴇʟɪᴀɴᴏ ᴅɪᴅ ɴᴏᴛ leave Melquíades' room for a long time. He learned by heart the fantastic legends of the crumbling book, the synthesis of the studies of Hermann the Cripple, the notes on the science of demonology, the keys to the philosopher's stone, the *Centuries* of Nostradamus and his research concerning the plague, so that he reached adolescence without knowing a thing about his own time but with the basic knowledge of a medieval man. Any time that Santa Sofía de la Piedad would go into his room she would find him absorbed in his reading. At dawn she would bring him a mug of coffee without sugar and at noon a plate of rice and slices of fried plantain, which were the only things eaten in the house since the death of Aureliano Segundo. She saw that his hair was cut, picked off the nits, took in to his size the old

N

clothing that she found in forgotten trunks, and when his mustache began to appear she brought him Colonel Aureliano Buendía's razor and the small gourd he had used as a shaving mug. None of the latter's children had looked so much like him, not even Aureliano José, particularly in respect to the prominent cheekbones and the firm and rather pitiless line of the lips. As had happened to Úrsula with Aureliano Segundo when the latter was studying in the room, Santa Sofía de la Piedad thought that Aureliano was talking to himself. Actually, he was talking to Melquíades. One burning noon, a short time after the death of the twins, against the light of the window he saw the gloomy old man with his crow's-wing hat like the materialization of a memory that had been in his head since long before he was born. Aureliano had finished classifying the alphabet of the parchments, so that when Melquíades asked him if he had discovered the language in which they had been written he did not hesitate to answer.

"Sanskrit," he said.

Melquíades revealed to him that his opportunities to return to the room were limited. But he would go in peace to the meadows of the ultimate death because Aureliano would have time to learn Sanskrit during the years remaining until the parchments became one hundred years old, when they could be deciphered. It was he who indicated to Aureliano that on the narrow street going down to the river, where dreams had been interpreted during the time of the banana company, a wise Catalonian had a bookstore where there was a Sanskrit primer, which would be eaten by the moths within six years if he did not hurry to buy it. For the first time in her long life Santa Sofía de la Piedad let a feeling show through, and it was a feeling of wonderment, when Aureliano asked her to bring him the book that could be found between *Jerusalem Delivered* and Milton's poems on the extreme right-hand side of the second shelf of the bookcases. Since she could not read, she memorized what he had said and got some money by selling one of the seventeen little gold fishes left in the workshop, the whereabouts of which, after being hidden the night the soldiers searched the house, was known only by her and Aureliano.

Aureliano made progress in his studies of Sanskrit as Melquíades' visits became less and less frequent and he was more distant, fading away in the radiant light of noon. The last time that Aureliano sensed him he was only an invisible presence who murmured: "I died of fever on the sands of Singapore." The room then became vulnerable to dust, heat, termites, red ants, and moths, who would turn the wisdom of the parchments into sawdust.

There was no shortage of food in the house. The day after the death of Aureliano Segundo, one of the friends who had brought the wreath with the irreverent inscription offered to pay Fernanda some money that he had owed her husband. After that every Wednesday a delivery boy brought a basket of food that was quite sufficient for a week. No one ever knew that those provisions were being sent by Petra Cotes with the idea that the continuing charity was a way of humiliating the person who had humiliated her. Nevertheless, the rancor disappeared much sooner than she herself had expected, and then she continued sending the food out of pride and finally out of compassion. Several times, when she had no animals to raffle off and people lost interest in the lottery, she went without food so that Fernanda could have something to eat, and she continued fulfilling the pledge to herself until she saw Fernanda's funeral procession pass by.

For Santa Sofía de la Piedad the reduction in the number of inhabitants of the house should have meant the rest she deserved after more than half a century of work. Never a lament had been heard from that stealthy, impenetrable woman who had sown in the family the angelic seed of Remedios the Beauty and the mysterious solemnity of José

Arcadio Segundo; who dedicated a whole life of solitude and diligence to the rearing of children although she could barely remember whether they were her children or grandchildren, and who took care of Aureliano as if he had come out of her womb, not knowing herself that she was his great-grandmother. Only in a house like that was it conceivable for her always to sleep on a mat she laid out on the pantry floor in the midst of the nocturnal noise of the rats, and without telling anyone that one night she had awakened with the frightened feeling that someone was looking at her in the darkness and that it was a poisonous snake crawling over her stomach. She knew that if she had told Úrsula, the latter would have made her sleep in her own bed, but those were times when no one was aware of anything unless it was shouted on the porch, because with the bustle of the bakery, the surprises of the war, the care of the children, there was not much room for thinking about other people's happiness. Petra Cotes, whom she had never seen, was the only one who remembered her. She saw to it that she had a good pair of shoes for street wear, that she always had clothing, even during the times when the raffles were working only through some miracle. When Fernanda arrived at the house she had good reason to think that she was an ageless servant, and even though she heard it said several times that she was her husband's mother it was so incredible that it took her longer to discover it than to forget it. Santa Sofía de la Piedad never seemed bothered by that lowly position. On the contrary, one had the impression that she liked to stay in the corners, without a pause, without a complaint, keeping clean and in order the immense house that she had lived in ever since adolescence and that, especially during the time of the banana company, was more like a barracks than a home. But when Úrsula died the superhuman diligence of Santa Sofía de la Piedad, her tremendous capacity for work, began to fall apart. It was not only that she was old and exhausted, but overnight the house had plunged into a crisis of senility. A soft moss grew up the walls. When there was no longer a bare spot in the courtyard, the weeds broke through the cement of the porch, breaking it like glass, and out of the cracks grew the same yellow flowers that Úrsula had found in the glass with Melquíades' false teeth a century before. With neither the time nor the resources to halt the challenge of nature, Santa Sofía de la Piedad spent the day in the bedrooms driving out the lizards who would return at night. One morning she saw that the red ants had left the undermined foundations, crossed the garden, climbed up the railing, where the begonias had taken on an earthen color, and had penetrated into the heart of the house. She first tried to kill them with a broom, then with insecticides, and finally with lye, but the next day they were back in the same place, still passing by, tenacious and invincible. Fernanda, writing letters to her children, was not aware of the unchecked destructive attack. Santa Sofía de la Piedad continued struggling alone, fighting the weeds to stop them from getting into the kitchen, pulling from the walls the tassels of spiderwebs which were rebuilt in a few hours, scraping off the termites. But when she saw that Melquíades' room was also dusty and filled with cobwebs even though she swept and dusted three times a day, and that in spite of her furious cleaning it was threatened by the debris and the air of misery that had been foreseen only by Colonel Aureliano Buendía and the young officer, she realized that she was defeated. Then she put on her worn Sunday dress, some old shoes of Úrsula's, and a pair of cotton stockings that Amaranta Úrsula had given her, and she made a bundle out of the two or three changes of clothing that she had left.

"I give up," she said to Aureliano. "This is too much house for my poor bones."

Aureliano asked her where she was going and she made a vague sign, as if she did not have the slightest idea of her destination. She tried to be more precise, however, saying that she was going to spend her last years with a first cousin who lived in Riohacha. It was not a likely explanation. Since the death of her parents she had not had contact with anyone in town or received letters or messages, nor had she been heard to speak of any relatives. Aureliano gave her fourteen little gold fishes because she was determined to leave with only what she had: one peso and twenty-five cents. From the window of the room he saw her cross the courtyard with her bundle of clothing, dragging her feet and bent over by her years, and he saw her reach her hand through an opening in the main door and replace the bar after she had gone out. Nothing was ever heard of her again.

When she heard about the flight, Fernanda ranted for a whole day as she checked trunks, dressers, and closets, item by item, to make sure that Santa Sofía de la Piedad had not made off with anything. She burned her fingers trying to light a fire for the first time in her life and she had to ask Aureliano to do her the favor of showing her how to make coffee. With time he was the one who took over the kitchen duties. Fernanda would find her breakfast ready when she arose and she would leave her room again only to get the meal that Aureliano had left covered on the embers for her, which she would carry to the table to eat on linen tablecloths and between candelabra, sitting at the solitary head of the table facing fifteen empty chairs. Even under those circumstances Aureliano and Fernanda did not share their solitude, but both continued living on their own, cleaning their respective rooms while the cobwebs fell like snow on the rose bushes, carpeted the beams, cushioned the walls. It was around that time that Fernanda got the impression that the house was filling up with elves. It was as if things, especially those for everyday use, had developed a faculty for changing location on their own. Fernanda would waste time looking for the shears that she was sure she had put on the bed and after turning everything upside down she would find them on a shelf in the kitchen, where she thought she had not been for four days. Suddenly there was no fork in the silver chest and she would find six on the altar and three in the washroom. That wandering about of things was even more exasperating when she sat down to write. The inkwell that she had placed at her right would be on the left, the blotter would be lost and she would find it two days later under her pillow, and the pages written to José Arcadio would get mixed up with those written to Amaranta Úrsula, and she always had the feeling of mortification that she had put the letters in opposite envelopes, as in fact happened several times. On one occasion she lost her fountain pen. Two weeks later the mailman, who had found it in his bag, returned it. He had been going from house to house looking for its owner. At first she thought it was some business of the invisible doctors, like the disappearance of the pessaries, and she even started a letter to them begging them to leave her alone, but she had to interrupt it to do something and when she went back to her room she not only did not find the letter she had started but she had forgotten the reason for writing it. For a time she thought it was Aureliano. She began to spy on him, to put things in his path trying to catch him when he changed their location, but she was soon convinced that Aureliano never left Melquíades' room except to go to the kitchen or the toilet, and that he was not a man to play tricks. So in the end she believed that it was the mischief of elves and she decided to secure everything in the place where she would use it. She tied the shears to the head of her bed with a long string. She tied the pen and the blotter to the leg of the table, and she glued the inkwell to the top of it to the right of the place where she normally wrote. The problems were not solved overnight, because a few hours after she had tied the string to the shears it was not long enough for her to cut with, as if the elves had shortened it. The same thing happened to her with the string to the pen and even with her own arm, which after a short time of writing could not reach the inkwell. Neither Amaranta Úrsula in Brussels nor José Arcadio in Rome ever heard about those insignificant misfortunes. Fernanda told them that she was happy and in reality she was, precisely because she felt free from any compromise, as if life were pulling her once more toward the world of her parents, where one did not suffer with day-to-day problems because they were solved beforehand in one's imagination. That endless correspondence made her lose her sense of time, especially after Santa Sofía de la Piedad had left. She had been accustomed to keep track of the days, months, and years, using as points of reference the dates set for the return of her children. But when they changed their plans time and time again, the dates became confused, the periods were mislaid, and one day seemed so much like another that one could not feel them pass. Instead of becoming impatient, she felt a deep pleasure in the delay. It did not worry her that many years after announcing the eve of his final vows, José Arcadio was still saying that he was waiting to finish his studies in advanced theology in order to undertake those in diplomacy, because she understood how steep and paved with obstacles was the spiral stairway that led to the throne of Saint Peter. On the other hand, her spirits rose with news that would have been insignificant for other people, such as the fact that her son had seen the Pope. She felt a similar pleasure when Amaranta Úrsula wrote to tell her that her studies would last longer than the time foreseen because her excellent grades had earned her privileges that her father had not taken into account in his calculations.

More than three years had passed since Santa Sofía de la Piedad had brought him the grammar when Aureliano succeeded in translating the first sheet. It was not a useless chore, but it was only a first step along a road whose length it was impossible to predict, because the text in Spanish did not mean anything: the lines were in code. Aureliano lacked the means to establish the keys that would permit him to dig them out, but since Melquíades had told him that the books he needed to get to the bottom of the parchments were in the wise Catalonian's store, he decided to speak to Fernanda so that she would let him get them. In the room devoured by rubble, whose unchecked proliferation had finally defeated it, he thought about the best way to frame the request, but when he found Fernanda taking her meal from the embers, which was his only chance to speak to her, the laboriously formulated request stuck in his throat and he lost his voice. That was the only time that he watched her. He listened to her steps in the bedroom. He heard her on her way to the door to await the letters from her children and to give hers to the mailman, and he listened until late at night to the harsh, impassioned scratching of her pen on the paper before hearing the sound of the light switch and the murmur of her prayers in the darkness. Only then did he go to sleep, trusting that on the following day the awaited opportunity would come. He became so inspired with the idea that permission would be granted that one morning he cut his hair, which at that time reached down to his shoulders, shaved off his tangled beard, put on some tight-fitting pants and a shirt with an artificial collar that he had inherited from he did not know whom, and waited in the kitchen for Fernanda to get her breakfast. The woman of every day, the one with her head held high and with a stony gait, did not arrive, but an old woman of supernatural beauty with a yellowed ermine cape, a crown of gilded cardboard, and the languid look of a person who wept in secret. Actually, ever since she had found it in Aureliano Segundo's trunks, Fernanda had put on the moth-eaten queen's dress many times. Anyone who could have seen her in front of the mirror, in ecstasy over her own regal gestures, would have had reason to think that she was mad. But she was not. She had simply turned the royal regalia into

N*

a device for her memory. The first time that she put it on she could not help a knot from forming in her heart and her eyes filling with tears because at that moment she smelled once more the odor of shoe polish on the boots of the officer who came to get her at her house to make her a queen, and her soul brightened with the nostalgia of her lost dreams. She felt so old, so worn out, so far away from the best moments of her life that she even yearned for those that she remembered as the worst, and only then did she discover how much she missed the whiff of oregano on the porch and the smell of the roses at dusk, and even the bestial nature of the parvenus. Her heart of compressed ash, which had resisted the most telling blows of daily reality without strain, fell apart with the first waves of nostalgia. The need to feel sad was becoming a vice as the years eroded her. She became human in her solitude. Nevertheless, the morning on which she entered the kitchen and found a cup of coffee offered her by a pale and bony adolescent with a hallucinated glow in his eyes, the claws of ridicule tore at her. Not only did she refuse him permission, but from then on she carried the keys to the house in the pocket where she kept the unused pessaries. It was a useless precaution because if he had wanted to, Aureliano could have escaped and even returned to the house without being seen. But the prolonged captivity, the uncertainty of the world, the habit of obedience had dried up the seeds of rebellion in his heart. So that he went back to his enclosure, reading and rereading the parchments and listening until very late at night to Fernanda sobbing in her bedroom. One morning he went to light the fire as usual and on the extinguished ashes he found the food that he had left for her the day before. Then he looked into her bedroom and saw her lying on the bed covered with the ermine cape, more beautiful than ever and with her skin turned into an ivory casing. Four months later, when José Arcadio arrived, he found her intact.

It was impossible to conceive of a man more like his

mother. He was wearing a somber taffeta suit, a shirt with a round and hard collar, and a thin silk ribbon tied in a bow in place of a necktie. He was ruddy and languid, with a startled look and weak lips. His black hair, shiny and smooth, parted in the middle of his head by a straight and tired line, had the same artificial appearance as the hair on the saints. The shadow of a well-uprooted beard on his paraffin face looked like a question of conscience. His hands were pale, with green veins and fingers that were like parasites, and he wore a solid gold ring with a round sunflower opal on his left index finger. When he opened the street door Aureliano did not have to be told who he was to realize that he came from far away. With his steps the house filled up with the fragrance of the toilet water that Úrsula used to splash on him when he was a child in order to find him in the shadows. In some way impossible to ascertain, after so many years of absence, José Arcadio was still an autumnal child, terribly sad and solitary. He went directly to his mother's bedroom, where Aureliano had boiled mercury for four months in his grandfather's grandfather's water pipe to conserve the body according to Melquíades' formula. José Arcadio did not ask him any questions. He kissed the corpse on the forehead and withdrew from under her skirt the pocket of casing which contained three as yet unused pessaries and the key to her cabinet. He did everything with direct and decisive movements, in contrast to his languid look. From the cabinet he took a small damascene chest with the family crest and found on the inside, which was perfumed with sandalwood, the long letter in which Fernanda unburdened her heart of the numerous truths that she had hidden from him. He read it standing up, avidly but without anxiety, and at the third page he stopped and examined Aureliano with a look of second recognition.

"So," he said with a voice with a touch of razor in it, "you're the bastard."

"I'm Aureliano Buendía."

"Go to your room," José Arcadio said.

Aureliano went and did not come out again even from curiosity when he heard the sound of the solitary funeral ceremonies. Sometimes, from the kitchen, he would see José Arcadio strolling through the house, smothered by his anxious breathing, and he continued hearing his steps in the ruined bedrooms after midnight. He did not hear his voice for many months, not only because José Arcadio never addressed him, but also because he had no desire for it to happen or time to think about anything else but the parchments. On Fernanda's death he had taken out the next-to-the-last little fish and gone to the wise Catalonian's bookstore in search of the books he needed. Nothing he saw along the way interested him, perhaps because he lacked any memories for comparison and the deserted streets and desolate houses were the same as he had imagined them at a time when he would have given his soul to know them. He had given himself the permission denied by Fernanda and only once and for the minimum time necessary, so without pausing he went along the eleven blocks that separated the house from the narrow street where dreams had been interpreted in other days and he went panting into the confused and gloomy place where there was barely room to move. More than a bookstore, it looked like a dump for used books, which were placed in disorder on the shelves chewed by termites, in the corners sticky with cobwebs, and even in the spaces that were supposed to serve as passageways. On a long table, also heaped with old books and papers, the proprietor was writing tireless prose in purple letters, somewhat outlandish, and on the loose pages of a school notebook. He had a handsome head of silver hair which fell down over his forehead like the plume of a cockatoo, and his blue eyes, lively and close-set, revealed the gentleness of a man who had read all of the books. He was wearing short pants and soaking in perspiration, and he did not stop his writing to see who had come in. Aureliano had no difficulty in rescuing the five books that he was looking for from that fabulous disorder, because they were exactly where Melquíades had told him they would be. Without saying a word he handed them, along with the little gold fish, to the wise Catalonian and the latter examined them, his eyelids contracting like two clams. "You must be mad," he said in his own language, shrugging his shoulders, and he handed back to Aureliano the five books and the little fish.

"You can have them," he said in Spanish. "The last man who read these books must have been Isaac the Blindman, so consider well what you're doing."

José Arcadio restored Meme's bedroom and had the velvet curtains cleaned and mended along with the damask on the canopy of the viceregal bed, and he put to use once more the abandoned bathroom, where the cement pool was blackened by a fibrous and rough coating. He restricted his vest-pocket empire of worn, exotic clothing, false perfumes, and cheap jewelry to those places. The only thing that seemed to worry him in the rest of the house were the saints on the family altar, which he burned down to ashes one afternoon in a bonfire he lighted in the courtyard. He would sleep until past eleven o'clock. He would go to the bathroom in a shabby robe with golden dragons on it and a pair of slippers with yellow tassels, and there he would officiate at a rite which for its care and length recalled Remedios the Beauty. Before bathing he would perfume the pool with the salts that he carried in three alabaster flacons. He did not bathe himself with the gourd but would plunge into the fragrant waters and remain there for two hours floating on his back, lulled by the coolness and by the memory of Amaranta. A few days after arriving he put aside his taffeta suit, which in addition to being too hot for the town was the only one that he had, and he exchanged it for some tight-fitting pants very similar to those worn by Pietro Crespi during his dance lessons and a silk shirt woven with thread from living caterpillars and

373

with his initials embroidered over the heart. Twice a week he would wash the complete change in the tub and would wear his robe until it dried because he had nothing else to put on. He never ate at home. He would go out when the heat of siesta time had eased and would not return until well into the night. Then he would continue his anxious pacing, breathing like a cat and thinking about Amaranta. She and the frightful look of the saints in the glow of the nocturnal lamp were the two memories he retained of the house. Many times during the hallucinating Roman August he had opened his eyes in the middle of his sleep and had seen Amaranta rising out of a marble-edged pool with her lace petticoats and the bandage on her hand, idealized by the anxiety of exile. Unlike Aureliano José, who tried to drown that image in the bloody bog of war, he tried to keep it alive in the sink of concupiscence while he entertained his mother with the endless fable of his pontifical vocation. It never occurred either to him or to Fernanda to think that their correspondence was an exchange of fantasies. José Arcadio, who left the seminary as soon as he reached Rome, continued nourishing the legend of theology and canon law so as not to jeopardize the fabulous inheritance of which his mother's delirious letters spoke and which would rescue him from the misery and sordidness he shared with two friends in a Trastevere garret. When he received Fernanda's last letter, dictated by the foreboding of imminent death, he put the leftovers of his false splendor into a suitcase and crossed the ocean in the hold of a ship where immigrants were crammed together like cattle in a slaughterhouse, eating cold macaroni and wormy cheese. Before he read Fernanda's will, which was nothing but a detailed and tardy recapitulation of her misfortunes, the broken-down furniture and the weeds on the porch had indicated that he had fallen into a trap from which he would never escape, exiled forever from the diamond light and timeless air of the Roman spring. During the crushing insomnia brought on by his asthma he would measure and remeasure the depth of his misfortune as he went through the shadowy house where the senile fussing of Úrsula had instilled a fear of the world in him. In order to be sure that she would not lose him in the shadows, she had assigned him a corner of the bedroom, the only one where he would be safe from the dead people who wandered through the house after sundown. "If you do anything bad," Úrsula would tell him, "the saints will let me know." The terror-filled nights of his childhood were reduced to that corner where he would remain motionless until it was time to go to bed, perspiring with fear on a stool under the watchful and glacial eyes of the tattletale saints. It was useless torture because even at that time he already had a terror of everything around him and he was prepared to be frightened at anything he met in life: women on the street, who would ruin his blood; the women in the house, who bore children with the tail of a pig; fighting cocks, who brought on the death of men and remorse for the rest of one's life; firearms, which with a mere touch would bring down twenty years of war; uncertain ventures, which led only to disillusionment and madness—everything, in short, everything that God had created in His infinite goodness and that the devil had perverted. When he awakened, pressed in the vice of his nightmares, the light in the window and the caresses of Amaranta in the bath and the pleasure of being powdered between the legs with a silk puff would release him from the terror. Even Úrsula was different under the radiant light in the garden because there she did not talk about fearful things but would brush his teeth with charcoal powder so that he would have the radiant smile of a Pope, and she would cut and polish his nails so that the pilgrims who came to Rome from all over the world would be startled at the beauty of the Pope's hands as he blessed them, and she would comb his hair like that of a Pope, and she would sprinkle his body and his clothing with toilet water so that his body and his clothes would have the fragrance of a Pope. In the courtyard of Castel Gandolfo he had seen the Pope on a balcony making the same speech in seven languages for a crowd of pilgrims and the only thing, indeed, that had drawn his attention was the whiteness of his hands, which seemed to have been soaked in lye, the dazzling shine of his summer clothing, and the hidden breath of cologne.

Almost a year after his return home, having sold the silver candlesticks and the heraldic chamberpot—which at the moment of truth turned out to have only a little gold plating on the crest—in order to eat, the only distraction of José Arcadio was to pick up children in town so that they could play in the house. He would appear with them at siesta time and have them skip rope in the garden, sing on the porch, and do acrobatics on the furniture in the living room while he would go among the groups giving lessons in good manners. At that time he had finished with the tight pants and the silk shirts and was wearing an ordinary suit of clothing that he had bought in the Arab stores, but he still maintained his languid dignity and his papal air. The children took over the house just as Meme's schoolmates had done in the past. Until well into the night they could be heard chattering and singing and tap-dancing, so that the house resembled a boarding school where there was no discipline. Aureliano did not worry about the invasion as long as they did not bother him in Melquíades' room. One morning two children pushed open the door and were startled at the sight of a filthy and hairy man who was still deciphering the parchments on the worktable. They did not dare go in, but they kept on watching the room. They would peep in through the cracks, whispering, they threw live animals in through the transom, and on one occasion they nailed up the door and the window and it took Aureliano half a day to force them open. Amused at their unpunished mischief, four of the children went into the room one morning while Aureliano was in the kitchen, preparing to destroy the parchments. But as soon as they laid hands on the yellowed sheets an angelic force lifted them off the ground and held them suspended in the air until Aureliano returned and took the parchments away from them. From then on they did not bother him.

The four oldest children, who wore short pants in spite of the fact that they were on the threshold of adolescence, busied themselves with José Arcadio's personal appearance. They would arrive earlier than the others and spend the morning shaving him, giving him massages with hot towels, cutting and polishing the nails on his hands and feet, and perfuming him with toilet water. On several occasions they would get into the pool to soap him from head to toe as he floated on his back thinking about Amaranta. Then they would dry him, powder his body, and dress him. One of the children, who had curly blond hair and eyes of pink glass like a rabbit, was accustomed to sleeping in the house. The bonds that linked him to José Arcadio were so strong that he would accompany him in his asthmatic insomnia, without speaking, strolling through the house with him in the darkness. One night in the room where Úrsula had slept they saw a yellow glow coming through the crumbling cement, as if an underground sun had changed the floor of the room into a pane of glass. They did not have to turn on the light. It was sufficient to lift the broken slabs in the corner where Úrsula's bed had always stood and where the glow was most intense to find the secret crypt that Aureliano Segundo had worn himself out searching for during the delirium of his excavations. There were the three canvas sacks closed with copper wire, and inside of them the seven thousand two hundred fourteen pieces of eight, which continued glowing like embers in the darkness.

The discovery of the treasure was like a deflagration. Instead of returning to Rome with the sudden fortune, which had been his dream maturing in misery, José Arcadio converted the house into a decadent paradise. He replaced the curtains and the canopy of the bed with new velvet, and he had the bathroom floor covered with paving stones and the walls with tiles. The cupboard in the dining room was filled with fruit preserves, hams, and pickles, and the unused pantry was opened again for the storage of wines and liqueurs which José Arcadio himself brought from the railroad station in crates marked with his name. One night he and the four oldest children had a party that lasted until dawn. At six in the morning they came out naked from the bedroom, drained the pool, and filled it with champagne. They jumped in en masse, swimming like birds flying through a sky gilded with fragrant bubbles, while José Arcadio floated on his back on the edge of the festivities, remembering Amaranta with his eyes open. He remained that way, wrapped up in himself, thinking about the bitterness of his equivocal pleasures until after the children had become tired and gone in a troop to the bedroom, where they tore down the curtains to dry themselves, and in the disorder they broke the rock crystal mirror into four pieces and destroyed the canopy of the bed in the tumult of lying down. When José Arcadio came back from the bathroom, he found them sleeping in a naked heap in the shipwrecked bedroom. Inflamed, not so much because of the damage as because of the disgust and pity that he felt for himself in the emptiness of the saturnalia, he armed himself with an ecclesiastical cat-o'nine-tails that he kept in the bottom of his trunk along with a hair-shirt and other instruments of mortification and penance, and drove the children out of the house, howling like a madman and whipping them without mercy as a person would not even have done to a pack of coyotes. He was done in, with an attack of asthma that lasted for several days and that gave him the look of a man on his deathbed. On the third night of torture, overcome by asphyxiation, he went to Aureliano's room to ask him the favor of buying some powders to inhale at a nearby drugstore. So it was that Aureliano went out for a second time. He had to go only two blocks to reach the small pharmacy with dusty windows and ceramic bottles with labels in Latin where a girl with the stealthy beauty of a serpent of the Nile gave him the medicine the name of which José Arcadio had written down on a piece of paper. The second view of the deserted town, barely illuminated by the yellowish bulbs of the street lights, did not awaken in Aureliano any more curiosity than the first. José Arcadio had come to think that he had run away, when he reappeared, panting a little because of his haste, dragging legs that enclosure and lack of mobility had made weak and heavy. His indifference toward the world was so certain that a few days later José Arcadio violated the promise he had made to his mother and left him free to go out whenever he wanted to.

"I have nothing to do outside," Aureliano answered him.

He remained shut up, absorbed in the parchments, which he was slowly unraveling and whose meaning, nevertheless, he was unable to interpret. José Arcadio would bring slices of ham to him in his room, sugared flowers which left a springlike aftertaste in his mouth, and on two occasions a glass of fine wine. He was not interested in the parchments, which he thought of more as an esoteric pastime, but his attention was attracted by the rare wisdom and the inexplicable knowledge of the world that his desolate kinsman had. He discovered then that he could understand written English and that between parchments he had gone from the first page to the last of the six volumes of the encyclopedia as if it were a novel. At first he attributed to that the fact that Aureliano could speak about Rome as if he had lived there many years, but he soon became aware that he knew things that were not in the encyclopedia, such as the price of items. "Everything is known," was the only reply he received from Aureliano when he asked him where he had got that information from. Aureliano, for his part, was surprised that José Arcadio when seen from

379

close by was so different from the image that he had formed of him when he saw him wandering through the house. He was capable of laughing, of allowing himself from time to time a feeling of nostalgia for the past of the house, and of showing concern for the state of misery present in Melquíades' room. That drawing closer together of two solitary people of the same blood was far from friendship, but it did allow them both to bear up better under the unfathomable solitude that separated and united them at the same time. José Arcadio could then turn to Aureliano to untangle certain domestic problems that exasperated him. Aureliano, in turn, could sit and read on the porch, waiting for the letters from Amaranta Úrsula, which still arrived with the usual punctuality, and could use the bathroom, from which José Arcadio had banished him when he arrived.

One hot dawn they both woke up in alarm at an urgent knocking on the street door. It was a dark old man with large green eyes that gave his face a ghostly phosphorescence and with a cross of ashes on his forehead. His clothing in tatters, his shoes cracked, the old knapsack on his shoulder his only luggage, he looked like a beggar, but his bearing had a dignity that was in frank contradiction to his appearance. It was only necessary to look at him once, even in the shadows of the parlor, to realize that the secret strength that allowed him to live was not the instinct of self-preservation but the habit of fear. It was Aureliano Amador, the only survivor of Colonel Aureliano Buendía's seventeen sons, searching for a respite in his long and hazardous existence as a fugitive. He identified himself, begged them to give him refuge in that house which during his nights as a pariah he had remembered as the last redoubt of safety left for him in life. But José Arcadio and Aureliano did not remember him. Thinking that he was a tramp, they pushed him into the street. Then they both saw from the doorway the end of a drama that had begun before José Arcadio had reached the age of reason. Two policemen who had been chasing Aureliano Amador for years, who had tracked him like bloodhounds across half the world, came out from among the almond trees on the opposite sidewalk and took two shots with their Mausers which neatly penetrated the cross of ashes.

Ever since he had expelled the children from the house, José Arcadio was really waiting for news of an ocean liner that would leave for Naples before Christmas. He had told Aureliano and had even made plans to set him up in a business that would bring him a living, because the baskets of food had stopped coming since Fernanda's burial. But that last dream would not be fulfilled either. One September morning, after having coffee in the kitchen with Aureliano, José Arcadio was finishing his daily bath when through the openings in the tiles the four children he had expelled from the house burst in. Without giving him time to defend himself, they jumped into the pool fully clothed, grabbed him by the hair, and held his head under the water until the bubbling of his death throes ceased on the surface and his silent and pale dolphin body slipped down to the bottom of the fragrant water. Then they took out the three sacks of gold from the hiding place which was known only to them and their victim. It was such a rapid, methodical, and brutal action that it was like a military operation. Aureliano, shut up in his room, was not aware of anything. That afternoon, having missed him in the kitchen, he looked for José Arcadio all over the house and found him floating on the perfumed mirror of the pool, enormous and bloated and still thinking about Amaranta. Only then did he understand how much he had begun to love him.

Amaranta Úrsula returned with the first angels of December, driven on a sailor's breeze, leading her husband by a silk rope tied around his neck. She appeared without warning, wearing an ivory-colored dress, a string of pearls that reached almost to her knees, emerald and topaz rings, and with her straight hair in a smooth bun held behind her ears by swallow-tail brooches. The man whom she had married six months before was a thin, older Fleming with the look of a sailor about him. She had only to push open the door to the parlor to realize that her absence had been longer and more destructive than she had imagined.

"Good Lord," she shouted, more gay than alarmed, "it's obvious that there's no woman in this house!"

382

The baggage would not fit on the porch. Besides Fernanda's old trunk, which they had sent her off to school with, she had two upright trunks, four large suitcases, a bag for her parasols, eight hatboxes, a gigantic cage with half a hundred canaries, and her husband's velocipede, broken down in a special case which allowed him to carry it like a cello. She did not even take a day of rest after the long trip. She put on some worn denim overalls that her husband had brought along with other automotive items and set about a new restoration of the house. She scattered the red ants, who had already taken possession of the porch, brought the rose bushes back to life, uprooted the weeds, and planted ferns, oregano, and begonias again in the pots along the railing. She took charge of a crew of carpenters, locksmiths, and masons, who filled in the cracks in the floor, put doors and windows back on their hinges, repaired the furniture, and whitewashed the walls inside and out, so that three months after her arrival one breathed once more the atmosphere of youth and festivity that had existed during the days of the pianola. No one in the house had ever been in a better mood at all hours and under any circumstances, nor had anyone ever been readier to sing and dance and toss all items and customs from the past into the trash. With a sweep of her broom she did away with the funeral mementos and piles of useless trash and articles of superstition that had been piling up in the corners, and the only thing she spared, out of gratitude to Úrsula, was the daguerreotype of Remedios in the parlor. "My, such luxury," she would shout, dying with laughter. "A fourteen-year-old grandmother!" When one of the masons told her that the house was full of apparitions and that the only way to drive them out was to look for the treasures they had left buried, she replied amid loud laughter that she did not think it was right for men to be superstitious. She was so spontaneous, so emancipated, with such a free and modern spirit, that Aureliano did not know what to do with his body when he saw her arrive. "My, my!" she shouted happily with open arms. "Look at how my darling cannibal has grown!" Before he had a chance to react, she had already put a record on the portable phonograph she had brought with her and was trying to teach him the latest dance steps. She made him change the dirty pants that he had inherited from Colonel Aureliano Buendía and gave him some youthful shirts and two-toned shoes, and she would push him into the street when he was spending too much time in Melquíades' room.

Active, small, and indomitable like Úrsula, and almost as pretty and provocative as Remedios the Beauty, she was endowed with a rare instinct for anticipating fashion. When she received pictures of the most recent fashions in the mail, they only proved that she had not been wrong about the models that she designed herself and sewed on Amaranta's primitive pedal machine. She subscribed to every fashion magazine, art publication, and popular music review published in Europe, and she had only to glance at them to realize that things in the world were going just as she imagined they were. It was incomprehensible why a woman with that spirit would have returned to a dead town burdened by dust and heat, and much less with a husband who had more than enough money to live anywhere in the world and who loved her so much that he let himself be led around by her on a silk leash. As time passed, however, her intention to stay was more obvious, because she did not make any plans that were not a long way off, nor did she do anything that did not have as an aim the search for a comfortable life and a peaceful old age in Macondo. The canary cage showed that those aims were made up on the spur of the moment. Remembering that her mother had told her in a letter about the extermination of the birds, she had delayed her trip several months until she found a ship that stopped at the Fortunate Isles and there she chose the finest twenty-five pairs of canaries so that she could repopulate the skies of Macondo. That was the most lamentable of her numerous frustrated undertakings. As the birds reproduced Amaranta Úrsula would release them in pairs, and no sooner did they feel themselves free than they fled the town. She tried in vain to awaken love in them by means of the bird cage that Úrsula had built during the first reconstruction of the house. Also in vain were the artificial nests built of esparto grass in the almond trees and the birdseed strewn about the roofs, and arousing the captives so that their songs would dissuade the deserters, because they would take flight on their first attempt and make a turn in the sky, just the time needed to find the direction to the Fortunate Isles.

A year after her return, although she had not succeeded in making any friends or giving any parties, Amaranta Úrsula still believed that it was possible to rescue the community which had been singled out by misfortune. Gaston, her husband, took care not to antagonize her, although since that fatal noon when he got off the train he realized that his wife's determination had been provoked by a nostalgic mirage. Certain that she would be defeated by the realities, he did not even take the trouble to put his velocipede together, but he set about hunting for the largest eggs among the spiderwebs that the masons had knocked down, and he would open them with his fingernails and spend hours looking through a magnifying glass at the tiny spiders that emerged. Later on, thinking that Amaranta Úrsula was continuing with her repairs so that her hands would not be idle, he decided to assemble the handsome bicycle, on which the front wheel was much larger than the rear one, and he dedicated himself to the capture and curing of every native insect he could find in the region, which he sent in jam jars to his former professor of natural history at the University of Liège, where he had done advanced work in entomology, although his main vocation was that of aviator. When he rode the bicycle he would wear acrobat's tights, gaudy socks, and a Sherlock Holmes cap, but when he was on foot he would dress in a spotless natural linen suit, white shoes, a silk bow tie, a straw boater, and he would carry a willow stick in his hand. His pale eyes accentuated his look of a sailor and his small mustache looked like the fur of a squirrel. Although he was at least fifteen years older than his wife, his alert determination to make her happy and his qualities as a good lover compensated for the difference. Actually, those who saw that man in his forties with careful habits, with the leash around his neck and his circus bicycle, would not have thought that he had made a pact of unbridled love with his wife and that they both gave in to the reciprocal drive in the least adequate of places and wherever the spirit moved them, as they had done since they had begun to keep company, and with a passion that the passage of time and the more and more unusual circumstances deepened and enriched. Gaston was not only a fierce lover, with endless wisdom and imagination, but he was also, perhaps, the first man in the history of the species who had made an emergency landing and had come close to killing himself and his sweetheart simply to make love in a field of violets.

They had met two years before they were married, when the sports biplane in which he was making rolls over the school where Amaranta Úrsula was studying made an intrepid maneuver to avoid the flagpole and the primitive framework of canvas and aluminum foil was caught by the tail on some electric wires. From then on, paying no attention to his leg in splints, on weekends he would pick up Amaranta Úrsula at the nuns' boardinghouse where she lived, where the rules were not as severe as Fernanda had wanted, and he would take her to his country club. They began to love each other at an altitude of fifteen hundred feet in the Sunday air of the moors, and they felt all the closer together as the beings on earth grew more and more minute. She spoke to him of Macondo as the brightest and most peaceful town on earth, and of an enormous house, scented with oregano, where she wanted to live until old age with a loyal husband and two strong sons who would be named Rodrigo and Gonzalo, never Aureliano and José Arcadio, and a daughter who would be named Virginia and never Remedios. She had evoked the town idealized by nostalgia with such strong tenacity that Gaston understood that she would not get married unless he took her to live in Macondo. He agreed to it, as he agreed later on to the leash, because he thought it was a passing fancy that could be overcome in time. But when two years in Macondo had passed and Amaranta Úrsula was as happy as on the first day, he began to show signs of alarm. By that time he had dissected every dissectible insect in the region, he spoke Spanish like a native, and he had solved all of the crossword puzzles in the magazines that he received in the mail. He did not have the pretext of climate to hasten their return because nature had endowed him with a colonial liver which resisted the drowsiness of siesta time and water that had vinegar worms in it. He liked the native cooking so much that once he ate eighty-two iguana eggs at one sitting. Amaranta Úrsula, on the other hand, had brought in by train fish and shellfish in boxes of ice, canned meats and preserved fruits, which were the only things she could eat, and she still dressed in European style and received designs by mail in spite of the fact that she had no place to go and no one to visit, and by that time her husband was not in a mood to appreciate her short skirts, her tilted felt hat, and her seven-strand necklaces. Her secret seemed to lie in the fact that she always found a way to keep busy, resolving domestic problems that she herself had created, and doing a poor job on a thousand things which she would fix on the following day with a pernicious diligence that made one think of Fernanda and the hereditary vice of making something just to unmake it. Her festive genius was still so alive then that when she received new records she would invite Gaston to stay in the parlor until very late to practice the dance steps that her schoolmates described to her in sketches and they would generally end up making love on the Viennese rocking chairs or on the bare floor. The only thing that she needed to be completely happy was the birth of her children, but she respected the pact she had made with her husband not to have any until they had been married for five years.

Looking for something to fill his idle hours with, Gaston became accustomed to spending the morning in Melquíades' room with the shy Aureliano. He took pleasure in recalling with him the most hidden corners of his country, which Aureliano knew as if he had spent much time there. When Gaston asked him what he had done to obtain knowledge that was not in the encyclopedia, he received the same answer as José Arcadio: "Everything is known." In addition to Sanskrit he had learned English and French and a little Latin and Greek. Since he went out every afternoon at that time and Amaranta Úrsula had set aside a weekly sum for him for his personal expenses, his room looked like a branch of the wise Catalonian's bookstore. He read avidly until late at night, although from the manner in which he referred to his reading, Gaston thought that he did not buy the books in order to learn but to verify the truth of his knowledge, and that none of them interested him more than the parchments, to which he dedicated most of his time in the morning. Both Gaston and his wife would have liked to incorporate him into the family life, but Aureliano was a hermetic man with a cloud of mystery that time was making denser. It was such an unfathomable condition that Gaston failed in his efforts to become intimate with him and had to seek other pastimes for his idle hours. It was around that time that he conceived the idea of establishing an airmail service.

It was not a new project. Actually, he had it fairly well advanced when he met Amaranta Úrsula, except that it was not for Macondo but for the Belgian Congo, where his family had investments in palm oil. The marriage and the decision to spend a few months in Macondo to please his wife had obliged him to postpone it. But when he saw that Amaranta Úrsula was determined to organize a commission for public improvement and even laughed at him when he hinted at the possibility of returning, he understood that things were going to take a long time and he re-established contact with his forgotten partners in Brussels, thinking that it was just as well to be a pioneer in the Caribbean as in Africa. While his steps were progressing he prepared a landing field in the old enchanted region which at that time looked like a plain of crushed flintstone, and he studied the wind direction, the geography of the coastal region, and the best routes for aerial navigation, without knowing that his diligence, so similar to that of Mr. Herbert, was filling the town with the dangerous suspicion that his plan was not to set up routes but to plant banana trees. Enthusiastic over an idea that, after all, might justify his permanent establishment in Macondo, he took several trips to the capital of the province, met with authorities, obtained licenses, and drew up contracts for exclusive rights. In the meantime he maintained a correspondence with his partners in Brussels which resembled that of Fernanda with the invisible doctors, and he finally convinced them to ship the first airplane under the care of an expert mechanic, who would assemble it in the nearest port and fly it to Macondo. One year after his first meditations and meteorological calculations, trusting in the repeated promises of his correspondents, he had acquired the habit of strolling through the streets, looking at the sky, hanging onto the sound of the breeze in hopes that the airplane would appear.

Although she had not noticed it, the return of Amaranta Úrsula had brought on a radical change in Aureliano's life. After the death of José Arcadio he had become a regular customer at the wise Catalonian's bookstore. Also, the freedom that he enjoyed then and the time at his disposal awoke in him a certain curiosity about the town, which he came to know without any surprise. He went through the dusty and solitary streets, examining with scientific interest the inside of houses in ruin, the metal screens on the windows broken by rust and the dying birds, and the inhabitants bowed down by memories. He tried to reconstruct in his imagination the annihilated splendor of the old banana-company town, whose dry swimming pool was filled to the brim with rotting men's and women's shoes, and in the houses of which, destroyed by rye grass, he found the skeleton of a German shepherd dog still tied to a ring by a steel chain and a telephone that was ringing, ringing, ringing until he picked it up and an anguished and distant woman spoke in English, and he said yes, that the strike was over, that three thousand dead people had been thrown into the sea, that the banana company had left, and that Macondo finally had peace after many years. Those wanderings led him to the prostrate red-light district, where in other times bundles of banknotes had been burned to liven up the revels, and which at that time was a maze of streets more afflicted and miserable than the others, with a few red lights still burning and with deserted dance halls adorned with the remnants of wreaths, where the pale, fat widows of no one, the French great-grandmothers and the Babylonian matriarchs, were still waiting beside their phonographs. Aureliano could not find anyone who remembered his family, not even Colonel Aureliano Buendía, except for the oldest of the West Indian Negroes, an old man whose cottony hair gave him the look of a photographic negative and who was still singing the mournful sunset psalms in the door of his house. Aureliano would talk to him in the tortured Papiamento that he had learned in a few weeks and sometimes he would share his chicken-head soup, prepared by the great-granddaughter, with him. She was a large black woman with solid bones, the hips of a mare, teats like live melons, and a round and perfect head armored with a hard surface of wiry hair which looked like a medieval warrior's mail headdress. Her name was Nigromanta. In those days Aureliano lived off the sale of silverware, candlesticks, and other bric-a-brac from the house. When he was penniless, which was most of the time, he got people in the back of the market to give him the chicken heads that they were going to throw away and he would take them to Nigromanta to make her soups, fortified with purslane and seasoned with mint. When the great-grandfather died Aureliano stopped going by the house, but he would run into Nigromanta under the dark almond trees on the square, using her wild-animal whistles to lure the few night owls. Many times he stayed with her, speaking in Papiamento about chicken-head soup and other dainties of misery, and he would have kept right on if she had not let him know that his presence frightened off customers. Although he sometimes felt the temptation and although Nigromanta herself might have seemed to him as the natural culmination of a shared nostalgia, he did not go to bed with her. So Aureliano was still a virgin when Amaranta Úrsula returned to Macondo and gave him a sisterly embrace that left him breathless. Every time he saw her, and worse yet when she showed him the latest dances, he felt the same spongy release in his bones that had disturbed his great-great-grandfather when Pilar Ternera made her pretexts about the cards in the granary. Trying to squelch the torment, he sank deeper into the parchments and eluded the innocent flattery of that aunt who was poisoning his nights with a flow of tribulation, but the more he avoided her, the more the anxiety with which he waited for her stony laughter, her howls of a happy cat, and her songs of gratitude, agonizing in love at all hours and in the most unlikely parts of the house. One night, thirty feet from his bed, on the silver workbench, the couple with unhinged bellies broke the bottles and ended up making love in a pool of muriatic acid. Aureliano not only could not sleep for a single second, but he spent the next day with a fever, sobbing with rage. The first night that he waited for Nigromanta to come to the shadows of the almond trees it seemed like an eternity, pricked as he was by the needles of uncertainty and clutching in his fist the peso and fifty cents that he had asked Amaranta Úrsula for, not so much because he needed it as to involve her, debase her, prostitute her in his adventure in some way. Nigromanta took him to her room, which was lighted with false candlesticks, to her folding cot with the bedding stained from bad loves, and to her body of a wild dog, hardened and without a soul, which prepared itself to dismiss him as if he were a frightened child, and suddenly it found a man whose tremendous power demanded a movement of seismic readjustment from her insides.

They became lovers. Aureliano would spend his mornings deciphering parchments and at siesta time he would go to the bedroom where Nigromanta was waiting for him, to teach him first how to do it like earthworms, then like snails, and finally like crabs, until she had to leave him and lie in wait for vagabond loves. Several weeks passed before Aureliano discovered that around her waist she wore a small belt that seemed to be made out of a cello string, but which was hard as steel and had no end, as if it had been born and grown with her. Almost always, between loves, they would eat naked in the bed, in the hallucinating heat and under the daytime stars that the rust had caused to shine on the zinc ceiling. It was the first time that Nigromanta had had a steady man, a bone crusher from head to toe, as she herself said, dying with laughter, and she had even begun to get romantic illusions when Aureliano confided in her about his repressed passion for Amaranta Úrsula, which he had not been able to cure with the substitution but which was twisting him inside all the more as experience broadened the horizons of love. After that Nigromanta continued to receive him with the same warmth as ever but she made him pay for her services so strictly that when Aureliano had no money she would make an addition to his bill, which was not figured in numbers but by marks that she made with her thumbnail behind the door. At sundown, while she was drifting through the shadows in the square, Aureliano was going along the porch like a stranger, scarcely greeting Amaranta Úrsula and Gaston, who usually dined at that time, and shutting himself up in his room again, unable to read or write or even think because of the anxiety brought on by the laughter, the whispering, the preliminary frolics, and then the explosions of agonizing happiness that capped the nights in the house. That was his life two years before Gaston began to wait for the airplane, and it went on the same way on the afternoon that he went to the bookstore of the wise Catalonian and found four ranting boys in a heated argument about the methods used to kill cockroaches in the Middle Ages. The old bookseller, knowing about Aureliano's love for books that had been read only by the Venerable Bede, urged him with a certain fatherly malice to get into the discussion, and without even taking a breath, he explained that the cockroach, the oldest winged insect on the face of the earth, had already been the victim of slippers in the Old Testament, but that since the species was definitely resistant to any and all methods of extermination, from tomato slices with borax to flour and sugar, and with its one thousand six hundred three varieties had resisted the most ancient, tenacious, and pitiless persecution that mankind had unleashed against any living thing since the beginnings, including man himself, to such an extent that just as an instinct for reproduction was attributed to humankind, so there must have been another one more definite and pressing, which was the instinct to kill cockroaches, and if the latter had succeeded in escaping human ferocity it was because they had taken refuge in the shadows, where they became invulnerable

o

because of man's congenital fear of the dark, but on the other hand they became susceptible to the glow of noon, so that by the Middle Ages already, and in present times, and *per omnia secula seculorum,* the only effective method for killing cockroaches was the glare of the sun.

That encyclopedic coincidence was the beginning of a great friendship. Aureliano continued getting together in the afternoon with the four arguers, whose names were Álvaro, Germán, Alfonso, and Gabriel, the first and last friends that he ever had in his life. For a man like him, holed up in written reality, those stormy sessions that began in the bookstore and ended at dawn in the brothels were a revelation. It had never occurred to him until then to think that literature was the best plaything that had ever been invented to make fun of people, as Álvaro demonstrated during one night of revels. Some time would have to pass before Aureliano realized that such arbitrary attitudes had their origins in the example of the wise Catalonian, for whom wisdom was worth nothing if it could not be used to invent a new way of preparing chick peas.

The afternoon on which Aureliano gave his lecture on cockroaches, the argument ended up in the house of the girls who went to bed because of hunger, a brothel of lies on the outskirts of Macondo. The proprietress was a smiling *mamasanta,* tormented by a mania for opening and closing doors. Her eternal smile seemed to have been brought on by the credulity of her customers, who accepted as something certain an establishment that did not exist except in the imagination, because even the tangible things there were unreal: the furniture that fell apart when one sat on it, the disemboweled phonograph with a nesting hen inside, the garden of paper flowers, the calendars going back to the years before the arrival of the banana company, the frames with prints cut out of magazines that had never been published. Even the timid little whores who came from the neighborhood: when the proprietress informed them that customers had arrived they were nothing but an invention. They would appear without any greeting in their little flowered dresses left over from days when they were five years younger, and they took them off with the same innocence with which they had put them on, and in the paroxysms of love they would exclaim good heavens, look how that roof is falling in, and as soon as they got their peso and fifty cents they would spend it on a roll with cheese that the proprietress sold them, smiling more than ever, because only she knew that that meal was not true either. Aureliano, whose world at that time began with Melquíades' parchments and ended in Nigromanta's bed, found a stupid cure for timidity in the small imaginary brothel. At first he could get nowhere, in rooms where the proprietress would enter during the best moments of love and make all sorts of comments about the intimate charms of the protagonists. But with time he began to get so familiar with those misfortunes of the world that on one night that was more unbalanced than the others he got undressed in the small reception room and ran through the house balancing a bottle of beer on his inconceivable maleness. He was the one who made fashionable the extravagances that the proprietress celebrated with her eternal smile, without protesting, without believing in them, just as when Germán tried to burn the house down to show that it did not exist, and as when Alfonso wrung the neck of the parrot and threw it into the pot where the chicken stew was beginning to boil.

Although Aureliano felt himself linked to the four friends by a common affection and a common solidarity, even to the point where he thought of them as if they were one person, he was closer to Gabriel than to the others. The link was born on the night when he casually mentioned Colonel Aureliano Buendía and Gabriel was the only one who did not think that he was making fun of somebody. Even the proprietress, who normally did not take part in the conversations, argued with a madam's wrathful passion that Colonel Aureliano Buendía, of whom she had indeed heard speak at some time, was a figure invented by the government as a pretext for killing Liberals. Gabriel, on the other hand, did not doubt the reality of Colonel Aureliano Buendía because he had been a companion in arms and inseparable friend of his great-great-grandfather Colonel Gerineldo Márquez. Those fickle tricks of memory were even more critical when the killing of the workers was brought up. Every time that Aureliano mentioned the matter, not only the proprietress but some people older than she would repudiate the myth of the workers hemmed in at the station and the train with two hundred cars loaded with dead people, and they would even insist that, after all, everything had been set forth in judicial documents and in primary-school textbooks: that the banana company had never existed. So that Aureliano and Gabriel were linked by a kind of complicity based on real facts that no one believed in, and which had affected their lives to the point that both of them found themselves off course in the tide of a world that had ended and of which only the nostalgia remained. Gabriel would sleep wherever time overtook him. Aureliano put him up several times in the silver workshop, but he would spend his nights awake, disturbed by the noise of the dead people who walked through the bedrooms until dawn. Later he turned him over to Nigromanta, who took him to her well-used room when she was free and put down his account with vertical marks behind the door in the few spaces left free by Aureliano's debts.

In spite of their disordered life, the whole group tried to do something permanent at the urging of the wise Catalonian. It was he, with his experience as a former professor of classical literature and his storehouse of rare books, who got them to spend a whole night in search of the thirty-seventh dramatic situation in a town where no one had any interest any more in going beyond primary school. Fascinated by the discovery of friendship, bewildered by the enchantments of a world which had been forbidden to him by Fernanda's meanness, Aureliano abandoned the scrutiny of the parchments precisely when they were beginning to reveal themselves as predictions in coded lines of poetry. But the subsequent proof that there was time enough for everything without having to give up the brothels gave him the drive to return to Melquíades' room, having decided not to flag in his efforts until he had discovered the last keys. That was during the time that Gaston began to wait for the airplane and Amaranta Úrsula was so lonely that one morning she appeared in the room.

"Hello, cannibal," she said to him. "Back in your cave again?"

She was irresistible, with a dress she had designed and one of the long shad-vertebra necklaces that she herself had made. She had stopped using the leash, convinced of her husband's faithfulness, and for the first time since her return she seemed to have a moment of ease. Aureliano did not need to see her to know that she had arrived. She put her elbows on the table, so close and so helpless that Aureliano heard the deep sound of her bones, and she became interested in the parchments. Trying to overcome his disturbance, he grasped at the voice that he was losing, the life that was leaving him, the memory that was turning into a petrified polyp, and he spoke to her about the priestly destiny of Sanskrit, the scientific possibility of seeing the future showing through in time as one sees what is written on the back of a sheet of paper through the light, the necessity of deciphering the predictions so that they would not defeat themselves, and the *Centuries* of Nostradamus and the destruction of Cantabria predicted by Saint Milanus. Suddenly, without interrupting the chat, moved by an impulse that had been sleeping in him since his origins, Aureliano put his hand on hers, thinking that that final decision would put an end to his doubts. She grabbed his index finger with the affectionate innocence with which she had done so in childhood, however, and she held it while he kept on answering questions. They remained like that, linked by icy index fingers that did not transmit anything in any way until she awoke from her momentary dream and slapped her forehead with her hand. "The ants!" she exclaimed. And then she forgot about the manuscripts, went to the door with a dance step, and from there she threw Aureliano a kiss with the tips of her fingers as she had said good-bye to her father on the afternoon when they sent her to Brussels.

"You can tell me later," she said. "I forgot that today's the day to put quicklime on the anthills."

She continued going to the room occasionally when she had something to do in that part of the house and she would stay there for a few minutes while her husband continued to scrutinize the sky. Encouraged by that change, Aureliano stayed to eat with the family at that time as he had not done since the first months of Amaranta Úrsula's return. Gaston was pleased. During the conversations after meals, which usually went on for more than an hour, he complained that his partners were deceiving him. They had informed him of the loading of the airplane on board a ship that did not arrive, and although his shipping agents insisted that it would never arrive because it was not on the list of Caribbean ships, his partners insisted that the shipment was correct and they even insinuated that Gaston was lying to them in his letters. The correspondence reached such a degree of mutual suspicion that Gaston decided not to write again and he began to suggest the possibility of a quick trip to Brussels to clear things up and return with the airplane. The plan evaporated, however, as soon as Amaranta Úrsula reiterated her decision not to move from Macondo even if she lost a husband. During the first days Aureliano shared the general opinion that Gaston was a fool on a velocipede, and that brought on a vague feeling of pity. Later, when he obtained deeper information on the nature of men in the brothels, he thought that Gaston's meekness had its origins in unbridled passion. But when he came to know him better and realized that his true character was the opposite of his submissive conduct, he conceived the malicious suspicion that even the wait for the airplane was an act. Then he thought that Gaston was not as foolish as he appeared, but, quite the contrary, was a man of infinite steadiness, ability, and patience who had set about to conquer his wife with the weariness of eternal agreement, of never saying no, of simulating a limitless conformity, letting her become enmeshed in her own web until the day she could no longer bear the tedium of the illusions close at hand and would pack the bags herself to go back to Europe. Aureliano's former pity turned into a violent dislike. Gaston's system seemed so perverse to him, but at the same time so effective, that he ventured to warn Amaranta Úrsula. She made fun of his suspicions, however, without even noticing the heavy weight of love, uncertainty, and jealousy that he had inside. It had not occurred to her that she was arousing something more than fraternal affection in Aureliano until she pricked her finger trying to open a can of peaches and he dashed over to suck the blood out with an avidity and a devotion that sent a chill up her spine.

"Aureliano!" She laughed, disturbed. "You're too suspicious to be a good bat."

Then Aureliano went all out. Giving her some small, orphaned kisses in the hollow of her wounded hand, he opened up the most hidden passageways of his heart and drew out an interminable and lacerated intestine, the terrible parasitic animal that had incubated in his martyrdom. He told her how he would get up at midnight to weep in loneliness and rage over the underwear that she had left to dry in the bathroom. He told her about the anxiety with which he had asked Nigromanta to howl like a cat and sob gaston

399

gaston gaston in his ear, and with how much astuteness he had ransacked her vials of perfume so that he could smell it on the necks of the little girls who went to bed because of hunger. Frightened by the passion of that outburst, Amaranta Úrsula was closing her fingers, contracting them like a shellfish until her wounded hand, free of all pain and any vestige of pity, was converted into a knot of emeralds and topazes and stony and unfeeling bones.

"Fool!" she said as if she were spitting. "I'm sailing on the first ship leaving for Belgium."

Álvaro had come to the wise Catalonian's bookstore one of those afternoons proclaiming at the top of his lungs his latest discovery: a zoological brothel. It was called The Golden Child and it was a huge open-air salon through which no less than two hundred bitterns who told the time with a deafening cackling strolled at will. In wire pens that surrounded the dance floor and among large Amazonian camellias there were herons of different colors, crocodiles as fat as pigs, snakes with twelve rattles, and a turtle with a gilded shell who dove in a small artificial ocean. There was a big white dog, meek and a pederast, who would give stud services nevertheless in order to be fed. The atmosphere had an innocent denseness, as if it had just been created, and the beautiful mulatto girls who waited hopelessly among the blood-red petals and the outmoded phonograph records knew ways of love that man had left behind forgotten in the earthly paradise. The first night that the group visited that greenhouse of illusions the splendid and taciturn old woman who guarded the entrance in a wicker rocking chair felt that time was turning back to its earliest origins when among the five who were arriving she saw a bony, jaundiced man with Tartar cheekbones, marked forever and from the beginning of the world with the pox of solitude.

"Lord, Lord," she sighed, "Aureliano!"

She was seeing Colonel Aureliano Buendía once more as

she had seen him in the light of a lamp long before the wars, long before the desolation of glory and the exile of disillusionment, that remote dawn when he went to her bedroom to give the first command of his life: the command to give him love. It was Pilar Ternera. Years before, when she had reached one hundred forty-five years of age, she had given up the pernicious custom of keeping track of her age and she went on living in the static and marginal time of memories, in a future perfectly revealed and established, beyond the futures disturbed by the insidious snares and suppositions of her cards.

From that night on Aureliano took refuge in the compassionate tenderness and understanding of his unknown great-great-grandmother. Sitting in her wicker rocking chair, she would recall the past, reconstruct the grandeur and misfortunes of the family and the splendor of Macondo, which was now erased, while Álvaro frightened the crocodiles with his noisy laughter and Alfonso invented outlandish stories about the bitterns who had pecked out the eyes of four customers who misbehaved the week before, and Gabriel was in the room of the pensive mulatto girl who did not collect in money but in letters to a smuggler boyfriend who was in prison on the other side of the Orinoco because the border guards had caught him and had made him sit on a chamberpot that filled up with a mixture of shit and diamonds. That true brothel, with that maternal proprietress, was the world of which Aureliano had dreamed during his prolonged captivity. He felt so well, so close to perfect companionship, that he thought of no other refuge on the afternoon on which Amaranta Úrsula had made his illusions crumble. He was ready to unburden himself with words so that someone could break the knots that bound his chest, but he only managed to let out a fluid, warm, and restorative weeping in Pilar Ternera's lap. She let him finish, scratching his head with the tips of her fingers, and without his having revealed that he was

o*

weeping from love, she recognized immediately the oldest sobs in the history of man.

"It's all right, child," she consoled him. "Now tell me who it is."

When Aureliano told her, Pilar Ternera let out a deep laugh, the old expansive laugh that ended up as a cooing of doves. There was no mystery in the heart of a Buendía that was impenetrable for her because a century of cards and experience had taught her that the history of the family was a machine with unavoidable repetitions, a turning wheel that would have gone on spilling into eternity were it not for the progressive and irremediable wearing of the axle.

"Don't you worry," she said, smiling. "Wherever she is right now, she's waiting for you."

It was half past four in the afternoon when Amaranta Úrsula came out of her bath. Aureliano saw her go by his room with a robe of soft folds and a towel wrapped around her head like a turban. He followed her almost on tiptoes, stumbling from drunkenness, and he went into the nuptial bedroom just as she opened the robe and closed it again in fright. He made a silent signal toward the next room, where the door was half open and where Aureliano knew that Gaston was beginning to write a letter.

"Go away," she said voicelessly.

Aureliano smiled, picked her up by the waist with both hands like a pot of begonias, and dropped her on her back on the bed. With a brutal tug he pulled off her bathrobe before she had time to resist and he loomed over an abyss of newly washed nudity whose skin color, lines of fuzz, and hidden moles had all been imagined in the shadows of the other rooms. Amaranta Úrsula defended herself sincerely with the astuteness of a wise woman, weaseling her slippery, flexible, and fragrant weasel's body as she tried to knee him in the kidneys and scorpion his face with her nails, but without either of them giving a gasp that might not have been taken for the breathing of a person watching the meager April sunset through the open window. It was a fierce fight, a battle to the death, but it seemed to be without violence because it consisted of distorted attacks and ghostly evasions, slow, cautious, solemn, so that during it all there was time for the petunias to bloom and for Gaston to forget about his aviator's dreams in the next room, as if they were two enemy lovers seeking reconciliation at the bottom of an aquarium. In the heat of that savage and ceremonious struggle, Amaranta Úrsula understood that her meticulous silence was so irrational that it could awaken the suspicions of her nearby husband much more than the sound of warfare that they were trying to avoid. Then she began to laugh with her lips tight together, without giving up the fight, but defending herself with false bites and deweaseling her body little by little until they both were conscious of being adversaries and accomplices at the same time and the affray degenerated into a conventional gambol and the attacks became caresses. Suddenly, almost playfully, like one more bit of mischief, Amaranta Úrsula dropped her defense, and when she tried to recover, frightened by what she herself had made possible, it was too late. A great commotion immobilized her in her center of gravity, planted her in her place, and her defensive will was demolished by the irresistible anxiety to discover what the orange whistles and the invisible globes on the other side of death were like. She barely had time to reach out her hand and grope for the towel to put a gag between her teeth so that she would not let out the cat howls that were already tearing at her insides.

P<small>ILAR</small> T<small>ERNERA</small> died in her wicker rocking chair during one night of festivities as she watched over the entrance to her paradise. In accordance with her last wishes she was not buried in a coffin but sitting in her rocker, which eight men lowered by ropes into a huge hole dug in the center of the dance floor. The mulatto girls, dressed in black, pale from weeping, invented shadowy rites as they took off their earrings, brooches, and rings and threw them into the pit before it was closed over with a slab that bore neither name nor dates, and that was covered with a pile of Amazonian camellias. After poisoning the animals, they closed up the doors and windows with brick and mortar and they scattered out into the world with their wooden trunks that were lined with pictures of saints, prints from magazines, and the portraits of sometime sweethearts, remote and fantastic, who shat diamonds, or ate cannibals, or were crowned playing-card kings on the high seas.

It was the end. In Pilar Ternera's tomb, among the psalms and cheap whore jewelry, the ruins of the past would rot, the little that remained after the wise Catalonian had auctioned off his bookstore and returned to the Mediterranean village where he had been born, overcome by a yearning for a lasting springtime. No one could have foreseen his decision. He had arrived in Macondo during the splendor of the banana company, fleeing from one of many wars, and nothing more practical had occurred to him than to set up that bookshop of incunabula and first editions in several languages, which casual customers would thumb through cautiously, as if they were junk books, as they waited their turn to have their dreams interpreted in the house across the way. He spent half his life in the back of the store, scribbling in his extra-careful hand in purple ink and on pages that he tore out of school notebooks, and no one was sure exactly what he was writing. When Aureliano first met him he had two boxes of those motley pages that in some way. made one think of Melquíades' parchments, and from that time until he left he had filled a third one, so it was reasonable to believe that he had done nothing else during his stay in Macondo. The only people with whom he maintained relations were the four friends, whom he had exchange their tops and kites for books, and he set them to reading Seneca and Ovid while they were still in grammar school. He treated the classical writers with a household familiarity, as if they had all been his roommates at some period, and he knew many things that should not have been known, such as the fact that Saint Augustine wore a wool jacket under his habit that he did not take off for fourteen years and that Arnaldo of Villanova, the necromancer, was impotent since childhood because of a scorpion bite. His fervor for the written word was an interweaving of solemn respect and gossipy irreverence. Not even his own manuscripts were safe from that dualism. Having learned Catalan in order to translate them, Alfonso put a roll of pages in his pockets, which were always full of newspaper clippings and manuals for strange trades, and one night he lost them in the house of the little girls who went to bed because of hunger. When the wise old grandfather found out, instead of raising a row as had been feared, he commented, dying with laughter, that it was the natural destiny of literature. On the other hand, there was no human power capable of persuading him not to take along the three boxes when he returned to his native village, and he unleashed a string of Carthaginian curses at the railroad inspectors who tried to ship them as freight until he finally succeeded in keeping them with him in the passenger coach. "The world must be all fucked up," he said then, "when men travel first class and literature goes as freight." That was the last thing he was heard to say. He had spent a dark week on the final preparations for the trip, because as the hour approached his humor was breaking down and things began to be misplaced, and what he put in one place would appear in another, attacked by the same elves that had tormented Fernanda.

"*Collons*," he would curse. "I shit on Canon Twenty-seven of the Synod of London."

Germán and Aureliano took care of him. They helped him like a child, fastening his tickets and immigration documents to his pockets with safety pins, making him a detailed list of what he must do from the time he left Macondo until he landed in Barcelona, but nonetheless he threw away a pair of pants with half of his money in it without realizing it. The night before the trip, after nailing up the boxes and putting his clothing into the same suitcase that he had brought when he first came, he narrowed his clam eyes, pointed with a kind of impudent benediction at the stacks of books with which he had endured during his exile, and said to his friends:

"All that shit there I leave to you people!"

Three months later they received in a large envelope twenty-nine letters and more than fifty pictures that he had accumulated during the leisure of the high seas. Although he did not date them, the order in which he had written the letters was obvious. In the first ones, with his customary good humor, he spoke about the difficulties of the crossing, the urge he had to throw the cargo officer overboard when he would not let him keep the three boxes in his cabin, the clear imbecility of a lady who was terrified at the number thirteen, not out of superstition but because she thought it was a number that had no end, and the bet that he had won during the first dinner because he had recognized in the drinking water on board the taste of the nighttime beets by the springs of Lérida. With the passage of the days, however, the reality of life on board mattered less and less to him, and even the most recent and trivial happenings seemed worthy of nostalgia, because as the ship got farther away, his memory began to grow sad. That process of nostalgia was also evident in the pictures. In the first ones he looked happy, with his sport shirt which looked like a hospital jacket and his snowy mane, in an October Caribbean filled with whitecaps. In the last ones he could be seen to be wearing a dark coat and a silk scarf, pale in the face, taciturn from absence on the deck of a mournful ship that had come to be like a sleepwalker on the autumnal seas. Germán and Aureliano answered his letters. He wrote so many during the first months that at that time they felt closer to him than when he had been in Macondo, and they were almost freed from the rancor that he had left behind. At first he told them that everything was just the same, that the pink snails were still in the house where he had been born, that the dry herring still had the same taste on a piece of toast, that the waterfalls in the village still took on a perfumed smell at dusk. They were the notebook pages again, woven with the purple scribbling, in which he dedicated a special paragraph to each one. Nevertheless, and although he himself did not seem to notice it, those letters of recuperation and stimulation were slowly changing into pastoral letters of disenchantment. One winter night while the soup was boiling in the fireplace, he missed the heat of the back of his store, the buzzing of the sun on the dusty almond trees, the whistle of the train during the lethargy of siesta time, just as in Macondo he had missed the winter soup in the fireplace, the cries of the coffee vendor, and the fleeting larks of springtime. Upset by two nostalgias facing each other like two mirrors, he lost his marvelous sense of unreality and he ended up recommending to all of them that they leave Macondo, that they forget everything he had taught them about the world and the human heart, that they shit on Horace, and that wherever they might be they always remember that the past was a lie, that memory has no return, that every spring gone by could never be recovered, and that the wildest and most tenacious love was an ephemeral truth in the end.

Álvaro was the first to take the advice to abandon Macondo. He sold everything, even the tame jaguar that teased passersby from the courtyard of his house, and he bought an eternal ticket on a train that never stopped traveling. In the postcards that he sent from the way stations he would describe with shouts the instantaneous images that he had seen from the window of his coach, and it was as if he were tearing up and throwing into oblivion some long, evanescent poem: the chimerical Negroes in the cotton fields of Louisiana, the winged horses in the bluegrass of Kentucky, the Greek lovers in the infernal sunsets of Arizona, the girl in the red sweater painting watercolors by a lake in Michigan who waved at him with her brushes, not to say farewell but out of hope, because she did not know that she was watching a train with no return passing by. Then Alfonso and Germán left one Saturday with the idea of coming back on Monday, but nothing more was ever heard of them. A year after the departure of the wise Catalonian the only one left in Macondo was Gabriel, still adrift at the mercy of Nigromanta's chancy charity and answering the questions of a contest in a French magazine in which the first prize was a trip to Paris. Aureliano, who was the one who subscribed to it, helped him fill in the answers, sometimes in his house but most of the time among the ceramic bottles and atmosphere of valerian in the only pharmacy left in Macondo, where Mercedes, Gabriel's stealthy girl friend, lived. It was the last that remained of a past whose annihilation had not taken place because it was still in a process of annihilation, consuming itself from within, ending at every moment but never ending its ending. The town had reached such extremes of inactivity that when Gabriel won the contest and left for Paris with two changes of clothing, a pair of shoes, and the complete works of Rabelais, he had to signal the engineer to stop the train and pick him up. The old Street of the Turks was at that time an abandoned corner where the last Arabs were letting themselves be dragged off to death with the age-old custom of sitting in their doorways, although it had been many years since they had sold the last yard of diagonal cloth, and in the shadowy showcases only the decapitated manikins remained. The banana company's city, which Patricia Brown may have tried to evoke for her grandchildren during the nights of intolerance and dill pickles in Prattville, Alabama, was a plain of wild grass. The ancient priest who had taken Father Ángel's place and whose name no one had bothered to find out awaited God's mercy stretched out casually in a hammock, tortured by arthritis and the insomnia of doubt while the lizards and rats fought over the inheritance of the nearby church. In that Macondo forgotten even by the birds, where the dust and the heat had become so strong that it was difficult to breathe, secluded by solitude and love and by the solitude of love in a house where it was almost impossible to sleep because of the noise of the red ants, Aureliano and Amaranta Úrsula were the only happy beings, and the most happy on the face of the earth.

Gaston had returned to Brussels. Tired of waiting for the airplane, one day he put his indispensable things into a small suitcase, took his file of correspondence, and left with the idea of returning by air before his concession was turned over to a group of German pilots who had presented the provincial authorities with a more ambitious project than his. Since the afternoon of their first love, Aureliano and Amaranta Úrsula had continued taking advantage of her husband's rare unguarded moments, making love with gagged ardor in chance meetings and almost always interrupted by unexpected returns. But when they saw themselves alone in the house they succumbed to the delirium of lovers who were making up for lost time. It was a mad passion, unhinging, which made Fernanda's bones tremble with horror in her grave and which kept them in a state of perpetual excitement. Amaranta Úrsula's shrieks, her songs of agony would break out the same at two in the afternoon on the dining-room table as at two in the morning in the pantry. "What hurts me most," she would say, laughing, "is all the time that we wasted." In the bewilderment of passion she watched the ants devastating the garden, sating their prehistoric hunger with the beams of the house, and she watched the torrents of living lava take over the porch again, but she bothered to fight them only when she found them in her bedroom. Aureliano abandoned the parchments, did not leave the house again, and carelessly answered the letters from the wise Catalonian. They lost their sense of reality, the notion of time, the rhythm of daily habits. They closed the doors and windows again so as not to waste time getting undressed and they walked about the house as Remedios the Beauty had wanted to do and they would roll around naked in the mud of the courtyard, and one afternoon they almost drowned as they made love in the cistern. In a short time they did more damage than the red ants: they destroyed the furniture in the parlor, in their madness they tore to shreds the hammock that had resisted the sad bivouac loves of Colonel Aureliano Buendía, and they disemboweled the mattresses and emptied them on the floor as they suffocated in storms of cotton. Although Aureliano was just as ferocious a lover as his rival, it was Amaranta Úrsula who ruled in that paradise of disaster with her mad genius and her lyrical voracity, as if she had concentrated in her love the unconquerable energy that her great-great-grandmother had given to the making of little candy animals. And yet, while she was singing with pleasure and dying with laughter over her own inventions, Aureliano was becoming more and more absorbed and silent, for his passion was self-centered and burning. Nevertheless, they both reached such extremes of virtuosity that when they became exhausted from excitement, they would take advantage of their fatigue. They would give themselves over to the worship of their bodies, discovering that the rest periods in love had unexplored possibilities, much richer than those of desire. While he would rub Amaranta Úrsula's erect breasts with egg whites or smooth her elastic thighs and peachlike stomach with cocoa butter, she would play with Aureliano's portentous creature as if it were a doll and would paint clown's eyes on it with her lipstick and give it a Turk's mustache with her eyebrow pencil, and would put on organza bow ties and little tinfoil hats. One night they daubed themselves from head to toe with peach jam and licked each other like dogs and made mad love on the floor of the porch, and they were awakened by a torrent of carnivorous ants who were ready to eat them alive.

During the pauses in their delirium, Amaranta Úrsula would answer Gaston's letters. She felt him to be so far away and busy that his return seemed impossible to her. In one of his first letters he told her that his partners had actually sent the airplane, but that a shipping agent in Brussels had sent it by mistake to Tanganyika, where it was delivered to the scattered tribe of the Makondos. That mixup brought on so many difficulties that just to get the plane back might take two years. So Amaranta Úrsula dismissed the possibility of an inopportune return. Aureliano, for his part, had no other contact with the world except for the letters from the wise Catalonian and the news he had of Gabriel through Mercedes, the silent pharmacist. At first they were real contacts. Gabriel had turned in his return ticket in order to stay in Paris, selling the old newspapers and empty bottles that the chambermaids threw out of a gloomy hotel on the Rue Dauphine. Aureliano could visualize him then in a turtleneck sweater which he took off only when the sidewalk cafés of Montparnasse filled with springtime lovers, and sleeping by day and writing by night in order to confuse hunger in the room that smelied of boiled cauliflower where Rocamadour was to die. Nevertheless, news about him was slowly becoming so uncertain, and the letters from the wise man so sporadic and melancholy, that Aureliano grew to think about them as Amaranta Úrsula thought about her husband, and both of them remained floating in an empty universe where the only everyday and eternal reality was love.

Suddenly, like a stampede in that world of happy unawareness, came the news of Gaston's return. Aureliano and Amaranta Úrsula opened their eyes, dug deep into their souls, looked at the letter with their hands on their hearts, and understood that they were so close to each other that they preferred death to separation. Then she wrote her husband a letter of contradictory truths in which she repeated her love and said how anxious she was to see him again, but at the same time she admitted as a design of fate the impossibility of living without Aureliano. Contrary to what they had expected, Gaston sent them a calm, almost paternal reply, with two whole pages devoted to a warning against the fickleness of passion and a final paragraph with unmistakable wishes for them to be as happy as he had been during his brief conjugal experience. It was such an unforeseen attitude that Amaranta Úrsula felt humiliated by the idea that she had given her husband the pretext that he had wanted in order to abandon her to her fate. The rancor was aggravated six months later when Gaston wrote again from Léopoldville, where he had finally recovered the airplane, simply to ask them to ship him the velocipede, which of all that he had left behind in Macondo was the only thing that had any sentimental value for him. Aureliano bore Amaranta Úrsula's spite patiently and made an effort to show her that he could be as good a husband in adversity as in prosperity, and the daily needs that besieged them when Gaston's last money ran out created a bond of solidarity between them that was not as dazzling and heady as passion, but that let them make love as much and be as happy as during their uproarious and salacious days. At the time Pilar Ternera died they were expecting a child.

In the lethargy of her pregnancy, Amaranta Úrsula tried to set up a business in necklaces made out of the backbones of fish. But except for Mercedes, who bought a dozen, she could not find any customers. Aureliano was aware for the first time that his gift for languages, his encyclopedic knowledge, his rare faculty for remembering the details of remote deeds and places without having been there, were as useless as the box of genuine jewelry that his wife owned, which must have been worth as much as all the money that the last inhabitants of Macondo could have put together. They survived miraculously. Although Amaranta Úrsula did not lose her good humor or her genius for erotic mischief, she acquired the habit of sitting on the porch after lunch in a kind of wakeful and thoughtful siesta. Aureliano would accompany her. Sometimes they would remain there in silence until nightfall, opposite each other, looking into each other's eyes, loving each other as much as in their scandalous days. The uncer-

413

tainty of the future made them turn their hearts toward the past. They saw themselves in the lost paradise of the deluge, splashing in the puddles in the courtyard, killing lizards to hang on Úrsula, pretending that they were going to bury her alive, and those memories revealed to them the truth that they had been happy together ever since they had had memory. Going deeper into the past, Amaranta Úrsula remembered the afternoon on which she had gone into the silver shop and her mother told her that little Aureliano was nobody's child because he had been found floating in a basket. Although the version seemed unlikely to them, they did not have any information enabling them to replace it with the true one. All that they were sure of after examining all the possibilities was that Fernanda was not Aureliano's mother. Amaranta Úrsula was inclined to believe that he was the son of Petra Cotes, of whom she remembered only tales of infamy, and that supposition produced a twinge of horror in her heart.

Tormented by the certainty that he was his wife's brother, Aureliano ran out to the parish house to search through the moldy and moth-eaten archives for some clue to his parentage. The oldest baptismal certificate that he found was that of Amaranta Buendía, baptized in adolescence by Father Nicanor Reyna during the time when he was trying to prove the existence of God by means of tricks with chocolate. He began to have that feeling that he was one of the seventeen Aurelianos, whose birth certificates he tracked down as he went through four volumes, but the baptism dates were too far back for his age. Seeing him lost in the labyrinths of kinship, trembling with uncertainty, the arthritic priest, who was watching him from his hammock, asked him compassionately what his name was.

"Aureliano Buendía," he said.

"Then don't wear yourself out searching," the priest exclaimed with final conviction. "Many years ago there used to be a street here with that name and in those days people had the custom of naming their children after streets."

Aureliano trembled with rage.

"So!" he said. "You don't believe it either."

"Believe what?"

"That Colonel Aureliano Buendía fought thirty-two civil wars and lost them all," Aureliano answered. "That the army hemmed in and machine-gunned three thousand workers and that their bodies were carried off to be thrown into the sea on a train with two hundred cars."

The priest measured him with a pitying look.

"Oh, my son," he sighed. "It's enough for me to be sure that you and I exist at this moment."

So Aureliano and Amaranta Úrsula accepted the version of the basket, not because they believed it, but because it spared them their terror. As the pregnancy advanced they were becoming a single being, they were becoming more and more integrated in the solitude of a house that needed only one last breath to be knocked down. They restricted themselves to an essential area, from Fernanda's bedroom, where the charms of sedentary love were visible, to the beginning of the porch, where Amaranta Úrsula would sit to sew bootees and bonnets for the newborn baby and Aureliano would answer the occasional letters from the wise Catalonian. The rest of the house was given over to the tenacious assault of destruction. The silver shop, Melquíades' room, the primitive and silent realm of Santa Sofía de la Piedad remained in the depths of a domestic jungle that no one would have had the courage to penetrate. Surrounded by the voracity of nature, Aureliano and Amaranta Úrsula continued cultivating the oregano and the begonias and defended their world with demarcations of quicklime, building the last trenches in the age-old war between man and ant. Her long and neglected hair, the splotches that were beginning to appear on her face, the swelling of her legs, the deformation of her former lovemaking weasel's body had changed Amaranta Úrsula from the youthful creature she had been when she arrived at the house with the cage of luckless canaries and her captive husband, but it did not change the vivacity of her spirit. "Shit," she would say, laughing. "Who would have thought that we really would end up living like cannibals!" The last threat that joined them to the world was broken on the sixth month of pregnancy when they received a letter that obviously was not from the wise Catalonian. It had been mailed in Barcelona, but the envelope was addressed in conventional blue ink by an official hand and it had the innocent and impersonal look of hostile messages. Aureliano snatched it out of Amaranta Úrsula's hands as she was about to open it.

"Not this one," he told her. "I don't want to know what it says."

Just as he had sensed, the wise Catalonian did not write again. The stranger's letter, which no one read, was left to the mercy of the moths on the shelf where Fernanda had forgotten her wedding ring on occasion and there it remained, consuming itself in the inner fire of its bad news as the solitary lovers sailed against the tide of those days of the last stages, those impenitent and ill-fated times which were squandered on the useless effort of making them drift toward the desert of disenchantment and oblivion. Aware of that menace, Aureliano and Amaranta Úrsula spent the last months holding hands, ending with the love of loyalty for the child who had his beginning in the madness of fornication. At night, holding each other in bed, they were not frightened by the sublunary explosions of the ants or the noise of the moths or the constant and clean whistle of the growth of the weeds in the neighboring rooms. Many times they were awakened by the traffic of the dead. They could hear Úrsula fighting against the laws of creation to maintain the line, and José Arcadio Buendía searching for the mythical truth of the great inventions, and Fernanda praying, and Colonel

416

Aureliano Buendía stupefying himself with the deception of war and the little gold fishes, and Aureliano Segundo dying of solitude in the turmoil of his debauches, and then they learned that dominant obsessions can prevail against death and they were happy again with the certainty that they would go on loving each other in their shape as apparitions long after other species of future animals would steal from the insects the paradise of misery that the insects were finally stealing from man.

One Sunday, at six in the afternoon, Amaranta Úrsula felt the pangs of childbirth. The smiling mistress of the little girls who went to bed because of hunger had her get onto the dining-room table, straddled her stomach, and mistreated her with wild gallops until her cries were drowned out by the bellows of a formidable male child. Through her tears Amaranta Úrsula could see that he was one of those great Buendías, strong and willful like the José Arcadios, with the open and clairvoyant eyes of the Aurelianos, and predisposed to begin the race again from the beginning and cleanse it of its pernicious vices and solitary calling, for he was the only one in a century who had been engendered with love.

"He's a real cannibal," she said. "We'll name him Rodrigo."

"No," her husband countered. "We'll name him Aureliano and he'll win thirty-two wars."

After cutting the umbilical cord, the midwife began to use a cloth to take off the blue grease that covered his body as Aureliano held up a lamp. Only when they turned him on his stomach did they see that he had something more than other men, and they leaned over to examine him. It was the tail of a pig.

They were not alarmed. Aureliano and Amaranta Úrsula were not aware of the family precedent, nor did they remember Úrsula's frightening admonitions, and the midwife pacified them with the idea that the tail could be cut off when the child got his second teeth. Then they had no time to think about it again, because Amaranta Úrsula was bleeding in an uncontainable torrent. They tried to help her with applications of spiderwebs and balls of ash, but it was like trying to hold back a spring with one's hands. During the first hours she tried to maintain her good humor. She took the frightened Aureliano by the hand and begged him not to worry, because people like her were not made to die against their will, and she exploded with laughter at the ferocious remedies of the midwife. But as Aureliano's hope abandoned him, she was becoming less visible, as if the light on her were fading away, until she sank into drowsiness. At dawn on Monday they brought a woman who recited cauterizing prayers that were infallible for man and beast beside her bed, but Amaranta Úrsula's passionate blood was insensible to any artifice that did not come from love. In the afternoon, after twenty-four hours of desperation, they knew that she was dead because the flow had stopped without remedies and her profile became sharp and the blotches on her face evaporated in a halo of alabaster and she smiled again.

Aureliano did not understand until then how much he loved his friends, how much he missed them, and how much he would have given to be with them at that moment. He put the child in the basket that his mother had prepared for him, covered the face of the corpse with a blanket, and wandered aimlessly through the town, searching for an entrance that went back to the past. He knocked at the door of the pharmacy, where he had not visited lately, and he found a carpenter shop. The old woman who opened the door with a lamp in her hand took pity on his delirium and insisted that, no, there had never been a pharmacy there, nor had she ever known a woman with a thin neck and sleepy eyes named Mercedes. He wept, leaning his brow against the door of the wise Catalonian's former bookstore, conscious that he was paying with his tardy sobs for a death that he had refused to weep for on time so as not to break the spell of love. He smashed his fists against the cement wall of The Golden Child, calling for Pilar Ternera, indifferent to the luminous orange disks that were crossing the sky and that so many times on holiday nights he had contemplated with childish fascination from the courtyard of the curlews. In the last open salon of the tumbledown red-light district an accordion group was playing the songs of Rafael Escalona, the bishop's nephew, heir to the secrets of Francisco the Man. The bartender, who had a withered and somewhat crumpled arm because he had raised it against his mother, invited Aureliano to have a bottle of cane liquor, and Aureliano then bought him one. The bartender spoke to him about the misfortune of his arm. Aureliano spoke to him about the misfortune of his heart, withered and somewhat crumpled for having been raised against his sister. They ended up weeping together and Aureliano felt for a moment that the pain was over. But when he was alone again in the last dawn of Macondo, he opened up his arms in the middle of the square, ready to wake up the whole world, and he shouted with all his might:

"Friends are a bunch of bastards!"

Nigromanta rescued him from a pool of vomit and tears. She took him to her room, cleaned him up, made him drink a cup of broth. Thinking that it would console him, she took a piece of charcoal and erased the innumerable loves that he still owed her for, and she voluntarily brought up her own most solitary sadnesses so as not to leave him alone in his weeping. When he awoke, after a dull and brief sleep, Aureliano recovered the awareness of his headache. He opened his eyes and remembered the child.

He could not find the basket. At first he felt an outburst of joy, thinking that Amaranta Úrsula had awakened from death to take care of the child. But her corpse was a pile of stones under the blanket. Aware that when he arrived he had found the door to the bedroom open, Aureliano went across the porch which was saturated with the morning sighs of oregano and looked into the dining room, where the remnants of the birth still lay: the large pot, the bloody sheets, the jars of ashes, and the twisted umbilical cord of the child on an opened diaper on the table next to the shears and the fishline. The idea that the midwife had returned for the child during the night gave him a pause of rest in which to think. He sank into the rocking chair, the same one in which Rebeca had sat during the early days of the house to give embroidery lessons, and in which Amaranta had played Chinese checkers with Colonel Gerineldo Márquez, and in which Amaranta Úrsula had sewn the tiny clothing for the child, and in that flash of lucidity he became aware that he was unable to bear in his soul the crushing weight of so much past. Wounded by the fatal lances of his own nostalgia and that of others, he admired the persistence of the spiderwebs on the dead rose bushes, the perseverance of the rye grass, the patience of the air in the radiant February dawn. And then he saw the child. It was a dry and bloated bag of skin that all the ants in the world were dragging toward their holes along the stone path in the garden. Aureliano could not move. Not because he was paralyzed by horror but because at that prodigious instant Melquíades' final keys were revealed to him and he saw the epigraph of the parchments perfectly placed in the order of man's time and space: *The first of the line is tied to a tree and the last is being eaten by the ants.*

Aureliano had never been more lucid in any act of his life as when he forgot about his dead ones and the pain of his dead ones and nailed up the doors and windows again with Fernanda's crossed boards so as not to be disturbed by any temptations of the world, for he knew then that his fate was written in Melquíades' parchments. He found them intact among the prehistoric plants and steaming puddles and luminous insects that had removed all trace of man's passage on earth from the room, and he did not have the calmness to bring them out into the light, but right there, standing, without the slightest difficulty, as if they had been written in Spanish and were being read under the dazzling splendor of high noon, he began to decipher them aloud. It was the history of the family, written by Melquíades, down to the most trivial details, one hundred years ahead of time. He had written it in Sanskrit, which was his mother tongue, and he had encoded the even lines in the private cipher of the Emperor Augustus and the odd ones in a Lacedemonian military code. The final protection, which Aureliano had begun to glimpse when he let himself be confused by the love of Amaranta Úrsula, was based on the fact that Melquíades had not put events in the order of man's conventional time, but had concentrated a century of daily episodes in such a way that they coexisted in one instant. Fascinated by the discovery, Aureliano read aloud without skipping the chanted encyclicals that Melquíades himself had made Arcadio listen to and that were in reality the prediction of his execution, and he found the announcement of the birth of the most beautiful woman in the world who was rising up to heaven in body and soul, and he found the origin of the posthumous twins who gave up deciphering the parchments, not simply through incapacity and lack of drive, but also because their attempts were premature. At that point, impatient to know his own origin, Aureliano skipped ahead. Then the wind began, warm, incipient, full of voices from the past, the murmurs of ancient geraniums, sighs of disenchantment that preceded the most tenacious nostalgia. He did not notice it because at that moment he was discovering the first indications of his own being in a lascivious grandfather who let himself be frivolously dragged along across a hallucinated plateau in search of a beautiful woman who would not make him happy. Aureliano recognized him, he pursued the hidden paths of his descent, and he found the instant of his own conception among the scorpions and the yellow butterflies in a sunset bathroom where a mechanic satisfied his lust on a woman who was giving herself out of rebellion. He was so absorbed that he did not feel the second surge of wind either as its cyclonic strength tore the doors and windows off their hinges, pulled off the roof of the east wing, and uprooted the foundations. Only then did he discover that Amaranta Úrsula was not his sister but his aunt, and that Sir Francis Drake had attacked Riohacha only so that they could seek each other through the most intricate labyrinths of blood until they would engender the mythological animal that was to bring the line to an end. Macondo was already a fearful whirlwind of dust and rubble being spun about by the wrath of the biblical hurricane when Aureliano skipped eleven pages so as not to lose time with facts he knew only too well, and he began to decipher the instant that he was living, deciphering it as he lived it, prophesying himself in the act of deciphering the last page of the parchments, as if he were looking into a speaking mirror. Then he skipped again to anticipate the predictions and ascertain the date and circumstances of his death. Before reaching the final line, however, he had already understood that he would never leave that room, for it was foreseen that the city of mirrors (or mirages) would be wiped out by the wind and exiled from the memory of men at the precise moment when Aureliano Babilonia would finish deciphering the parchments, and that everything written on them was unrepeatable since time immemorial and forever more, because races condemned to one hundred years of solitude did not have a second opportunity on earth.

GABRIEL GARCÍA MÁRQUEZ

CHRONICLE OF A DEATH FORETOLD

COLLECTED STORIES

IN EVIL HOUR

INNOCENT ERENDIRA AND OTHER STORIES

LEAF STORM

LIVING TO TELL THE TALE

LOVE IN THE TIME OF CHOLERA

MEMORIES OF MY MELANCHOLY WHORES

NEWS OF A KIDNAPPING

NO ONE WRITES TO THE COLONEL

OF LOVE AND OTHER DEMONS

ONE HUNDRED YEARS OF SOLITUDE

STRANGE PILGRIMS

THE AUTUMN OF THE PATRIARCH

THE GENERAL IN HIS LABYRINTH

THE STORY OF A SHIPWRECKED SAILOR

He just wanted a decent book to read ...

Not too much to ask, is it? It was in 1935 when Allen Lane, Managing Director of Bodley Head Publishers, stood on a platform at Exeter railway station looking for something good to read on his journey back to London. His choice was limited to popular magazines and poor-quality paperbacks – the same choice faced every day by the vast majority of readers, few of whom could afford hardbacks. Lane's disappointment and subsequent anger at the range of books generally available led him to found a company – and change the world.

'We believed in the existence in this country of a vast reading public for intelligent books at a low price, and staked everything on it'
Sir Allen Lane, 1902–1970, founder of Penguin Books

The quality paperback had arrived – and not just in bookshops. Lane was adamant that his Penguins should appear in chain stores and tobacconists, and should cost no more than a packet of cigarettes.

Reading habits (and cigarette prices) have changed since 1935, but Penguin still believes in publishing the best books for everybody to enjoy. We still believe that good design costs no more than bad design, and we still believe that quality books published passionately and responsibly make the world a better place.

So wherever you see the little bird – whether it's on a piece of prize-winning literary fiction or a celebrity autobiography, political tour de force or historical masterpiece, a serial-killer thriller, reference book, world classic or a piece of pure escapism – you can bet that it represents the very best that the genre has to offer.

Whatever you like to read – trust Penguin.